*The book jolted loose from her arm
and fell to the ground.*

Opening her mouth to apologize to the man she'd bumped into, Rose turned around. And stopped.

"*A History of the New World,*" he read, straightening with the book in his hands.

Eyes black as pitch regarded her. She'd never seen eyes like that before. The effect of their direct, level gaze was . . . unsettling. Beside her, Maggie gave a small gasp. "Thank you for retrieving my book, sir," she said, finding that her voice wanted to quaver and fighting against it. "May I have it back?"

His head tilted a little to one side, a strand of coal black hair falling forward across his forehead. He was all in black, she realized, from his beaver hat to his gloves to the soles of his boots. Only a white shirt collar and simply-tied white cravat leavened his stark appearance. No, not stark, she amended as he glanced down at the book again. Predatory. All six lean feet of him.

"Do the Americas interest you?" he asked, his voice a low, cultured drawl that seemed to resonate down her spine.

"Learning things interests me," she replied, and held out her hand.

The corner of his mouth quirked, and he slowly placed the book into her fingers. "Well, then. I could teach you such things, Lady Rosamund," he murmured.

By Suzanne Enoch

Historical Titles

Contemporary Titles

SUZANNE ENOCH

Always A SCOUNDREL

THE NOTORIOUS GENTLEMEN

AVON

An Imprint of HarperCollinsPublishers

AVON BOOKS
An Imprint of HarperCollins*Publishers*
10 East 53rd Street
New York, New York 10022-5299

Copyright © 2009 by Suzanne Enoch
ISBN 978-0-06-145675-6
www.avonromance.com

First Avon Books paperback printing: May 2009

Avon Trademark Reg. U.S. Pat. Off. and in Other Countries, Marca Registrada, Hecho en U.S.A.
HarperCollins® is a registered trademark of HarperCollins Publishers.

Printed in the U.S.A.

10 9 8 7 6 5 4 3 2 1

Always A SCOUNDREL

Prologue

February 1815
London

"I don't want a well-ordered life." Lord Bramwell Lowry Johns finished off his glass of whiskey and reached for the bottle and a refill. "I would die from boredom in a fortnight."

"You only think that because you equate well-ordered with dull," Sullivan Waring observed from across the table, dipping his voice below the cacophony of noise that filled Jezebel's establishment after midnight. "For someone of your reputation, you're amazingly naive."

"*You're* naive," Bramwell retorted, annoyance touching him. He was also a bit surprised the word hadn't combusted in mid-air upon being applied to him. *Naive. Ha.* "Can you imagine me married and sitting down to . . . what, do embroidery? Play whist with the darling empty-headed leg shackle? Drink tea and attempt a conversation?" He shuddered, not even having to pretend the horror likely reflected in his expression.

The third member of their party, Phineas Bromley, snorted. "Don't blame the institution of marriage for the fact that you'd never wish to be wed to any of the women whose skirts you've lifted. You need to choose better for a bride, is all."

Bram made a derisive sound. "I'm not talking about your ladies, so don't bother with being offended. You've managed to find the only two decent women in England—and even so, I wouldn't wish to trade places with either of you."

"I find that somewhat comforting," Sullivan noted, sipping his own drink.

"And so you should. It's only so you'll appreciate that I do possess some restraint, and that with the exception of your ladies, I choose not to exercise it."

"You've not found a bride due to your own squeamishness, then."

Bram eyed Phineas. "I would put it to equal parts horror and compassion, myself. I may be heartless, but I have no desire to inflict myself on a permanent basis upon some chit, innocent or otherwise. It's not my duty to continue the family bloodline, and I can't think of another reason to drag myself into a church before I'm put into a box."

"So you intend to spend the remainder of your life whoring, drinking, wagering, and being as outrageous as you can manage?"

Bram shook himself. He made it a point to be serious as little as possible, and neither did he want to argue with two newly married men about the merits of being leg-shackled. "Please, Phin," he said aloud. "I would never think so small. You know my ultimate goal is to lower the standards of morality enough that everything I do becomes acceptable."

"That's likely what happened at Sodom and Gomorrah," Sullivan observed.

"One can only hope. And what are you two doing anyway, trying to preach the gospels of morality and domesticity to me? Besides it being a bloody waste of time, one of you is a former housebreaker, and the other a former highwayman. Hardly occupations any true gentleman would seek to emulate. It's notorious of you. And selfish, to think you should be the only ones permitted to misbehave."

His two closest friends shared a glance. He'd known them for years, since the three of them had ended up serving together in the First Royal Dragoons on the Peninsula. He'd known Sullivan for even longer—since Oxford. And he recognized the look. He was about to be counseled. Good God. If he'd had anything better to do this evening, he would have left—and taken the bottle with him. No sense walking away from fine liquor. But London during the little Season had few amusements to offer.

"Speaking of *our* particular escapades," Phin, the more logical-minded of the two of them, began again, "in all seriousness, Bram, what the devil do you think you're doing? This new game of yours is both reckless and pointless. And dangerous."

"Recklessness is the point, Phin." He pinned Sullivan

with a look before the horse breeder could enter the fray as well. "And you gave me the idea, Sully. I've just perfected it."

"I don't want credit for inspiring your new hobby, thank you very much," Sullivan retorted. "I had reason for what I did."

"Yes, the things you burgled were yours to begin with. I'm pleased you had a cause to fight for. I don't."

"Then don't rob anyone."

"I said I didn't have a cause. I do have a reason."

"Such as?"

"None of your damned business. You're beginning to bore me."

Sullivan sat forward. "I'm not ashamed of what I did. I would do it again, considering that it led me to Isabel. But there are consequences, Bram. I nearly hanged. I would have, if—"

"If I hadn't pretended to be you and committed another robbery." He sent a glance at Phin. "And I pretended to be you, as well, to save your ungrateful life. And your brother's estate. So stop lecturing, and instead help me finish off this bottle. I know perfectly well what I'm doing. I don't need your approval."

"The question," Phin put in, offering his glass for a refill, "is whether you will know when to stop. Self-restraint—"

"Is an excuse invented by those without the spleen to see something through. It's dull as dirt," Bram interrupted, his annoyance deepening. "And so are the two of you, now that you're married. Old hens, clucking and complaining about the fun the rooster is having." He took a long swallow.

"Bram, the—"

"Fun they *used* to have," he broke in, "and now can only criticize because they've been castrated and Mrs. Waring and Mrs. Bromley won't allow them to play any longer." They certainly didn't play with him as often as they'd used to. The three of them had once been notorious, and now two had sunk into amiable domesticity. Zooks, it was shocking. A disgrace, even.

With a deep breath, Phineas shrugged. "God knows I'm no saint, and I won't lecture you on the hazards of lawbreaking. We've ridden into battle and mayhem together, and you know quite well what you're getting yourself into."

"Yes, I do. My aims are simply different than yours. You're happy, and that's fine for you. As for myself, I don't wish to live a long and proper life." Bram gestured for another bottle. "And I've listened to enough of this nonsense for one damned evening. For a cart full of them."

"You say you know there will be consequences," Sullivan said after a moment, his voice quieter. "I just hope you truly realize that."

"Oh, I do." Bram curved his mouth in a smile. "I look forward to them."

Chapter 1 _____

May 1815

Lord Bramwell Lowry Johns ducked into the foyer just ahead of the house's butler. Pressing back against the wall, the satchel of jewelry close against his chest, he listened as the servant walked within three feet of him to pass through the nearest door. The candles inside the room began going out one by one.

With a shallow breath, Bramwell moved to the front door, edged it open, and slipped silently outside. As soon as he closed the heavy oak door behind him, he trotted down the shallow front steps and out to the street.

That had gone smoothly—the Marquis of Braithe-waite needed to hire servants with better hearing. He also needed better taste in friends if he wanted to escape being targeted for any more robberies. Smiling darkly, he rounded the corner, strolled down the next street, and stopped beside the massive black coach waiting there in the deep shadows. "Back to Ackley House," he said, stepping inside and taking a seat on the well-cushioned black leather. "But stop on Brewer Street. I'll walk from there."

"Very good, my lord." With a cluck to the horses, Graham sent the coach rolling down the street.

That had been easy. No fuss, minuscule chance of discovery, and a well-sprung carriage waiting not too far away. The only thing lacking was a pounding heart and a rush of his pulse. He had never questioned why he craved that sense of excitement, or why he had to risk more each time to achieve it. But he did crave it. The choice of victims was satisfying and integral, but secondary. The items he took were a very distant third.

Without bothering to look at the contents in the satchel, Bram pulled open the hidden drawer beneath the opposite seat, tossed the bag inside, and closed it again. St. Michael's Church in Knightsbridge would find a nice surprise in its alms box this Sunday, not that he would ever admit to the charity. He wasn't any damned Robin Hood; it was only that he didn't have need of the things. Low as he prided himself on sinking, it seemed somehow beneath him to covet the valuables owned by his peers. With the notable exception of their wives, of course.

Tomorrow Mayfair would be abuzz with the news—the Black Cat had struck once more, relieving another member of the aristocracy of a selection of very fine baubles and trinkets. He was far from the first burglar to terrorize the London nobility, but he did consider that he brought the largest share of style to the profession. And unless something more . . . interesting came along, he had no intention of stopping his activities. Unlike certain other gentlemen of his acquaintance, he absolutely didn't wish to bag a few items and then find true love, become a pious fool, and live trapped ever after.

"My lord?" Graham's voice came from above, and the coach rumbled to a stop. "Brewer Street."

His tiger hopped to the ground and flipped down the steps, and Bram descended to the street. "That'll be all for the night. I'll find my own way home." He cracked a grin. "Or somewhere."

His servants were accustomed to not knowing his whereabouts by night, and Graham nodded. "Aye, my lord." The coach rolled back into the lane without him.

With a quick look around, Bram hopped the stone wall bordering the backside of Ackley House's gardens, dusted off his black jacket and black trousers, and strolled past the small fish pond and up to the terrace. Twenty minutes away, and no one the wiser. Now for a stiff drink, or better yet, a stiff—

A hand wrapped around his sleeve. "There you are," Lady Ackley murmured breathily. "I'd begun to think you'd found someone else."

And there it was. A very nice way to combat the edginess running through him. "Someone else? Not this evening, Miranda. Now why don't you show me the lovely fresco you mentioned earlier?"

Her fine brow furrowed, her exquisite blue eyes puzzled. "What fresco, Bram?"

"That was a ruse I utilized on the chance that some-one might overhear us," he said patiently, reflecting that if he'd wanted her for conversation, he would be sadly disappointed.

"Oh. No one's about. I checked very closely. And Lord Ackley is in the library showing off the new atlas he acquired."

"Very well, then. Where shall we go so we might commit the deadly sin of lust without being inter-rupted?"

This time she giggled. Apparently she understood that. "The gazebo, then. It has padded chairs and a chaise longue."

"Excellent."

Lady Rosamund Davies wondered for a moment whether her family would ever arrive at any event to-gether and in a timely manner if she didn't set strategic clocks forward or back depending on who would see them. Her mother, the Countess of Abernathy, would arrive before the orchestra, because she hated the idea of missing any gossip.

Her older sister, Beatrice, would think she was ar-riving exactly at the moment of being fashionably late, because of course Bea was perfection in human form—the reason she'd married at age eighteen, and to such an important and gracious man. In reality she would dawdle about changing her hair and her ear bobs until only the servants remained awake.

Thankfully Beatrice and her important and gra-cious husband Peter, Lord Fishton (good God, what a name), had decided to spend the London Season with the rest of the family at Davies House, because managing to keep two separate households on schedule would simply be too much work. Rose sighed, gazing around at the crowded Ackley ballroom.

And then there was her father, the Earl of Abernathy, who insisted on arriving precisely at the moment specified on the invitation, which of course would never do. Despite the fact that thanks to her . . . management they always managed to arrive in a timely manner, if any of her family members ever bothered to compare timepieces, she would be in for it.

Straightening her shoulders, Rose stepped forward to grasp the arm of the youngest family member in attendance, the one most likely to become lost on the way to any given soiree and never arrive at all. He didn't require a clock; he needed a caretaker, and for more than one reason. "Dance with me, James."

Her younger brother shook his tawny head. "Can't, Rose. Might miss him."

With a sigh Rose tugged again. "Might miss whom?" she asked.

"I saw him earlier. He's the only fellow ever to win all the wagers he made at White's during a single Season, you know. Every wager, Rose."

She wasn't certain whether it would be more prudent to humor James Davies, Viscount Lester, or to attempt a distraction. "Who is this sterling statistician?"

"Ha. A statistician. That's like calling . . . Captain Cook a fellow who did a bit of traveling. Or Shakespeare a fellow who wrote some plays. Or—"

"I said 'sterling,' " she repeated, thinking, and not for the first time, that her parents needed to invest in a very strong padlock for her brother's bedchamber door.

"Well, Lord Bram Johns ain't a statistician. He's a . . . a . . . god."

"Oh, please," Rose returned skeptically, mentally wincing at the name. Why her brother couldn't have befriended a parson or a kindly old whist player, she had no idea.

"A demigod, then. At the least." He sent her a glare, gray eyes narrowed. "And how is it that you've never heard of Lord Bram Johns? I talk about him all the time."

"I didn't say I've never heard of him. You wouldn't tell me who you were looking for." She tugged on his arm again. "And I still wish a dance. We're at a very nice soiree, for heaven's sake."

"A soiree with a card room."

Rose sighed. "Haven't you considered that this demigod of yours might have left the Ackleys' for more . . . underhanded pursuits by now?"

"By Jove, you may be right." He pulled free of her grip. "Tell Father I'm off to Jezebel's. If Johns ain't there, I know who will be."

She suppressed a responding shudder. "James, please stay. Keep me company."

He flashed a smile over his shoulder. "Don't worry, Rose. I won't step in over my head."

He would *begin* the evening at Jezebel's in over his head—if he managed to gain entry. But chasing after him would only leave the eighteen-year-old more determined to prove his skill with cards or dice or kittens or whatever it was they would be wagering over tonight.

And she had certainly heard of Lord Bramwell Lowry Johns. From the reverence with which her brother had spoken of him over the past month, he seemed more of a myth than a man. At the least she couldn't recall ever setting eyes on him. If she ever did, she would be very much inclined to punch this Hercules of scandal in the nose for being such a successful blackguard that an idiotic young man with no Town bronze would want to emulate his awful behavior.

Desiccated old Lord Ogilvy creaked through the substantial crowd and stopped in front of her. "May I have this dance, Lady Rosamund?" he rasped.

Only if you promise not to expire in the middle of it. "Of course, my lord," she said aloud, forcing a smile. At least a dance would distract her from the volcanic destruction in which James, and by extension the rest of her family, seemed determined to be swept away. Setting clocks clearly wouldn't suffice here, but she still hadn't found the appropriate lure to keep her younger brother out of trouble. And she needed to discover it quickly.

Because as much as she dreaded whatever tales of loss her brother would share with her tomorrow, part of her almost hoped that he *would* run across Lord Bramwell Johns at Jezebel's. At least there were still some unknowns to the equation that was Johns. The man James was more likely to run into meant definite trouble. She could only hope that even Jezebel's Club had become too tame this evening for the Marquis of Cosgrove. For all their sakes.

Lord Bramwell Lowry Johns straightened his coat and strolled back into the ballroom. Lord and Lady Ackley's soirees were always well attended, and tonight the crowd had nearly been reduced to adopting the tactics of fish in a barrel—all having to swim in the same direction in order for them to make any headway at all.

As fish were wont to do, however, when they came upon a predator they broke apart and swam well around before re-forming their school. And so a pocket of space remained directly around Bram. The closest of the brightly colored fish sent him nervous glances, undoubtedly fearing his appetite. This particular shark, though, had just fed, and at the moment more than anything else he wanted a glass of Polish vodka.

He found a footman toting a tray of weak Madeira and sweet port, and placed his request. With a quick nod the fellow scampered away. The butler announced a quadrille, his voice barely audible through the cacophony, and several dozen fish split away from the school and re-formed on the dance floor.

His drink arrived, and he took a long, grateful swallow. Busy as his evening had been, what with a robbery and sex and it barely being midnight, restlessness continued to creep through his limbs. Bram sent a glance in the direction of the refreshment table, where Lord Braithewaite stood stuffing his jowls with biscuits and sugared orange peels.

The damned fat sloth had made the burglary too easy. That's what it was. Putting the family's finest gems in a Gibraltar-sized box of fine, carved mahogany, and then placing *that* squarely beneath the bed in the master bedchamber—the only thing easier to find and empty would have been a bag hanging out a window and embroidered with the words "expensive jewelry." Bram wanted a challenge, and stealing from

Braithewaite would barely appease a boy in short pants.

Another figure joined the marquis at the sweets table, though he didn't touch any of the refreshments. Bram's jaw tightened. *That* was the man Braithewaite could thank for the removal of his valuables. The bloody Duke of Levonzy. Braithewaite needed to acquire better taste in both his desserts and his friends.

The two men continued to converse—round-cheeked sycophant and arrow-straight, sharp-angled tyrant. Two demons for the price of one.

Damn. Now he was being witty, and had no one with whom to share it. Taking a breath, he turned his back on the duke and went to find two of the four people in attendance tonight whose company he could tolerate.

A moment later he spied them, dancing. Married for just over six months, Phineas and Alyse Bromley looked only at each other as they twirled about the floor, both of them wearing the sickeningly sweet expression of happiness and true love. Well, no one was perfect, and Phin had simply succumbed to being more or less . . . human. Poor fellow.

"Your expression is distressingly dour," a voice drawled from low by Bram's side, "especially to be looking at two very happy people."

Ah, the third person he could tolerate. Viscount Quence sat in his wheeled chair, his ever-present valet at the handles behind him. "William," Bram said, offering his hand. "I don't mind that your brother and his bride are happy; it's only that they exude a sweetness that's likely to rot my teeth."

Quence chuckled. "I'll take your rotted teeth over Phin returning to the army. She saved his life, I think."

Bram thought it more likely that the life saving had been mutual, but he offered a half grin rather than saying that bit aloud. "And the lives of untold French soldiers." He sent a glance behind the viscount. "Speaking of lives being saved, is your sister about?"

"Beth is safely on the dance floor with the latest fellow to be smitten with her. Now that she's out, I think she may be over her infatuation with you."

"Thank God for that. You know she terrifies me."

"Mm hm. If you don't wish to admit that you're being honorable by sparing her from your dismal reputation, I won't contradict you."

"I freely admit to being admirable about my god-awful reputation. As you know, it's been painstakingly earned by multiple misdeeds and unconscionable wagers and drinking, and I'm quite proud of it."

The older man shook his head. "I'll agree that you're quite good at it."

Despite Quence's title and ownership of a very promising mineral hot springs property, the viscount sat alone. Bram swallowed his impatience and another mouthful of vodka and continued conversation with him until the country dance ended. He had worse things he could be doing, but certainly nothing better.

When Phineas and Alyse joined them, he was halfway through his second glass. Taking the chestnut-haired Alyse's hand and bowing over it, he curved his lips. "Are you certain you don't want to change your mind about this unpleasant fellow?" he asked smoothly. "I'm far more charming, and handsome, and I know people who could see him shipped off to Australia at a moment's notice."

She laughed. "Thank you for the offer, Lord Bram, but I find myself rather . . . happy with my circumstance."

He lifted an eyebrow. "But it's been half a year."

"I don't rot after a week or two like old fruit," Phin broke in, capturing her hand back. "And leave my wife be, you blackguard."

Anyone else would probably have been wise to warn him away from a female to which that person had a prior claim. If there was one line that Bram hadn't crossed, though, it was loyalty. And Phineas Bromley was his friend. But for Lucifer's sake, if he couldn't at least pretend to be a wolf, he might as well hang himself. "The only reason I appeared here tonight was for a waltz with your wife," he said aloud. "Or with you. I'm not particular."

"Mm hm." Phin glanced beyond him, his expression sharpening a little. "Alyse, give me a moment, will you?"

She nodded. "I'm expecting you to appear for the second waltz tonight," she said in Bram's direction, then joined Quence in greeting the frighteningly cheerful Beth as she returned from the dance with her partner.

"You wouldn't be the reason that Lady Ackley is missing one ear bob and Lord Ackley looks as though he's about to go pull a saber off the wall, would you, Bram?" Phineas asked, stepping closer and lowering his voice.

Phin had always been the observant sort. "Damnation. At times I appreciate a woman who can't keep her mouth shut, but outside the bedchamber I would prefer a little discretion."

"You are in the man's bloody house," Phin returned. "Isn't that a bit bold, even for you?"

Bram snorted, "A few minutes ago I was in the man's bloody wife. And you're no saint, yourself."

"I never claimed to be. But I have more than myself to consider now. And if Ackley's going to be challenging you to a duel, I don't want you anywhere around Alyse."

"Well, that's lovely, isn't it? Enjoy your sugar-coated domesticity, Phin."

As a rule, Bram didn't allow censure to trouble him, but Phin Bromley's conversion to piety was damned annoying. Together he and Phin and Sullivan Waring had left a well-marked trail of mayhem across half the Continent—or at least the bits that England was attempting to keep from Bonaparte. Sex, gambling, fighting, killing—they'd done it all. But now, a bare two years since he and Sully had returned, and one year less for Phin, he seemed to literally be the last man standing. They might call it a shame and say he would be happier married, but neither had they dared send any respectable, marriageable females in his direction.

"Bram?"

He blinked at Phin. "What?"

"I need to go dance with my sister. Are we still arguing, or are you going to stomp off?"

"I can't very well stomp off now that you've suggested it."

"Ah. Apologies."

Bram took a breath, the thought of wandering about

the ballroom for another two hours while avoiding both Lord and Lady Ackley making him want to gag. "Come to Jezebel's with me."

"I don't—"

"I'll tell you who I robbed this evening."

Phin opened his mouth, then closed it again. It must be difficult for Phineas, Bram reflected, to be morally superior in front of someone who knew of his every previously committed misdeed. At the moment Bram had no sympathy for him at all.

"Let me guess," the former highwayman and present loving husband finally said, sending a glance in the direction of the refreshment table. "Braithewaite, or Abernathy."

"Abernathy?" Bram turned around. A third oaf had indeed joined the ranks of the overly pompous. "Now this is a fortunate turn of events. I rescind my invitation to Jezebel's."

"Damn it all, Bram, you can't burgle the household of everyone who says a word to Levonzy."

"You know I hate to be contradictory, but I believe I can." He smiled, his so-called heart accelerating. A second robbery in one night. Everyone would be talking of the Black Cat tomorrow. Even Levonzy.

"Does the duke have any idea what you're doing?"

"Who gives a damn? Not I."

"The man is your father."

"That is the one thing in my life that isn't my fault. Pray don't remind me."

Phin rolled his shoulders. "I can see this isn't going anywhere. But didn't I see you at the Society the other day with Abernathy's son?"

"Yes. Viscount Lester. He's been following Cosgrove and me about like a lost puppy."

Phin's jaw clenched for the briefest of moments, but Bram saw it, nevertheless. If he was in for another damned lecture, he was going to flee.

"So you'd burgle the house of a friend."

"I didn't say Lester was a friend. And that wasn't your complaint. Come now. Don't spare the horses, Phin."

"No. I am not going to wade into that with you."

Bram forced a chuckle. "Go dance with Beth, then. And give Alyse my apologies for missing the waltz."

Sketching a lazy bow, he strolled out of the ballroom. He'd been seen by all and sundry, so no one would name him as the Black Cat. And now he had another task to occupy the remainder of his evening. He only hoped that burglarizing Abernathy's home would be a more interesting excursion than the visit to Braithewaite's had been. If it wasn't, he had no idea how to amuse himself next, or even which hobby, which activity, even remained undiscovered, unexplored, and undiscarded.

Considering both the ease and the lack of satisfaction he'd felt in making off with Braithewaite's valuables, Bram concocted a different strategy for visiting Lord Abernathy's home.

Other than the annoying son, James, Viscount Lester, he wasn't acquainted with the family. That in itself added an element of danger—he'd never been invited through the front doors of Davies House, and had no idea of the floor plan. Of course there were certain givens: the bedchambers would be upstairs, the silver would be locked in its closet, and the most valuable items would be kept closest to the master of the household.

Bram leaned back against the dark wall of the Davies stable. The family had returned home from the Ackley soiree nearly thirty minutes ago, and a few lights still glowed from the upstairs windows. He could have slipped in and been gone before they ever arrived, but he'd already done that once this evening, and he hated repeating himself.

He chewed on a stalk of straw and watched the house. Phineas had become bloody sanctimonious in the last six months. He frowned at the idea of thefts when he'd committed the same sins himself, and he practically suffered an apoplexy at the mere mention of Cosgrove's name. Kingston Gore, the Marquis of Cosgrove, had never done harm to Phin or Sullivan or their families—and that was because of Bram. They should be grateful for his friendship with the marquis.

And he'd known Cosgrove longer than he'd been acquainted with Phin, or even Sullivan. The man had practically raised him—or at least proved to be a very efficient tutor—after he and Levonzy had parted moral company shortly after he'd turned sixteen.

Another candle went out upstairs, and Bram straightened. No sense making it too easy—and aside from that, it was bloody cold out in the stable yard. He tossed the straw aside, pulling a black half mask from his pocket and tying it across his eyes. Low excitement stirred in his gut, and he slowed a moment to enjoy the sensation.

Too damned few deeds left him feeling alive—much less interested—these days.

Perhaps his next task should be to concoct an eighth deadly sin. Or he could work toward finding an even dozen. The devil knew he'd worn out the original seven. With a slight smile he reached a ground floor window and peered inside. Dark and empty. If he'd been one for self-reflection, that might have symbolized something—but he wasn't, and he curled his fingers under the frame and pulled. The glass swung open.

Very foolish of the Davies family, to leave their windows unlatched. A burglar was terrorizing the wealthiest residents of Mayfair, after all. Carelessness was this family's second sin, then. The first was their patriarch being caught in friendly conversation with the Duke of Levonzy.

As soon as he climbed inside, Bram closed the window again. He stood in what looked to be the breakfast room. A few baubles and bits decorated the walls and sideboard, but nothing that caught his eye. He hoped there would be something worth stealing upstairs. A lucrative satchel might even inspire the flock at St. Michael's to pray on their mysterious benefactor's behalf—or at least for his salvation.

Silently Bram pushed down on the door handle and cracked the door open an inch or so. A single candle still burned in the foyer, probably for young Viscount Lester's benefit, since the boy hadn't returned in the family coach. He was probably out somewhere, losing his shirt to Cosgrove. Again. Idiot pup.

The main stairway stood just in front of him. Taking another few seconds to listen and hearing only silence,

Bram made for the stairs and swept up to the first floor. In the dark with his black greatcoat, he probably looked like a fast-moving shadow.

Who would be in residence? He'd gone over the list as he waited outside—the earl and the countess, James, and an unmarried daughter whose name escaped him but who'd obviously been too virginal or too ordinary or both to catch his attention. The married daughter seemed to be staying there as well, and had an irritating laugh and an irritatingly dull husband.

He'd call it six, then, and more than likely three times that many servants. Just the right recipe to provide a good theft without leaving him overly stuffed or wanting more—at least not until tomorrow.

A low, muffled voice sounded off to his left. Bram froze. Abernathy. A second, female voice answered, and he tilted his head, listening. The voices came from a partially closed door on the north side of the hallway, probably the library or an upstairs sitting room. That was actually a bit reassuring; he wouldn't have to creep into the earl's private rooms while the man slept, anyway. There might remain a thing or two that could scar even his sensibilities.

First, though, he needed to *find* the earl's private rooms. Given his own dislike for the morning sun, he would start with the rooms on the west side of the house. Unable to help the dark smile curving his mouth, Bramwell started silently along the hallway.

If he hadn't been so restless tonight, he would have conceded that he should have done a bit more research into his target. Whereas with Braithewaite he'd known that the marquis had a particular fondness for his wife's

pearl necklace and matching ear bobs, he had no idea
what jewelry Lord and Lady Abernathy even owned.
Ah, well. He'd wanted a challenge.

"—understand how marrying me off to that blackguard can save us from him," the female voice said.

Bram stopped his advance. The door in front of
him stood ajar by an inch or so—not enough to see
through, but enough to hear fairly clearly now that he
was directly on top of it. He'd always had the curiosity
of a cat, and this conversation perked up his ears.

"Because most of the debt James has incurred is to
him," the deeper voice, Abernathy's, responded. "Do
you think this family has ten thousand pounds to
hand?"

"I'm certain Cosgrove would rather give us some additional time to repay him than see us bankrupted."

Not bloody likely, Bram thought. He'd been called
heartless, but Cosgrove had long ago gambled away
his own soul. But the chit had mentioned marriage.
How did that play into anything? Bram frowned,
moving closer to the door, clenching his fingers
against the temptation to push it open just another
fraction.

"You read his letter, Rose. He's made it quite clear
that he wants either the debt made good or your hand.
I can likely put him off until the end of the month to
make it look more respectable, but that's all. If neither
occurs, then we *will* be bankrupted."

"For heaven's sake, Father. I am not a box of bread to
be traded to satisfy a debt."

"That is precisely what you are. You are a member of
this family, and you will do your duty."

She made a scoffing sound. "This was James's doing—let him marry Cosgrove. He spends more time with that man and his awful cronies than he does with his own family, anyway."

"If you're going to argue, at least have something useful to say."

"You didn't ask me in here to be the voice of reason. Good night, Mother. Father."

Bram swept sideways, ducking into the dark doorway of the next room over. The library door slammed open, and a swoosh of silk passed him. The light scent of lavender followed. Seized by the abrupt desire to see this chit, Bram stepped halfway back into the hall. The tail end of a green patterned gown disappeared around the corner.

Well, this was unexpected. Most surprising of all, Cosgrove seemed to have decided to marry—and had put it in writing. He'd ruined men's fortunes and lives before, so that was nothing new. But marriage . . .

"She won't go along with it, you know," another female voice took up. The Countess of Abernathy, no doubt. "You should have let me put it to her. I've always been able to reason with her."

"Bah. We don't need to reason with her, Joanna. This is her duty. You had to let her sister marry that useless Fishton, so she's not available."

"But Fishton's a viscount, my dear. And mind your voice; they're sleeping just down the hallway."

"Yes. Another burden. And James is an idiot, but he's the heir. It has to be Rose, whatever her protests may be. She certainly isn't good for anything else."

"Are you certain this is the best use for her? She

might marry one of Prinny's circle, or someone higher in the government than Fishton. Or—"

"She doesn't show well enough for that. Bookish and flat-chested. No, it's Cosgrove. I have no idea why he wants her. Just be grateful he does. At the least he's wealthy, and titled. And we have no other way to pull ourselves out of this hole James has dug for us all."

"Cosgrove's reputation is nothing to brag about."

"His reputation is horrific. But at least it will be a marriage, and we will no longer be in debt to him. Perhaps Rose will lend him some respectability. Anyway, it's done. I've agreed in principle, and I'm to meet with Cosgrove tomorrow to see to the details. Just hope he agrees to the month delay, or everyone will know just how much monetary distress we're in."

Bram returned to the dark sitting room and sank back against the wall beside the door. So Abernathy was another man who saw his progeny as pawns and puppets. There was nothing new or unusual about that. He was one of those pawns, himself—though Levonzy would be worse than daft to attempt to use him as such now.

What struck him, though, was to hear it said so plainly, and in words that sounded so familiar. It didn't wound, because, well, nothing did any longer, but appreciating irony as he did, he wished there was someone else to recognize that thirteen years ago when he'd heard a very similar speech, he'd gone out and found Cosgrove with whom to commiserate. And now this Lady Rose Davies was being pushed at Cosgrove because of the same sentiment.

Hm. Bram listened for another few minutes, but the lord and lady of the house seemed to have finished discussing the interesting bits. Straightening, he slipped back down the stairs and out the window through which he'd entered. He now had something on his schedule for tomorrow: Talk to Cosgrove and discover why the devil's spawn now wanted to marry some obscure chit. And since the Black Cat's curiosity had been roused, who knew what else he might find to do tomorrow?

Chapter 2 _____

"Rose, may we please go now?"

Rose finished signing her name and picked up *A History of the New World* from the counter. "Thank you, Mr. Simms," she said. "I'll have it back to you in a fortnight."

The tall librarian dipped his head. "I'll see if I can locate that book on seafaring legends for you by then. Good day, Lady Rose, Lady Margaret."

With a pinched smile Lady Margaret Havendish led the way outside, practically dragging Rose behind her. "I did not escape tea with Mama and Aunt Joanna to go to the lending library," she stated. "Ascott will never wish to call on me again if he thinks I'm a bluestocking."

"Reading does not make you a bluestocking, Maggie. Quoting aloud what you've read makes you a bluestocking." Rose smiled. "And it's Ascott now, is it? What happened to Lord Benthem?"

Her petite cousin blushed to the roots of her fashionable blonde hair. "He begged me to address him as Ascott. I didn't wish him to expire from despair."

"Heavens, no. Especially if something as simple as calling him by his Christian name can save him."

"Oh, don't make fun."

Rose took a breath, tucking the book beneath her arm as they strolled toward Bond Street. Brightly colored muslins and polished boots and jackets of the finest cloth thronged in front of the shops, with carriage traffic on the street slowed to a near snail's pace. Generally she enjoyed the bustle of Mayfair, but today the crowds served to remind her that it was nearly noon. Less than an hour before her father would be sitting down to luncheon with the Marquis of Cosgrove.

It hadn't helped at all that James had lost another forty pounds at faro last night—a small loss for him, but another blow that the family was ill-equipped to weather. She'd tried speaking with him, reasoning with him, but Cosgrove clearly had more influence over her brother than she did.

She supposed she should be grateful that the marquis had offered the family an alternative to debtors' prison—though why he'd decided that marriage to her was worth ten thousand pounds, she had no idea. They'd met on two occasions, very briefly, and both times she'd made it clear that she despised him.

"Rose," Maggie said, interrupting her thoughts, "Ascott's uncle is quite wealthy. If your father can put Cosgrove off until after we're married, Ascott could likely persuade Lord Palbridge to loan your father the money."

"You haven't received a proposal yet, Maggie. You've only begun using his familiar name within the last day or two."

"You think he won't ask m—"

"All I'm saying is that Cosgrove expects my father to make good on James's debt. At the most, Father will be able to delay a public announcement of our betrothal until the end of the month. Twenty-six days. I prefer to deal in facts rather than fairy tales. And yes, I think Ascott will offer for you."

Her cousin's frown smoothed away. "Very well. I'm appeased. The facts, though, can't be very pleasing to you."

The facts deeply troubled her. She'd lain awake all night, trying to figure a way for the family to raise ten thousand pounds. Nothing had come to mind other than selling James to pirates; amusing as that thought had been, at the moment she simply felt . . . overwhelmed.

"Come along, Rose. Let's purchase some hair ribbons. That should cure your doldrums."

A sack of money falling from the sky would cure her doldrums better. Rose nodded, pasting a smile on her face. "Yes, that's just the th—"

The book jolted loose from her arm and fell to the ground. Opening her mouth to apologize to the man she'd bumped into, Rose turned around. And stopped.

"*A History of the New World*," he read, straightening with the book in his hands.

Eyes black as pitch regarded her. She'd never seen

eyes like that before. The effect of their direct, level gaze was . . . unsettling. Beside her, Maggie gave a small gasp. "Thank you for retrieving my book, sir," she said, finding that her voice wanted to quaver and fighting against it. "May I have it back?"

His head tilted a little to one side, a strand of coal black hair falling forward across his forehead. He was all in black, she realized, from his beaver hat to his gloves to the soles of his boots. Only a white shirt collar and simply tied white cravat leavened his stark appearance. No, not stark, she amended as he glanced down at the book again. Predatory. All six lean feet of him.

"Do the Americas interest you?" he asked, his voice a low, cultured drawl that seemed to resonate down her spine.

"Learning things interests me," she replied, and held out her hand.

The corner of his mouth quirked, and he slowly placed the book into her fingers. "Well, then. I could teach you such things, Lady Rosamund," he murmured. With a last look from those midnight eyes, he turned away and vanished into the crowd as if he'd never been there at all. As if she'd imagined him.

"Oh, my word," Maggie whispered, and clutched her arm.

Rose jumped. "What? Do you know him?"

Blonde hair shook vigorously. "Never. I know *of* him, though. So do you."

"Who is he, then? For heaven's sake. He knew my name." And the way he'd said it, and what he'd said . . . It had made her want to blush, but on the inside.

"Heaven has nothing to do with him. My father pointed him out to me once and told me to stay well away from him."

"Maggie."

"That was Lord Bramwell Lowry Johns."

Bram flipped open his pocket watch. If Abernathy was to meet Cosgrove at noon, then he was running very late. "Up, Titan," he ordered, nudging the black in the ribs. They moved into a canter, the fastest pace possible in the environs of Pall Mall at this hour.

If the chit hadn't spent so long in the bloody lending library—or if he'd been able to tolerate the idea of crossing the threshold to see her up close inside, he might have saved a bit of time. There were some things, though, not even he would stoop to. And entering a lending library was one of them.

The book he'd pushed out of her hands had surprised him, when he hadn't expected anything about her to be of much interest. He'd summed her up in advance. She would be mousy, with a weak character, close-set eyes, a dress up to her chin, a simpering laugh, no conversation, and the book would be one of those frightful gothic escapades all the young chits seemed to find so romantic.

Her eyes had not been close-set, but they annoyed him. They were green, he recalled quite clearly, complementing well her ginger hair, and they'd gazed directly at him. Women didn't often do that. Virginal, mousy chits certainly didn't.

Her father had been correct in saying that she wasn't striking, for her chest was less than ample, and her mouth a touch too wide. She stood several inches above anything that might be considered petite, and he'd spied at least a half-dozen freckles across the bridge of her nose.

As he reached the front door of the Society Club he swung down from Titan and tossed the end of the reins to the groom who came puffing up behind him. "Walk him, Redding," he instructed. "I shan't be long."

"Very good, my lord."

The doorman greeted him as he stepped inside. "Lord Bramwell. Good afternoon."

"Jones. Is Cosgrove here?"

"In the dining room. He's expecting g—"

"Yes, I know." Bram walked through the square foyer and into the large, dark, wood-paneled dining room.

The place smelled of roast pheasant and red wine, and already at this early hour better than half the tables were occupied by the cream of London's male aristocracy. Even with the growing noontime crowd, the lone figure seated at the back of the room seemed to have at least one empty table between him and the rest of the diners.

"King," he said, taking the seat opposite the marquis. He generally didn't like sitting with his back to the room, but Cosgrove didn't either, and the marquis had arrived first.

"Bramwell. Surprised to see you in such proper company." The marquis lifted the bottle of port that decorated the center of the table and poured Bram a glass.

"I could say the same about you."

Pale blue eyes regarded him for a moment. "I've a luncheon engagement. Business. I'd avoid it myself, if I could."

"Yes, you're arranging your marriage." Bram took a sip of the too-sweet wine, the only thing Cosgrove ever drank before nightfall. "Came to congratulate you in advance."

Bram could count on one hand the number of times Kingston Gore had ever been truly surprised, and this was one of them. His expression didn't change except for a slight narrowing of his eyes, but it was enough.

To anyone just setting eyes on him, the Marquis of Cosgrove looked very like an angel fallen from heaven. Unruly golden hair, fair skin, those pale blue eyes, tall, lean—poets wept for such subjects. Having been acquainted with him for thirteen years, though, Bram knew that his skin was pale both because he rarely ventured out of doors during daylight hours and because of the absinthe the marquis drank nearly nightly. The angelic features were as much a mask as anyone else would wear to a masquerade ball, and the creature that lurked behind it was both heartless and soulless, and was perfectly at ease with being so. As for his age, he'd never given it, but Bram would guess him to be somewhere in his middle thirties.

"One of these days," Cosgrove finally said, "you're going to tell me who you pay to get your information."

"I keep an oracle in my wine cellar. For the price of a selection of small animals and the occasional infant she tells me everything I wish to know."

"Mm hm. Everything?" King shifted his attention to the room, as he frequently did. He likely had more men wishing him dead than even Bram did.

Under other circumstances Bram would have found it annoying to be a runner-up at anything—wagering, sex, inappropriate conversation, unsavory habits, or friends. When the winner of the contest was Kingston Gore, however, second place was still left with enough notoriety to please Genghis Khan. Or Bram Johns. "Everything of any significance," he said aloud.

"Then you know who's decided to join Lord Abernathy for his luncheon appointment today."

With a frown, Bram leaned forward. "What I want to know is why you've decided to marry, and why to that Davies chit?"

Cosgrove's lips curved in a humorless smile. "Because she's of good stock, and her family has no choice in the matter. And because she'll give me an heir and won't dare protest my . . . habitual activities." The marquis looked past Bram again. "Abernathy, Your Grace, thank you for meeting me here. I'm afraid my schedule is frightfully tangled these days."

Bram's spine snapped to attention before he could stop it. Damned Cosgrove. *That* was what he'd been talking about—that the Duke of Levonzy was coming up behind him. And from the marquis's lifted eyebrow as he gestured for the two men to sit, he knew of Bram's abrupt discomfiture.

"I'm only here at Abernathy's request," the duke said, steel gray eyes passing over Bram and moving beyond him to Cosgrove. "You have a reputation for not dealing fairly."

"A well-earned one," Cosgrove returned easily. "Are you staying, Bramwell? I know how you detest business."

King might have supplied him an excuse to go without losing face, but the marquis cared only for his own interests, as did Bram. He considered staying, but when he weighed that against the prospect of listening to his father discuss anything for an hour, the decision was an easy one. He pushed away from the table and stood. "I'm leaving." Bram nodded at Abernathy. "You may sell your daughter in peace."

The earl's skin darkened. "I—"

"Pay that fool no mind, Lewis. He has no concept of duty or propriety." The duke gestured for a bottle of wine.

"I can't argue with that, except to say that I've never been happier not to be considered a proper gentleman. Cosgrove." With a nod Bram made his way through the maze of tables and back outside again.

Redding trotted up, Titan in tow, and Bram swung into the saddle. The problem was, he didn't have a destination in mind. He could go home and nap until a decent hour, or he could visit Phin and bully him into going to luncheon.

What he wanted to do, though, was have a longer chat with Lady Rosamund Davies. Nothing about this should have interested him in the least; for Lucifer's sake, arranged marriages were older than Egypt's pyramids. But at the same time, this one made him curious.

He understood Cosgrove and his motivations. The marquis had decided he wanted an heir of his own blood and name, which would remove his milk toast younger cousin Thomas Wyatt from the race. Being Cosgrove, he'd chosen a wife whom he could control, and who would continue to show a respectable face while the marquis continued with his whoring and drinking and wagering unabated.

And what was wrong with that? Nothing he supposed, except that King's betrothed-to-be borrowed books on the history of the Colonies. He was used to assessing character quickly, and even with the few words they'd exchanged, she didn't seem the moronic, spineless chit who would acquiesce to being a laughingstock without protest. Still, he'd been wrong before. Rarely, but it did happen.

Perhaps, then, his perception of her had been wrong. Bram sent a glance back in the direction of the Society Club. He loved deciphering a mystery, and this smelled like one. After all, Cosgrove might have been a good teacher, but Bram had been an excellent student. And anything that could be turned to his advantage needed to be looked into.

He consulted his pocket watch again. Not quite half twelve. Where had that whelp James Davies said he was going today? Generally Lord Lester prattled so much that Bram ceased listening altogether. But there had been something . . .

"Come along, Redding," he said over his shoulder, urging Titan into a trot. "We're off to Gentleman Jackson's."

The groom didn't even blink. "Very good, my lord."

As he entered the boxing establishment twenty minutes later, he'd begun to question just what it was he thought he was doing. Chasing after Cosgrove's plots and machinations had never netted anyone a reward, and he didn't believe in pursuing anything that held no profit for him. That damned curiosity of his, he supposed. Ah, well. A bit of knowledge rarely served him poorly.

"I say! Lord Bram!"

Stifling a sigh, Bram turned around to see the Earl of Abernathy's only son and heir. At least he hadn't had to scour the rest of London for the boy. "Lester."

The pup grinned happily. "I never expected to see you at Gentleman Jackson's."

Bram lifted an eyebrow. "And why is that? Do you think me incapable of defending myself in a row?"

Lord Lester flushed. "No. Of course not. It's merely that you seem more the . . . sword and pistol sort."

"Precisely so. Fisticuffs are messy." He sent a glance past the lad at Jackson himself, and nodded. With a short smile the boxer continued with the lesson he was delivering. Bram returned his attention to the young viscount. "Since we've run across one another, why don't you join me for luncheon?"

"Absolutely, old blade. Give me a moment to fetch my coat, will you?"

While the boy scampered off, Bram hoped this little play he'd discovered would be worth it. He'd originally planned to visit Miss Heloise Blanchard for a bit of sport after the actress's morning rehearsal. He'd done this to himself, though, and he was the one person whose consequences he was willing to suffer. Even if it meant an afternoon's celibacy so he could dine with an idiot.

"White's?" Lester commented, as they dismounted and handed the horses over to Redding.

"They serve a fine pheasant," Bram returned, reminding himself again that he'd instigated this. Considering that, Lester would have to behave in an even stupider manner than usual before he could let his own . . . displeasure be known. "Where did you think we were going?"

"I'd hoped you might take me to Jezebel's. Cosgrove's been singing its praises for weeks. I attempted to go last night, but apparently there's a password or secret knock or something involved."

Or a payment of a shilling to the fellow at the door. The viscount's wistful look was almost amusing. "One does not go to Jezebel's for food, James."

"Yes, but the faro tables are legendary."

As the doorman collected their hats and gloves, Bram felt a brush of annoyance touch him. He'd been known to wager heavily himself, but he had never lost more than he could afford. Clearly the young fool had no idea of his own limitations. "Do you think we'll encounter your father here?" he asked offhandedly.

Lester shook his head. "No. Father's having luncheon with Cosgrove. He forbade me to join them." He shrugged as a waiter escorted them to a table by the front window. "I told him I should be there. Cosgrove's *my* friend, after all."

Cosgrove was no one's friend; even knowing him for better than a decade, Bram thought of King as a mentor, but more recently as more of an acquaintance with whom he shared some interests and a general penchant for cynical observation and decadence. "Not to intrude, but what does your father want with Kingston Gore?"

For a moment Lester actually looked embarrassed. "I owe a little blunt to Cosgrove. They're deciding the terms of payment."

"Ah."

"I told Father I could win the funds back, but he'd rather treat me like a bloody infant."

Bram tried to remember when he'd been as stupidly naive as James Davies, but nothing came to mind. And any inclination to be so had vanished utterly during his sixteenth year. He even knew the date. The seventeenth of May. And he distinctly recalled that it had been two days afterward that he'd first encountered Kingston Gore and knowingly sold his soul to the devil.

Perhaps that was the difference between how *he'd* fared in Society's underbelly and how young James was progressing. The viscount wanted to be seen as an adult by his family. Bram had wanted to master every vice known to man, and if possible to invent several new ones. But King's claws were difficult to avoid, and he'd experienced that, too.

He shook himself as a waiter approached. Reminiscing left a sour taste in his mouth, and he made a point of never indulging in the practice in public. It had only been that damned conversation he'd overheard last night. The Earl of Abernathy and the Duke of Levonzy had more in common than even they probably realized.

"Your preference, my lord?"

Good God, he was *still* reminiscing. "The pheasant," he said. "And a bottle of your best claret."

The waiter bowed. "Right away, my lord."

"What do you think of Vauxhall Gardens?" Lester asked, leaning forward on his elbows. "My father says it's generally no place for gentlemen, but I heard that Prinny attends."

"I avoid it whenever possible. Unless your taste runs to penny-a-tumble doxies, I see little attraction."

The viscount's brow furrowed. "Oh. But what about—"

"How will your father settle your debts? Cosgrove's not the only fellow you owe." His own uncollected winnings amounted to only a few hundred quid; when Cosgrove began toying with a new pup, Bram tended to stand clear of the slaughter. But the blunt did give him a reason to ask the question.

Lester made a dismissive gesture. "Seeing that he didn't want me included, I reckon it's nothing that concerns me."

"Just so." Bram poured himself a glass of claret and took a drink. "Which soiree does your family attend next?"

"We're all to go to Clacton House tonight. Lady Clacton's my mother's aunt. Dull as stones, but Father will take a stick to me if I don't attend."

Bloody hell. Lord and Lady Clacton. The two of them still powdered their damned hair. During a less-than-sober moment he'd made a vow once to fall on a sword before he ever attended one of their soirees. As soon as he returned home this afternoon, however, he would be sending over a belated acceptance to their invitation.

As to why, precisely, he'd decided to make such a sacrifice, he couldn't come up with a decent explanation even for himself. He had to be missing something in all this, though, and he hated letting a mystery pass by without solution. Even when he'd probably dislike the answer.

Chapter 3 _____

Rosamund Davies took her time choosing a gown and putting up her hair. She subscribed to the idea that a woman's outer appearance served the same function as did a knight's armor, and this evening she was definitely dressing for battle.

"You look lovely, Lady Rose," her maid said with an uncomfortable-looking smile.

"Thank you, Martha. And I think I'd prefer to wear the pearls," Rose answered, eyeing herself critically in the mirror. The faux emeralds complemented both her eyes and the light green and gray of her gown, but the pearls felt more . . . sophisticated. And this evening she at least wanted to appear intelligent and unruled by emotion, however scattered she felt.

She'd always been the one to see to things, to make certain that the household ran smoothly and that the family showed itself as well as possible. Most of the time they more than likely weren't even aware of what she contributed. Choosing the daily menu, overseeing the staff, approving household purchases. And now she felt as though she'd been kicked. After twenty years, she'd abruptly become valuable in their eyes—as a bargaining chip to settle a debt. And for the first time she had to wonder whether they were asking—no, demanding—too much of her.

Her bedchamber door rattled. "Come along, Rose," her mother called. "Your father doesn't wish to be late."

They were already late, though she was the only one who knew that. Rosamund didn't answer the summons, mostly because she wanted to see whether Lady Abernathy would dare step into the room. Considering that both of her parents had been avoiding her since her father had returned from luncheon, she wasn't surprised when her mother's footsteps retreated in the direction of the stairs.

She sniffed. *Good.* It was certainly easier to be indignant and angry than to sit back and consider what lay before her. How lovely to know that in her family's eyes she could finally serve a purpose. In a sense, though, she was glad that it hadn't been Beatrice sent headlong into this mess; her sister could barely tolerate anyone looking at her crosswise. She would certainly be no match for Cosgrove.

The door shook again. "Rose?"

James. With a grimace she stood, gesturing for her white kid gloves. Yesterday her brother's carelessness had only annoyed and appalled her. Now his actions seemed almost criminal. And he would of course be the one who escaped any consequences. Taking a breath, she pulled open her door.

Her brother blinked and took a step backward. "There you are. Thought maybe you were going to hide all night."

"I haven't done anything for which I need to hide." She looked him directly in the eyes, trying to decide when his youthful obliviousness had gone from amusing to exasperating. She was unsurprised when he quickly averted his gaze. "Do you feel any responsibility at all for the mess you've made for this family? For me?"

Her younger sibling frowned. "Father mishandled the situation," he muttered, falling in behind her as she descended the stairs. "He should have let me talk with Cosgrove. He's *my* crony, and I could have played him for the blunt. I'm nearly unbeatable at faro. He's told me so himself."

"James, you owe him more than the value of this house. Clearly you are not unbeatable at faro. I daresay *I* could play the game better than you do. At the least I would have stopped when I began losing."

"If you stop when you're behind, you'll never recover your losses."

"Idiot."

"You can't talk like that to me, Rose," he snapped. "I'm not fifteen any longer."

"No, you're eighteen. And you're behaving like a two-year-old."

"That is not so," he stated. "And I don't know why your hackles are up, anyway. Cosgrove thinks you're worth ten thousand quid. You're the Queen of Sheba."

"If you think so highly of him, *you* marry him."

"You don't even know him. He's coming to the soiree tonight, and he don't ever do that. He wants to see you."

A quiver of uneasiness slithered up her spine. "He wants to see me," she repeated. "If he'd wanted to . . . court me, he might have called here and offered to take me driving. Not purchase me for the price of a gambling debt."

"Father got him to agree to wait until the end of the month to announce anything, so now he can take you driving. I daresay you might even decide that you like him."

That seemed extremely unlikely. As she reached the foyer, her father sent her a stern look and then led the way out to the waiting coach. None of them saw the true problem. Cosgrove might have agreed to forgive James's debt, but in marrying her the marquis would secure a permanent position in her softheaded brother's life. In all their lives. Ten thousand pounds could very well be nothing but an aperitif.

Whatever Cosgrove's plans, though, he'd miscalculated; he could insinuate himself into their lives, but at the same time she would be in the middle of his. And however angry she might be with her family at the moment, she was still a Davies. The one who kept them all in order. And she was not about to sit by and let them be ruined. Not if she had any say at all in the matter.

She took her seat in the coach, perfectly resigned to sit in silence all the way to Clacton House. At the moment she preferred being left to stew, and imagining with some satisfaction how her parents meant to inform Mayfair at large that their daughter would be marrying a notorious blackguard after a month of supposed courtship. Yes, being affronted and indignant was much better than finally having to pause and consider that she was the daughter expected to wed that awful man.

"Rosamund," her father said abruptly, "you know that none of us is pleased to be in this position." He sent a glare at James, seated beside her. "But I expect you to behave, and to keep a civil tongue in your head."

"Of course, Father."

James shifted. "I don't see why this is such a sacrifice for Rose, anyway. I think Cosgrove is being very generous. And he knows everything about everything."

"Lord Cosgrove has forgiven your current debts, James," their father grunted. "I have nothing else to give him—or anyone, so pray don't do it again."

"Yes, James," Rose seconded, "nearly destroy the family a second time, and you might just have to face a consequence."

"Ha. You think Cosgrove and his cronies have reckoned me an easy touch. Well, that's not so. Bram Johns had me to luncheon just today, and we went to White's. No wagering at all, and he even asked what my plans were for tonight and said he might attend, as well."

Another shiver ran down Rose's spine. Lord Bramwell must have met up with James immediately after their . . . unusual little conversation. What was he up to? She had enough trouble. All she needed was for Lord Bramwell Lowry Johns to make a few more of those comments he undoubtedly found clever and oh, so effective at stirring female hearts. Well, she might be obligated to behave toward Lord Cosgrove, but no one had made any such stipulation where Lord Bram was concerned.

Generally, attending Great Aunt and Uncle Clacton's annual soiree was a dull chore. The staid festivities seldom attracted any but the white-haired set who all had to be home in bed by eleven o'clock in the evening at the latest. So the large crowd of vehicles lining the drive and the street outside Clacton House was something of a surprise.

"Good heavens," her mother said as they stepped down from the coach. "Is there no other entertainment to be had tonight?"

"Apparently not," Lord Abernathy answered, his own expression growing grimmer by the moment. And not because they were coming closer to the moment of sighting the man to whom he'd sold his daughter, but more likely because there would be more witnesses than he'd anticipated.

The harried-looking butler ushered them into the foyer. "Lord Abernathy," he panted, gesturing to one of the dozen footmen scurrying about the entryway. "Desmond will take your wraps."

"What's afoot tonight, Wiltern?"

"A very many last-minute acceptances to the soiree, my lord. Lord Clacton is quite put out that we shall likely run out of Madeira before the second set."

"There's always his wine cellar," Rose's father returned.

"That is what he's afraid of."

Before Rosamund was ready, they found themselves inside the upstairs ballroom. It was so crowded that she could barely keep her mother in view. Hope flashed through her. Perhaps Cosgrove would miss her entirely. Perhaps he'd seen the crush of vehicles in front of the house and decided to forgo the evening entirely in favor of visiting one of those infamous dens of iniquity.

Then she caught sight of him, and her heart turned to ice. He wore a light brown coat that somehow accented his golden hair, an angel's costume concealing a demon. Dread trickled deeper through her, and involuntarily she took a step backward. The longer she could go without engaging in any conversation with him, the better.

Swiftly she turned around before he could see her—only to spy the other blackguard in the room. Lord Bramwell stood by the stairs, accompanied by two young ladies and a tall, dark-haired man with a narrow scar down his right cheek. The two ladies laughed at something the Duke of Levonzy's second son said.

Laughing? With a glance again at Cosgrove across the room, she edged closer to the conversation. Laughter and James's black-hearted cronies didn't seem at all compatible.

"—don't think you were ever afraid of me at all," the younger of the ladies said. "Until I arrived in London, I had no idea your reputation was as awful as Phin kept telling me. You were being nice by running away from me."

Bram Johns coughed. "*I* kept telling you that my reputation is abominable. And you were trying to frighten me by being . . . innocent. It still makes me shudder, Beth."

"Well, I'll never say anything bad about you, no matter how much you want me to."

"You are a cruel chit, my dear. What about you, Alyse? Surely you can conjure something vile about me."

"Why don't you ask me?" the fellow with the scar put in, grinning.

"Don't interrupt, Phin."

The second woman leaned into this Phin's shoulder. "I'm glad to be your friend, Bram. And I'm even more glad not to be your enemy."

Bram nodded. "That at least sounds like a backhanded compliment."

As he spoke he caught sight of Lady Rosamund Davies. She quickly turned away, only to head off in a third direction after a glance toward Cosgrove, retreating from a man who hadn't even seen her yet. Was it distaste, or was it fear? Either sentiment intrigued him, probably more than it should.

"Excuse me, Bromleys," he said, and left his friends to trail after Lady Rosamund. "I wouldn't recommend running," he drawled from behind her. "You're not dressed for it."

Her shoulders stiffening, she turned around. "Lord Bramwell Johns," she stated, her voice nearly steady.

He inclined his head. "You've discovered my identity."

"Yes. Your misdeeds have made you quite famous. Or infamous, rather. I'd been hoping James would introduce us before today."

A slight smile curved his mouth. Not fear, then. And yet she didn't seem foolish, which she would have to be to want an acquaintance with him. "And why were you hoping for an introduction, Lady Rosamund?" he prompted, liking the way her name felt on his tongue.

"Because I wanted to punch you in the nose for encouraging my brother into a life of nonsense and depravity."

Bramwell laughed. God, women surprised him so seldom any longer, and yet she'd managed to do so. Twice in one day, if he counted that ridiculous history tome she'd been toting about. "Nonsense, I shall admit to," he said, continuing to chuckle. "Every man must find his own depravity. I'll take no credit for that."

"Do you take credit for his losses at the table?"

He shrugged. "He owes me a few hundred quid." Cocking his head at her, he assessed his next move on this chessboard. "Do one thing for me, and I'll erase the debt."

Rose narrowed her eyes. "What is it, exactly, that you want from me?"

That was a more interesting question than she probably realized. And he hadn't an answer. Not yet. He damned well meant to find one. "A dance," he said aloud.

Blinking, Lady Rosamund folded her arms across her not-quite-generous-enough chest. "I am not going to dance with you."

Yes, you are. The force of that thought unsettled him a little, but for the moment he would humor himself. He certainly had nothing better to do. "If a marriage is valued at ten thousand, surely I might have a waltz for three hundred."

Her fingers clenched into very determined-looking fists. "So you know about the debt."

He nodded. "If I'd known the prize, I might have wagered a larger sum against your brother."

"I am not for sale."

Clearly he could argue with that, but from the abrupt horror in her grass green eyes, she'd realized that at the same moment she'd spoken. *Horror*. He'd been forced into things he didn't relish by the lure of funds—or of having them cut off—but the blunt had been the reward for compliance. What was her reward? Marriage to Cosgrove?

As she started to turn her back on him, he touched her shoulder. Lightly. Even through the green silk of her gown, his fingers felt scalded, and he withdrew them swiftly.

"A trade, then," he continued, as she faced him again. He flexed his fingers, resisting the urge to shake them.

"I have no idea what you're talk—"

"Once the rest of Mayfair hears you're to marry Kingston Gore, very few gentlemen will be willing to risk stepping onto the floor with you. If you dance with me tonight, though, I will dance with you later, when no one else will. *And* I'll forgive your brother's debt."

He wanted to touch her again, to see whether that odd heat would repeat itself, but at the same time the idea worried him. He enjoyed sex, but one woman served as well as another. Touching a female's arm did not scorch him, and certainly not through cloth.

Green eyes studied his face in that direct, disconcerting way he'd already noticed that she had. "You'll forgive James's debt."

"Yes."

"And you will not wager with him again."

"That will take two dances."

Rosamund glanced in the direction of her parents, who'd been foolish enough to wander halfway across the room without her. Of course they'd been foolish enough to let their son bury them in debt, and to send their daughter off as a sacrifice, so their lack of attention wasn't unexpected. "I doubt you'll hear a waltz played tonight."

He grimaced. Damned powder-wigged drudges. "A quadrille, then, for tonight. And the promise of a waltz at the next soiree you attend."

"Very well," she said slowly.

His mouth curved again. "Good." Bram stuck out his hand. "Let's shake on our agreement, shall we?"

Her mouth opened again, and he abruptly wanted to kiss her. Another oddity, because he rarely kissed. Whatever the devil was wrong with him, it seemed to involve her. When she touched her palm to his and curled her fingers around his, warmth shot through his hand down his spine, and slammed into his groin. It took more self-restraint than he generally showed to keep from pulling her into his arms.

Lady Rosamund made a small sound and swiftly withdrew her hand, flexing her fingers as she did so. For God's sake, she'd felt it too. He looked at her, for once not certain what to say.

An arm draped across his shoulder. "Ah, Bramwell, I see you've met my intended," King drawled, gazing at Rosamund.

"Yes. I was just congratulating her," he heard himself say, noting that King's almost-betrothed had lost several shades of color. "And I've gotten myself a quadrille," he continued, "because apparently waltzing is forbidden here."

"That is a shame," Cosgrove said. "Where but a waltz or a marriage bed can a man and a woman be so intimate?" The marquis grinned. "Other than the odd brothel or broom closet or closed carriage or . . . more discriminating soiree, that is?"

Rosamund's color returned in a rush. "Excuse me, my lords," she said, bobbing a stiff curtsy. "I think I hear my mother calling me."

Bram's gaze lowered to the curve of her hips as she hurried away from them. He'd heard Cosgrove give a near duplicate of that speech before, but the female in that instance had been neither shocked nor virginal.

"Ah, I suppose I'll have to chase after her now." King sighed. "I imagine her mother and sister are equally as frigid."

"Then why bother?" Bram asked, managing just the right degree of cynical amusement. For once the tone sounded odd on his lips, because surprisingly he didn't feel much amused at all.

" 'Why bother?' " King repeated. "Because it will be very, very amusing. I daresay in six months you won't even recognize proper, clenched Lady Rose Davies." He tightened his grip on Bram's shoulder. "And her damned father forced a month's delay on me. Apparently he wants it to look like a love match. *I* think that was Levonzy's doing, but it does make the game more interesting, I suppose. So keep the agreement to yourself, will you?"

More interesting, indeed. "I'll be silent as the grave."

"Good." Blue eyes slanted in Rosamund's direction. "Look at her, Bramwell. She thinks she can stand up to me. It puts me all aflutter."

Cosgrove released his grip to stroll over to where Rosamund stood beside her mother and tried to look interested in whatever inane conversation the woman was having with her husband. Bram gestured for a glass of whiskey. Uncomfortable with the tight sensation in his chest, he took a long swallow and turned his back on them in favor of the equally crowded corridor.

He'd seen the Marquis of Cosgrove dig his claws into people before. King probably had urns full of dusty, ill-used souls lining the mantel of Gore House. Some had been eager to learn what they thought would be the ways of a popular bounder. Others had been snatched unawares simply because they took King's fancy for some reason or other. Bram conceded that he was more than likely the only one of Cosgrove's former fledglings who had known precisely what he was walking into and had welcomed every black, twisted moment of his so-called education.

This time Cosgrove's game bothered him. Rosamund Davies wanted nothing to do with the marquis, and she was being forced into it against her will. Neither did she seem to want anything to do with *him*, Bram reflected, but he could hardly blame her for that. He knew full well that he was as black as pitch inside and out. And Lady Rosamund was . . . good.

Bram downed the whiskey and set the glass aside. Yes, she was good, and he was definitely not good, and he was going to dance a bloody quadrille with her because he'd given his word.

"I don't think we need to wait to make the announcement," Lord Cosgrove said in a low voice.

Ostensibly he was speaking to her father, but Rose hadn't been able to avoid noticing that his light blue gaze remained on her the entire time. It made her want a bath.

"You agreed to the delay, Cosgrove. It will better serve all of our reputations."

The marquis nodded. "I suppose so. Everyone will be convinced that Rose and I have made a love match, and no one need know how close your family came to ruination and the poorhouse. Very clever of you, Abernathy."

Her father didn't like that, Rose could see, but since it was true there wasn't much he could say about it. It might have been satisfying to see him put in his place, except that she remained the one paying the highest price in all of this.

Bram Johns had turned her into a bargaining piece as well, but at least he'd bargained *with* her. And she'd had the choice of agreeing to his terms or not. She hadn't expected that from someone of his reputation, but perhaps she simply wasn't familiar yet with all the machinations of blackguards. At the same time, if she hadn't overheard his amiable conversation with proper ladies who apparently liked him, she didn't think she would be dancing a quadrille with him later.

She glanced at Cosgrove and then away again. Apparently she was going to become a great deal more familiar with at least this blackguard—unless she could conjure a way to aid her family's predicament that didn't include marriage. Failing that, she would be forced into his life. Hm. It therefore seemed wise to learn about it—especially if she meant to be able to use any of her knowledge to keep Cosgrove away

from James. If no one else could do it, she would
have to do it herself. There was also the matter of
self-preservation, though she had no idea yet how she
would protect herself.

The first quadrille of the evening was announced,
and her heart shuddered a little in her chest. Lord
Bramwell hadn't said which quadrille he wanted, but
with Cosgrove standing so close to her, no one else had
approached her for a place on her dance card—not that
she'd ever seen it filled past halfway under the best of
circumstances. Her evening tonight seemed to be wide
open. Bramwell Johns had been very correct about that.
It seemed her days of dancing for the joy of it had vanished before she'd had a chance to bid them goodbye.

"Excuse me," the low voice she'd already come to
recognize drawled from behind her, "but I believe this
is our dance, Lady Rosamund."

As she turned to face him, she caught the quick look
that flashed from Cosgrove to Lord Bramwell. That
was curious. She knew them to be fast friends, and yet
the look in the marquis's eyes hadn't been friendly at
all. Trying to ignore the unhappy throat-clearing from
her mother, as if associating with Cosgrove was better
in any way than accepting a dance with Johns, she held
out her hand.

Awareness crept up her fingers as he clasped them.
Wordlessly he led her to a space on the dance floor and
released her to take a step back into the long line of
gentlemen. The music began, her side curtsied while
his bowed, and they turned into the dance.

"Answer a question for me, Lord Bramwell," she
began after a moment, as the dance brought them together.

"Perhaps," he returned, regarding her again with that unreadable gaze of his.

"Are you and Lord Cosgrove not allies?"

A muscle in his jaw jumped. "We generally end on the same side of opinions. Why do you ask?"

"I'm attempting to discover what your part in all of this might be. And don't try to tell me that our meeting this morning was a coincidence. You've known James for nearly a month, yet I only make your acquaintance on the morning that Cosgrove deigns to settle my brother's debt? You came specifically to see me."

"You have me deciphered, then."

"And yet, I don't think a groom-to-be's friend would say to a wife-to-be what you said to me."

They parted, turning with other partners before he made his way back to her side. "I'm not much for formality of acquaintance," he drawled, keeping his voice pitched low.

Rose drew a breath. "So you think we should become . . . lovers."

His grip on her fingers tightened briefly. "Oh, I definitely think that."

Goodness. "What would your friend think about that?" she asked when she could steady her voice again.

"Lady Rosamund, if you're attempting to play one of us against the other, I would recommend another course of action. Neither of us is terribly particular, and though for some reason I seem to be feeling . . . nice this evening, it's not an emotion you should wager on where I'm concerned."

"You were very pleasant to those ladies, earlier."

"Alyse and Beth Bromley? They are my friends. I don't touch my friends." He gazed at her. "You are not my friend."

For the first time since she'd set eyes on him tonight, a stir of uneasiness went through her. This man she danced with and exchanged words with had ruined people before. He'd ruined women with scandal, and men with money. He'd fought in the war on the Peninsula, and the rumors were that he'd killed both before and after that expedition. Drinking, wagering, women—according to James, Lord Bramwell hadn't set foot inside a church in ten years for fear that he would be struck dead beneath the entryway.

"Why are you here then, sir?"

The dance ended, and he stopped in front of her, ignoring the applause of the guests around them. He gazed at her levelly, a black-haired, black-clothed demon of impeccable proportion and symmetry. A handsome devil, literally.

"I've decided to do you a favor," he said finally, the lazy drawl just touching his voice and stirring down her spine in response.

She folded her hands in front of her. "And what favor is that, pray tell?"

"Kingston Gore will eat you alive," he returned even more quietly, taking a slow step closer among the milling guests. "Beginning with your honor, and ending with your soul."

"I—"

"I know this, because I fed him mine a very long time ago." Lord Bramwell took her hand, lifting it in his to examine it thoughtfully before he raised her knuckles to his sensuous lips. She wanted to close her eyes at the sensation of his warm mouth touching her skin. Good heavens.

"Then you've warned me," she said, more stiffly than she meant to, and snatched her hand away. "Thank you. My family requires me to make a union with Lord Cosgrove, and so I will do so. I daresay I can manage him as well as he manages me."

He shook his head, one black strand of hair falling across his eyes. "Not without my help, you won't." Lord Bramwell took her hand again, this time placing it more properly over his sleeve. "I know him better than anyone other than Satan himself," he continued, strolling with her in the direction of her parents and Lord Cosgrove, who continued to gaze at her with those angelic blue eyes.

"What could you possibly do to help me?"

"Make off with you."

"Don't jest."

"I find myself surprised, but I seem to be utterly serious."

"No!" Rose tried to regain some composure before she suffered an apoplexy in the middle of Great Aunt Clacton's ballroom. "For heaven's sake. Keeping me hidden away in some . . . cellar wouldn't help my family."

"But they're selling you to Cosgrove."

She looked up into his eyes. They were very different people, she realized, and while he obviously had no grasp of right from wrong, or loyalty and honor, she did. "I don't like my family," she whispered as they drew near, "but they are my family. They depend on

me. This is how I am required to render my assistance."
As for her private feelings about that circumstance, she
wasn't about to enlighten him.

Slowly he slipped his arm from hers, stopping as she
continued to advance. "Then allow me to teach you
how to play the game," he murmured from behind her.

His voice echoed into her chest. Heaven knew she did
need some help. The . . . horrified dismay she felt when
she looked again at the Marquis of Cosgrove made that
clear enough. Marriage. The rest of her life, entwined
with his. She was in well over her head. And to her surprise, she didn't feel that same horror when she looked
at his friend.

She supposed beggars, as the saying went, couldn't
be choosers. Without turning around, Rosamund
nodded her head. She would have to learn whatever
Bram Johns could teach her about the devils inhabiting
London. And soon.

Chapter 4 _____

Bram rose early the next morning. It was early for him, anyway. Before noon, and by several damned hours. "Mostin," he said, as he sat at his dressing table to shave, "how long have you been in my employ?"

The valet finished opening the heavy curtains that covered every window of the large bedchamber. "Seven years, my lord."

"And in all of that time, have you ever known me to do anything selfless?"

"Selfless, my lord?"

"Don't play coy, Mostin. You know perfectly well what I mean. An action without any gain, monetary or otherwise, for me. And be honest."

"Honest, my lord?"

Bram slanted a look at the servant. "Honest."

"Then yes, my lord. I have seen you behave in a self-less manner."

"You have not." Damn it all, that was not what he wanted to hear this morning. Not after the oddness of last night. "When?"

The valet cleared his throat. "I have several times seen you leaving for luncheon with Lord Quence, even to the point of canceling engagements with . . . young ladies to do so."

"Oh, that. Allow me to clarify. I refer to selfless actions that do not involve the families of Phin Bromley or Sullivan Waring."

"Ah. Then no, my lord. I have never known you to perform a single selfless act."

"Precisely."

"Though you did spend three years on the Continent, where I know very little of your activities."

"That was war. One is never selfless in war."

"As you say then, my lord."

The question became, then, what did he hope to gain from his offer to enlighten Lady Rosamund Davies as to the abyss that was Kingston Gore's soul? And what had prompted her to accept his offer? Aside from the fact that his own kettle was nearly as black as Cosgrove's, all he was likely to accomplish was to make his friend into an enemy. His suggestion hadn't been selfless, clearly; he found Rosamund interesting—even intriguing and compelling—and that baffled him. He'd known duchesses and opera singers and courtesans and even a female mercenary working against the French in Spain. A round-hipped, small-chested, green-eyed young woman with no worldly experience and a penchant for reading histories should barely have caught his eye, much less his attention.

Was that it, then? He needed to spend another hour or so chatting with her, telling her to stay away from absinthe and laudanum—and Cosgrove when he imbibed them—and take a bedchamber with a locking door as far away from Cosgrove's as she could manage. Then he could go back to burgling the homes of his father's friends and being as much of an annoyance as possible again.

"Will there be anything else, my lord?" Mostin asked as he put the last touches on Bram's cravat.

"Hm? No. Yes. Have Graham saddle Titan."

The valet nodded. "I shall inform him, my lord."

Bram dropped his pocket watch, money, a cigar, a handkerchief, and several calling cards into various pockets, then headed downstairs. Lowry House where he lived had been in the Johns family for three generations now. He'd moved into the house on Stratton Street as soon as he'd returned from Oxford, and his father had been only too happy to have him and his circle of acquaintances gone from the patriarchal abode of Johns House.

Lately he'd been receiving hints—well, closer to outright statements—that his days at Lowry House were numbered. After all, his older brother, August, the Marquis of Haithe, had managed to produce a male offspring, and the Johns progeny and heir to the heir was nearing his tenth birthday. The golden child would need his own abode in a decade or so, and Lowry House was the third finest London property the family owned.

So apparently if he wanted to avoid being removed from his own house, Bram would have to expire within the next ten years. And that happenstance wasn't all that unlikely. On the heels of that uplifting thought, his butler pulled open the front door as Bram reached the stair landing. "Good morning, Lord Haithe," Hibble intoned.

Bram stopped. "Oh, good God," he muttered, and turned on his heel, ascending the stairs again.

"Ah, Bram. Surprised to see you up and about already," his brother said, handing his hat to Hibble and beginning his own trot up the stairs. "I thought I'd have to sit in your morning room for hours and wait for you to come downstairs."

"That's precisely what you'll have to do, August," Bram returned, topping the stairs and making for his bedchamber. "I've just returned home from last night's festivities, and I'm off to bed. Good day." Thankfully the door of the master bedchamber had a very sturdy lock on it. One never knew when a jealous husband might make an appearance.

"You're not dressed for the evening."

Bram glanced down at his attire, black as it always was. "How can you tell?"

"Did you burgle Braithewaite?"

Clenching his jaw, Bram stopped his retreat. "That depends," he returned, facing the top of the stairs again. "Who's asking?"

"Father's already convinced it was you, so I suppose *I'm* asking."

"Then yes, it was me."

As older brothers went, he supposed that August Johns was at least no less than average. At eleven years his junior, Bram would never have called his brother a friend. Other than the black Johns hair they'd never looked much alike, and August's additional years and general . . . satisfaction with his life had rendered him five stone heavier and exceedingly smug.

"You have to stop robbing our friends, Bram."

"They're not *my* friends."

August frowned, clearly attempting to decipher him—something that Bram truly disliked. As if the pampered firstborn son would ever be able to understand what motivated the second. As if Bram knew even half the time what motivated him.

"They may not be your friends, but they've certainly committed no more sins than you have," the marquis finally decided. "And they can have you arrested if any of them realizes it's you who's been burgling them."

"I look forward to it. Was there anything else you wanted? Because I do have some plundering and pillaging on my calendar for today."

"Yes. Come to dinner tomorrow. The children want to see you again."

Bram lifted an eyebrow. "That invitation is a bit stunted, even for you."

"I won't apologize for not being as glib as you are. Bring some of your cronies if that makes your attendance more likely. Just not that damned Cosgrove. I won't have him in my home."

"I'll consider it."

Giving a nod, August turned to descend the stairs again. Just as Bram let out his breath in relief, though, his brother stopped. "Will you answer me one question honestly, Bram?"

"That depends on the question."

The Marquis of Haithe topped the stairs again. "Cosgrove. For five years, even when you weren't at war on the Peninsula, you barely had any communication with him. Now over the past year or so you two seem to be fast friends again. Why?"

For a moment Bram considered ignoring the question, simply retreating to his bedchamber until August left the house. If it had been his father asking, he would have said something about anything being an improvement after a conversation with Levonzy.

"I had two very dear friends," he said finally. "In their absence, I suppose the old saying 'the devil you know' applies."

"Your friends, did they die in the war? If I'd known, if you'd said something, I might have—"

"A fate worse than death befell them," Bram interrupted, unwilling to listen to August's account of how he would have provided sage advice and brotherly affection. "They both married and became insufferably happy about it. Disgusting, really." Even if their spouses were among the most tolerable females he'd ever met.

"Bram, that—"

"Good day, August. I actually do have an appointment this morning."

"Very well. And I expect to see you tomorrow evening, promptly at seven."

With a noncommittal grunt, Bram watched his brother out the front door. He gave the marquis five minutes to dilly about or think of another abysmally obvious question or observation, and then headed back downstairs.

"I'll be out all day, I imagine," he informed Hibble as he pulled on his black leather gloves and black great-coat. "If anyone calls to inquire, tell them I've . . . gone to Scandinavia."

The butler nodded. "Very good, my lord. Will you be returning for dinner?"

"Doubtful. Just on the odd chance, have Cook put on a pot of something."

"I'll see to it."

He collected Titan and rode off in the direction of Davies House. Since, as Mostin had agreed, he never did anything that didn't have a benefit in it for himself, he merely needed to decipher what he hoped to accomplish by befriending Rosamund Davies. Last night he'd dreamed of her mouth. It had done all the things he liked female mouths to do, and very well, but more interesting had been the talking. They'd chatted about all sorts of nonsense in his dream, and he'd enjoyed it. Talking. With a female. And *after* having sex with her. Some very excellent sex, if he said so himself.

Shocking. Best to become better acquainted with her and her family's circumstances, and with the details of King's plan, and then he could decide what it was that he wanted in all of this. Aside from bedding Rosamund Davies while wide awake, that was. And considering the circumstances and his supposed friendship with her groom-to-be, that was not going to be easy.

"What the devil is he doing here?" the Earl of Aber-nathy said as he lifted the embossed calling card off the butler's silver salver.

Rosamund looked up from her book as her father stood. All morning, every time someone called at the front door, her heart had leaped into her throat. After four hours of it, she was surprised she could still breathe. Still, no one had yet elicited the heated response that might signify one of James's supposed cronies. Until now.

"Shall I inquire, my lord?" Elbon asked in his usual toneless voice.

"No. I'll see to—"

"Bram Johns!" James's excited voice came from out in the hallway. "What the devil brings you here?"

It was amazing, Rose reflected, setting her book aside to cover the sudden shaking of her fingers, that James and her father could use nearly identical phrases and have nearly opposite sentiments behind them. As for herself, she couldn't decide yet how she felt. Anyone with insight into Cosgrove's character would ostensibly be welcome, but when that person had nearly as black a reputation as the marquis, the entire business became a bit muddy.

The two men entered the room, James with sunny green eyes and light brown hair, and Bram Johns with his pale skin and midnight features and clothes. He must have had some Spanish in his blood. Mesmerizing. And dangerous. Rosamund stood when her mother did, both of them curtsying. Somewhat to her surprise, Lord Bramwell sketched a shallow bow in response. The man did have manners, whether she'd ever heard of him using them before now or not.

Black eyes swept the room and focused on her, where they remained. "Good morning," he said. "I thought I'd ask James if he'd care to go riding with me this morning. And perhaps Lady Rosamund might wish to take the air with us as well. It's a fine day."

"Lady Rose is to join me on Bond Street for shopping," her mother said stiffly, disapproval in the straight line of her shoulders.

"Oh, but Mama, James and I get to go riding together so rarely these days. And that situation is not likely to improve." She didn't add that after a marriage to Cosgrove none of them would likely see her very often, but hopefully they understood that.

Her parents exchanged a glance, and then her father nodded. "Very well. At least with Rose present, James isn't likely to step into a card game."

"Father," the viscount complained, his cheeks flushing. "We have a guest."

By the door, Lord Bramwell flicked an imaginary speck of dust from the black sleeve of his coat. Whether he was annoyed or amused, Rose couldn't tell. "In all honesty, James," she ventured, hoping she wasn't about to find herself uninvited from the outing, "I don't think you need to dissemble. Lord Bramwell is probably quite familiar with your skills at wagering."

"That I am," Bramwell returned easily. "And since I rarely wager during daylight hours, everyone's purse is safe. Shall we?"

Rosamund picked up her book, since her mother hated seeing books lying about the house. "Give me five minutes," she said, and hurried out the morning room door without waiting for an answer.

As she passed by Lord Bramwell, his fingers brushed hers. She didn't know whether it had been an accident or not, but the way her pulse sped at the contact made one thing perfectly clear—she could not trust her own body where he was concerned. If he was to teach her how to deal with Cosgrove, she needed to realize her own odd . . . susceptibility to him. If there was one thing she *didn't* need, it was more trouble where James's cronies were concerned.

As soon as she fastened the last button of her gray riding jacket, she hurried down the stairs again. She could see James and his friend through the open front door, and when a hand grabbed her arm and yanked her sideways back into the morning room, she nearly shrieked.

"Mama!"

"Hush, Rose. We only have a moment."

She frowned. "What is it?"

"That man's reputation is as tarnished as Lord Cosgrove's. Attempting to play one man against the other will only ruin you and send this family to the poorhouse."

Rosamund shrugged free of her mother's too-tight grip. "I'm not playing at anything," she returned. "Instead of censuring me for wishing to go riding, you might have tried speaking with James before he lost ten thousand pounds he didn't have."

"Mind your duty," Lady Abernathy hissed after her as she left the house.

As if she needed to be reminded. She was the one who saw to everyone else's. What they would begin to do without her, she had no idea.

"I do wish you'd let me ride him once," James was saying, his admiring gaze on Lord Bramwell's enormous black stallion. "Titan is stellar. Might I?"

"No," Bramwell returned smoothly, walking over to help Rosamund onto her chestnut mare, Birdie, when her brother showed no inclination to do so.

She held her breath as Lord Bramwell slid his hands around her waist and lifted her. His hands remained there for a heartbeat, warm and intimate, before he released her to swing up onto his own mount.

A day ago she'd wanted to punch him in the nose. He had a reputation for being charming when he wished to be, but she knew that. And she didn't feel as though he was attempting to trick her into liking him. At the same time, she should be hating him for his role in helping to lead James astray. And she wasn't. "Thank you, my lord," she said belatedly.

"Bram," he responded, circling his horse to bring it even with hers.

She nodded. "Br—"

"Your Titan makes my Swift look dull as rocks," James complained from beyond Bram. "I'll wager you for him."

"No."

"But he's from Waring's stable, ain't he?"

"Yes. Sullivan Waring is my good friend. Ride on your sister's other side."

"But—"

"A lady should always be protected. And I don't want you gawking at my damned horse all morning."

With clear reluctance James moved to her right, so she had one of them on either side of her. Whether Lord Bramwell—Bram—was attempting to show her respect or whether James's pestering did bother him, she didn't know, but she appreciated the gesture. And she liked the way he claimed Sullivan Waring as a friend. He said it plainly, as a fact not to be questioned. Simple, brief as it was, it spoke well of him. And that was something she'd never expected.

"When you returned my book to me," she began conversationally, "you said you could teach me a great many things. I assume those things were not what you were referring to when you made that same offer again last night."

Obsidian eyes met hers, unreadable and assessing. Men didn't generally pay her much attention except to make an even number in a dance. And now she had a secret nearly-betrothed and a supposed teacher, one who looked like an angel and one a devil, and both with awful reputations. Best to remember that neither of them likely had anything good in mind for her.

"So today you're unblushing and unafraid?" he asked after a moment, using the same low tone that she had. "Wise to the ways of men and unable to be shocked?"

"Given my present circumstances, I prefer to think of it as being practical."

He nudged his big black a breath closer. "Do you think you can stand toe-to-toe with me, Lady Rosamund?"

Oh, dear. "I think words are just words. Air with sound."

He continued to gaze at her levelly. "If you think that," he finally said, his voice a low, sensual murmur, "then you don't know the same words I do."

"I assure you, I am quite well edu—"

"Fuck, for example," he interrupted. "Or cunt."

Bramwell said the words so . . . matter-of-factly that it stunned her. Rose took a breath. If this was how he meant to proceed, then, well, she would simply be above it. "The vocabulary of fishmongers and whores doesn't impress me."

"It's not meant to impress you, Rosamund."

"Then what, precisely, is it meant to do?"

Bram looked beyond her, at her idiot brother who'd gotten her into this quagmire and didn't seem to care a whit about what he'd done. And however sophisticated she played at being, those two words had obviously nearly given her an apoplexy. Cosgrove wouldn't even need the six months he'd boasted it would take to destroy her. And that wasn't taking into account what the marquis would do to her in bed.

"Well?" she prompted. "Or are those words all you have to offer?"

"It was a demonstration," he returned, annoyed that the abrupt image of her in Cosgrove's bed angered him. More than angered him. Infuriated him. He set his reaction aside for later consideration. "Put a princess among pigs, and eventually she'll smell like one of them."

"But she'll still sound like a princess rather than a pig. And even a pig can learn to do tricks."

"And a princess can be made to walk on all fours and squeal. Pretty tones or not, she still becomes a pig. Or worse."

Rosamund blushed. "*I* will not become a pig. Or worse."

"I've seen pretty princesses once Cosgrove has finished with them. And they began with more experience about men than you have."

Fear flickered in her grass green eyes, and he told himself that was a good thing. She needed to understand the facts of what lay before her if she meant to survive Cosgrove with any bit of herself left at all. And so he wasn't angry with himself for frightening her; he was angry with her for being so naive that she required his assistance.

"If I'm to be forced to . . . wallow in the mud, then what can you possibly *say* that will help me?"

Sweet Lucifer, she had spleen. He glanced at her brother again, but now that they'd reached Hyde Park the pup seemed absorbed by all the carriages and pretty colors. "I would say once again that perhaps you might consider taking the air in a place other than London," he whispered.

He didn't need or want Cosgrove for an enemy. Apparently, though, he'd just discovered that there was at least one line he wouldn't cross—or allow her to cross. Not without saying something, at any rate. How far his convictions would carry him next, he had no idea.

"You were being serious?" She looked truly shocked for the second time that morning. "What good would that possibly do?"

"It would keep you from having to marry Cosgrove. If you're as well-educated as you claim, I could find you employment as a governess somewhere. I know a handful of people who aren't completely despicable."

"And Cosgrove would attempt to collect the ten thousand pounds from my family, and they would be twice ruined. Once by James's actions, and once by mine."

"Yes, well, it could all actually be traced back to James. His actions force you to react to save yourself."

"What of my parents, then?"

He blinked. "They've sold you to a monster. They can go hang themselves."

Rosamund gazed at him, meeting his eyes in that disconcertingly direct way she had. The expression on her face puzzled him. What was that? Pity? For herself, or for him?

"I hadn't realized the help you offered was to advise me to do something that would harm and betray my family," she said softly. "I won't do that, so thank you for your time, but I cannot use your assistance."

The twists and cankerous pits of human nature rarely surprised Bram any longer. This surprised him. She surprised him. "You're a fool, Rosamund."

"Perhaps. But I'm a loyal fool. Even if I had no obligation to my parents for raising me, I have a sister and brother-in-law, and a young niece and nephew back in Somerset. They would pay for my selfishness, more than I would. And you must agree that while Cosgrove may attempt to . . . alter my character, I have an equal chance of altering his."

"You have no chance in hell."

"But he's never wished to marry before. Perhaps now he is willing to change."

"Who, precisely, are you attempting to delude? Because it's not working on me, my dear."

She swallowed, looking down at her hands. "Then you have your opinion and I have my duty to help my family, and I suppose we have nothing left to discuss."

Bram had caused women to cry before, but this was new. And he felt distinctly as though he had just descended into a lower level of Hades. He must be fairly close to the bottom, by now. Was it worse, though, to say nothing and watch Rosamund Davies walk down the aisle to her destruction all unawares, or to remove any vestige of hope from her beforehand?

He shook himself, disliking the tension in his gut. And when he came across a sensation he didn't like, he took action to dispense with it. *Damnation.* "The lessons that would have the greatest benefit for you," he said slowly, "are the ones a proper young lady is only supposed to receive from her husband."

Rosamund lifted her head again. "A lesson is only words."

He nodded, a sensation very like hope running through him. He certainly recognized it in *her* face. This was a definite improvement. "Air with sounds."

"There's certainly nothing wrong with talking and such. And I think it might be to my benefit to know what to expect."

"I agree." His lips curved. "You can't be rid of me yet, anyway, because you still owe me a waltz."

"You may not be as awful as I first believed, Bram Johns."

"I suggest you withhold your opinion on that count. It's early yet."

Since he'd apparently just agreed to teach a young lady—one he found oddly compelling—about the ways and whims of a rake and blackguard without actually touching her, he wasn't about to vouch for his judgment or his sanity. It almost made housebreaking seem . . . simple.

"What are the odds that Sullivan Waring would sell me a horse?" Viscount Lester asked abruptly.

"The odds would be better if you had any blunt to spend," Bram returned. He considered himself self-absorbed, and happily so, but James Davies had raised that particular merit—or fault, he supposed—to an art form.

"Loan me the funds," the boy said. "Or I'll play you for them."

It would have been an easy way to make another hundred quid or so, but he didn't need Rosamund looking over at him to know that it wasn't something he wanted to do at the moment. "I don't play where I can't lose," he returned. "If you haven't realized it by now, Lester, you are an abysmal gambler."

The boy's face fell. "I say! That's unkind of you, Bram. Rotten, even."

"What would you have me say? The very first rule of wagering is to never risk more than you can afford to lose. You've failed at that one, I would say."

"Cosgrove says you have to lose before you can win. That's how you learn the mettle of the other players."

Good God. Lester sounded even younger than the barely grown boy he was. Bram didn't think he'd ever been that young, himself. He wanted to cuff the pup on the back of the head. "You lost ten thousand quid, James. I think you've shown everyone in Mayfair *your* mettle."

"Cosgrove says—"

"I'm going to dinner at my brother's house tomorrow night," Bram interrupted hurriedly, before he could change his mind. "You and Lady Rosamund join me. We play faro after dinner. We'll test your mettle there."

Rosamund clearly didn't like that, but it was the best way he could think of to keep her brother from getting into even more trouble for which she would somehow have to pay. At least if Lester was under his supervision, he could control the amount being lost.

The brother would be the easy part, though. Keeping his word to Rosamund while not crossing Cosgrove was another task altogether. Especially when he wasn't feeling the least bit brotherly about her. And restraint had never been his strong suit. In fact, he couldn't recall ever having attempted to use it before.

Chapter 5 _____

Had she made a mistake? Rosamund tied on her bonnet, preparing to go down to the small Davies House garden to pick some fresh flowers for her bedchamber—and to give herself a moment without the sounds of her mother's and Beatrice's voices echoing through both her head and the entire house.

Her parents had sold her to the devil. Then she'd turned around and willingly made what amounted to a bargain with a second devil. They'd done it to save the family, but she'd acted only to help herself. But then, her family wouldn't be living under Cosgrove's roof. And if Bram could somehow lay out for her what she could expect from the marquis, then at least she could prepare herself a little.

Nothing Bram Johns had said thus far had made her feel any better at all—just the opposite, actually.

For a hardened, heartless rake to call another man, his own friend, a monster, was terrifying. Especially when she only had a little less than a month before she was supposed to spend the remainder of her life with him.

A shiver ran down her spine. For another week or so she would be able to pretend that it wasn't truly going to happen, that she had just dreamed her upcoming marriage or that her father would find the money to repay James's debt. The closer the date came, the more real the circumstances would become. And then Bram's suggestion that she flee would be much more difficult to ignore.

As she passed her father's downstairs office, she could hear James complaining about something, probably the reduction of his monthly allowance. Her father's lower voice answered. All James needed to do was have a bit of patience; in a month the family's debt would be erased, and he could return to his former debauchery.

"The garden, is it, my lady?" Elbon queried with a smile as he pulled open the front door for her.

She nodded. "I'll pick some fresh lilies for the foyer, as well."

"They would be most welcome."

Even with the sounds of Mayfair and the neighboring households all around, the garden had always felt peaceful. Not to the degree of the one at Abernathy in Herefordshire, but the nearest thing to that anywhere in London. She could stand a bit of peace after the chaos of the past few days.

Fleetingly she wondered whether Lord Cosgrove had a garden, but she just as quickly banished the thought.

She didn't want to think about it until she absolutely had to. Duty, duty, duty. Why had she learned that lesson so well when James seemed not to have been required to do so?

Blast it all. Kneeling, she used her scissors to cut a handful of lily stems, laying the flowers in the basket she'd brought outside with her. For her own room she preferred roses, but the plants had bloomed early this year.

"A Rose among lilies," a deep voice drawled from the direction of the carriage drive.

Her heart jumped, then began skittering as she realized the man moving up behind her wasn't who she'd first thought. *Oh, dear.* "Lord Cosgrove," she said, glancing over her shoulder and then returning to the lilies. They could use some pruning, she decided. "My brother and father are both inside the house."

"Have you wondered," he continued, as though she hadn't spoken, "why it is that I consider you to be worth ten thousand pounds?"

He leaned against the oak tree several feet behind where she knelt. She didn't like having her back to him, but neither did she want to turn around and somehow give the impression that she welcomed a conversation. She was without a chaperone, after all, and no one but her family—and Bram Johns—knew of their particular agreement.

"I'm certain I have no idea, my lord," she answered after she'd waited in silence for as long as she could stand.

"Shall I tell you?"

Rose drew a breath, closing her eyes for just long

enough to wish that someone would look out a window and come to her rescue. "Do as you wish, my lord."

"I always do." He paused again. "Ask me, why don't you?"

"Beg pardon?"

She heard him straighten, heard him move forward so that he stood directly behind her. "Perhaps it's early yet to give orders," he said in a low voice. "We are barely acquainted, after all."

"Of course. I'm certain that once I've come to better know your character, and you mine, we will find ourselves compatible." She jumped on the excuse, knowing she was prattling and unable to stop. "Love isn't always necessary at the beginning of a marriage, because with familiarity comes affection. And—"

"I thought familiarity bred contempt."

"Oh, no. I don't think that's so, at all. The—"

"Are you going to dig that hole all the way to China?" he interrupted.

Rosamund looked down. She'd pruned the lily in front of her into oblivion, and ruined her scissors stabbing them into the dirt. "The plant had worms," she improvised.

Lord Cosgrove circled her, stopping his finely polished Hessian boots directly over the lily's carcass. "Look at me, Rose."

Oh, she should have stood up when she first heard his voice. *Idiot.* Pasting a friendly smile on her face, she lifted her head, swiftly looking past the crotch of his trousers and up at his face. The lazy, cool expression in his blue eyes turned her insides to ice. Every rumored affair, every whispered degradation, flooded her mind. And clearest of all was Bram Johns's voice talking about pigs and squealing and women with more experience than she had.

"You show very well, looking up from down there," the marquis murmured. "We'll have to remember that."

Summoning every bit of courage she had, Rosamund lifted her hand. "Help me to my feet, if you please."

At the same moment he took her hand, she realized that he'd never touched her before. His grip was firm enough as he pulled her upright, but despite a brief, wordless hope, all she felt at the contact was a chilly, growing dread.

Cosgrove kept her fingers in his, pulling her up against him. "Do you know how difficult it is, dearest Rose," he murmured, "to find a woman of exactly your qualities?"

"And what qualities are those, my lord?" Her voice wasn't quite steady, but that couldn't possibly surprise him. The marquis was clearly trying to intimidate her, and he was doing a very fine job of it.

His lips curled in a smile that didn't touch his eyes. "I imagine you'll discover that soon enough."

He placed his fingers beneath her chin, not forcing her face up, but leaving her with the distinct impression that he would if she resisted. *Please don't kiss me*, she prayed fervently, though at the same time she wondered why she bothered. In a month he would kiss her whenever he wished. And he wouldn't have to stop there. As she looked up into those angelic blue eyes, she knew that Bram had been utterly, absolutely correct; she didn't have a chance in Hades against this man. She didn't know enough to fight this battle, much less to have a hope of winning it. Of even surviving it.

"Are you afraid of me?" he continued in the same soft tone, their faces inches apart. "I suggest you say yes."

"Y-yes," she managed.

The marquis licked her mouth.

"You taste of it," he said, releasing her and stepping back at the same time. "Delicious." With another faint smile he took her in from head to toe, then turned his back and strolled away down the carriage drive.

"Good heavens." Scrubbing at her mouth, Rosamund made her way to the garden's stone bench and half collapsed on it. "Good heavens." What in the world would she do when he didn't walk away? When he wanted her to—made her—perform her wifely duty? Even Beatrice shuddered when she mentioned that, and she claimed to have made a love match.

"Oh, blast it, he's gone," James said as he panted up from the servants' entrance.

"You saw Cosgrove out here with me?" Her voice lifted into an indignant squeak.

"Well, yes. Wanted to give you two a moment of privacy, so maybe you'd be convinced he ain't so awful, but now I've missed him. Did he ride, or drive?" Her brother trotted past her toward the street.

"How the devil should I know?"

Frowning, James glanced over his shoulder at her. "Don't bark at me. It's not my fault he came to see you while you was wearing your gardening clothes. Cosgrove don't care about th—"

"*What?*" Rosamund shot to her feet and stalked after her brother. "Not your fault, James? Of course it's your fault. If you had a single ounce of common sense you would realize that what I'm doing is trying to save this family from its ruination at your hands!"

He backed up, putting his hands out to keep her away from him. "There's no need for hysterics, Rose. You're twenty as it is. All winter Mother complained about you not being married yet. Now I suppose I've seen to it. That's doing my duty, ain't it?"

There was every need for hysterics. Clearly, though, James wasn't the one with whom she needed to speak. And Bram Johns had best not have changed his notoriously mercurial mind. Because she definitely needed his help. Even more than she'd realized previously.

"This is a very bad idea," Bramwell muttered, eyeing himself in the dressing mirror.

"My lord?"

"The next time I agree to attend dinner with August and his progeny, you are to shoot me, Mostin. Is that clear?"

"As glass, my lord," the valet returned, as calmly as if they'd been discussing cutlery. He continued brushing out the shoulders of the black coat Bram had donned.

"And if I mention that I've invited anyone else to join me there, reload and shoot me again."

"Yes, my lord."

Generally his valet's toneless, obedient responses served to put Bram back into his usual, properly cynical humor. Tonight, though, he couldn't shake off the sense that he'd blundered badly. Not only had he sent a note yesterday accepting August's invitation, but he'd stated that he would be bringing friends.

Friends. He'd only asked Lester because his sister would require a chaperone, and he'd thereafter barely given the pup a second thought. He'd been thinking about Rosamund, and not about himself. The one bloody place he never felt like himself was in the presence of his own family. For Lucifer's sake, he didn't even know whether the duke meant to make an appearance. And now with Rosamund attending as well . . . He groaned. Christ. Levonzy knew about Abernathy's agreement with Cosgrove.

"Idiot," he muttered fiercely.

"My lord?"

Bram shook himself. "Not you, Mostin. Me."

"If I may say, my lord, you don't look at all well. Perhaps you should stay in tonight."

"I should most definitely stay in tonight." He set his black beaver hat on his head and pulled on his black leather gloves, then dropped a plump bag into one pocket. "Don't wait up for me."

Mostin nodded. "Have a good evening then, my lord."

That wasn't likely. The weather was mild, at least, and he supposed he might have taken his curricle or the barouche. But on the off chance that the duke would be in attendance, he'd had the coach brought around. Massive and black, it required two matched black teams to pull it, and as far as Bram was concerned its best feature was the absence of the family crest on the door panels. Levonzy likely had the Johns crest tattooed on his backside, but no one would find it anywhere at Lowry House.

Bram gave the direction to Davies House to his driver and sat back as Hibble closed the coach's door. It was a damned good thing that he enjoyed inciting chaos, because he was going to be in the middle of a bloody cartload of it tonight.

He was accustomed to women meeting his coach rather than him having to disembark and call at their front door, but apparently proper manners needed to be observed for a proper chit. Bram stifled a sigh a few minutes later as Viscount Lester galloped down the staircase to meet him in the Davies House foyer. The idiot had of course dressed all in black, so that together they looked like a pair of pallbearers.

"You two look like a pair of pallbearers," a rich female voice said from the landing.

The hair on his arms lifted. Taking an uncharacteristic shallow breath, Bram looked up. He'd seen Rosamund dressed in her finery at the Clacton soiree. Intriguing as he'd found her then, that was nothing to now, when he could tell himself that tonight perhaps she'd dressed for him. Her ginger hair was piled artistically atop her head, with loose strands over her ears and across her forehead. She wore a yellow and violet gown with a froth of lace at the sleeves and throat, somehow demure and daring all at the same time.

"And you do *not* look like a pallbearer," he returned, inclining his head as she joined them in the foyer.

This was ridiculous. He had to flex his fingers to keep from touching her. Even if he did consort with virginal females, which he did not, Rosamund Davies was tall, outspoken, and otherwise unremarkable. It had to be the temptation of forbidden fruit—Cosgrove had claimed her, and so logically she was supposed to become a . . . nonfemale in his eyes, an entity to be tolerated and talked to if necessary, but not anyone he would ever think of in a sexual manner.

Except that he did think of her that way. And that wasn't even the worst of it. He'd put himself in the position of being some sort of tutor to her, which was both absurd and so far out of character that he couldn't quite believe it, himself.

"How many guests will be in attendance tonight?" Lady Rosamund asked as the butler helped her with her shawl.

"Just us," Bram answered, then frowned. "And perhaps one other." Unless the duke had something more important with which to occupy himself, which he more than likely did.

" 'One other'?" she repeated.

Her voice sounded tight and tense. Bram looked from her to James, then stepped forward and offered his arm. "The Duke of Levonzy, possibly," he said, walking with her down the front steps to the waiting coach. "He was with your father when the agreement was made with Cosgrove."

"His Grace is one of my father's good friends."

The mere mention of Levonzy would be nearly enough to give *him* an apoplexy, but her fingers around his arm relaxed a little. It wasn't the prospect of the duke, then, that bothered her. "What's amiss?" he murmured, gesturing for Lester to precede them into the vehicle.

"Nothing."

He put his hand over hers before she could pull away. "I am unaccustomed to sensitivity," he continued. "If you want my help, I therefore suggest you be forthright and honest."

She met his gaze for a moment, then nodded. "Lord Cosgrove came by today. He . . . kissed me. In a manner of speaking."

The way her fingers convulsively clenched actually alarmed him. "Which manner?"

Her cheeks darkened. "He . . . licked my mouth," she whispered, so quietly he almost couldn't make out what she'd said.

Lord Lester leaned out the coach door. "Are you two going to stand there chatting all night?"

"Yes," Bram said shortly.

"But—"

Damned pup. "Shut up and sit down, James."

With a look of surprised affront, the viscount retreated back into the depths of the coach.

"He's correct," Rosamund said. "We should—"

"Cosgrove knows perfectly well the preferred way to kiss a woman," he interrupted, tugging her closer so he could lower his voice still further. "He also knows precisely what would shock a proper young lady. He's trying to send you reeling, Rosamund."

She nodded, but turned half away from him. "He—that—I didn't want my first kiss to be like that. Certainly not the first kiss from my future . . ." A tear ran down her cheek as she trailed off.

Something dark and unpleasant wrenched at his insides. If her first encounter with Cosgrove had upset her to this degree, she would be dead by her own hand within a month of her marriage. Why the devil wasn't she running? "We'd best go," he said stiffly, shifting his grip to hand her up into the coach. "To Marsten House, Graham," he instructed his driver, and pulled the door closed.

"I've brought twenty quid with me for faro," James said, patting his pocket. "What are my odds?"

Bram regarded him for a moment. "You'll return with at least that much, I imagine."

"That's splendid. I mean, it's your family and so I don't wish to make them turn out their pockets, but you must know I've been improving."

"Your skill is plain to see, Lester." He faced Rosamund, seated beside her brother. "Do you play, Lady Rosamund?"

"I do not. And if my brother had any sense, he wouldn't play, either. And neither would you, Bram."

It was good to hear the anger in her voice, even if it was partly meant for him. And she'd used his Christian name. If she could still muster anger, then Cosgrove hadn't done more than shock her. Yet. "I think you'll enjoy this game. I'll be happy to instruct you."

"She don't play," the viscount broke in. "And she won't spend her pin money on wagering. Believe me, I've tried to convince her otherwise."

"I'll provide all of the stake you'll need, my dear," Bram said. "You won't lose a penny. I give you my word."

She continued to look skeptical, but then she obviously didn't know him well enough to realize that he very seldom gave his word—and that when he did so, he kept it. If that meant he would have to learn how to be helpful, then so be it.

One of August's footmen pulled open the coach door as they reached the foot of the steps outside Marsten House. Bram blew out his breath, watching the Davies siblings descend from the carriage. His older brother's

thoughts and opinions had never been of much importance to him, and in the past he'd brought some rather
despicable companions, both male and female, to the
family dinner—to the point that his nephew and nieces
had been sent from the room. For the first time he wondered why August continued not just to invite him, but
to insist that he come.

And tonight he wanted his brother to . . . like at least
one of his guests. Not that she'd be allowed back to
Marsten House once she married Cosgrove.

"Uncle Bram!"

A pocket-sized blur flashed down the main staircase
and thudded against his waist. A second and a third of
varying size followed, and in a heartbeat he was being
mobbed.

"Good God, what sticky-fingered urchins are these?"
he asked. "Does Lord Haithe know you're living under
his roof?"

"Yes!" they answered in a ragged chorus, laughing.
The two girls remembered their manners and broke
away first, curtsying to Rosamund and Lester.

"Lord Lester, Lady Rosamund, may I present Oscar,
Lord Kerkden; Lady Louisa; and Lady Caroline Johns?
Short persons, my friends, James and Rosamund
Davies."

Children. Rosamund looked on, stunned, as Lord Bram
Johns took the two youngest around the waist, and carrying one under each arm, climbed the stairs to the
drawing room.

With his reputation, she'd half thought he wouldn't
know what children were, much less be capable of
chatting and jesting with them. His nephew and two

nieces, though, clearly adored him. And that deep cynicism he wore like a second coat seemed missing, as though he'd left it at the front door along with his hat and gloves.

She wondered how many of his supposed friends had ever seen this side of him, and why he'd chosen to allow James and her to do so. It seemed very out of character for a man who'd won every wager he'd made at White's last Season.

"What the devil is this?" James muttered from behind her. "I thought we were playing cards."

"He said it was to be a family dinner, James. Come along."

Her brother was clearly dismayed to see children running about, but Rosamund abruptly felt like smiling. And that was quite something, after the day she'd had. How odd that the only person she could talk to, the only one who seemed the least bit sympathetic or understanding, was reputed to be one of the worst blackguards in London. Or it could be that he was simply better at hiding his true intentions than was Cosgrove.

Oh, dear. That was a dismaying thought. Because she didn't have any idea what her future husband might have in mind for their next encounter, and she desperately wanted Bram to be able to tell her.

As she entered the drawing room, Bram slung the shrieking young ones onto a couch and then sketched an elegant bow to the large man and the tiny woman standing in front of the hearth. She'd seen the Marquis and Marchioness of Haithe on several occasions, but they'd never been introduced. And if she hadn't known, she wouldn't have suspected in a hundred years that Haithe and Bram were brothers.

Yes, they had the same fair skin and dark features, but where Bram was lean and sleek like a panther, his older brother more closely resembled a great bear, broad and loud and not at all subtle. Or dangerous, because it would be so easy to see him coming.

"August, Emily, may I introduce Viscount Lester and his sister Lady Rosamund? James, Rosamund, Lord and Lady Haithe."

The couple exchanged a quick glance that she couldn't quite interpret, and then the marchioness came forward. "Welcome to our very noisy home," she said, smiling all the way up to her light gray eyes.

"Thank you for inviting us," Rose returned, dipping a curtsy.

"Uncle Bram," the boy, Oscar, broke in, grabbing Bram's sleeve, "did you bring enough blunt to cover your losses?"

"I brought enough to ensure my victory," Bram commented, pulling a very full-looking cloth bag from his pocket and handing it over.

James finally perked up. "I say, that looks to be quite a—"

The young viscount dumped out the bag on an end table. Shelled peanuts spilled out everywhere. "Oh, gads," he exclaimed. "I'll have a stomach ache for a week! Sterling!"

"Only if you win. Back in the bag with them, midget." As he finished speaking he glanced sideways, black eyes dancing, to look at Rosamund. "I told you that you wouldn't lose a penny."

"You play for peanuts?" James burst out, sounding not much older than Oscar.

"Much easier on the purse," Bram returned. "Especially if you'd care to learn how to play."

"I know how to play."

"Ah, yes. Allow me to clarify. I'm offering to teach you how to play and win, James."

"I say," her brother responded, edging closer and lowering his voice, "I find that a bit insulting, Bram."

"Then sit there and lose to a ten-year-old. If I'm feeling amused, I may offer assistance once. Don't expect me to offer again."

"But I—"

"August, do you still have that hideous old Turkish tapestry in the library?"

The marquis frowned. "Yes. And it's not hideous."

"Oscar, you and Lester divide up my blunt into three equal portions. Lady Rosamund and I will be back in just a moment." He took her hand, wrapping it around his sleeve.

"Shall I—"

"I know the way," Bram interrupted his brother. "Lady Rosamund enjoys history."

"American history, mostly," she corrected, feeling her cheeks heat. Clearly Haithe didn't think it wise for her to venture off somewhere with Bramwell, and she had to agree. She was in enough trouble.

"American history? I have several books on red Indians. They're in the back right corner, beside the Greek vases."

"Do you?"

"Come on." Bram tugged her toward the door. "Let's find them."

"That wasn't very subtle," she whispered, as they headed down the hallway.

"Wasn't it? Apologies. I told you I didn't have much practice with that."

"Yes, but now your family will think you and I are . . . up to something."

"We are."

"No, we're not." She pulled her hand free. "Nothing nefarious, anyway."

He smiled, the expression astoundingly handsome on his lean face. " 'Nefarious.' That is a splendid word." Pushing backward, he slipped through a door. "This way."

Scowling, Rosamund followed him. Whatever he was up to, he still offered her the best chance of learning something—anything—that could help her not feel so frightened and ill whenever she set eyes on Lord Cosgrove. "You are . . ." She trailed off as she caught sight of the large, square tapestry mounted on the north wall of the library. "That's magnificent. How old is it?"

"It supposedly depicts the creation of the Hanging Gardens of Babylon. Very old, I would say. August knows more, but I warn you that he'll talk your ear off if he has the chance."

Rosamund looked at the vivid reds and golds and greens woven through the tapestry. Old, familiar curiosity pulled at her, but not because of the ancient artwork before her. "What did you need to tell me?" she asked. "Clearly we're not here to talk about the tapestry."

"No, we're not." Silently he closed and latched the door, then crossed the room to her. "I didn't want to do this." A muscle in his jaw jumped. "Another thing at which I don't have much practice."

Her own heart had begun thudding the moment she heard the library door close. "What are you talking about? Have you changed your mind about helping me?"

"No. I'm talking about self-restraint." Bram took a short breath. "You've never been kissed, you said."

Oh. She swallowed hard. "That may not have been a proper kiss that Lord Cosgrove gave me, but—"

"No, it wasn't. It doesn't count."

His gaze held hers. She was tall for a female; she'd certainly heard that from her mother often enough. But she still had to look up to meet his dark eyes. Not for the first time, she wished she knew what he might be thinking.

"A kiss is about intimacy," he murmured, reaching out to stroke the back of his forefinger along her cheek. "Cosgrove stepped past the line where you felt comfortable, and he did it deliberately."

Rose's mind seized on the word "intimacy." Bram had made himself an ally. Whether he was one she would have chosen under other circumstances, she had no idea. She'd certainly been ready to hate him a few days ago. But since actually meeting him, he'd surprised her by being astute, intelligent, and witty, and by being more of a gentleman than certain others she'd met at the same time.

"You haven't given me much time to consider this," he continued, "but I see only one way to make you more comfortable with a man's advances."

"Oh, yes?" Her voice sounded breathy and nervous even to her own ears. Of course she probably wanted him to continue much more than a proper lady in her circumstances would ever have admitted.

"Yes."

Bram took one slow step closer. His gaze still holding hers, he cupped both her cheeks in his palms, leaned down, and touched his lips to hers. Her eyes fluttered closed of their own accord at the soft caress. When he retreated an inch or so, as though assessing the taste of her to see whether he liked it, she felt . . . disappointed. Still, that was much better than what she'd felt with Cosgrove. And under the circumstances, it had been almost honorable.

"That was—"

He closed on her again. His mouth sought hers, molded to her, soft and persistent at the same time. Desire, shocking in its sudden heat, speared through her. Goodness, he knew how to kiss. Rose gasped, putting her hands on his chest to push him away as she should. But she didn't want him to stop. Instead she twisted her fingers into his lapels and pulled herself up on her toes to get still closer to him.

Bram deepened the kiss, his tongue flicking against hers. He pressed her backward until she came up against a bookcase, teasing and nipping at her lips until she couldn't breathe. Nothing was supposed to feel so very good. Certainly nothing from anyone of Bram Johns's reputation.

One hand left her face to skim down her side. Everywhere he touched her, even through the material of her gown, felt heated. Molten, almost. When his fingers closed over her bottom and pulled her forward against his lean, hard body, she groaned.

Blinking, blood roaring through his ears and downward to his cock, Bram stepped back. He couldn't disguise the jutting evidence of his arousal, because he felt utterly blindsided. Rosamund's stunned gaze seemed locked to his face, thank Lucifer, though she must have felt him. He'd practically torn her clothes off, after all. In his mind, he had. His own eyes became abruptly fascinated by the scarlet flush of her soft cheeks and the damp beckoning of her swollen, slightly parted lips. *Good God.*

Taking a breath, he turned his back. His reaction to her troubled him for so many different reasons that he couldn't settle on any one as being worse—or better—than the others.

Say something, damn it all, he ordered himself. "Now you've been kissed," he ground out.

"I think I need to sit down for a moment," she breathed, her own voice unsteady.

"Yes," he said over his shoulder, taking another breath and madly trying to conjure a procession of old, sagging, warty females—men, even—anything to reduce the pressure in his groin. "Take a minute. And don't forget to select one of those books my brother recommended."

He heard her sit. "Bram?"

Her soft voice stopped him with his hand on the door. *Damnation.* "What?"

She cleared her throat. "That was a good lesson. But I don't think he means to stop with kissing me."

The sudden anger her words caused in his chest helped him to pull himself back under control. Bram faced her again. "No, I don't expect that he will."

"You aren't . . . finished then, are you?" she asked, folding her hands primly in her lap so that he almost didn't notice them shaking. "With assisting me, I mean."

He scowled. "In all honesty, Rosamund, telling you how much it will hurt to be punched doesn't make the pain less when you *are* hit."

Rose stood and walked up to him. He half thought she meant to kiss him again, but without warning her hand flashed out, toward his face. Instinctively Bram blocked the blow with his wrist before it could connect. "If I knew what to expect," she said, lowering her hand again, "I might know how to avoid being hit in the first place. Though I do hope you were speaking metaphorically."

Not necessarily. "So you still won't listen to reason?"

"I still won't abandon my family to ruin. Will you still assist me?"

"I— Yes. Of course. But this isn't the place." He gazed at her face again, but he felt himself sinking into her meadow green eyes. "A few faro lessons come first," he said, and made his escape.

Lucifer's ballocks. He hadn't felt that aroused and awkward since he'd first bedded a female at age sixteen. Thankfully in that instance she'd both known what she was doing and been a consummate actress. Lillian Maybury's performance as Ophelia on stage had been nothing compared to her skills in her rather cramped dressing room.

"Shut up," he growled at himself as he stalked back down the hallway. Why in Lucifer's name had a kiss with the virginal Lady Rosamund sent him back thirteen years to his first sexual encounter?

Probably because he'd felt so . . . alive that night. Aware of everything—every touch, every breath, every sound. And that was precisely how he'd felt kissing Rosamund. Alive.

Considering that for better than the past two years the most overwhelming emotion in his life had been boredom, this was extremely troubling. Because as he recollected, he hadn't felt bored from the moment he'd first set eyes on Rosamund Davies. Not in the least.

Chapter 6 _____

Dinner, once Rose had recovered her senses enough to return to the festivities, was loud and boisterous and very amusing. Even James appeared to rouse from his disappointment about the wagering currency enough to take part in the silliness.

"You never did that, Uncle Bram!" seven-year-old Caroline exclaimed around a mouthful of beef and gravy.

Bram nodded solemnly. "I did. Backwards, all the way from Dover to the Tower bridge."

"You rode a horse sitting backwards for all that way and never once fell off? I don't believe you."

"I saw it in the book at White's," James put in. "Nearly fifty men wagered over the outcome. It's noted as a successfully completed wager."

"You see? I told you, Caro!" Oscar crowed. "I'm

going to ride backwards all the way from Brighton to London. It will be very difficult, but I'm a sterling rider."

"I don't think so, young man," a new, deeper voice said from the doorway. "If you break your head then your uncle Bramwell will inherit, and none of us want that."

The children, followed by Lady Haithe and her husband, then James, hurriedly stood. Instinctively Rose followed suit, though Bram beside her remained seated, and in fact shoveled another mouthful of stew off his plate.

The Duke of Levonzy strolled into the room, eyeing each of the occupants in turn. His gaze lingered on her for a moment before it moved past her to Lord Haithe. "Apologies for my tardiness, August," he rumbled, taking the seat at the foot of the table as footmen hurried to serve him. "I had a meeting with Prinny and Melbourne."

"No apology is necessary of course, Father. Have you met Lord Lester and his sister Lady Rosamund? My father, the Duke of Levonzy."

"Your Grace," she said, curtsying. Across the table from her, James bowed before they all seated themselves again.

"Yes, we've met, though Lester there wasn't yet in breeches, and the girl barely talking. The oldest girl, Beatrice, was the pretty one."

Rose returned her attention to the meal. Hearing the duke's assessment of her appearance was nothing new; she'd known precisely who the beauty in the family was since before she could walk. It did seem a bit of a slap in the face to hear a near stranger say it, but

Levonzy and her father had known each other for ages. The duke was undoubtedly very aware of her family's opinion of her.

"So says a crow among snowy doves," Bram commented, reaching for another roll and gesturing for the butter.

The Marquis of Haithe made a choking sound. "How is the Duke of Melbourne these days?" he asked swiftly.

"Considering that his family doesn't insult him to his face, I would say he's quite well." The duke finally looked at Bram. "I hadn't realized you were here."

"I'd prefer if you continued not to realize that. Or better yet, notice enough to keep your mind-numbingly heavy-handed insults aimed in my direction and leave August's guests be."

"He didn't invite them," Levonzy returned. "They are *your* guests. And why is that, pray tell?"

Rosamund's cheeks heated despite her best efforts. Was the duke's query because of Bram's invitation, or because she was promised to Cosgrove? Neither one seemed likely to make her very popular.

"This is *my* house," Haithe unexpectedly broke in. "Everyone here is my guest. And since Oscar is determined to end the evening with a pound of peanuts in his possession, I think the old axiom 'The more, the merrier' applies."

"Two pounds," young Oscar amended. "Did you bring any blunt, Grandfather?"

"I am not engaging in your ludicrous games."

Bram chuckled, no trace of humor in the sound. "He's embarrassed that he might lose, Oscar. No worries. You and I understand that the challenge is half the fun."

"I think it's a silly game, too," Caroline stated.

"That's because you don't know your addition."

"I do know my addition, Oscar. You cheat."

"Now, now, Caro. You know we don't make accusations like that." Lady Haithe looked as though she would prefer to be standing outside in a rain shower. Rose hoped she hid her own dismay a bit better than that.

"Tell me, young Lord Kerkden, what do you think of Lowry House?" His Grace asked, turning his nose up at the potatoes one of the footmen offered him.

"Uncle Bram's house? It's very nice."

"You know it's going to be yours when you reach your majority. You are your father's heir, and thus, my heir."

The boy frowned, his dark eyes puzzled. "But where is Uncle Bram going to live?"

"Me? I'm going to become a farmer and raise sheep. I imagine your grandfather will be my largest purchaser." He winked at the young viscount. "Or perhaps I'll move to the tropics and grow peanuts."

Oscar laughed. "You'll be rich."

"Yes, I believe I will be. Speaking of which, Your Grace, how is Braithewaite these days? I heard he'd been burgled. By the Black Cat, yet."

The duke's skin paled. "You go too far."

"There's no such thing."

Rose looked from son to father. For heaven's sake. She was to be married to a monster to aid her family, and Bram was apparently to be removed from his own home for his family's convenience. They had more in common than she'd realized.

And being hurt by others' expectations—that was

something she could understand. Bram sent her a side-ways glance that plainly told her not to be alarmed. But she wasn't alarmed by the duke's blustering. She was intrigued. And she very much wanted another lesson in kissing.

Phineas Bromley sent a glance around the long room for perhaps the seventh time. The former army colonel had a strong survival instinct, but Bramwell doubted that he suspected an ambush in the Egyptian display at the British Museum.

"What are we doing here again?" Phin asked, slanting him a glance.

"I'm trying to be unnefarious today. I haven't seduced anyone here, at least not to my recollection, so I thought it would serve."

"You're aware that's not a word. 'Unnefarious.'"

"I've just invented it. And you owe me a shilling because you've used it."

"Mm hm. I'm supposed to be meeting with an architect this morning."

"Then I've saved you, and you owe me a favor *and* a shilling."

"I wanted to meet with him. We've nearly finalized the building design for the mineral baths at Quence."

Bram wandered over to a highly decorated sarcopha-gus. "Don't you miss it?"

"Miss what?"

"For ten years you risked your skin on a daily basis, Phin. War, women, wagering, drinking, danger—hell's bells, you rode as a highwayman."

Phin took a quick step closer. "Lower your damned voice, will you? And no, I don't miss it. I am very pleased with the life I've found." He slapped his gloves against his palm. "Is that what this is about? You feel the need to lure me into admitting that I enjoy being domesticated so you can then insult me and call me a gelded bull again? We've been through this. You need a new path, Bram, because you've worn all the vegetation off this one. Has some woman rejected you and you're bored?"

"No. That's not it." If only that was the problem. "I haven't slept in other than my own bed in a week. And I've slept *alone* in my bed, if you meant to ask about that."

His friend laughed. "I'm so sorry. Are you not feeling well? Bits and pieces begun falling off, finally?"

Bram narrowed his eyes. "Damnation. I knew I should have gone to speak with Sullivan. The damned horse breeder won't come to London, though."

"He'd come, if you asked." Phin eyed him again. "Stop beating around the subject and tell me what's troubling you."

"I don't know what's troubling me." He hadn't felt like himself in days. And he couldn't very well ride off to Sussex to see Sullivan Waring, because Rosamund had only three weeks before her engagement would be made public, and only days after that before she would be married. To Cosgrove. He shook himself. "I burgled Lord Villiers night before last, and even that hasn't helped."

"Bram, damn it all," Phin murmured, "you have to stop doing that. I've heard the talk. The Black Cat is being sought by every Bow Street Runner in London. Prinny's going to send out soldiers if one more nobleman complains."

"I should hope so; it would be a great deal of wasted effort on my part if no one noticed."

Levonzy had noticed, of course, but all he'd done was more of his general ill-tempered grumbling and spitting. In all fairness Bram hadn't been putting his all into his nighttime activities—any of them—over the past week, but neither had he been summoned for a formal dressing-down since before the beginning of the month.

"I don't know how to advise you then, my friend. Come to dinner tonight. Beth has become infatuated with Lord John Elliot, so you should be safe."

"Your sister is a menace."

"Only to you."

Bram hesitated. "Might I bring a pair of friends?"

Immediately Phin's expression grew wary. "Which friends?"

Stifling his annoyance, Bram curved his lips. "Not Cosgrove, if that's what's troubling you."

"I'm afraid I'm even more particular than that, these days. I'm responsible for an eighteen-year-old menace, and I have a wife who's seen enough scandal."

"Good God," Bram exclaimed, "you *have* been gelded."

"Bram, that is n—"

"Lord Lester and his sister. I'm . . . taking the lad under my wing." And he hadn't seen Rosamund in three days, since the night he'd kissed her. Banishing himself from her presence, though, hadn't done a damned thing to remove the troubling and annoying batting about in his chest that occurred whenever he thought about her.

"Bring them along, then. Seven o'clock." Phineas pulled out his pocket watch and flipped it open. "I think

I can still manage my meeting. I'm leaving you now. Don't steal anything from the museum, or I'll turn you in, myself."

"Yes, yes. Run along, you henhouse Harry."

With a grin, Phin clapped him on the shoulder and hurried off to meet with his architect. Bram was happy for him, he supposed, though it was damned inconvenient that his friends' evenings—when they even came to London—were full of family dinners and evenings that ended early so that they could return home to their adoring wives.

Taking a breath, he left the museum himself. He needed to inform Lester that they'd been invited to another dinner. A note would be the most appropriate, but he'd been neglecting his so-called duties to Rosamund. And, damn it all, he wanted to see her.

With that idiocy in mind, he rode to Davies House and knocked the rapper against the front door. A few seconds passed before it opened. "My lord," the butler said, bowing.

"Is Lester to home?"

"No, my lord. I believe him to be at luncheon with Lord Cosgrove."

Damnation. "Lady Rosamund?"

"If you'd care to wait in the morning room, I shall inquire."

She was home, at least. And he'd been allowed into the house. There were occasions, more and more frequently, in fact, when he wasn't welcomed beyond the foyer.

Now that Rose had had three days to consider whether his assistance would help at all in her next encounter with Cosgrove, he had to wonder whether she'd wish to see him. Unaccountably restless, he paced the morning room and waited.

"Bram."

He whipped around at the sound of her voice. She wore a green and yellow sprigged muslin walking dress, an old-looking mauve pelisse over it. Only being blind would have kept him from taking her in, from her walking boots, to her pretty gown with its swooping neckline, to the pulse jumping at her throat, to her ginger hair with a damp strand caressing one cheek.

"Rosamund. I— Did I interrupt something?"

She brushed at her hair. "I was helping rearrange some furniture in the drawing room."

A maid entered the room behind her, and deeper annoyance pushed at him. Bloody propriety. "Shall I go, then?"

"I don't know. Why are you here?"

His mind went blank as a new painter's canvas for a moment. Then he remembered. "I'm inviting you and your brother to join me again for dinner, at Lord Quence's home. Bromley House. On St. George Street. Do you know it?"

"You're acquainted with Lord Quence?"

"More closely with his brother, Phin, but yes. Do you wish to go?"

Her soft lips twisted. "Martha, give me a moment, will you?"

"But your mama said—"

"I think my reputation has been established," Rosamund interrupted. "A moment, if you please."

The maid bobbed and scurried out of the room, closing the door behind her. Bram, though, stayed where he was, with half the room between them. Generally he could read a person's character and intentions in a heartbeat; it was a gift that came in very handy both when wagering and when avoiding duels with cuckolded husbands. Today, though, he had no idea what Rosamund might be thinking.

"I thought perhaps you'd changed your mind," she said after a moment. "That you'd kissed me and had your amusement, or won some sort of wager with Lord Cosgrove or something, and gone on to your next conquest."

Bram lifted an eyebrow. "You're angry with me? For what? Stopping with one kiss? For not ruining you?"

"No. Yes."

For one of the few times in his life, Bram found himself utterly baffled. "I thought I was being honorable. I suppose I could be in error about that; I don't have much practice."

Rosamund snorted.

Finally he stalked closer. "Oh, you think that's amusing, do you? If you had any idea what I'd like to do with you, you would run the other way."

The humor faded from her meadow-colored eyes. "Are you trying to convince me that there's no difference between you and Lord Cosgrove?"

Unable to resist touching her, he stroked a finger along her bare arm. "There isn't much," he conceded. "We're both self-serving hedonists more concerned with our own pleasure than anything else."

"But you offered to help me."

Yes, he had, and the reason for that seemed to be becoming more complicated by the moment. "I know. That struck me as odd, too. But I gave my word, and I do attempt to keep that whenever possible."

"You are a very interesting man," Rosamund stated. "And you have female friends. Actual friends. I don't think Lord Cosgrove can claim that."

He smiled, sincerely complimented. "Why thank you, my lady. So, as long as I'm here, shall we kiss again, or do you wish to proceed along the garden path a bit further?"

She backed up a step. "That's not very romantic."

It took more control than he expected to remain where he was and not pursue her. "Neither is your prospective husband. Don't expect posies. If you do receive them, they're more than likely deadly nightshade."

Rosamund hesitated. "Does he mean to murder me?"

What a question for any young woman to have to ask. "I would guess that he doesn't." Bram studied her face for a moment, the light freckles sprinkled across the bridge of her nose. "King manipulates people," he said slowly, still not certain how or whether he should proceed. "In order for him to win a game, his prey needs to step beyond where they would otherwise never care—or dare—to tread. A number of them have ended up ruined. Destroyed, rather. Some of them have ended up dead, by another's hand or by their own."

She gave a shaky, forced-sounding laugh. "Oh, my. I don't suppose you have ten thousand pounds you'd care to lend me?"

It was his turn to smile grimly. "I receive a monthly allowance, just as your brother does. Generally. At the moment I'm cut off yet again." He was also mainly earning his keep by wagering, but she didn't wish to hear that any more than he wanted to say it.

"This isn't your disaster, anyway, Bram. I shouldn't have asked you for help."

Fresh anger rose in him. Cosgrove, Lester, Lord and Lady Abernathy, they'd all made deals to suit themselves and set her, the only innocent party in this, to pay the price. Indignation was a new emotion, and he was fairly certain he didn't like it. "There is one service I *can* provide, Rosamund."

Before he could consider that in his own way he was using her just as much as anyone else, Bram reached down for her hands and tugged her closer. King had given him reason to help her, but the truth was that he hadn't kissed her to assist her; he'd kissed her because he'd wanted to do so, and with a hungry desperation that truly troubled him.

This time as their lips met he was ready for the tingling, jangling warmth that shot down his spine. He tilted her head back, deepening the embrace of their mouths. It was odd, he thought fleetingly as her soft lips parted against his—as a man who didn't particularly enjoy kissing, he'd certainly looked forward to this. With her.

The thought shook him a little, and he took a step back. Yes, he was an animal who enjoyed rutting with a select number of pretty females. But he had no business lusting after a woman Cosgrove had chosen for himself. He was doing her a favor by showing her what King would do to try to hurt her. To remove the shock of the first kiss, first touch, first whatever she would allow of him. Nothing more. It was charity. Nothing more than a twisted, enjoyable good deed.

"Bram?"

He blinked. "I'm debating," he improvised, "what to show you next. Mouth or hands."

"You've shown me mouth." As she spoke, her gaze focused on his lips.

At the responding heat lowering to his crotch, Bram narrowed his eyes. "If you think that, I have a bit more to show you," he murmured.

This time when he closed on her, he avoided her lifted, expectant lips and instead ran his mouth along her jaw, starting with her chin and moving back to her ear. She gave a feminine gasp of surprised pleasure, and he went hard. *Damnation*. Well, if he was teaching her, he might as well make it a true lesson.

Bram slipped his fingers beneath the shoulder of her gown and slid the material down her arm, following the trail of bare skin with his lips and teeth and tongue. She stiffened perceptibly when his tongue flicked against the base of her throat, but a moment later tangled her fingers into his hair. One hurdle overcome. With a sigh Bram continued his assault.

Though he'd had a great many lovers, Bram couldn't recall ever previously being so . . . aware of the woman softly in his arms. He'd never bedded a virgin, but it wasn't that. Her quick, shallow breaths, the shifting of her legs, the soap and lavender scent of her skin—she was quite the most intoxicating chit he'd ever tasted.

So intent was he that at first he didn't hear the voices in the hallway. The door rattled, and his keen sense of self-preservation took over. Pulling her sleeve back up her shoulder, he pushed Rosamund backward to sit on the couch, and then vaulted over the back of it.

The door shoved open. "Rose! Lord Bramwell! What do you—"

Bram straightened onto his knees, clutching the back of the couch with one hand while he madly pulled and tugged at the front of his trousers with the other, trying to settle his raging arousal. "Lord Abernathy," he said calmly, and ducked down again. "I don't see it, Lady Rosamund," he continued. "Not that I'd recognize an embroidery needle if I stabbed myself with it."

Beneath the legs of the couch he made out the mother's shoes crowding in behind the earl's. They had every right to be wary of having him under their roof, especially unchaperoned and in their daughter's company, but they'd waited long enough before they'd barged in that he could well have made off with her and half their belongings.

"It's silver in color, and curved," Rosamund's unsteady voice took up.

Good girl, he applauded silently. She had wits, and knew precisely how and when to best apply them. "Are you certain it's not stuck into the upholstery somewhere?" Finally feeling—and looking—a bit more composed, Bram made a show of climbing to his feet and dusting off his poor, abused trousers. "I think you'll have to give in and purchase a new one."

"Yes, I suppose I shall."

Walking around the couch, Bram offered his hand to Abernathy. "I apologize for calling without Lester present," he drawled as they shook hands, "but I thought he and I were to go to Tattersall's together."

"And when you realized he wasn't here, you thought what, that Rose might join you instead?" the countess suggested.

So it was the Davies females who had the larger measure of intelligence. He would remember that. "Since I was already here, I invited Lady Rosamund and your son to join me for dinner with Lord Quence," he returned.

"And then I mentioned that I'd lost a needle in here somewhere, and Lord Bram said that he has the senses of a foxhound, and here we are," Rosamund finished, climbing to her own feet.

Abernathy looked from one of them to the other. "No harm done then, I suppose. Lord Bramwell, a word with you before you leave?"

Bloody splendid. He sent a last glance at Rosamund, not willing to risk taking her hand. "Of course. I'd best be off now, anyway. I'll come by for you and Lester at twenty before seven." Sketching a bow, he left the room to wait for the earl in the hallway.

A moment later Abernathy appeared to lead the way to his office. "Your father and I are friends," he said, once they had some privacy.

"I'm aware of that. I shan't hold it against you." Except for the near burglary, but he hadn't gone through with that, so it didn't count. The sale of the earl's daughter to Cosgrove, though, was another matter entirely.

"I only inform you so that you understand that that friendship is the only reason I didn't just toss you out on your arse. I assume you're aware both of James's debt and of the arrangement I've made with Lord Cosgrove to settle it."

Torn between whether to point out that any attempt to throw him anywhere would likely lead to bloodshed and scoffing at the earl's idea of an "arrangement," Bram settled for nodding. "I'm aware of it."

"Then whether your presence is on Cosgrove's behest or your own, you are to leave Rose be until such time as her welfare and reputation are no longer in my hands. I won't have you further mucking up an already unpleasant matter."

Bram took a slow breath. "As her welfare will only be in your hands for another three weeks, I will assume that you realize allowing her to make friends among Cosgrove's circle can only benefit her. I've asked her and Lester to join me for dinner with Viscount Quence and his family. Surely you have no objection to your daughter dining at the house of a man of such impeccable reputation as William Bromley."

"No, I don't suppose I do. But watch yourself, sir, for I shall certainly be doing so."

And you've been tremendously effective with that, Bram thought, but only nodded again. He'd gotten what he wanted for the moment—dinner with Rosamund. After that, he supposed he'd best come to his senses before Abernathy or Cosgrove cut off his balls.

Chapter 7 _____

"I've brought Cosgrove back with me, Rose," James stated, strolling into the upstairs sitting room. "I mentioned that you weren't happy about marrying a fellow you didn't know well, and he said that wouldn't do."

Before Rose could curse at James, the marquis entered the room. She climbed hurriedly to her feet. Despite the abrupt panic pushing at her, she tried to remind herself that she knew what to expect now. If he kissed her, lips or . . . tongue, she wouldn't be shocked. She knew what it felt like and what his reasoning was, thanks to Bram. Perhaps a show of inner strength and courage on her part might convince Kingston Gore that she was not to be trifled with. At the least he might treat her with a bit more respect the next time they met—and after they married.

If she could avoid it, she didn't want a war. Particularly not with an opponent who had much more experience than she did. While it was true she'd already been gathering information, she didn't want him to know that. And this strategy, of course, had absolutely nothing to do with the surprising fact that she liked kissing, and being kissed by, Bram Johns—and that she absolutely needed to keep that fact a secret.

"Good afternoon, my lord," she said, offering a smile and a curtsy.

Cosgrove inclined his head. If circumstances hadn't caused him to be introduced to her as a villain, his appearance would have placed him firmly in the role of a potential beau. Golden hair, light blue eyes, a smile angels must envy—at first glance his looks belied everything she knew about him. Only his pale, almost translucent skin and the . . . deadness behind his eyes spoke about his true nature. Unless he had a reason— a very good reason—for his previous nastiness, she was not about to let her guard down in his presence. Oh, thank goodness her father had at least gotten her a month to prepare for this.

"I know we're not well acquainted," he drawled, gesturing her to sit and taking a seat on the couch directly beside her, "but we should make every effort to become so before our engagement is made public, don't you think?"

Hm. Was this a test of her spirit and fortitude, or her memory? She wanted him to be conciliatory and honorable, certainly, but she also wanted him to realize that she was not a fool. "I think we could become friends," she said slowly, "if individually we can manage to keep civil tongues in our heads. Our own heads."

He smiled. "James, go sit over there and give us a little privacy." As he spoke he gestured at the far side of the room.

Immediately her brother moved to the doorway and sat down, then stood and grabbed a book off a shelf and took his seat again. The mere act of James voluntarily touching pages with writing on them said a great deal about Cosgrove's influence over him. Generally all she had to do to escape her brother's prattling was walk into the library.

"So you want me to keep my tongue to myself, Rose?"

"Yes, I do. I've done nothing to you to cause you to treat me with anything less than respect and kindness."

"Indeed. And are you willing to show me the same respect and kindness?"

Unexpected hope pushed at her. It didn't seem likely at all, but perhaps Lord Cosgrove was . . . merely awkward around females. Very awkward. "Of course I am. I might have wished for a . . . a love match, but I have no illusions. I understand my father's inability to otherwise repay as substantial a debt as my brother's foolishness has caused us to owe you. And I've always done my duty by my family."

"Very well said. I might be offended by the idea that if you had a choice in the matter you wouldn't have chosen to marry me, but knowing that you mean to make the best of this arrangement truly pleases me."

"I am very glad to hear that, Lord Cosgrove."

"I mean to say that *you* please me," he continued, placing his hand over hers where it rested on her knee. "I battered at your pride, and you decided it was a test, that if you showed strength and compassion, or turned the other cheek, as it were, that I would also make an effort to be kinder."

"Has it worked, then?" she ventured.

His smile deepened. "On our wedding night I mean to put you on all fours and mount you as a dog mounts a bitch. And you will remain on your hands and knees until such time as I permit you to rise. Do you not appreciate my new willingness to be forthright with you?"

Rose stared at him, her entire body turning to ice. "I see no need for you to say such shocking things to me." No wonder Bram had scoffed when she'd dismissed the ability of words to cause pain. She'd had no idea. No idea at all.

"Too true," he replied. "I might have kept my intentions from you until we recited our vows—me to cherish, and you to obey. But I want you to anticipate that night as much as I do." The marquis took a deep breath. "In fact, just telling you about it brings me pleasure." Tightening his grip on her hand, he lifted it from her knee and drew it toward his own lap. "Allow me to demonstrate to you the degree of pleasure I am feeling at this very moment."

She jerked her hand free. "Do not touch me," she hissed, climbing gracelessly to her feet.

"I shan't touch you again until the next time I do so," he said in a low voice, rising when she did. "And while I don't doubt that you've somehow managed to catch Bram Johns's interest, I will warn you that he only enjoys trouble and strife as long as he's the one causing it. At the first whisper of his own comfort and ease being disturbed, he will walk away without a backward glance. I have seen it. And now I trust that you have no illusions."

"I don't know what you're talking about. And I do not bid you good day, because I only want you to be gone." With that, she hurried out of the room, and didn't stop until she reached the relative safety of her own bedchamber.

Every time Cosgrove said a word to her, her future became more dire. For a long time Rose paced back and forth as swiftly as she could. Only when she was out of breath and her heart raced from exertion rather than from panic did she let herself collapse on the bed.

It abruptly occurred to her that his words weren't rendering her future more dire; they merely gave her a clearer idea of what he'd already planned. And she knew enough about war to be fairly certain that one side didn't tell the other its plans. He'd made a mistake, both by talking and by admitting that her fear increased his own enjoyment.

Bram had called Cosgrove a monster. For the first time she realized that he was absolutely correct. And the worst of it was that though her perception might have been altered so that she could now see the road ahead more clearly, the road itself still led to precisely the same place—marriage to the Marquis of Cosgrove.

An hour later, James stuck his head around the library door. "Elbon said you was looking for me. I was only trying to help by having King stop by, you know."

"I know." Setting aside her book and trying to steady her still shaky nerves, Rose motioned at him to come into the room. "I need to ask you something."

His expression wary, as though he expected the tomes in the room to fly off the shelves and hit him, her brother walked over to sit in the chair opposite her. "By the by, I won thirty quid off Cosgrove and his cronies today. Bram knows how to play cards, even if he does play for peanuts with children."

Wonderful. She didn't suppose James would be willing to put his thirty pounds toward reducing the debt to Cosgrove, but asking him would only set his back up, and she did want to talk to him. "I meant to tell you earlier, Bram asked us to join him for dinner again this evening. With Lord Quence and his family."

Her brother grinned. "Sterling. I'll have another go at learning some of his wagering skills."

Good. If James didn't wish to attend, then she couldn't very well do so. She could contemplate why she wanted to see Bram again so keenly, though, later. "Tell me about Lord Cosgrove."

He sank back, scowling. "I don't want to. He's my friend, and I know you and Father and Mother don't like him. Even if I hadn't known that before, the way you ran off when he tried to flirt with you made that clear enough."

Rose stifled an unsettled breath. If that was how he flirted, she likely wouldn't survive their first married encounter. And that might be a good thing. "Perhaps you should try telling me about some of his positive qualities. Tell me why you consider him a friend. Something drew you together."

"You're bamming me, ain't you?"

"No, I'm not." She set her book onto the chair beside her. "You made some mistakes, James," she began. "The re—"

"Oh, you see?" Her brother shot to his feet. "Father already told me that I'm a half-witted nickninny. I don't need you to chew my ear off, as well."

"I'm not chewing your ear off! I wanted to say that the result of your . . . friendship is that I'm to be married." Rose grabbed her brother's hand, pulling him back down into the chair. "I'm frightened, James. Please, please understand that this is important for me. It's my life, forever. And I want you to tell me that Lord Cosgrove's reputation has been exaggerated. Tell me that he's hurt and bitter and strikes out without thinking, but has a good heart and only needs the love of a good woman to return him to propriety."

James looked at her, his expression slowly going from defiant and defensive to troubled and very, very young. "You'll . . . you'll suit well, Rose. He's very intelligent, and I've heard him laugh at, well, at things. You like to laugh."

Oh, dear. If even jovial James couldn't conjure anything pleasant about his dear friend, things were even worse than she'd been imagining over the past hour. She shivered a little. "Have you seen how he treats women?" she pursued, desperation edging at her voice. "Does he like to dance? Has he ever courted anyone?"

"Gads, no. He says dancing is for dandies who can't play cards. And as for . . ." He trailed off, then leaned forward and put his hands on her knees. "Like I said, Bram's been showing me some of his tricks, and my game's shockingly improved. With his help, I may be able to win back the blunt I owe Cosgrove. Then you'll have nothing to worry over."

Bram had been showing her some of his tricks, as

well. She hoped they would serve her better than the card tricks were likely to aid James's efforts, though they both seemed beyond assistance. "Don't make it worse," she said quietly. "Our parents don't have the means to erase another ten-thousand-pound debt."

After he escaped the library, Rose opened her book again. Reading, though, remained an impossibility. Slowly she touched her fingers to her lips. If—when—Cosgrove next approached her, she would have to restrain her instinct to hit him and flee. She would have to listen, and to learn everything she could about what he meant to do.

Perhaps if she could use some of the so-called tricks to which Bram had introduced her, she could exert a little influence on her future husband. As much as Cosgrove's overtures had frightened and sickened her, Bram's caresses had left her weak in the knees. Had it been that way for him?

She shook herself. The important question was whether she could positively affect Cosgrove—not Bram. If she could somehow convince the marquis not to wager with James any longer, that would be something. For some reason Cosgrove did find her interesting. Enough so to insinuate himself into her life and attempt to control it. The more . . . persuasive she could be, the better for her, and her brother, and anyone else with whom Cosgrove might choose to toy.

And now she had one more thing to think about. If every moment of her marriage was going to be a hideous nightmare, she wanted something pleasant to remember. And kissing, being kissed by, Bram Johns was very pleasant, indeed.

At the same time, she had to wonder what Lord Bramwell Lowry Johns was getting out of this little exchange. He'd several times declared himself to be self-absorbed and self-serving, and Cosgrove said the same thing. He had to be enjoying kissing her, or he wouldn't have done it. Aside from the logic of that, she wasn't blind. As he'd pushed her onto the couch she'd very clearly seen the evidence of his interest.

Of course, being Bram Johns, he'd most likely been interested in more women than she could count. Great beauties of the age, exotic, forbidden women, females who knew all the secrets of the bedchamber. She wasn't any of those things, and yet he'd kissed her a second time. Heavens, he'd practically rendered her naked. Just as interesting, he'd protected her reputation when her parents had barged into the room. She somehow doubted that Cosgrove would have bothered to do that.

She knew what she wanted from Bram, and she very much believed that he would do it if she asked. It would give her an advantage in her dealings with Cosgrove, and at the least it would be a revenge for the awful plots about which the marquis had already informed her. This was no longer about being told how much a punch would hurt before she experienced a blow. This was about being able to remember a caress from one man while she was being threatened and bullied by another.

But there was another difficulty in this path, and it belonged entirely to her. Because even after just a week, she was becoming very fond of the Duke of Levonzy's second son. The question became whether she was willing to risk a possible broken heart in order to save her soul.

*   *   *

Bramwell descended his main staircase to the foyer. Uncharacteristically he was early, but he'd debated whether to pace his drawing room or that of Davies House, and the Davies's floorboards had lost.

He needed to stop this obsession with Rosamund Davies. Aside from the fact that there would be no reward at the end of the chase, what with his one rule regarding virgins, every time he set eyes on her she made his life more complicated. He detested anything complicated when it applied to him. Dinner tonight, and perhaps one more kiss, and he would move on.

"You have a note, my lord," Hibble said, holding out the letter salver. "It only just arrived."

For a moment Bram thought Abernathy might have come to his senses and declined to allow his children to go about in a blackguard's company. The keen disappointment that followed that thought surprised him, but he didn't allow it to show on his face as he took the folded missive.

He immediately recognized the handwriting, but he wouldn't quite have called the resulting sensation that ran through him relief. Cosgrove. With a glance at his pocket watch, he opened the note.

Bramwell, he read to himself, *Do grace me with your presence tonight. We haven't chatted for nearly a sennight, and we have a great many things about which to converse. I think three o'clock at Jezebel's would be appropriate. Bring along as much blunt as you'd care to lose. KG.*

This was interesting. He could count on one hand the number of times he'd received a summons from Cosgrove. And in this instance he would be willing to

wager that the little tête-à-tête would concern Rosamund Davies. Considering that he'd already resolved
to distance himself from her after tonight, anyway,
the timing of his meeting with Cosgrove couldn't have
been better.

"Any difficulties, my lord?" the butler queried, Bram's
black beaver hat in his hands.

Taking a breath, Bram shoved the note into a
pocket. "No more than usual. I'll be out all night.
Have Mostin set out some brandy before he retires for
the evening."

"I'll see to it, my lord."

Whatever he'd said to his butler, tonight didn't feel
usual. And it wasn't simply because Cosgrove's invitation was likely to delay the Black Cat's visit to Lord
Montgrieve's home. Damned shame, that, but the odd
anticipation making him so restless wasn't about either
King or a burglary. He didn't know what it was, but he
was fairly certain he didn't like it.

"I don't suppose we'll be playing cards this evening,"
Lester said without preamble as the Davies siblings met
his coach at their front drive.

They were early then, as well. "Not tonight," he
answered, leaning out to offer his hand to Rosamund. In a gown of soft mauve and gray, she looked
elegant. On a wispier female frame he would have
described the gown as ethereal, but with her the
adjective "regal" seemed a better fit. "And how are
you, Lady Rosamund?" he asked, pulling her onto
the seat beside him before she could join her brother,
opposite.

"Quite well, thank you," she replied.

The curve of her ear beckoned him, and to cover his

sudden discomfiture he turned away and leaned out the door again. "Bromley House, Graham."

The coach rolled back onto the street, and Bram took the moment to consider that having Rosamund sit beside him was a mistake. Not only could he practically feel the soft folds of her gown beneath his fingers, but he couldn't look into her face when they spoke.

"I'd hoped you might give me a few more pointers, Bram," her brother began again. "I won thirty quid from Cosgrove at luncheon today, thanks to you."

Was that what the summons was about, then? Teaching a no-talent pup a few tricks to save himself losing a quid or two at the tables? He could hope so, but Lester seemed too trivial to both him and King to warrant a late-hour conversation. Aside from that, Bram had ceased relying on hope several years ago. Pragmatism and cynicism served him much better. And both told him that Cosgrove wanted to discuss Rosamund.

He shook himself. "Did you inform Cosgrove that I've been tutoring you, James?"

"He knew. I won a hand, and damn me if he didn't sit back in that way of his and say, 'Bramwell's been busy, hasn't he?' Remarkable, the way he knows things when no one else does."

More remarkable was the marquis's well-placed network of spies in most of the wealthiest households within Mayfair. "Indeed. You feel at ease, then, continuing to have luncheon and wager with the man who's to marry your sister?"

"He'll be my brother-in-law. Who else should I be comfortable hanging about?"

"Don't you have another brother-in-law?"

"Fishton? He's made stones weep with boredom. I have no idea how Bea has kept from stabbing herself in the ears to escape his prattling."

Bram sent a sideways glance at Rosamund, to find her gazing out the coach window. "I've never met Fishton. Is he as dull as all that?"

She stirred, looking at him and then away again. "I'm afraid so. The main benefit is that with only twenty-four hours in a day, he and Bea together can only talk for twelve hours each at the most. It's reduced Bea's conversation by half, I'm certain."

He laughed. "You have a very delightful tongue," he said deliberately, enjoying the sight of her soft blush.

"Fishton don't think so," Lester replied. "She never agrees with what he says, and he turns red as tomatoes and begins a chorus of 'but, but, but.'"

"It's only that he's so certain he has the one and only solution to every difficulty."

"Ah. Did he advise you on your upcoming marriage, then?" Bram asked more quietly, curling his fingers to keep from brushing against hers.

"Oh, yes. 'No man can be displeased with an efficiently run household.' And I'd apparently do well to learn Cosgrove's favorite drink in the evening so I can prepare it for him when he returns home at night."

"Absinthe," Bram said. "Not anything you should be getting near."

"I tried a bit of it once," Lester broke in yet again. "Heady stuff. Twenty minutes later I cast up my accounts all over the street."

"Will you teach me how to prepare it?" Rosamund asked, facing Bram full-on this time.

"No."

"I will be near it," she said, lowering her voice a little. "If you show me, then he won't have to do so. I'll take any opportunity I can to avoid conversation with him."

"I can show you, Rose," James offered, "though I'm a bit unsure of the sugar."

Bram met her gaze. She seemed to be talking about more than just a potent drink, but he couldn't question her with her damned brother sitting two feet away. "Very well," he muttered. Staying away from her had been more about avoiding the kissing and touching, but he didn't do well with temptation of any kind. Still, an hour of showing her how to prepare absinthe meant he could stay across a table from her. Much safer, that way.

"Thank you."

Once the coach stopped, Lester made it to the door and hopped to the ground before Bram or Rosamund even stirred. "That pup is too impatient for everything," he grumbled, offering his hand. "Nothing is worth looking lathered-up over."

Rosamund wrapped her fingers around his, tighter than he expected. "I need to speak with you in private before the end of the evening," she whispered, and brushed past him to descend the folded-down steps.

Bram held his breath for a moment, then let it out again. He knew exactly what he needed to do once he'd finished with Cosgrove tonight—go find Lady Ackley or Charlotte DuCampe or Sarah Vischer or any of the other myriad energetic females with whom he was acquainted. He hadn't had sex in more than a week. That was the problem. The celibacy was rotting his brain, making him susceptible to the lures of a practically flat-chested, forthright young lady who would only be trouble. More trouble.

And while he generally welcomed that sort of thing, he did try to avoid it with his friends. He frowned as he stepped out of the coach. Cosgrove *was* a friend. After all, without his tutelage and influence, Bram's life today would be very different. And it was only in the past few days that he'd felt any real . . . reservations about his friend's actions. As if someone like him had a right to question anyone else's motives or actions.

"Lord Bramwell," the Bromley House butler said with a shallow bow. "You'll find Lord Quence in the billiards room."

"Thank you, Graves," he replied, placing Rosamund's fingers over his sleeve as they ascended the stairs. "Might you give me a hint?" he murmured, deciding the noise Lester made clomping along behind them would drown out the conversation.

"My brother brought his luncheon companion home to see me after you left," she said in a tight, barely audible voice, "and I would like you to attempt to talk me into fleeing again so I might conjure a new reason or two to remain and do my duty. The current reasons are beginning to seem rather inadequate."

"What?" Bram didn't realize he'd stopped until Lester knocked into him from behind.

"Dash it, Bram, you've nearly made me break my nose."

"What did he do?" Bram demanded, ignoring the pup's wailing.

Rosamund swallowed, visibly pulling her emotions back into check. "Later," she muttered.

Shaking off the sensation of troubled dread running through him, Bram pushed open the door to the Bromley House billiards room and stepped inside. "Be careful with that," he said, as Phin Bromley leaned over the billiards table to take a shot. "I've seen him bring down a horse with a cue."

"The penalty for riding a horse through an inn," Phin returned with a grin, straightening. The scar bisecting his right eyebrow and running down his cheek made most females consider him charming and rakish. Bram had seen what happened to the French officer who'd attacked him, and had a slightly more circumspect view of his friend.

"Rosamund, James," he said, gesturing, "my friends Lord Quence; Phin Bromley and his wife, Alyse; and Miss Beth Bromley. Bromleys, Lord Lester and his sister, Lady Rosamund Davies."

"Welcome." With a smile of his own, William, Lord Quence, motioned to his ever-present valet, and the man pushed his wheeled chair around the billiards table to greet them.

"Thank you for inviting us, my lord," Rosamund said with a curtsy. "Or rather, thank you for allowing Lord Bramwell to bring us along with him."

"Nonsense." Phin set aside his cue to clap Bram on the shoulder and shake hands with Lester. "We only continue to invite him on the chance that he'll introduce us to more interesting persons."

After a few minutes the group was talking and laughing together like old friends. Despite his . . . unsettled gut, he supposed it was, over Rosamund's whispered request that he talk her into fleeing, Bram felt himself relax a little. The Bromleys were good friends; he certainly felt more at ease with them than he did with his own family.

"Isn't Lester the one who lost his inheritance to . . . your friend?" Phin asked in a low voice as they finished dinner and the ladies retreated to the drawing room.

"If you won't even mention Cosgrove's name, then I won't answer any questions about him," Bram said without heat, accepting a glass of port from his former comrade-in-arms.

Phin dropped into the chair beside him. "There's no need to be sharp with me. I was merely curious. I'm behind on my gossip since you've been coming about less often."

"I thought it would be cruel to remind you of the amusements you could be enjoying as a bachelor."

His friend eyed him. "I may be married, but I'm not dead."

"You think not? Let's go off to the Society Club, then. Or Lord Belmont is holding one of his masqued parties tonight."

"Bram, I don't—"

"You don't wish to abandon your wife while you go out and play. I have no one to neglect. If I decide then to go out, does that obligate me to go alone?"

"I fail to understand why you consider Cosgrove's company superior to your own."

"Bramwell," Lord Quence broke in with his usual impeccable timing, "Lord Lester here tells me that he and his sister joined you for dinner with your brother earlier this week."

Damnation. Why was everyone picking at his good deeds? No wonder he rarely committed them. "I thought he and Oscar could use some lessons in gambling."

"I lost nearly a pound of shelled peanuts," the pup contributed, showing some humor. Of course anyone who could lose ten thousand quid and not blow his own brains out probably didn't take much very seriously.

"I've met Oscar," Viscount Quence said, grinning. "In a few years he may challenge even his uncle with his wagering skills."

"I hope he finds something better to do with his time," Bram muttered, and pushed away from the table. "Excuse me for a moment." He leaned over Phin. "Keep the boy here," he whispered.

Phineas grabbed his wrist. "I'm not helping you ruin a young lady under my roof."

"When did you become so bloody proper?"

"Bram."

"It's not your roof, anyway; it's your brother's. And I'm not ruining her. I need to ask her a question, and her brother's an incurable wag."

With a tight nod, Phin released him again. "Behave."

"Almost never."

He could have been more subtle about it, waited until later in the evening and taken her aside with no one noticing. Her request had jabbed at him all through dinner, though. Previously the chit had seemed ready to drown herself if duty demanded it. The sooner he could learn what new thing Cosgrove had done to distress her, the sooner he could find something comforting to say to her. And if he could manage a kiss, then so much the better.

Then he would meet with King and attempt to diplomatically convince the marquis to . . . to what? To cease tormenting Rosamund? To be kinder and realize that he could have made a far worse choice as far as a spouse was concerned? Whatever he said, he needed to extricate himself from the middle of this mess. He didn't want the Marquis of Cosgrove for an enemy. And his encounters with Rosamund had served only to trouble his thoughts and disrupt his routine. And his sleep.

As he stopped at the entrance to the drawing room, the three ladies were laughing over something. He paused there in the doorway. At eighteen, young Beth Bromley was all dark hair and stunning hazel eyes, the most excitable and least reserved of the three. Alyse was quiet and thoughtful with nerves of iron, the perfect counter to Phin's well-explored wild side, the home he'd finally found to stop his wandering.

And then there was Lady Rosamund, ginger-haired and freckled, eyes the color of meadow grass after a rain. Practical, witty, and for some reason loyal to her damned family, she continued to baffle him. She deserved better than she would be receiving—both from Cosgrove and from her own blood.

She turned her head and looked at him. Drawing his thoughts back in, he nodded his chin toward the doorway. Immediately she swept to her feet. "Excuse me. I'll be back in a moment," she said, and he backed into the hallway to wait for her. As she emerged, he turned and led the way into the music room opposite.

"What happened?" he asked, quietly closing the door behind her as she entered the room after him.

For a long moment she looked at him, her expression tense and hesitant. "I dislike running to you every time Lord Cosgrove calls on me. I'm not some fainting flower."

Bram shrugged. "I don't mind." His chest tightening a little, he forced a smile. "Not as though I've dire matters to attend to." Just a few robberies and some drinking, but he could see to both of those again beginning tomorrow.

"Are you his friend?"

The question made him scowl before he could stop himself. "I've known him since I was sixteen. I give him some credit for making me the man I am today."

"Yes, but are you his friend?"

He'd claimed friendship with Cosgrove before, but he'd never been asked so directly to define what it was between himself and the marquis. And he wasn't an idiot; for some reason the answer would be significant. "I am social with him, but I wouldn't tell him my secrets," he said slowly. "Not any longer, at any rate. So to answer your question, yes, and no."

Rosamund nodded. "I am somewhat relieved."

"And why is that?"

"Lord Cosgrove spent several minutes describing his wedding night plans to me," she said, twisting her fingers. "He means to humiliate and degrade me, and he wanted me to know it."

Bram swallowed. There had been times he'd relished doing those very same things, when the female participant had shown an interest. Rosamund, though, had never been given a choice in the matter. All she'd done was catch Cosgrove's eye at the time the marquis happened to be looking for a new game to play. Machinations, manipulations—he understood them. Hell, Cosgrove had introduced him to the twin evils, and he'd embraced them wholeheartedly. Or so he'd thought, until now.

"You asked me to say this, but in all seriousness might I suggest again that you leave London?" he said, as she continued to gaze at him. "I understand that you feel some sort of obligation to your family, but truly, Rosamund, what do you owe them that would convince you to stay about for this?"

"They gave me life."

"So do cows to calves, every spring. The offspring don't volunteer to walk into the slaughterhouse to spare their parents."

"Yes, but I am not a cow." Fleeting humor touched her eyes, then was gone again. "I take care of my family, Bram. It seems as though I always have. They're . . . silly, for the most part. I'm not. And I have no idea how else they would survive this debt."

"So they will survive, and you . . . pay the price." He'd nearly said that they would survive and she wouldn't, but she would probably accuse him of being overly dramatic.

"Someone has to pay." She took a breath. "I know you dislike being pulled into the difficulties of others," she continued, "but I have one last favor to ask of you."

One last favor. It was as if she realized that he meant to remove himself from this tragedy after tonight. "What is it, then?"

"I want you to ruin me."

Bram blinked, the clever remark he'd been about to make dying on his lips. He might have been imagining stripping her out of her proper clothes for days, but to hear someone—her—say it aloud, very simply seemed too good to be true. "While I'm happy to oblige," he drawled, "I have to ask how my ruining you would be better for your family than your flight."

"Because it will be just between you and me. A . . . preemptive attack against Cosgrove's plans." She took a single quick step in his direction. "I want to know what is supposed to be between a man and a woman before he . . . educates me to his version of it."

"That's quite a burden you're setting on my shoulders, Rosamund." And it made him more uncomfortable than he would care to admit.

"If Cosgrove means to play games, then so do I. I will marry him because I must, but I shall not be a lamb— or a cow—led to the slaughter. If he intends to destroy my spirit, he will find it a difficult task. I am not some fly whose wings he can pull off and then step on. I'm . . . I'm a bee, and I shall sting him back."

Good God. Bram refrained from pointing out that a bee died as a result of its sting. She would know that already. He wanted her, and she wanted revenge for a forced marriage scheduled to take place in a few weeks' time. This was a damned flip-flop on his usual reality.

"Are you not up for it? You bed women all the time, do you not, Bramwell Lowry Johns?"

Not since he'd set eyes on her. "I am not the sort of man you tease, Rosamund Luisa Davies," he said in a low voice, another kind of heat entirely beginning low in his gut. "I have a certain reputation, and you may be sure that I have earned it. I'm going to ask you once, and that's one more chance than I generally give. Are you certain you want me to be the one to lift your skirts? Are you certain that what you experience at my hands will be better than what Cosgrove might do?"

"It has been so far," she returned. "Just don't disappoint me. Please."

He cracked a smile. Any other chit he would have had on her back by now, regardless of the setting. "Leave your door unlocked tonight. If you change your mind, you'd best find another bedchamber in which to sleep. Because I mean to call on you at midnight."

Chapter 8

If Bram's friends found it odd that he had another engagement after their dinner party, they didn't say anything about it. For all Rose knew, Bram always had late-night assignations after dinner parties.

Tonight, though, *she* was the assignation. Another tremor ran through her as she sat at her dressing table. She'd done it. Just where she'd gotten the courage, Rose wasn't certain, but at least now it was too late for her to change her mind. Well, she could, if she chose to leave the room and sleep elsewhere, but she wouldn't.

The longcase clock downstairs chimed twelve times. The house was quiet around her, but she had no idea if all the servants had yet retired for the night. She hoped so, but it might have been safer for

Bram to climb in through her window. Rose stood up and pulled aside the curtains to look outside. A lone carriage rolled down the street, but other than that everything was still.

She paced to the bed and back to her chair again. A dashing young man climbing up the trellis would certainly be more romantic than his calling at her door. This, though, was not about romance. It was about knowledge, and about changing the rules another man had decided would apply to her.

Her door swung open. For a moment against the black of the hallway she couldn't make anything out. Then he moved, black garments against black shadows, and stepped into the room.

"You decided not to flee," he drawled in a low voice, closing and latching the door behind him.

"This was my idea, if you'll recall," she said with more bravery than she felt. Oh, goodness, he'd come.

"I recall."

He tilted his head, watching her in the light of the one candle she'd left lit on the bed stand. And she remembered vividly their first encounter, before he'd become an odd ally. Back when he'd said that he could teach her some things, back before she'd known who he was and he'd been a pure, dangerous predator. Abruptly she realized that tonight he was that man again. Perhaps he had been all along, and he'd only been playing with her before.

That man, though, was who she needed tonight. She cleared her throat. "How should we proceed?"

One after the other he pulled off his black gloves and dropped them onto her dressing table. They looked strange there, surrounded as they were by her hairbrush and hat pins. "First, tell me precisely what Cosgrove said to make you wish to embark on this venture."

Her heart stuttered. "What does it matter? I do not want him to be my first and only experience."

Bram continued to regard her. "Tell me anyway. I realize that it must have been terrible, to make you want me to be your first experience." He shrugged out of his coat, setting it over the back of her dressing chair.

"Are you such a poor choice?"

He snorted. "The fact that you have to ask me that tells me I should leave. But I'm not that nice. Nor do I have that much self-restraint."

"I find that difficult to believe."

"Rosamund, if chatting is all you wish to do, then go fetch us some tea and biscuits. Otherwise, tell me what he said." Bram drew a breath. "If you're feeling missish about telling me the details, consider that in a very short time I shall see you naked, and you shall have very few secrets from me."

Oh dear, oh dear. Rose sat on the edge of her bed, then remembered that they would probably be conducting their business there and shot to her feet again. "He said that on our wedding night he would put me on all fours and mount me as a dog mounts a bitch."

Something crossed Bram's expression so swiftly that she couldn't tell what it might have been. Anger? Surprise? Shock? She had no idea. And those were more than likely her own sensibilities she was looking for in him, anyway. He'd likely heard—and said—worse things than that. "That . . . position," he said slowly, unbuttoning his waistcoat, "can be quite pleasurable for both participants, I believe."

"And then he said he would keep me on my hands and knees until he decided to give me permission to rise."

His fingers paused in their trail down his chest. "I can't assist you with that part."

"I know. He told me that you would walk away as soon as anything became unpleasant for you, so I imagine we will have parted company long before my wedding, anyway. But you wanted me to tell you precisely what he said, and I have."

"You are quite the logical chit tonight, aren't you?" His waistcoat landed on the seat of the chair, and his cravat followed a moment later. He sat on them and leaned down to tug his boots off, one by one, setting them down quietly on the floor.

Fleetingly she wondered how much experience he'd had at sneaking into boudoirs while husbands or parents slept close by. "I don't see the point of becoming emotional tonight," she returned, telling herself that her abrupt fascination with his bared throat merely meant that such a sight in the future wouldn't set her heart pounding as it was now.

"A fine sentiment shared by many a man." Bram stood again to pull the tail of his shirt from his trousers, letting the fine white lawn hang loose down to his hips. "Do you wish to undress yourself, or shall I do it for you?"

Her knees began to feel wobbly. "I . . . um, what do you think?"

"It can be a quite intimate experience," he said, sounding thoughtful. "Perhaps I should do it for you."

Oh, she wanted him to touch her. "Very well. You do have much more experience about these things than I do."

Unbuttoning his shirt cuffs as he walked, Bram closed the distance between them. As he stopped in front of her, she expected a kiss or at least a caress of her cheek, but instead he motioned for her to turn around. Rose complied, closing her eyes for just a moment. Tonight she'd chosen to best Lord Cosgrove. Her virginity would go to Bram, and not to her future husband. It was only lucky coincidence that she also wanted to do it, and with Bram Johns. The—

His fingers touched not her back, but her hair. Gently he pulled out the clips and pins, making short work of an artistic pile that had taken her maid twenty minutes to compose, and her hair tumbled past her shoulders. As she stood there he brushed his fingers down her tresses, making her shiver. "That's better," he murmured.

Then, with a slow, steady pull and tug, he opened the back of her gown. Warmth touched the nape of her neck, the soft caress of his lips against her bared skin. Goose bumps lifted on her arms. *Oh, heavens.* Bram's mouth trailed along her shoulders as he pushed her dress down her arms, his warm, soft breath as arousing as the touch of his lips.

In a moment she stood in only her shift, her back still to him and her breath sounding not at all normal. Her mauve and gray gown puddled around her bare feet. Rose swallowed, determined not to flinch or wince or make any sign that might convince him that she was a silly chit and not worth the trouble of seducing. Oh, she liked this seduction.

"Lift your foot," he said, sounding as cool as if they were discussing apple tarts.

She lifted one foot, then the other, as he squatted down to move her dress. Once she was free from its circle, he tossed the material into a corner and straightened again. "What do we do next?" she prompted after a moment.

His hands rested on her shoulders, then pressed down a little. "Firstly, relax a bit. I don't want you punching or kicking me, for God's sake."

"I am relaxed," she lied.

"Really?" he breathed into her ear, then swept his palms down her shoulders to cup her breasts.

She jumped, squeaking.

"Hm."

"You only surprised me," she managed, her voice quavering as he splayed his fingers.

"This is allowed to be pleasurable, whatever your reasons for wanting me to seduce you."

Rose took a deep breath, which only made her more aware of his hands on her breasts. "Very well."

"I have a French condom, by the by," he said. "To prevent you becoming with child."

She shook her head, something warm running through her muscles. "Don't bother. I'm to be married in less than a month."

"Are you certain about that? Because I'm not certain I like the idea of Cosgrove raising the fruit of my loins."

She hadn't considered that; she'd been more focused on how much she would prefer a child fathered by Bram. "You mean to say that you care about something?"

He chuckled quietly. "You make a fair point. Lean back against me."

"Fine."

Rose settled her back against his hard chest. She could feel his breathing, the play of the muscles beneath her back, and his growing arousal pressing against her hip. Then he moved his fingers again. Slowly he circled her breasts with his forefingers, her nipples growing tight and budding through the thin material of her shift. The sensation was exquisite, and when he flicked a nail across her aching nipple, she drew in a hard breath through her teeth.

"Is this n-necessary?" she quavered, stammering over the words.

"Do you like it?"

Oh, yes. "It's pl-pleasant, but do you think Cos—"

"As a point of information," he interrupted, his low voice rumbling into her, "discussing one man while another has his hands on you is generally a poor idea." Moving again, he slipped his fingers beneath the straps of her shift and slid them down her arms to bare her breasts. "And if you wish to be ruined, we may as well do it right."

Oh, he seemed to be doing quite well at it, because even with her shift still half on she was quaking and barely able to think.

"Any complaints thus far?" Bram murmured, trailing his mouth down her shoulder to the inside of her elbow.

"No," she breathed shakily. "Not yet."

He stepped back, then put a hand on her arm to turn her to face him. "Do let me know if anything should arise."

"I believe something is already arising," she said, stealing a glance down at the apex of his thighs, her breath hitching again.

"Indeed it is." For a long moment his gaze lingered on her face, though she had no idea what he saw there. Then those black eyes lowered, and he reached out to brush a finger down her throat and her bare breastbone. He pulled her arms from her shift, and let the garment fall past her hips and down to the floor.

Abruptly feeling very vulnerable, and very conscious of the fact that she stood naked before a practiced rake, Rose squared her shoulders. "Are you going to kiss me?" she whispered.

"There are better uses for mouths," he returned, lowering his head to kiss the outside of her left breast. He moved in slowly, kissing lightly, until he took her nipple into his mouth and flicked his tongue against it.

"Bram," she gasped, arching her back.

He ignored her exclamation, shifting his attention to her right breast and repeating his actions. Her insides turned to liquid fire. Rose lifted her shaking hands, tangling her fingers into his coal black hair and pressing harder against him.

"Time to put you on your back," he murmured, slipping a hand beneath her knees and lifting her in his arms.

Laying her down on the bed with his knees straddling her thighs, he bent down to lick and suck at one breast again while he teased at the other with his very capable fingers. A few moments later he straightened, and she moaned in protest. It couldn't be over with yet. Not with this . . . craving rising through her insides.

Bram yanked his shirt off over his head and cast it aside. A dusting of dark hair crossed his chest and narrowed on its path down his stomach, disappearing beneath the waistband of his trousers. Rose lifted a hand to place it over his breast, and the hard muscles beneath flinched.

"Do you enjoy my touch as much as I'm enjoying yours?" she asked.

"Yes." He took her hand and lowered it to his trousers. "Why don't you unbutton me, and I'll show you?"

Shifting a little, her hands shaking, she unfastened the top button. Somewhere she'd stopped thinking about Cosgrove, about how her family had not raised her to ruin herself at Bramwell Johns's capable hands. But if they'd raised her to be bartered in exchange for gambling debts, then she couldn't place much value on anything they'd done. And as for what *she'd* done, she was prepared to sacrifice herself to the marquis—but first she wanted this, and she wanted Bram Johns.

As the last button came open he shoved his trousers down to his thighs. His large, hard . . . manhood came free, erect and jutting. "You know what this is for, yes?" he whispered, following her gaze.

Her mouth felt dry. "I can surmise."

"Good. Then you don't need an anatomy lesson, and we can continue with the exploration of you."

"Of m—"

One hand trailed down her stomach, through her curls, and down *there*. She gasped again, bucking as his fingers parted her, pressed into her.

"You're damp," he announced softly.

"Is that bad?"

His lips curved. "No. It's very, very good." Kicking

out of his trousers, he bent down to suck at her breasts again. Then his mouth began a slow, delicious, breathless trail downward, following his very busy hand.

She was absolutely going to die. Nothing was supposed to feel this exciting. Slow lightning swirled through her, holding her more and more tightly in its heated grasp. Every touch from Bram's fingers, from his mouth, sent her spinning into fire. When he began kissing the insides of her thighs, she half expected her heart to burst, it was beating so hard and fast.

And yet he didn't seem to be in any hurry, at all. When his mouth joined his fingers, she shrieked, grabbing his hair.

"Shh, Rosamund," he murmured, humor in the sound. "And loosen your damned grip before you render me bald."

"Apologies," she whimpered. "I can't . . . This is too much, Bram."

"It's never too much." He lowered his head again.

Her eyes rolled back. Oh, she was going to die. "Bram, please."

Finally he relented, returning his attention to her tight, swollen breasts. "How do you feel?" he asked.

"On fire," she answered truthfully, breathless.

Nudging her knees apart, he settled between her thighs. "I have it on good authority that this is going to hurt," he said, gazing down at her from inches away. "But only this once. He can't do that to you, anyway."

The last part came out as a growl, but before she could ask for clarification, he angled his hips forward. The sensation of him pushing inside her was . . . indescribable. She felt pressure, felt him hesitate, then with a sharp pain he entered her fully.

"God," she gasped, muffling her cry against his shoulder.

"Rosamund."

She realized she'd closed her eyes, and opened them again to look up at him. Bram kissed her, softly at first, then deeper and more urgently. Her arms went around his shoulders as she lifted to meet his seeking mouth. His hips began a rhythm, forward and back, slowly and then harder and faster, following the tempo of his kisses.

The harder and deeper he stroked, the tighter she drew. Then, with a breathless pulse, she shattered. Everything went white and hot and exquisite. When she came a little back to herself Bram was still moving inside her, slow and deep, his gaze fixed on hers.

"Jesus," he whispered.

"I want to do that again," she panted.

He chuckled. "I haven't finished my first go yet," he murmured, his tone not quite steady. "Do you want me to show you what Cosgrove meant?" His voice caught on the marquis's name, as if he didn't want to say it.

Nor did she want him to. And yet, Kingston Gore was the reason for this. Her heart shivered. "Show me."

Bram withdrew, still hard and erect. "Turn over."

Rose rolled over, sinking onto her hands and knees as he shifted her into the position he wanted. Bram rose up behind her, parting her thighs, and then slid into her once more. There was no pain this time, just an incredible filling sensation that left her gasping again.

He reached around, lightly pinching her left nipple between his thumb and forefinger as he thrust into her. Immediately she began drawing tight again, each strong pump of his hips drawing her closer and closer to that edge that she now knew and wanted. Rose clenched her fingers into the bedsheets, stifling her cry as she came again. With a low growl Bram thrust hard and fast and then held himself inside her as he found his own release.

Pulling free, Bram collapsed onto the bed beside her and drew her down across his chest. "Now you are ruined," he said quietly, and kissed her again.

Bram lay on his back, Rosamund curled against his side, and tried to recover both his breath and his senses. He felt sated, unusual for him considering that he'd done most of the work this time. And his contentment wasn't the only unusual thing about the evening.

Candlelight flickered across Rosamund's smooth skin and turned her ginger hair to bronze and flame. Jaded as he considered himself, she'd aroused him from the moment he'd opened her door to find her sitting at her neat dressing table, waiting for him. Listening to her voice, to her questions as she'd tried to be logical and sensible about her choices and her situation, had actually shaken him a little.

She must have been desperate to not only welcome him into her bed, but to invite him to join her there. He could call it a good deed, he supposed, but good deeds weren't supposed to be so . . . pleasant. And even finished, he wanted to kiss her again. He wanted her to fall asleep in his arms, and to see her wake up in the morning.

"Bram?"

He blinked, shaking himself out of his terrifying domestic reverie. "Hm?"

"Thank you."

With a scowl he turned on his side to face her. "It wasn't any imposition for me, Rosamund. I do this sort of thing all the time, if you'll recall." She started to reply, but he shook his head. "You're now ruined, and you may be with child, which I shouldn't have risked whatever you said about it. So for God's sake, don't thank me."

"If I'm to be with child, I would rather it be conceived in kindness and gentleness than in spite and cruelty."

So she hadn't lost sight of her reasons for having him visit her. And she somehow still managed to maintain her practicality. He searched for something suitably cynical with which to respond. "You are an unusual chit, Rosamund." It didn't seem adequate, but it was the best he could manage.

She tilted her head, green eyes regarding him. "Is that a compliment?"

"I don't know. Tell me; is this what you wanted?"

She sat up, and he had to stifle the strong urge to take her arm and pull her back down beside him. What the devil had gotten into him? *He* was the one to leave the bed first, to announce that he had somewhere else to be and needed to leave before anyone could begin sighing or making moon eyes.

"Yes, it's what I wanted." With another glance at him, she slid to the edge of the bed and stood up. He sat up to watch as she bent down and picked up her shift, shaking it out and then pulling it on over her head.

It seemed a damned shame to cover up those lovely curves. When she retrieved his trousers and tossed them onto the bed, he scowled. "Excuse me, but are you trying to get me to leave?"

"I don't want anyone to find you here, Bram."

"I've adequately performed my services for you, then, and we're finished with one another?" He wasn't even entirely certain why he was asking the question. Once he'd bedded a woman she generally ceased to interest him unless he had nothing better to do. But previously he'd only been shoved out of bed or the house when a husband was expected home.

Rosamund grimaced. "I'll know what it should be like now," she finally said. "Gentle, and very, very nice. And he will know that I'm not the virginal flower he expected me to be. But having you found here wouldn't help me any. Being involved with you would do me no good."

"And why, pray tell, have you suddenly come to this decision?"

"Because you're his friend. You drink, you gamble, you . . . bed women you shouldn't. If it wasn't for this stupidity with Cosgrove, I would have wanted nothing to do with you."

Bram stayed where he was, fascinated by the recitation of his sins. When she paused, he motioned at her. "Go on."

Her frown deepened. "I will admit that you have on several occasions surprised me. But the fact remains, when I marry Cosgrove he will forgive a ten-thousand-pound debt, and I may have the opportunity to dissuade him from leading James into further trouble."

"Your brother's game has improved, thanks to me. Pray keep that in mind."

"Oh, yes. You're encouraging him to think he knows what he's doing. *I'm* better at cards than he is. He needs to stop playing. I can't force him to do that, but Cosgrove could."

"So you consider King a better candidate for a husband than I." Not that he wanted to marry her or anyone else, but he'd never heard himself so disparaged by anyone but his own father.

"Please get dressed and go, Bram."

With a sigh, covering a deep, growing annoyance, Bram stood up. Though he noted that her gaze lowered to his cock, for once he made no comment about it. Damnation, he'd thought to take her at least once more before he had to go meet Cosgrove and excuse himself from this mess. Insulting as she'd been, he still wanted her again.

"Bram, go," she repeated, turning her back to gather up the remainder of his clothes.

"But I find your insight into my character fascinating," he returned, shrugging into his trousers. "I had no idea you knew so much about human nature—that after a sennight of acquaintance you've been able to stick a pin through me and put me in your glass display box above the label marked 'Bram Johns, wrecked and wretched.' "

She threw his shirt at him, and he caught it against his chest. "You made yourself what you are. And why do you always wear black? You hardly need to advertise your character."

Bram pulled on his shirt and waistcoat without bothering with any of the buttons. He yanked on his coat, stuffing his cravat into his pocket, and picking up his boots, strode for the door. "Good night, Rosamund."

With her door halfway open, though, he paused. He knew people who cared for nothing but logic or profit or their own comfort. Rosamund Davies was not one of those people. Taking a breath, he turned around, walked up to her, and put a hand around the nape of her neck. And then he kissed her.

After a second her lips softened, opening to his. He molded his mouth against hers, enjoying the taste of her, of her excitement and passion. Then he backed away. "I thought so," he murmured, and slipped out the door.

Chapter 9 _____

By the time Bramwell put his clothes
back in order, recovered his horse, and made his way
across Cheapside to Jezebel's, it was several minutes
past three o'clock. In his present state of mind he would
have preferred to avoid a chat with Kingston Gore, but
he'd spent better than a decade balancing a half-dozen
schemes and women all at the same time, all without
missing a step. This situation wasn't much different.

King sat at his usual table at the back of the dim,
candlelit room. Dingy floors, bare wood, and cheaply
painted walls, most of the tables still occupied even at
this hour of the morning—he'd always been rather fond
of Jezebel's. Until tonight.

Bram noted the faces of the patrons sitting nearest
King's table, relegating them to memory and then otherwise ignoring them. He had enemies, and they would

be as happy to stab him in the back as in the chest. At least with him and the marquis at the same table, no sane man was likely to approach them.

He motioned for a bottle of whiskey and a glass. "Cosgrove," he drawled, taking the seat opposite. "I expected you to be involved with something else by this hour. Or someone else."

"Who was she?"

Omniscient as Cosgrove could seem at times, Bram knew it to be an illusion, created by a combination of astute guesses and his well-compensated network of spies and informers. And given the way Bram generally spent his evenings, the marquis's guess was a fair one.

Accepting the whiskey, he poured himself a glass and downed it. "Good God," he said aloud, "that was an hour ago. I've forgotten her name."

Cosgrove glanced up at him, then returned to pouring water over the lump of sugar and slotted spoon that lay balanced over his cloudy green glass of absinthe. "Doubtful. Mine wanted to know whether I would continue to call on her after her husband returned from the Peninsula next month."

"Will you?"

"I see no reason why not, considering she began entertaining me six weeks before he left."

"You will be married by the end of the month, if you'll recall. Won't you find your plate rather full?" He would have been wiser to stay well away from the topic of Rosamund, especially after she'd just booted him out of her bedchamber, but the damned chit—or something—had set him off kilter.

"Hm."

"Hm, what?"

"I merely find it interesting that you would think marriage would make anyone—much less me—faithful. How many other men's wives have you bedded?"

"I'm not talking about them; I'm discussing you. You've never seen fit to marry before now."

Setting the spoon aside, the marquis took a slow swallow of his potent drink. "I am six-and-thirty. I need a legitimate heir. For that, I require a wife. But I don't need her for anything beyond that. May as well have a bit of fun with the proper chit, then, as long as I'm purchasing her."

"Or you could leave her be, and find a female who shares your tastes."

"The amusement comes from the fact that she doesn't share my tastes." Cosgrove lit a cheroot off the table's candle. "And this is a unique opportunity. Her family owes me such a substantial sum that the dutiful chit's been left with absolutely no means of escape. She detests me, and she fears me. It's . . . delicious. Intoxicating, actually. I recommend it, if you should chance upon a pretty, proper chit with limited prospects and an impressionable fool for a brother." His mouth curved in a slow smile. "And however desperate she becomes, her family will never be able to purchase her freedom, because our relationship will ensure that I will always have the largest share of influence over young Lord Lester."

Bram had fairly well figured out all of that, but hearing it laid end to end, especially after the night he'd spent, he felt . . . sickened. And Rosamund considered King and him to be cut from the same cloth.

"What do you think of that?"

With a frown he didn't have to fake, Bram shrugged. "It might be amusing at the beginning, I suppose," he said in the most nonchalant tone he could manage, "but the end result is that you'll be married with a child and a wife. Neither of those seems like anything you'd enjoy."

"One I'll need, and the other is for me to do with as I please." Cosgrove took another drink, closing his eyes for a moment as he swallowed. "And as you know, I'm very particular about my pleasures."

"So you felt the need to terrorize someone, and because Lady Rosamund isn't a celebrated beauty, doesn't have a great fortune, and does have bastards for parents and an idiot for a brother, you've chosen her."

"Yes." Cosgrove lifted a golden eyebrow. "You sound angry, Bramwell. Have another drink and calm yourself."

Bram finished off his second glass of whiskey. He *was* angry. The muscles across his shoulders felt so tight they practically creaked, and above the queasiness that Cosgrove's plan inspired in him was the distinct urge to punch his mentor in the face. What he needed to figure out, immediately, was whether his sensibilities were finally being affected, or if his . . . growing fondness for Rosamund had sparked this mental mutiny.

If it was Rosamund in particular, she'd made it clear that she thought little better of him than she did of Kingston Gore. She hadn't wanted, asked for, or expected his assistance or protection. All she'd requested was that the deed be done, and as brilliantly as he'd performed, she'd kicked him out. And she might not like the idea of marrying King, but she still planned to go through with it.

Damnation. He detested this bloody morass of conflict and emotion. There was absolutely nothing in it for him, and stepping into the middle of it would likely gain him an enemy in Cosgrove, no appreciation at all from Rosamund, and a cartload of trouble for no damned good reason at all.

"Generally when you or I play one of our games, King," he said anyway, treading more carefully than he could ever recall doing before, "I've always thought that the fool we selected deserved some misery. This seems well beyond that."

"It is," Cosgrove agreed readily. "Leading a sinner to further sin isn't much in the way of a challenge. Corrupting someone who believes herself incorruptible, though—that is a true measure of skill."

Bram downed another glass. "Leave her be, King," he finally muttered. "Console yourself with the idea that I will owe you a favor."

"Well," the marquis said, sitting back, "this is interesting. Might I ask *why* you think I should spare Rose Davies?"

"I suppose it's because I rather like the idea that there are a few people of good character about to balance damned souls like ours."

Cosgrove sat silently for a long moment as he sipped at his absinthe. "And do you think that your climbing beneath the bedsheets with her would leave her less sullied than would a marriage to me?"

"That's not what I'm talking about."

"You've been escorting the Davies siblings to dinner with your beloved family and friends because you want to bugger the boy, then."

King's damned spies. "She's . . . refreshing. I find her innocence amusing."

"Then what's the difference between us?"

"I'm not attempting to drive her to madness or ruin or suicide."

"You chisel away at her every time you say a word in her presence." Light blue eyes met his gaze squarely. "And I won't have it."

"Beg pardon?"

"This isn't something I decided on a whim. Well, it is, actually, but since then it's taken me weeks to learn the ethics of Abernathy, lure in Lester, and bring him to the point of falling ten thousand quid into my debt. I have no intention of altering my plans because you see a way to salvation or some other horseshit when you look at her."

"I've said nothing of the kind," Bram protested, fighting against his growing desire to leap across the table and throttle his so-called friend. "I only asked you to leave her be."

"And I'm *telling you* to leave her be. Step back from my affairs, or I shall make you the target of my next game. I would prefer that we remain friends." He took a puff of his cheroot. "So consider, is this truly where you wish to take a stand against me, Bramwell?"

Sweet Lucifer, what was he doing, sticking out his neck for a chit who insulted him? Finishing off his fourth overfull glass of whiskey, Bram pushed to his feet. "I suppose we'll both find out," he said, and left the club.

He needed to talk to someone he could trust, and though surprisingly the first face that came to his mind was Rosamund, she clearly didn't wish him back in her bedchamber tonight. That narrowed it down quite a bit, as a matter of fact.

Phineas Bromley awoke to what sounded like a full-scale battle directly outside his bedchamber door. Alyse sat up beside him a heartbeat later, her hair a disheveled autumn-colored waterfall, and her brown eyes wide with alarm.

"Phin, wh—"

"Get behind the wardrobe," he barked, his old soldier's instincts taking over as he rolled to his feet and collected the pistol from his nightstand in the same motion.

The door burst open. Phin leveled his pistol as a dark streak slammed into the room, two lighter-colored globs attached to it and trying unsuccessfully to slow it down.

"Yes, that's it," Bram Johns's low, oddly pitched voice came, "blow my damned brains out. Save me the trouble."

With a breath, Phin lowered the weapon. At the same moment, candlelight flared from the hallway as another servant stumbled into the room to join the chaos. "Let him go," he ordered the nightshirt-wearing butler and footman.

Bram shrugged his coat back onto his shoulders. "You're naked, you know," he announced, his words slurring just a little.

"And you're drunk." For Bramwell Johns to be showing the effects of alcohol, he must have consumed a tremendous quantity of it, indeed. "Thank you, Graves. Please make certain William and Beth are well, and then return to bed. All of you." All he needed was for his crippled older brother to attempt to drag himself to the rescue, or for his younger sister to begin screaming and awaken the entire street.

The butler gave an annoyed nod. Lighting another candle and sending the two footmen out before him, he exited the bedchamber and pulled the door closed. As Phin eyed his friend, Alyse handed him a pair of trousers. With a grateful glance at her, he tossed the pistol onto the bed and shrugged into them. Evidently she'd grabbed the sheet as she fled the bed, because her slender figure was securely swathed in gold. A very good thing for all of them, considering the way Bram was eyeing her.

"It's past three o'clock in the morning, Bram," he said finally. "What's happened that couldn't wait another three or four hours?"

"I need to speak with you," his friend replied, still brushing the overzealous servants' fingerprints from his sleeves. "In private. Without any chits about."

Alyse motioned at the two of them. "I am going back to bed. You," and she motioned at Phin, "keep *him* out of here."

"The morning room, I think," he said, turning Bram toward the door. He agreed with Alyse. Bram sober could be relied on to honor a very few things, among them keeping his hands off a friend's wife. Drunk, he became much less predictable and much more dangerous.

"Good night, sweet Alyse."

"Good night, Bram."

Taking the candle with him, Phineas followed Bram downstairs to the morning room. His friend was still in the same clothes he'd worn to dinner, though his cravat looked as though it had been retied, and there was a certain . . . carelessness about his appearance that was highly unusual.

The liquor tantalus was locked, but just as Phin braced himself for an argument about more drinking, Bram walked past the table and dropped into one of the seats facing the hearth and the banked fire. Chilly without a shirt on, Phin stirred the coals and set another log into the fireplace before he sat in the opposite chair.

"You love Alyse," Bram said abruptly.

"Yes, I do."

"You would die for her."

"I'd prefer to remain alive to enjoy her company, but yes." Phin scowled. "What's this about? Did you go on another of your burglaries?"

"No. What about Isabel? Would you die for her?"

"Sullivan's wife? Yes."

"What about—"

"You and Sully are my closest friends. You're my brothers," Phin interrupted, unwilling to go through a list of people for whom he would fall on a sword. "I would lay down my life for either of you, and for any member of your families. But considering that you already knew that, might we move on to the reason you needed to speak to me at nearly four o'clock in the morning?"

"What did you think of Lady Rosamund?"

Phin blinked. This was about a woman? "She seemed pleasant," he offered, not certain on which side Bram's sentiments would fall. Now that he considered it, though, Bram wouldn't generally have tolerated being in the presence of a foolish boy like Lord Lester. Not unless he had something more in mind.

"She's annoying," Bram stated.

"Very well. So the sister of one of your friends annoys you."

Bram made a derisive sound. "That idiotic pup is the cause of all this."

"Mm hm. All what?"

"Having a monster for a friend doesn't make me a monster, you know. Does it?"

Cosgrove. "No, it doesn't."

"But if I call him friend, knowing who he is and what he does—what about the things I've done? Am I the sort of man to tell anyone else he's gone too far? Should anyone look to me for protection?"

"Bram, you're beginning to alarm me," Phin said, sending a glance in the direction of the tantalus. Bram might not need anything more to drink, but he wasn't so certain about himself. "What's afoot?"

Bram sat forward, rubbing at his forehead. "Nothing. Just something I need to decide." He pushed to his feet. "Apologies, Phin. Go back to your bed and your pretty wife."

Phineas stood up, as well. "Bram, if you need any assistance, tell me."

"I don't." He walked through the door to the foyer. "You may want to distance yourself from me, Phineas. I have a good idea that things are going to get very sticky." Pulling open the front door, he slipped outside and quietly closed it behind him again.

For a long moment, Phin stood where he was. Then he turned around and went back into the morning room for paper, ink, and pen. Bram embraced trouble, but clearly this was different. And worrisome. It seemed to be time to request reinforcements.

Whether Sullivan Waring disliked London or not, he was needed.

Rosamund held her sheets up to her nose and breathed in. Whether it was all in her imagination or not, Bram's scent seemed to linger, a masculine smell of soap and leather.

Thank goodness he'd left, especially after that kiss. If he'd stayed . . .

She sat up, pushing the sheets aside and going to splash water from the wash basin on her face. If he'd stayed she would have begun listening to his advice about fleeing, and she would have done something foolish like begin to fall for a man with no clear allegiances or morals and very questionable taste in certain friends.

He'd done as she'd asked, and not only allowed her to best Cosgrove in the only way she could think of, but he'd also shown her what Cosgrove's mysterious, awful-sounding threats had meant. She feared the act less now, though the thought of Cosgrove touching her as Bram had last night left her chilled and sick. So she'd exchanged one troubled thought for another, and at the moment she couldn't say whether she was the better for it.

Except that she felt better inside. Stronger. She'd had no idea that intimacy with a man could feel as alive and wondrous as it had. Was it always that way? Or was it just because she'd been with Bram Johns? She hoped not, because after what she'd said to him last night, she wasn't going to be seeing him again, for kisses or for anything else.

Her door opened. "Good morning, Lady Rose," her

maid said, hurrying inside to pull open the curtains. "Your sister says you're to join her for shopping."

"Tell her I've an aching head, Martha," Rose replied, collapsing back onto the bed. The last thing she wanted was to spend the morning being talked at by Beatrice. She wanted to think—though at this point she was in all likelihood beyond finding help through thought.

"She said you would say that, my lady, and that she won't take no for an answer."

"Come along, Rose," Bea's voice echoed up from downstairs at the tail end of Martha's comment. "We have a great deal to do."

"Oh, bother." Dragging herself upright again, she went to her dressing table while Martha found her a suitable morning gown to wear. "Did she happen to mention what we're to shop for?"

"I heard her telling your mother the countess that gathering her own wedding trousseau was such a delight, and she can't wait to help you with yours."

Rose's response to that couldn't be said in the maid's presence if she wanted to retain her standing as a lady. Instead she sighed and picked up her hairbrush to begin combing out her hair—and looked down at Bram's black leather gloves. With a squeak she swept them onto her lap.

"Is something amiss, my lady?"

"Oh, no. I hadn't realized my hair was in such a state," she offered, gesturing at the dressing mirror and making a face. "Would you open the windows? I feel the need for some fresh air."

"Right away."

As soon as Martha turned her back, Rose stood and

hurried over to shove the gloves into one of the less-used reticules in her wardrobe drawer. That done, she returned to her seat. "What time is it, anyway?" she asked.

"Half ten. You slept quite late."

"I was quite tired."

After she dressed in a white and yellow gown of sprigged muslin and Martha helped her put up her hair, she took a deep breath and went downstairs to the breakfast room. The rest of the family, including Bea and her husband Peter, Lord Fishton, sat around the table, chatting.

"There you are," Beatrice trilled. She'd always been far too happy, and that trilling had only gotten worse once she'd married and begun producing offspring. "Do come sit beside me. I was beginning to think you meant to sleep the day away."

"Apologies," she returned, selecting her breakfast from the sideboard before she took her seat. "I didn't sleep well."

"Is something troubling you, Rose?"

No, I had a man in my bed. She looked at her sister for a moment. "Nothing other than the fact that I would prefer not to marry the Marquis of Cosgrove."

"Oh, do stop complaining, dear," her mother said airily. "You're marrying a very wealthy and titled and handsome gentleman."

Rose had her doubts about the "gentleman" part, but arguing was clearly useless when no one cared to see the truth. "Do you think it's wise for me to purchase a trousseau when my engagement hasn't yet been announced?"

"You need to have one, goose," her sister countered.

"And Papa said that Lord Cosgrove means to marry you immediately after the end of the month."

"Do we know Cosgrove's politics?" Fishton asked abruptly.

"No, dear," Beatrice answered. "We will discover them. Oh, perhaps we could meet Lord Cosgrove for luncheon. The more everyone sees you together, the better."

"I don't want to have luncheon with Cosgrove." Just the thought of it spoiled her appetite for breakfast. "Why don't you dine with him, Fishton, Papa? If he's to be part of the family, the rest of you need to become better acquainted with him."

Fishton nodded as he sipped his tea. "You know, that's a fair idea, sister. The—"

"I say," James put in around a mouthful of poached egg, "I did notice that you left me out of that invitation. But it just so happens that *I'm* having luncheon with Cosgrove, so if any of you want to join us, you'd best tell me."

"Oh, we should all go," Bea seconded, clapping her hands together.

While James and Beatrice compared the merits of various dining establishments, Rose picked at her buttered toast. Why was it that the only one who'd even suggested a way for her to escape this mess was someone of equally poor reputation? Busy as her thoughts were with planning how she could avoid luncheon with her future husband, this morning visions of coal black eyes and elegant hands and warm skin crowded out even the dread of Cosgrove. It helped, but for how long could she steel herself against one man with thoughts of another?

"No," James was explaining, "he said something about fetching a special license from Canterbury. He said it would save waiting about for no good reason."

"Then I hope he's already begun making arrangements for a church. And if we're to hold an engagement ball, I certainly need to know when he plans to make the announcement."

A shudder ran through Rose at her mother's pronouncement. "I know you all want everything to appear happy and proper," she forced out, "but I would appreciate if in private you would at least acknowledge that you understand I would rather marry a fishmonger than Cosgrove."

"What's done is done," Beatrice said in her bright voice. "And of course we know you're not overly fond of him. But many a match has begun with bare acquaintance and ended in friendship and love."

"And what of his reputation?" Rose pursued.

"His connection with us can only improve it. And he is a marquis, after all."

She closed her eyes for a moment. It wasn't that her family didn't or couldn't understand her reservations. It was that they understood them and set them aside as insignificant. She fell into the same category; nothing more than goods with which they could settle a gambling debt. Didn't they see that she could run away if she chose to? That she'd decided instead to do as she always did—make certain everyone else was taken care of? For the first time she considered that a little blasted appreciation and gratitude might be appropriate.

"Then let's be off and purchase my trousseau, shall we?" she said as she opened her eyes again. "Clearly there's no reason to wait."

"You're being sarcastic," Bea returned, standing, "but I shall ignore it until your spirits improve. James, we shall be on Bond Street. Send a note to Cosgrove about luncheon and then come and inform us."

Anger tickled at the back of Rose's skull. Before now she'd never minded that no one knew of her contributions to the household. She could see for herself that she'd done well—with the notable exception of James and his wagering. As far as her family was concerned, though, she'd been . . . invisible. Until now.

Once she left, they would notice her absence. At the moment she had a value—ten thousand pounds. And she felt more unappreciated than ever. Was she simply expecting too much of them? Or too little of herself?

For the next two and a half hours she followed Beatrice from shop to shop, collecting armfuls of bonnets, hair ribbons, night rails, shawls, and other baubles that had little importance to her and were even less her own taste. When Bea selected a particularly pink and frilly hat, she shook herself and attempted to distract Lady Fishton from it. That, at least, kept her from dwelling on the fact that in less than twenty minutes she would be sitting across a table from Kingston Gore.

The very pink and very frilly matron's cap went into a hatbox and into her arms—and then vanished.

"This is interesting," a deep, familiar drawl came from beside her. Bram held the hat up in his fingers, looking at it as if it were some kind of insect.

The hairs on her arms lifted, warmth flowing like liquid fire down her spine. Rose took a hard beat of her heart to compose herself, then turned to face him. "What are—" She stopped, surprise pushing at her. "What are you wearing?"

He looked down at himself. "Clothes."

Rose reached out and touched a finger to his chest. "Your waistcoat is gray."

Black eyes, amusement in their depths, regarded her. "Dark gray. And you should probably stop touching me."

Oh, dear. Hurriedly she clenched her fingers and lowered her hand again. "Apologies."

"No need. I know I'm difficult to resist. As would you be, in this hat." He twirled it on his finger.

"Stop it," she muttered, snatching the chapeau back and trying to resist her silly urge to smile. But he'd come to see her, in a dress shop of all places, after she'd practically thrown him out of her bed last night. "Beatrice thinks I'll look fetching in it."

"You would look fetching in anything," he countered, "or nothing. But that does not change the fact that this is an ugly hat."

The unexpected humor and the even more surprising compliment made her pause—and immediately aroused her suspicions. "What are you doing here? I thought I made it clear that I appreciated your . . . assistance, and that I don't . . . trust you any further." Wanting him about was something else entirely, but it was also far too disruptive. She remained uncertain whether encountering Bram Johns was rendering her decision to do her duty easier or more difficult.

Deprived of the hat, Bram picked up one of her new night rails and examined it. "I got quite drunk last night after we parted company," he said in a thoughtful tone. "Generally I take most of the supposed insults people hand me—when they dare to say them to my face—as compliments."

Oh, dear. A shiver of much less warmth ran through her. She had enough trouble and misery ahead of her, and she absolutely did not want Bram Johns as an enemy. Not him. "We were both quite tired," she offered. "The—"

"I have to admit," he went on, as if she hadn't spoken, "since meeting you I've realized that, as far beyond propriety as I roam, I do seem to have my limits."

She gazed at his face, studying the inscrutable coal-colored eyes, the tired lines around them, the tight set of his jaw. He actually looked troubled. Whatever he'd been contemplating had clearly kept him from a good night's sleep, unless he'd simply had another assignation after he'd left her bed and that had caused his sleeplessness. Rose didn't like that idea, and she covered her abrupt discomfiture by retrieving her garment from him and stuffing it back into its box.

"You don't agree with me. I don't blame you; until last night, I wouldn't have believed me, either. I'm still not all that convinced."

He didn't sound either angry or resentful, but he was also a master of trickery and deceit. The last thing she needed was for him to announce to everyone in the shop that she'd invited him to stop by and ruin her last night, and that he'd done a very fine job of it. That was for Cosgrove to discover. "And what do you mean to do about this epiphany?" she asked carefully.

"I'm going to rescue you."

She snorted. Immediately horrified that she'd just made things worse, she tried to turn the sound into a cough.

Bram looked insulted, but recovered his expression so quickly that she couldn't be certain. Then he lifted an eyebrow. "Ungrateful chit."

"You've already helped me," she returned quickly, sending a glance at her sister as Lady Fishton had half the shop's staff running about to gather up their purchases. "I don't think there's anything more you can do."

"Then I'll have to prove you wrong."

"Bram, you—"

"Rose, come along or we'll be late," Beatrice broke in, hurrying over with still more packages in her arms. How nice that the bride-to-be wasn't needed in the purchasing of her own trousseau. Her sister abruptly stopped, her eyes widening. "Lord Bramwell Johns," she exclaimed, her warbling becoming distinctly wobbly.

"Lady Fishton, I presume," Bram returned, sketching a shallow bow.

Rosamund looked on with interest. Her sister's cheeks had paled, then darkened as Bram gazed at her. She'd felt the same sensation herself upon first meeting those eyes; she was being watched by a lean, dark predator, and while it was very unsettling, a good half of her wanted to be caught.

Beatrice was petite, slender, and had golden blonde hair and bright green eyes. Had Bram looked at her before? She very much seemed to be the sort of woman he would pursue. Rose found herself stepping forward, in between them.

"Lord Bram is a friend of James's," she explained, picking up an armload of packages only to have Bram take them from her.

"Where are you off to?" he asked, falling in beside her as they left the shop for the Fishton coach.

"We're meeting Lord Cosgrove for luncheon," Beatrice supplied as she stepped up into the carriage. "Good afternoon, my lord."

Bram took Rose's elbow to help her up the pair of steps, but instead of releasing her, he tightened his grip. "Ah, Cosgrove," he drawled. "Another friend of mine. Perhaps I shall invite myself along."

"We're to meet at the White Lion at one o'clock," Rose said, before Beatrice could open her mouth to declare that the meal was for family and prospective family only.

"Then I shall see you there."

As he closed the door and stepped back, the coach rolled off and Bea began chastising her for talking with unsavory characters. Rose barely heard it. Though Bram might be unsavory, she was rather glad he would be joining them. He seemed to be the only person who understood her revulsion for the man she was to marry, and he was certainly more qualified to stand up to Cosgrove than anyone in her party.

As for him rescuing her, she supposed he could amuse himself as he pleased, so long as he didn't listen to the last thing she'd asked of him—that he go away.

Chapter 10 _____

A luncheon with Cosgrove. Bram disliked
the timing, but if he meant to orchestrate his own ruin,
he might as well get on with it. Aside from that, knowing
Rosamund's feelings where Cosgrove was concerned,
and after his own conversation with the marquis early
this morning, he . . . couldn't leave her without an ally.
Even an ally she didn't particularly trust or even want
about. Even an ally who didn't have much practice in
that role.

Recovering Titan, he trotted off in the direction of
the White Lion, one of the tamest and most respectable public houses in Knightsbridge. He'd debated with
himself all morning, and even with Cosgrove's warnings and his own strong sense of self-preservation, the
thing that had troubled him most and stayed with him

the longest had been Rosamund's dismissal of him after he'd ruined her.

As he'd gotten older, his games had become darker and more elaborate. What he'd most been aware of had been fleeing a perpetual state of boredom, and of chasing toward the next thing that would annoy and affront his father. He hadn't liked Cosgrove's plans from the moment he'd gotten a whiff of them, but the more he'd learned, and the better he'd come to know Rosamund Davies, the less he'd been able to condone any of it.

But frowning about something and actively attempting to put a halt to it were two different things. *Very* different when Kingston Gore was involved. And that brought up a different question: If the woman Cosgrove had selected hadn't been witty and forthright or hadn't had a compelling sprinkle of freckles across her nose, would he now be attempting to play a hero?

Bram shook himself as the inn and Fishton's coach came into view. He enjoyed the company of women for one reason, and he'd already indulged in that with Rosamund. Anything else was nonsense. And he was about to stir up enough chaos without something beyond that, something even more absurd and ridiculous and . . . troubling coming into play.

Lester and Cosgrove were already seated at a table at the back of the public room when Bram trailed Rosamund and her very chirpy sister into the inn.

He kept his attention on the marquis, watching as Cosgrove looked up. King's gaze went immediately to Rosamund, and the possessive and proprietary look in his eyes made Bram clench his fists. Clearly, with his appearance and wealth, if King had been kinder and more solicitous about it, duty-minded Rosamund might well have gone along with the wedding plans without any protest at all. And for an absurd moment Bram was glad his so-called friend had chosen to woo in the way that he had.

The marquis's gaze moved past Rosamund, and his eyes narrowed as he spied Bram. Cosgrove would wait, though, before he acted on anything; after all, the two of them had worked schemes together in the past.

So for a moment, anyway, Bram had the advantage. Given his past actions, Cosgrove would expect that he'd decided to step back and avoid crossing his mentor. This time, however, Cosgrove was wrong.

"I say," Lester exclaimed with a happy grin, "where did you find Bram?"

"I was looking for a gown to match my eyes," he said dryly, deliberately taking the seat beside Rosamund. He wanted to touch her, to taste her soft lips, and with his sharp awareness of her it would be wiser to put someone else between them. At the moment, though, this was more about keeping Cosgrove from doing something else to frighten or intimidate her. "Who knew we favored the same dress shop?"

"Interesting choice of attire you've settled on," Cosgrove drawled, indicating his waistcoat. "What brought this about?"

Sweet Lucifer. Simply because he'd decided this morning that perhaps he did wear black to excess, everyone thought he must be up to something. "I'm expanding my horizons," he offered.

"Also interesting."

"We've been purchasing items for Rose's trousseau," Lady Fishton said brightly.

The blue eyes shifted again to Rose as she occupied herself with choosing a pasty from the platter on the table. "Ah," the marquis commented. "I've been purchasing some things for my wife-to-be, as well."

"Oh, how very sweet! What things? You must tell us."

Briefly Bram wondered whether Lady Fishton was merely obtuse or whether she was utterly without any common sense at all. People didn't banter with Cosgrove. Women especially. One of the marquis's favorite ripostes was that the only opening in a woman of any interest to him was the one between her legs. Or her mouth, if it was occupied with the thing between *his* legs.

"Things that are only between a husband and his wife," Cosgrove returned, giving a slight, brief smile that didn't touch his eyes. "I will be happy to tell Rose all about them later."

"Did you hear that Lady Gervais is holding one of her infamous masqued balls tonight?" Lester broke in. "Certainly you and Bram must have been invited, Cosgrove."

"Indeed I was," Cosgrove returned. "Do you wish to attend, James?"

"Sweet Saint Joan, yes!"

Bram felt Rosamund shift a breath closer to him on the bench. She hadn't said a word, which in itself was unusual for her, and when her fingers brushed against his beneath the table, it felt as though lightning had struck him full in the chest. Twisting his wrist a little, he briefly squeezed her fingers. "I'll be attending as well, Lester," he said aloud. "It's to be all three of us, it seems." That was all it took to encourage him to stand in front of a cannon, then; a single touch from a gently bred female seven years his junior.

For a time they sat and ate, Lady Fishton and Lord Lester doing most of the chatting. Rosamund had still barely said a word, and Bram began to feel somewhat frustrated that Cosgrove hadn't uttered any blatant threats or more obvious innuendos. Her unusual silence in itself spoke volumes, though. She was not only angry at her present circumstances, but she was frightened, as well. Bram clenched his jaw.

He didn't have much—any—practice at being a hero, but then he wasn't one yet. The damsel was in distress, and there he sat, trying to decide how many of his cards he should lay on the table. As Rosamund hunched her shoulders, Bram took a breath. Time to fish or cut bait.

"Any luck, Lester," he drawled, "with your father raising the ten thousand quid to pull Rosamund out of this predicament?"

Cosgrove's eyes narrowed a fraction, but he said nothing. Viscount Lester, though, frowned. "It ain't such a predicament, Bram. Rose is two-and-twenty. Don't you think it's time she married? And Cosgrove here is my friend, same as you."

Bram reached into his pocket and pulled out the two hundred–odd pounds' worth of notes the pup owed him. "Not quite the same," he said, and tore them in half before he handed them to Rose.

"I say, that's good of you, Bram." Lord Lester reached across the table to shake his hand.

"Is it?" he returned. "I have so little experience."

"Quite a coincidence that you happened to have those promissory notes in your pocket when you stumbled across the Davies family and invited yourself to luncheon." Cosgrove poured himself a glass of port. "I would like to point out that being owed a debt of a few quid is much different than being owed ten thousand."

"They might as well be the same, considering that neither of us labored very hard over gathering either amount."

"If you've . . . feelings for the chit, Bramwell, inform me now and perhaps we might work out an arrangement."

So Cosgrove could torment her six days out of the week and he could come calling on Tuesdays? Dismayed as the notion of the other six days left him, he wasn't about to admit to feeling any affection for any member of the Davies family. No chinks in his armor. This was about setting Cosgrove's attention away from Rosamund. Period. "I'm discussing easily acquired and unneeded blunt. Be a gentleman for once and let them escape."

The marquis leaned forward, planting his elbows on the table and resting his chin on the steeple of his fingers. "No. If you're interested in the lady, why don't you ask her which of us she prefers?"

She prefers me, Bram wanted to shout, but instead forced out a chuckle. "I'm discussing honor, not chits. Aside from that, with the weight of what you hold over her, it's not precisely a fair question, is it?"

"It's fair enough for me." The marquis turned his gaze on Rosamund. "I would like to hear my wife-to-be answer, anyway. Whose company do you prefer, Rose?"

"My own," she stated in a low, flat voice.

"Ah, but my dear, I wish you to say either my name or his. Tell us. Now."

"Yours, Lord Cosgrove."

As little as he liked the answer, Bram understood it. He reached beneath the table again for her hand, but she snatched it away.

"Please do not make things any worse," she muttered, lowering her head.

"You see, Bramwell? The lady prefers me. And no wonder. He's cut off, you know. Supports himself through wagering. And there he went, letting go of two hundred quid he probably needed to keep himself fed."

"I'm cut off at least thrice a year," Bram retorted, glad his jibes were working to focus Cosgrove's ire on him. "I've become an expert at coping, if I say so, myself."

"Is that what you call it? Coping? I prefer making a plan and following it. With that in mind, I shall escort Rose to the Hampton soiree on Friday. It's time we begin the public semblance of a courtship. Now, my dear, tell Lord Bramwell that you would like him to leave, before I become insulted that you hesitated in answering my question."

He didn't want to hear her say that again, coerced or not. Bram stood and stepped back from the bench. "No need. I have an appointment, anyway. Good day, all. I'll see you tonight, King, Lester."

"We will continue this fascinating conversation later, Bramwell," Cosgrove said as Bram turned his back.

"Yes, we shall," he returned. Hopefully after he had a strategy other than sitting beside Rosamund and touching her whenever possible, the ungrateful chit. Because unexpectedly pleasant as that was, it made for a very poor plan. Being a damned hero was more difficult than he'd imagined.

"I do enjoy a party," Beatrice said as the Davies and Fishton families gathered in the Davies House morning room and waited for *him* to arrive.

Him. The Marquis of Cosgrove. Rose had worn the most demure gown she owned. Sweltering as the very high neckline and long sleeves were, they provided the only portable barrier between Cosgrove and herself. If she could have managed it, she would have worn trousers, a wool shirt, and a very thick greatcoat.

"Did you have to wear that gown?" her sister asked on the tail of her thought. "You look like a governess."

"Considering that I'll be spending the evening in the Marquis of Cosgrove's company, dressing conservatively seemed as though it would better serve our family."

"She has a valid point, Lady Fishton," Lord Fishton commented. "I'm still half convinced that being seen in close proximity with Cosgrove could jeopardize my position in the cabinet."

As far as Rose knew, Beatrice and Peter always referred to each other as Lord and Lady Fishton. Now with her experiences expanded she wondered whether they did so in the privacy of the master bedchamber as well—though she had some difficulty imagining mild Fishton in flagrante delicto.

Once Fishton mentioned the possibility of being forced out of his employment as undersecretary to the secretary to the minister of finance, Beatrice's opinion of their outing changed remarkably. "You know," her sister said, her voice pitched even higher than usual, "we can't all possibly fit into one coach. Lord Fishton and I will go ahead and meet you at the Hamptons' party."

"Yes, do go," Rose agreed. "And perhaps Mama and Papa should join you. James and I will wait for Lord Cosgrove."

"Are you certain about that, dear?" her mother asked, though she'd already stood to leave the room. "Of course it *is* you whom he wants to see. And the reason your father asked for the delay was to avoid any gossip."

"I know what my part in this is," Rose returned, pushing back against the sick feeling in her stomach. Failing to deal with Cosgrove would ruin her entire family. This way, she would be the only one who would have to deal with the marquis. Overmatched as she felt, she was certainly more qualified for the task than the rest of the household.

The remainder of her family fled the house, leaving her to take a seat as far from the fireplace and its heat as she could manage, while James paced. Practically everyone had fled from her side, now. Her cousin Maggie had taken to corresponding with her, even when their two households were barely a quarter mile distant from each other. James hadn't stood by her for any selfless reason, but because he still considered the marquis practically a god. And she hadn't seen or heard from Bram Johns in three days.

At least he'd told the marquis to leave her alone before he'd vanished, making him the only one to speak a word on her behalf. Why he'd done it, she wasn't certain. Without eliminating either the debt or Cosgrove's influence over James, it had been a futile effort. And yet since he'd left the table at the White Lion, she'd felt as though her last, best hope had gone with him. And since then she'd been very much alone.

"He's generally late everywhere, Rose," James said into the silence. "Makes for a grander entrance, he says. So don't worry that he's forgotten us."

Nothing would please her more than to be forgotten. "You never told me, was the masqued ball at Lady Gervais's everything you'd hoped it would be?"

Her younger brother actually blushed. "Bram said it wasn't the sort of place to go with anyone you cared about, or if you cared for anyone. I didn't believe him at first, but after seeing the place, it made some sense."

"He attended, then?"

"No. Sent me a note, begging off. You've got him and King growling at one another."

Despite her resolve and her firm hold on reality, her heart skipped a beat. "It's nothing I asked him to do," she said.

"I don't know about that, but I ain't even seen Bram in three days to ask him. And he ain't exactly a hermit, you know."

She knew that quite well. Even before their arrival in London she'd heard and read tales about him, of his outrageous wagers and conquests and how he wasn't welcome in some houses because of his reputation. So he'd been more nuanced in person than she'd expected; no one had said he wasn't charming.

And yes, perhaps she'd enjoyed his attentions, and his kisses, and his more . . . intimate instruction. She hadn't expected him to cure all the ills around her. She'd only asked for what had to be, for him at least, a few very minor favors. That was all she'd expected. And to herself she could admit that the only thing worse than being forced to marry an uncaring, unrepentant blackguard would be to marry one and pine after another of the same character.

The front door opened, and a moment later Elbon appeared in the morning room doorway. "My lord, my lady, Lord Cosgrove," the butler intoned, bowing, and the marquis walked around him into the room.

"King," James said with a smile, hurrying forward to offer his hand.

Rose remained seated, somewhat surprised that James hadn't kissed his dear friend. At this moment she wasn't certain she could make herself voluntarily rise and greet the awful man. Marrying him would be terrible enough; dissembling and pretending he was tolerable seemed completely beyond her ability. Clear blue eyes looked her up and down, and she turned her gaze to the window.

"Are Lord and Lady Abernathy joining us?" the marquis asked.

"Oh. They—my parents, that is—went on ahead with Bea and Fishton. Not room enough for us all in one coach, you know," James returned brightly.

The marquis continued past her brother and stopped in front of her. "Do you think that ridiculous gown will convince me to leave you at home?"

"I like this gown," she retorted.

"I don't. Change it."

"No."

It took every ounce of courage she possessed to stand and face him. For once she was glad to be tall; at least she didn't have to crane her neck to meet his gaze. Bram was an inch or two taller than the marquis, in fact. It was an insignificant detail, of course, but she seized on to it and held it hard. Cosgrove might think himself powerful and controlling, but he couldn't manage to make himself taller.

"Lester, go have a look at my new team," he said, his gaze still on Rose.

Before she could open her mouth to order her brother not to go anywhere, he'd galloped out the door. Damnation. James hadn't the common sense to fill one of his own pockets. She squared her shoulders. "Go on."

"Go on with what?" Cosgrove murmured, taking one step closer to her.

Rose stifled the urge to back away. He'd only pursue her, and she'd be trapped in the corner. "Insult me, or lick me, or tell me what awful thing you're going to do to me after we're married. Isn't that why you sent James outside?"

The marquis looked at her, his expression utterly unreadable. Where she'd conjured the courage for that little speech and what the consequences might be she had no idea, but she was glad she'd said it. He couldn't control everything.

"He's bedded you," he said in the same quiet murmur.

A cold chill went down her spine at the words, and she abruptly remembered that she wasn't just defying a cruel man; she was standing face-to-face with a monster. "I beg your pardon?" she forced out, with all the injured dignity she could manage. Oh, she wanted him to discover that, but not already, and not when he could sound accusing and superior about it.

"That's why he wanted me to leave you be," the marquis went on. "This is extraordinary. He's had you and he still . . . likes you." His slow smile froze her blood. "Not what I had planned," he went on, his expression becoming more thoughtful, "but Bramwell Lowry Johns has always been a bit . . . unpredictable."

This time Rose did back away. "I have no idea what you're talking about, but all I ask is that you treat me with a modicum of resp—"

He slapped her.

The blow rocked her, and she grabbed on to the back of a chair to keep from falling. Her cheek stung, and she put a hand over it. *He'd hit her.* She turned for the door to escape.

Cosgrove got there first and closed it before she could slip through. "'Respect'?" he repeated, still smiling faintly, his blue eyes glittering. "Is that what you showed *me* when you allowed Bramwell between your legs? We're to be married, my dear."

"Get away from me," she rasped.

He leaned closer. "Never," he whispered. "The thing about hell, my dear, is that the devil hates being alone. You belong to me, just as my horse does. And Bramwell does now as well, I suppose."

"Go away."

"The only reason I won't put you on your back at this moment is that I want us both to appreciate the wait. I know I do."

"Open this door, or I shall scream. You don't own me yet, Lord Cosgrove."

With a slow breath, he lowered the latch and pulled open the door. "Was he gentle, Rose? Did he say your name? Did you come for him?"

Giving a half shriek, Rose shoved past him and up the stairs. It was awful. This was awful. Every time she thought she'd raised some sort of defense against him, bested him even, he found another way to attack.

Rushing into her bedchamber, she slammed the door and shoved a chair beneath the handle. Sobbing, Rose paced the floor and then sank down onto her knees. How could her parents ask her to marry that . . . that animal? She rubbed at her smarting cheek. He hadn't hit her hard, but he could have. And knowing that made it even worse.

A knock sounded on her door. "Rose?"

"I'm ill, James," she managed, sniffing. "Go to the ball without me."

"But Cosgrove wants you to join us."

Cosgrove could go hang himself. "I'm ill," she repeated.

"Very well, but he won't be pleased."

When she didn't answer, his footsteps retreated back to the stairs. Rose curled up on the floor. Even if she told her parents that Cosgrove had struck her, it wouldn't change the circumstances that had caused them to agree to the marriage in the first place. As things were now, they would likely accuse her of provoking him with her complaining.

As she lay there, the one face that gave her any sense

of peace and hope was Bram's. And now Cosgrove would be after him, as well. For a man who disliked entanglements, he was going to find himself in a very unpleasant situation. She might not yet be able to convince herself to flee and leave her family to their own troubles, but Bram Johns probably would have no trouble at all doing so to her.

Chapter 11 _____

"Are you waiting for someone?" A warm hand curled around Bram's arm. "Because I've sent Lord Ackley to fetch me sugared orange peels." Lady Ackley moved closer, breathing into his ear. "And there are no orange peels being served tonight."

Bram stifled his sigh. "A brilliant maneuver, Miranda," he returned, his gaze still on the doorway of the Hampton ballroom. Lord and Lady Abernathy and the tongue-wagging Lady Fishton with her vapid husband had already arrived. Where the devil was Rosamund?

Miranda tugged on his arm. "You haven't touched me in days, Bram. I long for you. But we must hurry. Ackley will come looking for me eventually."

The best thing about bedding Lady Ackley was that she lost the ability to speak once he removed her clothes. In fact, when they weren't having sex, he found her irritating. And over the past days, that irritation had for some reason deepened into dislike.

"I'm not going anywhere with you tonight, Miranda," he said in a low voice.

"Oh, does my devil not feel well?"

That would be an easier way of getting rid of her than telling her that he simply wasn't interested any longer in what she had to offer. "No, I don't," he agreed, slipping his arm from her grasp. "And it's best if we're not seen together for no reason."

"Oh, of course." She released him, but leaned up to whisper at him again. "I've been wanting to inform you that my husband is leaving for Ackley Abbey on Monday, and he will be away for the next fortnight." She giggled. "Can you imagine all of the fun we will have?"

Across the floor Lester and Cosgrove strolled into the ballroom. "Excuse me, Miranda."

"But—"

He didn't listen to the tail end of her prattling; all his attention was on Cosgrove. To anyone else the marquis probably looked his usual aloof, cynical self, but Bram had known him, studied him, on and off for better than a decade. Kingston Gore was angry. And considering that Rosamund hadn't appeared with either her parents or her brother, she was the likely cause of his ire. Good for her.

Passing behind Cosgrove as the marquis began his own perusal of the crowded room, Bram slipped up beside Lester. "James, good evening."

The viscount jumped. "Bram. Where the devil did you come from?"

"The shadows. It's my way. Where's your sister?"

"Damnedest thing, that. She was all dressed up, ready to go, and then Cosgrove sets eyes on her and says she must put on a different gown—and the one she was wearing did make her look like a pinchy old governess, with those long sleeves and—"

"And did she change clothes?" Bram interrupted, attempting to turn the tale back onto its path.

"Well, she and King chatted in private for a minute, and then she went upstairs, but when I tried to fetch her, she said she'd taken ill and wouldn't go out."

Taking a deep breath, Bram fought against an abrupt rise in his temper. "You left her alone with Cosgrove?"

"They are engaged, really. And King's got a sterling new pair for his coach."

"You idiot."

"I say, that's unkind. I don't—"

"Never leave your sister alone with a man unless *she* asks you to do so," Bram hissed. "No matter who the man is. Is that clear?"

A hurt expression on his face, Lester nodded. "But it was Cosgrove," he complained, as if that explained everything.

"And Rosamund is your sister. You've done her enough of a damned disservice, James. You can at least stand by her while she's still in your care."

As Bram finished his lecture, Lester gazed at him like the gullible, naive eighteen-year-old he was. For a moment Bram thought the pup might begin weeping. He took a breath. When had he become the one espousing propriety? With a half scowl he clapped the viscount on the shoulder.

"You listen to your heart, James," he continued more quietly. "There's nothing wrong with that. But a man listens to his head, as well."

"Was it your heart or your head, then, that wagered Lord Deverill over whether you could drive through Brighton blindfolded?"

"Ah. I don't always listen to either one, though I do acknowledge that they've spoken. But I'm a poor example, James. As is Cosgrove."

"You're daft, Bram," the pup returned. "You won every wager you made at White's last year. That ain't a poor example. That's bang up to the echo."

Very well, perhaps it was a rather spectacular feat, but that wasn't the point. The middle of the Hampton soiree, however, wasn't quite the place for a lecture on honorable behavior. Nor was he the ideal one to give it. Far from it. Aside from that, he wanted to know what Cosgrove had done to trouble Rosamund.

He turned around to see Miranda glaring at him, and Cosgrove now looking full at him, as well. Given the poor showing he'd made at luncheon the other day, the expression on the marquis's face, difficult as it generally was to read, should have been contempt or triumph. Instead, though, the anger that he'd first glimpsed on King's face deepened.

It was aimed at him, then. Perhaps on later reflection Cosgrove had realized that he'd erred in his treatment of Rosamund—though considering what Lester had just told him, that didn't make much sense. The marquis was still attempting to antagonize and frighten her, and he'd apparently been successful at it.

Bram supposed he could have turned around and made an escape, but little as he liked being embroiled in something that he hadn't intended, he liked turning his back on someone he didn't trust even less. And he'd never trusted Cosgrove.

"Bramwell," the marquis drawled, as Bram stopped in front of him. He sent a glance at an approaching footman, who immediately found another direction to walk.

"Cosgrove. You seem to be without your nearly-betrothed. A bit careless of you to misplace her, considering all the trouble you went through to catch her."

"You owe me an apology."

Bram raised an eyebrow. "Do I?"

"Yes, you do. And I expect you to deliver it by sinking down on your knees here in front of everyone and begging for my forgiveness."

Hm. That didn't sound good. And there he was, unarmed except for his wits and the knife in his boot. "It's beginning to sound as though you and I aren't friends any longer," he mused, noting that the open area around them had grown, as though the fellow guests felt danger in the air.

"It's beginning to seem that we're not," Cosgrove agreed. "You've had her. When I made it quite clear that she belonged to me."

"I've had so many of them, King," he replied with a slight smile that he didn't feel. "To which one are you referring?"

"If I'd wanted her publicly ruined, I would have done it by now," Cosgrove grunted, anger flaring again in his angelic eyes. "And you've made it worse for her; if words aren't effective, I'll be forced to use other means."

"Or you could choose a different victim."

"No. If you wish this to stop with our friendship ending, I suggest again that you apologize to me. Now."

Cocking his head, Bram noted that both his older brother and the Duke of Levonzy were standing just beyond the outer rim of onlookers. Bloody wonderful. Out of all the things he'd done, associating with Cosgrove had probably angered his father the most, and for that reason alone he was loath to let the duke see a public break with the man. On the other hand, he'd shoot himself in the head before he would kneel in public to apologize for something. Particularly when he considered himself in the right—which, unusually enough, he was. Probably.

"I've an offer for you," he said aloud, keeping his voice pitched low. "Let her be. Let the entire family be, and *I* won't take this beyond the end of our friendship. Pursue this game of yours any further, and I will see that you regret it."

"I'd pay to see you attempt to best me. Go to the devil."

Bram sketched a bow. "After you." With that he turned on his heel and strolled into the crowd.

"Bram," his brother said, reaching for his shoulder.

He ducked the embrace. "Excuse me, August. I'm in search of whiskey."

In truth, while a strong drink would be welcome, that wasn't what he was thinking of. The idea seemed to burst fully formed from his skull the moment he'd learned that Rosamund might be in distress. And for the devil's sake, he'd been breaking into houses while purportedly at parties for months. He'd already visited

Davies House twice under cover of darkness, as it was. A third time would be a very simple matter.

He lingered for a few minutes at the fringes of the room until the dancing began, and then he slipped out a side door of the ballroom and made his way outside through the gardens. This time he left his coach at the soiree and instead walked down the street and around the corner until he could hail a hack.

A hack—another of his own rules broken. He detested the ill-sprung monstrosities with their lumpy seats and indecipherable scents, but tonight he barely gave it a first thought—much less a second. Was it obsession, the way Rosamund had come to consume his thoughts over the past weeks? Perhaps it was a sign that he was becoming feeble-minded, which wasn't surprising considering the way he'd been living his life.

But why her? Why not Miranda Ackley, who certainly had more experience in the bedchamber than Rosamund? Or Sarah Vischer, who could suck the yolk from an egg? Not decent, freckled, annoyingly stubborn Rosamund Davies. It made no sense at all.

The hack stopped to let him out two streets away from Davies House, and he walked the rest of the way. Half the downstairs windows still glowed with candlelight, as did a handful of the rooms upstairs. Clearly he wouldn't be going through the front door tonight.

Irritated at his own driving need to see her and to touch her, Bram skirted the carriage drive and made his way along the base of the west-facing wall. Even three years after his return from the war on the Peninsula he kept fit with riding and boxing, but climbing walls to reach damsels in distress didn't seem terribly dignified, or in keeping with his cynical view of life.

That realization didn't keep him from working his way up the drainpipe that ran past Rosamund's window. As usual the glass stood open a few inches, and he was able to hook it with the toe of his boot and pull it toward him. Once the opening was wide enough, he swung across the open space and grabbed the windowsill with his gloved fingers.

Shifting his grip, Bram dug his toes into the wall and hefted himself up. Then something smacked him across the face, and he nearly lost his grip. "Rosamund," he rasped, scrambling to keep his precarious hold. "Stop bloody hitting me!"

She gasped, and then her head emerged from the window to look down at him. "Bram? Oh, my goodness! I thought you might be the Black Cat, coming to burgle the house."

The Black Cat had already been to the house, though the only thing he'd stolen had been her virginity. "James said you'd taken ill," he said, gazing up at her and aware of an odd thumping in his chest that had nothing to do with his hanging twenty feet above the ground. Next he would be quoting from *Romeo and Juliet*. "I came to see how you were."

"You might have called at the front door for that."

"If you don't step back and let me in, the constabulary is going to come calling at your front door, wondering why there's a very handsome dead man in your garden."

Rosamund moved back quickly. Feeling a bit unsettled—after all, he'd expected to find her cowering and witless—Bram hauled himself up over her windowsill and stepped down into her bedchamber.

"Hello," he said, brushing at the sleeve of his dark gray jacket.

Dropping the cricket bat with which she'd struck him, Rosamund abruptly threw herself forward. Faced with a female shoving herself into his chest, her hands clutching into his coat, and her face buried hard into his shoulder, Bram did the only thing that felt correct; he closed his arms around her.

"Rosamund, shh," he breathed, lowering his face into her soft, ginger-colored hair.

He wasn't very practiced at being comforting; hell, he could count on one finger the number of times he'd offered comfort. She lifted her face and began kissing the underside of his jaw, featherlight and filling him with longing.

"I'm attempting to be supportive and understanding," he whispered, tilting his head, his eyes rolling back, as she continued nibbling at him. *Good God.*

"Everyone left, and you came to see me," she murmured, her voice still unsteady. Her fingers lifted to pull at the knot in his cravat.

"This is not being comforting," he tried, steeling every muscle in his body to keep from returning her caresses.

"This is the comfort I want," Rosamund returned, pulling his cravat free and dropping it to the floor.

As her hands began tugging at the buttons of his waistcoat, Bram decided that he'd endured more than could be expected of any mortal man, and he lowered his head to take her mouth in a hard, hungry kiss. Part of him wondered whether this was her way of gaining revenge against Cosgrove again, this time for whatever he'd done to make her retreat to her bedchamber. At the sensation of her hands unfastening the buttons of his trousers, he ceased caring what her motivations might be.

Bram pulled the pins from her hair, letting the ginger waves cascade down around his hands. "You are dressed a bit conservatively this evening," he noted, reaching around her to loosen the top of her gown.

"It was intentional."

He nearly said something about the more skin she covered up, the more interested he was in exposing it, but he stopped himself just in time. Bram Johns only said such things when he was bent on seduction. This chit already had her hand down his— "Good God," he muttered, aloud this time, shifting as her slender fingers closed around his cock. "Don't pull it off; it's headed where you want it to be."

"Apologies," she whispered, removing her hand from his nether regions to shove his jacket and waistcoat onto the floor.

Pulling the shirt over his head himself, he turned her around and swiftly went to work on the remainder of her buttons. She was enclosed more tightly than a mummy, and he wanted at her. Badly.

As soon as he had her undone, he pulled down on her sleeves and twirled her around so that he could clamp his mouth over her left breast. Whatever her reasons for wanting him, at any moment she could come to her senses, and urgency pulled at him.

Lifting her, he half dropped her backward onto her bed. He yanked her dress up over her hips, wetting his lips as she lifted her hips to assist him. Then he shoved down his trousers.

"Your boots," she rasped, gasping as he pulled her toward the edge of the bed.

"Leave them." With a growl he slid inside her, relishing the tight, hot sensation. Still standing beside the bed, he pumped his hips hard and fast, leaning forward to place his hands over her breasts. Her nipples pebbled beneath his palms, and he bent further to replace one hand with his mouth again.

Moaning in time with his thrusts, she reached up to tangle her hands into his hair. "Bram," she gasped, and then came, pulsing around him.

Heat speared through him, turning his blood molten. Without any of his usual finesse he found his own release, deep inside her. *Sweet St. Christopher.* Whatever the devil she did to him, and much as he hated to admit it, he liked it. And he liked Rosamund Davies.

He released her hips and twisted to lie back on the bed beside her, reaching over to fling a blanket over the two of them. When she rested her head on his shoulder, her hand curled over his chest, he had the oddest sensation of simply wanting time to stop.

Clearly he needed to rid himself of this oddness. "Will you tell me what happened?" he asked, placing a subtle kiss into her hair.

For a moment she lay there in silence. "He knows," she finally said in a muffled, miserable voice. "Cosgrove knows that you . . . that we've been together. I didn't tell him, but I suppose I wasn't as frightened of him as he expected."

As he held her, listening, he sent his gaze around her room. Aside from the cricket bat on the floor, a chair stood jammed beneath the door handle. Most telling of all, though, was the portmanteau on the floor at the far side of the bed, the thing half filled with clothes and other personal items.

Something had happened. Something worse than Cosgrove's previous threats and promises. Something bad enough to make the absurdly loyal chit fly into his arms and pack her bags. Bram rubbed his hand down her back, pulling her closer against him, as she began shaking. Her fright troubled him. It troubled him a great deal. "What did he do?" he murmured.

"He said something about if his words didn't put me in my place, he would find something that would. And then he slapped me."

Bram abruptly regretted not making use of the knife he'd carried in his boot to the Hampton soiree. He could understand Cosgrove desiring her and wanting to control her. But to strike her . . . Bram was accustomed to being angry; he'd spent most of the past ten years in varying states of it. What he felt as he listened to Rosamund, though, to the shake of her words and the despair in her voice, was deeper and hotter than anything he'd ever experienced. Plainly and simply, it was fury. White-hot, blood-boiling fury.

"Hope that he enjoyed hitting you, Rosamund," he said in a low voice, "because he will never touch you again."

She lifted her head, green eyes gazing at him. "I won't let him. I'm going to leave."

His breath caught in sudden dismay. "I believe I suggested that before," he said as evenly as he could.

"And I should have listened. My family . . . my family will be destroyed, but I can't spend the remainder of my life in that man's company." Her voice broke. "I can't do it, Bram. I thought I could, but—"

"But at some point you need to begin looking after your own welfare," he finished. "I've found that that is the only way to live, Rosamund."

She frowned. "No, it's not. But I've been forced into it by his actions."

"I have an idea," he said slowly, about to break another of his rules. Three in one night. Someone should have made a wager. "Stay with me."

Rosamund's pale cheeks darkened. "What?"

"Stay at Lowry House. No one would suspect it. I would . . . I would protect you."

She leaned up and gave him a soft, slow kiss. Bram closed his eyes at the touch. A kiss freely given by her was almost better than sex.

"I'm not complaining, but what was that for?" he asked.

"You *would* protect me, wouldn't you?"

With his dying breath. "Yes."

"From Cosgrove, anyway. But you couldn't protect me from Society, and who would protect me from you?"

"You're the one who began undressing me."

"That's not what I mean."

"Explain, then."

"This"—and she ran a finger across his chest—"is . . . delicious. But this"—and she lifted her hand to place it over her own chest—"is something else entirely. Because I seem to desire you doesn't mean that I trust you."

This time Bram scowled. "Marry me, and Society and I will both be managed."

For a hard heartbeat he wasn't certain he'd spoken aloud, until she pulled away from him and sat up. *Christ.* What the devil was he thinking? He'd *proposed,* for God's sake. But now that he'd done so, he damned well wanted an answer.

"Well?" he prompted, rising beside her.

Rosamund cleared her throat. "Oh, my," she whispered. "I admit, I expected you to turn tail and run for Scotland or somewhere rather than put yourself directly in your friend's path."

"He's not my friend any longer. I made that rather clear this evening. And thank you for your faith in my character."

"It's not faith or a lack thereof. I've been studying up on you, Bram."

"Isn't that nice." Just what he wanted after a damned proposal; her picking at his character. Admittedly there was a great deal to take apart, but he was being the bloody hero, damn it all. "I could be mistaken, but I think I just asked you to marry me. Pray give me an answer."

"I insulted you when I said you were cut from the same cloth as Cosgrove. I apologize for that."

"Thank y—"

"But you're still trouble. A great deal of it. I won't flee one ill-conceived marriage that I had a good reason to go through with for another one that I don't."

Swallowing, Bram rose and yanked his trousers back over his hips. Just one bloody time he would like to lie in bed and quote poetry or some other damned thing with her before the blows began flying. "Very well, then," he growled. His first instinct was to throw open her door and walk down the stairs and out her damned front door with the entire household staff watching. Just as compelling, though, was the desire to know what she meant to do if she wouldn't have him. "If you're fleeing your home and you won't marry, you won't be able to stay in London."

"I thought I might find work as a governess or a companion. Perhaps in York, or in Cornwall. I like the sea."

Either place was too far away. Another worry entirely seized him. If she went away, he wouldn't be able to see her any longer. And that was unacceptable. "No."

" 'No'? I don't believe it's up to you."

He paced the length of her room and back again. Twice. And then once again. For years he'd amused himself with schemes and games and wagers. It was a simple procedure: Figure out what he wanted, and then the best way of getting it. "This is all about a ten-thousand-pound debt," he mused, half to himself.

She nodded. "Yes, I agree."

"Your engagement to Cosgrove won't be announced for better than a fortnight."

"Again, you have a wonderful grasp of facts."

Bram sent her a glare. "I'm thinking, if you don't mind."

"Think all you like. I'm not staying to be accosted by that man again."

Finally he faced her again, his heart pounding so hard he was surprised his chest didn't erupt. "Make me a bargain, Rosamund. Give me fourteen days. If I haven't removed you from Cosgrove's grasp by the time he's able to make your engagement public, I will see that you get safely to wherever you wish to go, with enough pin money to give you time and a chance to find decent employment."

She looked at him for a long moment as she found a night rail and pulled it on over her naked form. "What's in it for you, then?" she finally asked.

You. "You know I like a challenge. And if you can withstand him, with my assistance, for another fourteen days, then you have nothing to lose."

"You just proposed to me. Are you going to behave as a gentleman?"

He grinned, amused for the first time since he'd spoken to Lester. "I never said that. Do you agree?"

Finally she stuck out her hand. "Fourteen days, Bram. I'm trusting you."

He shook hands with her, then lifted her fingers to kiss her knuckles. "Fourteen days."

And if everything went according to his hurriedly constructed plan, at the end of the fortnight she would be free from Cosgrove, and she would instead be hopelessly—hopefully—entangled with him. This was going to be a seduction, and marriage to Lady Rosamund Davies would be his prize.

Chapter 12 _____

Rose made it halfway from the stairs to the breakfast room before her father emerged from his office. "There you are," he said in a tight voice. "Come in here. Now."

Squaring her shoulders, Rose turned down the hallway and followed him into his private domain of ledgers and newspapers and almanacs. This confrontation didn't trouble her as much as it might have a few days ago; she'd likely spent more time considering her actions and all their possible ramifications than he ever could. And she'd done her best to comply with his wishes, even when she knew no good would come of it for her. "I wanted to apologize for not attending the soiree last night," she said, deciding to bridge the topic before he could begin chastising her over it. "It must have been something I ate. I had to sleep beneath a damp compress all night."

He sat down behind his desk. "My income last year, from both estates, was seven thousand pounds," he said without preamble. "Expenses, including taxes, salaries, Oxford tuition for James, and food, among many other things, totaled six and a half thousand pounds."

"Papa, I—"

"Quite simply," he went on, raising his voice until she stopped talking, "I cannot afford to hand Lord Cosgrove ten thousand pounds. As he has the promissory notes to prove that James owes him that sum, I am at his mercy. He has offered me a way to escape from this debt. I have to accept his terms. Do you understand?"

She looked at him. Her first instinct was still to say that of course she understood, both the debt and that he had to do what was best for the family. Her growing . . . frustration at having all this put on her shoulders when she'd already done more for the family than any of them would ever realize, though, stopped her. "I understand that James has put you into a difficult situation," she agreed slowly. "I also understand that handing me over to Cosgrove is the easiest way for you to rectify matters."

" 'The easiest'?" he repeated, scowling.

"You have a great many wealthy friends, Papa. I should have considered that before, but now I realize that you would rather lose me than lose your pride." Rose took a breath. "If you truly had no alternative, I imagine I would be more compliant. Since you've given me your facts and figures, I shall give you mine. Cosgrove slapped me last night, because I didn't want to change my dress. My marriage to him might allow me to have some control over his future actions, but as

I've become acquainted with him it seems more likely that our connection will provide him with an unending influence over both James and this entire family. And so whatever *your* plans are, I haven't quite made up my mind yet."

He nodded. "How many proposals of marriage have you received, Rose? Excluding Cosgrove's of course."

She hesitated. Clearly she couldn't mention the one that had occurred in her bedchamber last night, either. "Two. I didn't feel I would be . . . compatible with either of them." And they'd both had even less sense than her own family.

"Then perhaps you are the architect of your own fate, my dear. If you had married, I would be *forced* to find other means to deal with Cosgrove—or if you happened to be wrong about the willingness of my so-called wealthy friends to loan me such an exorbitant sum, I suppose your mother and I might find ourselves without property or income. But you chose not to marry, and quite frankly, each year you grow older, you place more of a strain on my accounts."

Oh, she should have fled ages ago. To be so unvalued when she worked so hard—she'd known it forever, but to hear him say it flayed her to the heart. Even marriage to a dullard like Thomas Hankenridge would have been preferable to this. In that sense, she *had* done this to herself. But not quite yet; she still had thirteen days for Bram to play his part, and two more beyond that to arrange her flight if he failed.

"Then I think we understand one another," she said, lifting her chin. "Is that all?"

"Yes. As long as you keep in mind that this marriage

will happen. It will be better for everyone concerned, then, including you, if it looks to be a result of mutual affection."

"I will keep that in mind."

Her hands clenched into fists, Rose stalked into the breakfast room, spied her brother loading thick slices of ham onto his plate, and stalked out again. As if her contributions to the family amounted to less than James's. She doubted her father had spent ten thousand pounds on her upkeep.

A knock echoed from the foyer, and Elbon hurried past her to answer the door. She turned to watch, ready to flee up the stairs again if it should be Cosgrove. Whether she would be better off playing pretty with him or not, she was certainly not prepared to do so the morning after he'd struck her.

The silhouette in the doorway, though, was leaner and taller than Cosgrove, and her pulse stirred. For a time this morning she thought that perhaps she'd dreamed Bram's visit last night, because it made more sense that she would put her faith in a phantom Bram Johns than in the actual one.

After speaking for a moment to the butler, he entered the foyer. Black eyes lifted, and he saw her. "Good morning, Lady Rosamund," he drawled, bowing.

The smile that curved his mouth seemed to light even his dark eyes. Shaking herself, Rose curtsied to him. "Lord Bram. I didn't think you ever ventured out this early in the day."

"I'm a conundrum," he returned, stopping in front of her. "Lester told me you were ill last night. I hope you are feeling improved."

"Much improved. Thank you."

Bram leaned his face closer to hers. "Are you much improved?" he whispered, taking her hand to bow over it.

Rose nodded. "For the next thirteen days," she replied in the same tone.

"Hm." He straightened again, releasing her. "Is your brother about?"

"He's in the breakfast room."

"Ah. Escort me, my lady. I don't have much familiarity with anything having to do with morning or breakfast."

Smiling despite her earlier ire, Rose wrapped her fingers around his arm. As they walked, she examined him more closely. "Blue today? Your valet must be overset."

"You have no idea. He tried to gouge out his eyes this morning. But you were correct; I wear far too much black. I looked like a bookkeeper. Or worse, a solicitor."

He'd declared himself an ally, and when he appeared, she actually felt as though she needn't face the next few weeks entirely alone. His time and attention didn't make him an angel; he was nothing close to one, in fact. But he'd offered to help her escape. She would keep her eyes wide open, but she would also allow herself, for the moment, at least, to hold on to a small sliver of hope.

"Lester," Bram said, offering his hand to her brother.

"Bram. What brings you here?"

"You do. I'm off to Tattersall's. Care to join me?"

James cleared his throat. "I'm to attend luncheon with King and some of his cronies."

"Then attend if you wish." Bram shrugged. "If I know King's friends, which I do, they'll be too busy proving how clever they are to notice whether you're there or not."

"I—"

"Let's go to the horse market. You have a good eye for driving pairs, and I'm in need of one. Leave whenever you choose, or stay. I may make a day of it."

Finally James grinned. "Let me change my boots."

"I'll be here, eating your food."

As soon as her brother left the room, Rose faced Bram. "That was very direct of you."

"Was it? It must be the early hour. You know I prefer deviousness."

"Hm. What are you up to?"

"Taking your brother to Tattersall's," he returned, lifting an eyebrow. "Do you wish to join us?"

"Why aren't you attending Cosgrove's luncheon?"

"Because I wasn't invited."

That made her pause. "You truly have broken with him, then?"

"I said I had." He took a half step back in her direction. "Perhaps you should come with us. Cosgrove may decide he wants you to attend, and it's not anything you need to witness."

She couldn't stop the shiver that traveled down her spine. "What happens at these luncheons?"

Bram lifted his hand. Running a finger softly along her cheek, as though he couldn't help touching her, he lowered his gaze to her mouth. With two footmen and the butler in the room, she didn't think he would kiss her, but she abruptly wanted him to, anyway.

"People remove their clothes," he murmured, still

studying her face. "They drink and wallow about together. Some of them should really know better than to be seen nude."

And if she married Cosgrove, she would no doubt be expected to participate. His words were horrific, but the way he said it—dismissively, as though he was involved with something more interesting—lessened her own apprehension. Did he know that? Did he do it intentionally?

"Have you attended any of these luncheons?" she asked.

His hand dropped from her face. "On occasion," he said quietly. "Generally I prefer to pursue my amusements in private."

His amusements. She was one of those, she supposed. Even knowing that, she was still more inclined to join him looking at horses than to risk being at home if Cosgrove should send over an invitation. "Thank you for telling me," she commented. "And I think I'll go find something to wear to the horse auctions."

He flashed a smile. "Good."

Even as she spoke, Elbon edged toward the door. Oh, dear. If the servant told her father of her plans, she might be forbidden to leave the house. Before she could move, though, Bram stepped between the butler and the hallway.

"Elbon, is it?" he said. "I need to send a note to my home. Please guide me to a pen and some paper."

With another brief smile of her own, Rose fled the room. Having someone as quick-witted and astute as Bram Johns for an ally definitely had its advantages. And that wasn't even counting his proficiency with kissing and other, more intimate things.

* * *

Two hours later she stood on the bottom rail of a large show pen with Bram holding her elbow to help her keep her balance. A lovely chestnut hunter trotted around the ring on a longe line while a rather frantic, round man several yards away from her shouted out steadily rising numbers in opposition to another half-dozen members of the crowd.

"Who is that?" she whispered, indicating the nearest bidder.

"Francis Henning," Bram returned, his voice amused. "Poor fellow. That's his horse."

She stepped back down to the ground, not commenting when Bram kept his hand on her arm. "What?"

"He lost it in a wager last week. Now he's trying to get her back before his grandmother arrives in Town and catches him out at gambling."

"He shouldn't have wagered her, then," James said from the far side of Bram.

"He shouldn't have gotten into a game when he couldn't afford the loss," Bram said in a sharper voice. "Wagering is an amusement. Anyone who does it for any other reason is a fool."

Rose glanced from him to her brother. From his pinched expression, James had heard and understood the criticism. But if Bram was attempting to make her brother stalk off to Cosgrove's luncheon and leave her there alone with him, she didn't think even James was that self-absorbed.

"That don't make sense," her brother complained. "You win most of the time, but I've seen you lose."

"I do indeed." Bram reached into an inner pocket of his blue jacket and pulled out what looked to be fifty or so pounds. "This is the blunt I have to play with at the moment. If I lose it, my evening is finished."

"But what if the next hand is the one that could win it all back?"

With a sigh Bram put his money away. "Since I can afford to lose it, I don't mind letting it go. If I borrowed more and lost, I would be forced to apply to the duke for funds. Aside from the fact that I would never, ever do that, he would sooner see me clapped in irons than spend any additional blunt on me."

"Then you don't have a choice when you run through your money. I d—"

"No, you don't. You will owe something to somebody. And then you have lost your freedom, or that of someone you care for." He sent a glance at Rose. "What if Cosgrove had said the only way to make good on your debt was to shoot Earl Minster? Those two aren't precisely friends."

Blanching, shaking his head, James backed away. "He wouldn't ask such a thing. King is my—"

"He's your friend. And so he will be, until you decline to do something he asks of you, James. Trust me on this. I have been in your shoes."

"But you and Cosgrove were still friends until . . . very recently," Rose commented, not certain whether she should be intruding on this lesson, but too curious to keep silent.

Black eyes assessed her. "I did as he asked."

James gasped. "You never killed someone."

"Actually, I've killed a number of someones, but that was when I wore a uniform. No, his request was simpler than that. The ruby ring he wears on his left forefinger—do you recall it?"

Rose nodded, since he seemed to be addressing her. It was an exquisite piece, as she recalled.

"My father gave it to me on my sixteenth birthday. It had been in the Johns family for five generations. I, however, owed Cosgrove three thousand quid and had no means to pay it back."

The ring most likely wasn't worth three thousand pounds, but clearly that hadn't concerned the marquis. "What did His Grace do when he found out?" she pursued.

His expression hardened. "Several choice things."

Goodness. Was that ring the reason for the very strained relationship between father and son? It explained a great deal, but not why Bram had chosen to break with Cosgrove now. Rose studied his lean profile as he returned his attention to the bidding. The ruby hadn't ended their friendship, but had she?

That felt very significant. And the story made her review all over again what she knew about Bram. She couldn't imagine that he'd ever been as gullible as James was. Nor could she imagine the man she knew today ever being put in the position where he would have to do anything against his will. It must have been a very hard lesson, but he'd clearly learned it—unlike her own brother.

Heat traveled slowly through her insides, warming every corner of her being. Whoever this man was, it was becoming more and more clear that he was not a twin in either character or demeanor to Kingston Gore. And who he might be was beginning to intrigue her very, very much.

* * *

As he stood, pretending to watch the auctions, Bram couldn't help wondering whether he'd said too much. Today had been about hopefully tempering Lester's wagering, not about him telling tales of his own youthful stupidity. At least he hadn't mentioned the one benefit to losing the ring; the duke had finally and clearly declared precisely what he thought of his second son. And that had truly been enlightening.

A warm hand closed around his arm, and he stilled. "You said before that Cosgrove has abused other of his friends. How?" Rosamund asked.

He nearly declined to answer; she certainly didn't need another lesson about the horror that was Cosgrove. Lester still listened, though, and if Rosamund wanted her brother cured of wagering, he would do his best to see to it. "Do you know of John Easterling?"

Both of the Davies siblings shook their heads.

"He was Viscount Hammond's oldest son."

" 'Was'?" Rosamund repeated, astute as always.

Bram nodded. "About four years ago while I was away on the Peninsula, Cosgrove befriended Easterling, and ended up holding nearly thirty thousand quid in notes from the pup. As soon as he heard about it, Hammond disowned him, and two days later Easterling put a pistol in his mouth."

"If you were away," Lester demanded, his face pale, "then how do you know about this?"

"My brother was friends with Easterling." And August had been only too happy to write him with the tale. "I can't verify this last bit, but apparently upon learning of the lad's death, Cosgrove said it was a damned shame because he'd thought to get several more years of fun out of him first."

"I'm going to be ill," Lester said, and Bram pointed him toward the side of one of the buildings.

"You made up that last bit, didn't you?" Rosamund whispered, either unaware or uncaring that being on his arm was beginning to earn her looks from more than a few of the men and women present.

"Yes, but considering that King has yet to alter his game, I thought it plausible."

"More than plausible." She looked at him sideways. "And do you actually stop wagering when your pocket is to let?"

"My pocket is rarely to let, but yes, I do. I don't like being in debt to anyone. Ever."

He thought perhaps he'd spoken too vehemently, but Rosamund only sighed. "I wish James felt that way."

"You're not marrying Cosgrove." He blurted it out with all the finesse of a rutting bull, but at least she didn't laugh or announce that she no longer wanted his help and would make do on her own.

Her grip on his arm tightened. "I don't intend to marry him. Not any longer. But the more awful things you tell me about him, the more I worry that he's already anticipated all this."

That had begun to worry him, as well. But he'd stepped into this knowingly, and the hero was supposed to bear the bother on his own shoulders. "Now I'm insulted," he drawled aloud. "If there's one thing at which I excel, it's seeing trouble coming."

"Bram Johns, you scoundrel!"

Bram tensed, instinctively moving between Rosamund and the loud male bellow. As he faced the sound, the crowd at the south side of the auction pen stirred and parted, and a pair of tall, lean men emerged, striding toward him. Immediately he relaxed again, flexing his clenched fingers. *Thank Lucifer.* Some people might call this trouble, but he called it providence.

"Sullivan Waring," he said, stepping forward. "What the devil are you doing here?"

"I heard there might be trouble," Sullivan Waring, illegitimate son of the Marquis of Dunston, grinned and gave him a hard handshake. "I didn't want to miss it."

Bram glanced past his friend to Phin Bromley, who looked very pleased with himself. "You sent for him."

"I have no idea what you're talking about." Shifting his gaze, he nodded. "Lady Rose. Good afternoon."

With a muffled curse Bram took Rosamund's hand again and placed it over his arm. "Rosamund, you know Phin. This is my very good friend Sullivan Waring, the finest horse breeder in England. Sully, Lady Rosamund Davies."

Sullivan bowed. "Lady Rosamund. Are you here alone with Bram?"

The damned nosy nag even had the presumption to frown. Abruptly not so happy to see his comrade again, Bram forced a lazy grin. "Her brother's around the back of the building, casting up his accounts."

"Are you here for the auctions, Mr. Waring?" Rosamund asked.

"No. I generally hire someone to bring my stock to London. I'm just here for a visit."

Those cool green eyes beneath brown hair run through with gold looked amused—and more than likely very handsome to every chit in the area. Bram tightened his grip on Rosamund. "I assume Isabel is still at Amberglen? Isabel is expecting their first child, you know."

"Congratulations, Mr. Waring."

"Thank you, and no, Tibby insisted on joining me in London. We're staying at Bromley House." As he spoke, Sullivan returned his attention to Bram. "And what the devil are you wearing?"

Damnation. "Can't a fellow alter his attire a fraction without causing the shift of the continents?"

"Evidently not," Phin put in dryly.

"Gads," Lord Lester exclaimed, rejoining them, "you're Sullivan Waring!" He grabbed Sullivan's hand and shook it. "Bram owns one of your horses. Prime animal, Titan."

"Yes, one of my finest," Sullivan said, lifting an eyebrow.

"Sully, this is Rosamund's brother, Lord Lester."

"Ah. You've finished vomiting, then."

Lester blushed. "It weren't my fault. Bram's tales about Cosgrove are enough to make anyone need to lighten their ballast." He gave an uneasy laugh. "Though Bram does like to joke about."

All he needed was for his friends to agree with that. What he *did* need, though, was a moment with Sullivan. "James, Rosamund, would you be kind enough to show Phin the pair I favor?"

Rosamund stirred, stepping away from him to take her brother's arm. "Certainly. This way, Mr. Bromley."

"Phin, please, my lady."

Once they were out of earshot, Bram gripped Sullivan by the shoulders. "I am glad to see you, you annoying bastard."

"Likewise."

"Isabel— Tibby—is well?"

"Everything's grand, which you would know if you ever came to visit."

"I do. It's just that your happy domesticity rots my teeth."

"Very amusing."

With a glance around them, Bram led the way toward the lane and beyond the thickest part of the crowd. "Phin did write you, didn't he?"

"What did you expect, after you stumbled into his bedchamber in the middle of the night and nearly got your head blown off?"

"I'd overindulged a bit."

"Mm hm. What's Cosgrove got to do with the girl and her family?"

Sullivan had never been much for dancing around a topic when he could ride straight over it. It had gotten him into trouble on more than one occasion, but Bram had always appreciated his forthright manner. His friend was much like Rosamund, actually.

Keeping his voice pitched well below the excited chattering going on at the auction behind them, Bram told Sullivan as succinctly as he could about Cosgrove befriending Lester, the ten-thousand-pound debt, and how the marquis wanted it repaid. All he left out was some of his involvement, and his refused proposal to Rosamund. When he'd finished, his friend no longer looked the least bit amused.

"And they say I'm a bastard," he muttered. "I've never understood why you continue to call that barrow pig a friend, Bram. He—"

"I've stopped doing so," Bram interrupted.

Sullivan looked at him. "You have?"

Shrugging, Bram kicked the toe of his Hessian boot into the dirt. "There would be no point in my telling the story if I didn't intend to do something about it, now would there?"

"You frequently have no point."

"True enough." And how could he announce that he'd suddenly decided to become a hero when he'd never done such a thing before in his life, and was likely already making a muck of it? "I'm well acquainted with what King is," he went on, "and Rosamund is a genuinely good person. He can continue to feed on the carrion of society for all I care, but I won't let him have *her*."

Sullivan looked as though he wanted to say something more, but instead he only nodded. "What can I do to help?"

Help. Bram had *offered* help before—had even arguably saved the lives of both Sully and Phin on several occasions. But *asking* for help—that smacked of debt and obligation. "I believe I have it in hand at the moment, but I'll let you know. Of course if you should wish to remain in Town for a short time, I wouldn't argue."

"Fair enough. Tibby's got another few weeks before she needs to decide where she wants to settle for her confinement. I'm half hoping we end up in Cornwall with her family, because I am already frightened to death." Sullivan took a breath. "And what do you think you're doing, visiting Tattersall's when none of my animals are showing?"

"I'm not here to purchase anything," Bram returned, grateful for the change of subject. "Cosgrove's holding one of his orgies this afternoon, and I'm attempting to keep Lester clear of it."

"A few more good deeds like that, and I'll have to stop referring to you as a scoundrel."

"Don't you dare."

When she, James, and Phin Bromley rejoined the two men beside the auction pen, Rose couldn't keep her gaze off Bram. It wasn't just that he showed exceedingly well in his dark blue jacket with its gray waistcoat and black trousers, but the way he seemed to command the attention of everyone—male and female—around him. She'd never been notorious, but he made it look like a great deal of fun.

Those striking black eyes met hers, and heat shot through her again. Why Bram Johns—a man who'd seduced and apparently abandoned countless beautiful, exotic women—had fixated on her, she had no idea. But it felt . . . powerful to have the attention of a man that other women clearly wanted. Even if it was only for another handful of days, and even if he had positioned himself as some sort of tutor to her brother and protector to her.

"What say we collect Isabel and Alyse, and picnic in Hyde Park?" Sullivan Waring suggested, his gaze lingering on her for just a moment. Unlike Cosgrove's gaze, though, it didn't feel at all predatory or threatening, but more as if he was attempting to decipher a puzzle. She wondered what Bram had said to him.

"Splendid," James exclaimed, no doubt flattered to be included in the company of the men he had previously and repeatedly termed "notorious gentlemen" to the point that she wanted to throw things at him.

Beginning to wish she'd paid more attention to the Society pages and her brother's gossip before her family had arrived for James's first Season in London, Rose nodded her agreement. Anything to keep her brother and her away from Cosgrove today.

"We'll purchase luncheon then, and meet you in the middle of the park, on the north shore of the Serpentine," Bram said, offering her an arm.

She took it. Even if he didn't realize that such preferential treatment from him in public could damage her reputation, she did. And she welcomed it. At this moment anything that might discourage Cosgrove was welcome. Aside from that, Bram had already done a very fine job of ruining her.

"What are you smiling at?" he murmured, as they and James made their way past the other auction attendees to his coach.

"I was just thinking that I've enjoyed myself this morning," she answered. As if she would admit that she'd been remembering the weight of his naked body atop hers.

"I have, as well. Quite odd, really."

"Yes? Perhaps doing good deeds suits you."

Bram shook his head, a lock of black hair crossing the corner of one eye. "Chatting with someone who has more than half a wit suits me. But I'm in this game for the trouble it will cause."

A few weeks ago she would have believed that claim. Now, she wasn't nearly as certain. And nothing she witnessed over the next three hours served to convince her any further. He purchased them a splendid luncheon, better than anything she'd tasted for weeks. Far from behaving like an unrepentant, incurable rakehell, Bram was amusing, kind, and solicitous not only toward her, but toward the wives of his two closest friends, as well.

It was all blasted confusing. Which was the true Bramwell Lowry Johns—the black-hearted cynic, or the jaded but good-hearted man? And why in the world did it matter, as long as he continued helping her?

"You're staring at me," he said from the seat opposite her as they rode back to Davies House.

Rose blinked. "Am I?"

"Yes. I'm near to blushing from it."

James snorted from beside her. "I've yet to see anything make you blush, Bram."

"Excessive heat has done it," Bram countered, but his gaze remained on her. "You no doubt find me fascinating, but may I ask why? Unless the reasons are too many for you to name, of course."

"Actually, after hearing you conversing with your friends, I was wondering if there are any of the Ten Commandments you haven't broken."

"Number nine," he said promptly.

"Oh, really?"

"Absolutely. And quite possibly number two. At least I don't recall carving any statues, though I might of course have been drunk at the time."

"Carving ain't the sin; it's worshipping a carved image," James contributed. "But which one is the ninth? I get 'em confused."

"Bearing false witness against your neighbor," Rose

supplied with a grin. "You don't strike me as being a liar, Bram, so I can believe that."

He inclined his head. "Thank you. That does still leave a wide swath of broken commandments and deadly sins in my wake, however."

"What about number eight?" she pursued.

"Is that the Sabbath one?" her brother asked.

"It's the stealing one."

Bram continued to gaze at her, but he didn't say anything. Something in his eyes intrigued her mightily, and she very much wanted to know what, if anything, he might have stolen. At the same time, however, she absolutely wanted to remain ignorant. She had enough to worry over.

"I would wager he's stolen the virginity of dozens of chits," James chortled, laughing.

Oh, heavens. Had he? She hoped not. If he visited naive young ladies every other night or so, it made what he'd done for her—with her—somehow . . . less. And she didn't like thinking of it that way.

"James, one cannot steal that which is freely given," he drawled. "But rest assured that I don't make a habit of bedding virgins. I don't like to break hearts, and theirs are far too fragile." He finally turned his eyes away from her and toward the window. "For the most part."

She wasn't certain whether that was an insult or a compliment. And she couldn't very well ask him with James sitting a foot away from her. Considering that he'd proposed to her and she'd turned him down, it was a topic best left unpursued, anyway.

But there was something she did want to tell him,

whatever the outcome of this disaster. "You call the Bromleys and the Warings your friends," she said.

He nodded. "So they are. I've found it more prudent to keep a few close ones I may rely on, rather than a great many I can't."

"Oh." *Stupid girl.*

"What is it?" he pursued.

"I was going to say that I . . . consider you to be a friend to me."

Bram actually smiled. "I've already decided to include you in that number, Rosamund."

Rose smiled back at him. "Oh," she said again, this time hope making her feel just a little bit lighter. "Good. I'm glad that we are friends."

"As am I." He paused. "I happen to have somehow acquired a box at Drury Lane Theater," he went on after a moment. "I don't suppose you would be interested in seeing the latest production of *A Midsummer Night's Dream* on Thursday evening."

Rose wasn't certain how a night at the theater would help free her from Cosgrove's clutches, but even so, spending an entire evening in Bram's company tempted her far more than it should. If it wasn't a sin to be devilishly handsome and even more enticing, it should be. "I—"

"That's tomorrow night." Her brother scowled. "Faro at Jezebel's."

Rose, you halfwit. The invitation was for James's benefit, not hers. "But James, I would love to attend," she said aloud, trying to sound plaintive. "Say you'll go, so that I can."

"Bother. Very well." He jabbed a finger in Bram's direction. "But I mean to ask King if those tales you told me are true, you know."

Bram lifted an eyebrow. "I would hope so. You should never take anything—or anyone—at face value."

This time she thought he *was* speaking to her, but once again she couldn't be certain. Even so, it was good advice—and she meant to take it. Especially now that she'd been introduced to two ladies and their husbands, all of whom knew him better than she did.

The coach rolled to a stop, and James exited almost before a footman could flip down the steps. Rose started to her feet, but Bram shifted to the seat beside her, and she sat back again.

Slowly he leaned in, as though smelling her hair. Rose suppressed a shiver. "What are you doing?" she whispered.

"You are my only virgin," he murmured back.

She swallowed. Now that night felt significant again. "Oh."

His fingers brushed her arm. "Do you want me to kiss you right now?"

Oh, goodness. "Yes," she breathed.

Bram took her hand and brushed his lips against the inside of her wrist. "Good," he said softly, his mouth curving in a slow, delicious smile. "Out you go. I'll be by for you and Lester tomorrow at seven o'clock."

It would likely take that long for her heart to slow to a normal pace again.

Chapter 13 _____

Kingston Gore flipped the post boy a shilling and summoned his butler to show the boy out. Alone again, he sank back in the deep chair sitting beside his library hearth. So Sullivan Waring had come to Town, and with his pregnant whore. There would be only one reason for that—Bramwell had summoned reinforcements.

He sipped his glass of absinthe, relishing the potent, bittersweet slide down his throat. Then he rose and returned to the firelit drawing room to rejoin his one remaining luncheon guest. Welcome lust stirred him as she rose from the floor onto her hands and knees, presenting him with her round, smooth arse and watching him coyly over her shoulder.

"I hope your business was important," she cooed, licking her lips as he shed his robe.

"Nothing less would take me away, Miranda," he returned, sinking onto his knees behind Lady Ackley and then entering her with a hard shove. "We have some things to discuss," he grunted as he thrust into her.

So Bramwell had allies. He would need them.

Bram paced the floor of his library. The Lowry House library had been a particular favorite of his father's, so Bram had moved half the tomes into the attic—after announcing that he'd burned them—and replaced them with erotic art and statues, most of them from India and the Far East. The near apoplexy the duke had suffered the last time he'd set foot in the house had made the effort and expense more than worth the trouble.

Now, though, he stopped before an old water-color of a male and female making, as Shakespeare termed it, a two-backed beast, and scowled. What was the bloody point of it all? He could certainly never entertain Rosamund in the room; aside from its over-all lewdness, taken as a whole it looked juvenile and meaningless. Mindless bodies writhing and humping. He didn't want her to see the act of sex portrayed that way, as Cosgrove no doubt viewed it. As he had, until very recently.

Barely pausing to reflect that Rosamund would never have cause to see his library, he strode to the door and pulled it open. "Hibble!"

The butler hurried up the stairs. "Yes, my lord?"

"Bring me some boxes and a pair of footmen."

"You'll be removing the remainder of the books, then?"

Was that disapproval he heard in the blasted butler's voice? He generally enjoyed Hibble's stuffiness, but only when he was intentionally misbehaving. "I'm un-removing the ones in the attic. This is a library, after all—not a museum of carnality."

"Indeed, my lord. I'll have the boxes brought down immediately."

Not waiting for the boxes or the help, Bram shrugged out of his jacket and began placing paintings and draw-ings and figurines on the worktable at one side of the room. The duke had once owned a supremely well-endowed Burmese fertility statue, and though it had lost its cock due to an arranged accident a year ago, he'd hated seeing the idiotic thing every time he was called into Levonzy's office for a dressing-down. And here he'd gone and surrounded himself with the same sort of item. Who, precisely, was he spiting?

"Good God, you've become a Puritan."

Bram whipped around to see Sullivan Waring lean-ing in the doorway. "A Calvinist," he countered, and went back to removing items from the shelves.

"Even worse." Waring pushed upright. "I came by to inquire where you might be this evening. I didn't expect to find you at home and . . . decorating."

"Undecorating."

"I can see that. Why?"

"Because I wanted to. You know I always do as I please."

The footmen appeared, both of them lugging large boxes of books. Hibble hadn't wasted any time at all. "Put them by the window and fetch the rest," he de-cided. "We'll use the empty boxes for my erotica idi-otica."

Once the servants were gone again, Sullivan approached. "Not to pry, but are you removing all of it?" he asked.

"I'm rather fond of the Nepalese sculpture, but the rest of it, yes."

His friend lifted a small statue of a maiden and a donkey and carried it to the table. "From someone who once sent me half a library of erotic sketches, this is slightly . . . unusual. Unless you're planning on shipping it all to the duke. Is that it?"

Bram paused. That was a fair idea, actually. It would annoy Levonzy no end, but it would also alert him that the objects had been removed from the Lowry House library. "No, they're going into the attic until I can sell them off."

"Why?"

"I'm tired of them."

"When did this happ—"

"You're not very skilled at prying, Sullivan. And I just decided on a change of scenery. There's nothing significant about it."

Sullivan set down another figure. "Why don't we sit and have a brandy?" he suggested.

Taking a half-dozen steps, Bram shut the door just as one of the footmen reached it. "I'm occupied," he said shortly, wondering how he could escape this sensation of being restless in his own skin. It was damned unpleasant, and harder to ignore. "I'm not going to sit and pour out my heart to you, because we both know I haven't got one."

"Mm hm. Just how much do you like this Lady Rosamund Davies?"

Bram froze for a heartbeat. He thought he'd been

fairly clever about it, but Sullivan knew him better than most. Placing both hands flat on the table, he bowed his head for a brief moment. "She consumes me," he muttered, not entirely certain Sullivan had heard him until his friend dropped heavily into a chair.

"I didn't expect that," Waring said.

"Neither did I." With a growl, Bram dumped a box of books onto the floor and began flinging his lewd art into the empty container. "Once you've proposed to someone and she turns you down, I suppose going off whoring and drinking oneself into the grave is the proper response, but I seem to be cleaning."

Silence, except for the sound of things breaking as he dropped them into the box, answered him.

"You proposed to her?" Sullivan repeated, his voice cracking.

"Yes, but since I'm clearly not much of an improvement over Cosgrove, I also offered to either help repay her family's debt or spirit her away to safety."

"I need a damned drink."

"Help yourself."

While Sullivan poured them each a whiskey, brandy apparently no longer being sufficient, Bram allowed the footmen back in with more books and then sent them off again. This was not a conversation he ever wished to have, and particularly not when the turmoil of it still crashed about without resolution in his brain.

Sullivan handed him a glass and seated himself again. Not Bram, though—he needed to keep moving, as if his body was attempting to catch up to his thoughts, with neither entity having the least idea where it was going. The only cure seemed to be seeing Rosamund, and he couldn't break into her bloody bedchamber every night.

"What are you going to do?"

"Change her mind about me."

"And if you can't?"

He *would*. That was one thing about which every part of him agreed. "Then I'll get her to the north of the country somewhere and help her find employment, just as she asked me to do."

"God's sake, Bram. Either way, you'll be crossing Cosgrove. Have you considered that?"

"Of course I have. I even warned him to leave her be, which of course was a declaration of war. He'd be a fool to try to best me to my face, so I assume he'll be attempting something underhanded. I would." He glanced over his shoulder. "In fact, you may want to get you and your wife home before anything happens. And warn Phin of the same."

"So we should abandon you here to manage this on your own?"

Bram shrugged. "I would do it to you."

"Like hell you would." Sullivan blew out his breath. "When I received Phin's note, I thought this would have something to do with you and the Black Cat. I half expected you to be in the Old Bailey, and I would have to rob someone's house to convince the magistrate of your innocence."

"You should attempt to be more original than that," Bram returned, mustering a brief grin. "Something more akin to Guy Fawkes and explosives."

"They could bury what was left of us all in smaller coffins, at any rate."

"Precisely." Pausing, Bram faced his friend. "You've

never liked Cosgrove, and I'm . . . fairly certain I wandered back to him because you and Phin were occupied elsewhere. Whatever he attempts, it's my own damned fault for stepping into the middle of this. I don't want your help, Sullivan. You have other concerns."

"Duly noted. What's your next step?"

With a frown, Bram backed away from the table. "I'm not jesting. I may have no idea what I'm doing, but you're not to be part of it. You or Phineas. So good evening. Go back to your wife and contemplate infant names. I'm partial to Bramwell, myself."

"I would never burden a babe with so wretched a name." Clearly reluctant, Sullivan stood up and walked to the door. "I'll be in Town for a bit, seeing the sights and perhaps mustering up a horse or two for sale. Just for your information."

"Yes, we'll have to dine together sometime before you leave."

"Yes, we shall."

With that, Sullivan left the house. Bram picked up his glass of whiskey and downed it in one go.

Twelve days before Cosgrove would announce his engagement. He probably should be doing something besides cleaning. But for some damned reason, this seemed important, too. Perhaps if he could clear the clutter that was his life, he could manage to do the same with his mind. At the same time, he had a feeling it would only make room for more thoughts of Rosamund.

"Damnation." Grabbing up his jacket, he left the room for his office, retrieved a small pouch from his desk, and headed downstairs. "Hibble, see that the library's finished by tomorrow," he said.

"Of course, my lord. Will you be out late tonight?"

"I imagine so. You'll find me at White's or the Society or the Navy Club. I'm about to break another rule."

"Very good, my lord."

It was either this, or find himself climbing in through Rosamund's window again. He hefted the pouch in his pocket. He had the fifty quid he'd shown Lester, and another three hundred or so he'd kept back so he could manage his household until the duke decided to reinstate his allowance. Ten thousand quid would be a bit much to expect to win in one evening, but he could make a start. He had a few markers, and a few favors, he could call in if required. And he didn't intend to lose.

"My lady," Elbon said, as he stepped into the morning room, "you have callers."

Rosamund poked a hole in her embroidery. He had to be speaking to her, because her mother had taken to doing her sewing in an upstairs sitting room. Anything to avoid discussing . . . well, anything.

But callers. Plural. It couldn't be Bram, then, which was at least easier on her heart, or Cosgrove, which was easier on the rest of her. Either of them would come alone. "Who is it?" she asked.

The butler brought forward his salver with a pair of prettily embossed calling cards resting on its polished surface. Trying to steady the shaking of her hand, Rose picked them up. And frowned. Alyse Bromley and Isabel Waring. *Goodness.*

"Please show them in," she said, hurriedly setting her embroidery aside. She'd wanted to chat with them about Bram, but coherent and logical thought seemed to have escaped her completely these days. And second chances seemed rare enough in her experience that she wasn't about to let this one pass her by.

She stood as the two ladies entered the morning room. Yesterday at Bram's picnic she'd been so occupied with trying to keep James from behaving like a happy puppy that she hadn't much time to converse with either of them. If she'd learned anything from Bram, it was to make use of circumstances, and so she smiled. She'd met Alyse before—a petite, brown-eyed lady with hair the color of autumn. Isabel Waring was a bit taller, with brown, brightly inquisitive eyes framed by blonde, wavy hair. She had said she was five months into her pregnancy, and she did look a bit round in the middle despite her slender frame.

"Good morning, Mrs. Bromley, Mrs. Waring."

"You're surprised to see us," Mrs. Waring commented with an easy smile.

"I am, but happily so."

"Good. Alyse and I are going walking along Bond Street, as I feel the need for a bit of exercise. Would you care to join us?"

"You know of my . . . circumstances, do you not?" If they didn't, she would have to decide how much she wanted to tell them about Cosgrove. If they already knew, well, she couldn't call them allies yet, but at least she wouldn't have to dissemble.

This time it was Alyse who smiled. "Yes. We know. Some of it, anyway. And if I may say, we three are all acquainted with some very cunning men. Perhaps we might share our insights."

Rose found herself smiling in return. "Yes, please."

They took Lord Quence's coach to Bond Street, where

they disembarked. She learned that while Alyse and Tibby, as she liked to be called, had known each other for only a year, they'd discovered a kinship thanks to the close friendship of their husbands.

"They served on the Peninsula together, did they not? With Bram," Rose commented as they strolled along the street.

"Yes. Sullivan and Bram joined at the same time, and met Phin when they all ended up in the First Royal Dragoons," Alyse answered. "Phin served for ten years, but the other two returned home three years ago when Sullivan was wounded."

Rose took a breath. She'd expected them to be full of advice about escaping Cosgrove, but if they wanted to talk about Bram she certainly wasn't going to complain. Heaven knew she could use any possible insights. Because if she couldn't trust his word or his resolve, the sooner she could make her own plans, the better. "Bram doesn't precisely seem the sort of man who would join the army in the first place," she ventured.

Tibby grimaced. "I've spent the Season in London since I can remember," she said, "and I fairly clearly recall when Lord Bramwell was challenged to a duel by Lord Massenfield for, well, apparently for seducing Massenfield's wife. Massenfield was a good friend of the Duke of Levonzy, and His Grace ordered Bramwell to leave the country or be disowned."

"I remember my father talking about it," Alyse took up, nodding. "There were some wagers about whether Bram would leave the country for the army, or whether he would be forced to flee for shooting Massenfield. Apparently he preferred the army."

As they stopped to admire the bonnets in Mrs. Harmond's shop window, Rose edged closer so she could lower her voice. "Do you know why Bram and His Grace are estranged?"

The two ladies exchanged a glance. "You would have to ask Bram," Tibby said. "All I know is that it happened sometime before Bram even attended university, which is where he met Sullivan. I'm sure he and Phin know, but sometimes it's easier to make horses fly than to get them to talk about one another."

For another forty minutes they divided their time among chatting, strolling, and shopping. Rose liked Alyse and Tibby, and the idea that she might be making new friends at a time when her own family was avoiding her was more than heartwarming. And knowing that these witty, intelligent women were both acquainted with Bram *and* liked him at the least gave her hope that she wasn't completely mad.

"I have had some experience with scandal, Rose," Alyse was saying, "and Bram Johns lives on the far side of the line most of us try not to cross. But since his interest is in making your relationship legitimate, I would also say it's sincere. I—we—just wanted you to know that he does have positive qualities. Whether they're enough to outweigh his . . . penchant for badness, only you can decide. But whatever you decide about him, you *will* have friends."

What? "Oh, good heavens," Rose blurted, putting both hands over her mouth. Her face felt so hot it must be scarlet. This had all been about Bram. Did they even know about her difficulties with Cosgrove? "That is not—I mean, he didn't—the—"

"Take a breath, Rose," Tibby exclaimed, patting her on the back. "Alyse, we need a place to sit."

"The bakery," Alyse returned immediately, taking Rose's other arm.

The ladies led her into the bakery, and Alyse requested tea and biscuits as they sat at the small table beneath the window. Rose did as they suggested and concentrated on breathing and not fainting dead away. "What, precisely, do you know?" she whispered as one of the bakery employees set the requested items on their table.

"I don't want to upset you further," Tibby replied in the same low voice.

"But—you know that Bram proposed to me, don't you?" She wanted to trust these women, and hopefully her desire for a female confidante or two after her cousin Maggie's . . . escape, she supposed it was, hadn't caused her to lose her sensibilities.

For a moment she thought they wouldn't answer. Both of them looked embarrassed, as though they'd been caught gossiping. Finally Tibby covered Rose's hand with her own. "Yes. Sullivan told me that Bram offered for you, and that you refused him. Coming to see you today, though, was *our* idea. No one knows we're here. And no one will, unless you wish it."

Rose believed her. She believed both of them, and hoped it wasn't simply because she wanted to. "Bram only proposed to me because I'm in a great deal of trouble," she said, accepting the tea Alyse poured for her and taking a swallow, as she drank considering what she would tell them. "I thought that was why you called on me."

Tibby's brow furrowed. "More trouble than having Bram Johns after you?"

"That is a very good question." Rose took a breath.

"My younger brother, James, Viscount Lester, fell in with Bram and the Marquis of Cosgrove."

"Cosgrove," Alyse said, blanching.

"You know of his reputation, then. James took to gambling, mostly with Cosgrove, and he ended up owing the marquis ten thousand pounds. My family has no way to repay the debt."

"Rose, you don't have to tell us this."

"I know, Tibby. One thing I'm discovering about Bram, though, is that with the exception of Cosgrove, he has very good taste in friends." She offered a brief smile. "Cosgrove said that in exchange for my hand, he would forgive the debt. Since then, he's been . . . antagonizing me, threatening to make my life difficult once we marry."

"That devil."

She had no problem agreeing with Tibby's assessment of the marquis's character. "Bram didn't like what he saw. He's been quite a good friend. His offer to marry me was to prevent Cosgrove from doing so. Nothing more." Nothing she would let herself believe, anyway.

"I see," Alyse said slowly, fiddling with her teacup. "So you are going to wed the marquis?"

"No. Bram said that he would help me to leave London before the engagement is announced, and assist me in finding employment somewhere. If he doesn't, I'll do it myself." She took a breath. "It will ruin my family," she continued, her voice shaking as she considered what would happen to them and their reputations in her absence, "but I can't marry him. I had resigned myself to it, but I can't."

"Nor should you have to," Tibby said firmly.

"The silly thing is, if Cosgrove had been kind or even

if he'd kept his distance, I would have gone through with it."

"He's the kind of man who sets fire to cats for the fun of it," Alyse commented, her voice full of contempt. She bit a biscuit in two. "So you have no romantic feelings for Bram, or he for you? That's a blessing."

Yes, it would have been, if it were true. She had a great many romantic feelings for him. How was she supposed to look forward to being free of Cosgrove, when the same number of days remained for her to be around Bram?

Chapter 14 _____

Bram had no idea how it happened, but when Rosamund met him in front of the Drury Lane Theater, not only was James with her, but so were Lord and Lady Abernathy, and Lord and Lady Fishton. *Bloody hell.*

"Apologies," Rosamund whispered as he bowed over her gloved hand. "I think you're beginning to worry them."

Good. They should be worried. He nodded. "Cosgrove may have warned them that I intend to make a muck of things. Which I do. Luckily I have a very large box here tonight."

Luckily he'd convinced his brother, August, to give up his box, considering that he'd invited Rosamund to join him without having the first clue how he would get them seats, much less private ones. Offering her an arm, he led the way into the large foyer.

"Good heavens, what a sad crush," Lady Fishton exclaimed. "Do you think Prinny will make an appearance tonight?"

"I haven't a clue," Bram answered, though considering that Prinny was in Brighton at the moment, he seriously doubted it. If it distracted the chirping chit, he'd let her believe whatever she chose.

"James, you should take your sister's arm," Lady Abernathy said, closing in on Bram and Rosamund. "We must be mindful of her reputation."

"Ah," Bram whispered, leaning toward Rosamund. "That's a bit like blowing out the candle after the house has been burned down. Twice."

"Hush." She glanced over her shoulder. "Lord Bram is a friend, and we are in public. *And* he is our host."

His Rosamund had a backbone. And considering that she'd likely never questioned her own loyalty to her family before, or even whether or not they deserved her loyalty, that was impressive. He knew from personal experience that standing up to one's parents was never simple, or easy. With her beside him, he seemed aware of everything—the way the chandelier light deepened the red-gold of her hair, the mutterings of the other patrons around them as they wondered whether she was one of his mistresses, the glances of other women whom he'd never bothered to take to the theater. And he liked that she called him a friend.

"How is your rescue plan progressing?" she murmured, green eyes glancing up at his face and then away again.

Considering that last night he'd turned three hundred quid into two thousand, he thought it was going quite well. At the same time, he doubted she would smile at the idea of him attempting to earn money in the same way that her brother had lost it. And surprisingly, that mattered to him. "Suffice it to say that the fair maiden is not going to marry the foul-smelling ogre. I gave you my word."

She smiled. "So says the black knight."

He glanced down at his wardrobe. "Gray knight, if you please." After all, he might have begun this with an attempted burglary, but Cosgrove had surpassed him as a villain. It was a title he didn't particularly aspire to, at the moment.

Once they reached the long hallway behind August's box, he pulled aside the heavy curtains and ushered the extended Davies family in. If they'd brought along a maid or a large dog, they wouldn't all have fit inside.

Originally he'd planned to sit beside Rosamund at the front of the box, and set James behind them. Now, though, he had no doubt that he would end up in the back corner as far away from her as her family could manage. And the oddest part of this little gathering was that a few weeks ago he wouldn't have tolerated any of them for more than a minute. Abernathy was a friend of Levonzy's, making him utterly unacceptable. James was a half-witted pup, and the Fishtons were too bothersome for words.

And yet there they all were, Lady Fishton leaning over the edge of the box to wave at some acquaintance or other below, and her mother dictating the seating arrangements. Bram leaned back against the wall beside the curtain and folded his arms over his chest to watch.

"Mother, you can't put Bram in the back," Rosamund said, scowling. "He didn't even invite you, for heaven's sake."

"Though I'm pleased you've all come," Bram put in quickly, for once trying to avoid a row.

"Sit James back there," Rosamund continued. "He'll be asleep five minutes after the play begins, anyway."

Lady Abernathy clearly didn't like being spoken to like that; her lips thinned as she pressed them together. Rolling his shoulders, Bram pushed upright. "I'll sit wherever you wish," he drawled, "but I will confess that this is my favorite play."

"Yes, let me sit back here," James said, pushing past Bram and flopping into the padded chair.

Bloody wonderful. Now he would have to keep an eye on Lester and prevent him from escaping to the faro game at Jezebel's. Bram almost changed his mind and reclaimed the corner chair, but then Rosamund motioned to him and everything else fell away.

"*A Midsummer Night's Dream* is your favorite play?" she asked in a low voice, pointing him to the seat beside her. "Not *Doctor Faustus* or *Macbeth*?"

Grinning, he seated himself. "With *Faustus* I have to ask myself whether I've made a bargain with the devil, or I *am* the devil. Too much self-reflection. And *Macbeth*—well, too many females plotting. That makes me a touch uneasy."

With a surprisingly serious look, Rosamund shook her head. "I've met the devil, Bram, and you're not him."

"You've only seen my good side."

Her expression softened into a smile. "Yes. And why is that?"

He wanted to kiss her so badly it hurt to hold himself back. "I have no idea," he answered truthfully.

"Oh, it's to begin," Lady Fishton trilled. "Everyone sit, sit, sit."

No one tried to shove him out of his chair, so Bram settled in to watch. They might have been sweeping the floor, though, for all the attention he paid to the actors on the stage. Instead he listened—to every sigh and laugh, every held breath or clap of the hands of the woman seated beside him. For a man as self-concerned as he knew himself to be, it was a fascinating revelation.

Considering what she'd been through—was still going through—he was exceedingly pleased that he'd suggested an outing that amused her. Hell, he scarcely had a thought any longer that didn't somehow concern Rosamund. The moment they'd met everything had changed. For that reason, he was grateful to Kingston Gore. If Cosgrove hadn't begun this game of his, Bram would never have had cause to introduce himself.

Of course she was promised to someone else, and he'd proposed to her and been turned down, but that would change. He had the oddest sensation that his own life and sanity depended on it.

Rosamund kept glancing over at Bram. She shouldn't be doing that, both because her parents sat directly behind her and because she didn't want to like him as much as she did.

In the corner she could hear James snoring softly; at least he was there instead of losing more money to Cosgrove or anyone else who saw him as an easy target. If nothing else, she owed Bram thanks for that.

Her parents couldn't seem to stop her brother from doing as he pleased, but he listened to Bram. Unfortunately he also listened to Cosgrove—which was the only reason she could conjure for her to change her mind and marry the foul-smelling ogre, as Bram had called him.

She'd half thought Bram might turn tail and run when her entire family walked up to the front doors of the theater, but instead he seemed amused by their presence. His guess that Cosgrove must have said something to her parents was in all likelihood correct, though no one had spoken to her about it. But she couldn't think of another reason that her father would want to sit through an entire play.

Hearing the characters on stage soliloquizing about feelings and love and fate, Rose wished that even with the pining and misunderstandings and frustrations, she could have that. Just to be able to feel and to act, without considering how it would affect her family. Just to be able to say yes or no and be listened to.

Of course James did as he pleased, and the results had been disastrous—though not for him. Only for her. But James hadn't yet learned any common sense. She had. And she wanted . . . she wanted Lord Bramwell Lowry Johns. And her abundant common sense just as loudly proclaimed that that was a very bad idea.

He'd proposed because he didn't want Cosgrove to win the game. Perhaps he'd even done it because he'd considered it the gentlemanly thing to do. He had mistresses and drank and gambled and took terrible, dangerous chances with his life, and stirred up chaos because he enjoyed seeing the carnage. But she wanted him.

By intermission she was fairly shaking, the desire to touch him, to kiss him, burning through her like fire. As the audience in the seats below began to hurry for the common areas, she stood so quickly she nearly knocked over her chair. "I need a breath of air," she said, when Bram lifted an eyebrow at her.

"I'll escort you." He offered his arm.

If she put her hand on him now, she would burst into flames. "No," she blurted, and strode over to shake James until he sat up groggily. "Take me outside for a moment."

"What? Is it over?"

"Intermission." She tugged him to his feet. "Outside."

"I'm going! Don't pull my blasted arm off."

As she and James stepped through the curtain and into the crowded hallway, she nearly bumped into the slender woman hurrying in her direction. "Excuse me," she said, yanking James sideways.

"Just a moment, Lady Rose."

She turned around to face the high-pitched feminine drawl. "Have we met?"

"I believe we have a mutual friend. Lord Bramwell Johns?"

Alarm bells began ringing in the back of Rose's skull. Bram seemed to have only one kind of female friend. Even she fit into that category. "Bram's in the box, if you wish to see him," she muttered, and pulled on her brother again. "Excuse me."

"He's a very naughty boy, setting himself after a woman promised to another man." She giggled. "But then, he likes married women."

The curtain shoved aside, and Bram stood there, his

black eyes cold as stone. "Miranda. A word with you, if you please?" He gestured her to join him.

"Oh, I can't, Bram. I'm here with friends." She faced Rose again, who stood torn between flight and dread curiosity. "Lord Ackley's gone to the country and left me all alone in London. Bram was very interested to hear that, you know."

"Rosamund, go," Bram murmured, then took a step closer to this Miranda. "If you wish to cause a scene, my dear, let's do so where everyone can enjoy it. Where did you say Ackley was? The country? So you didn't want to risk setting him after me. Is that because you know that if you force a fight I will make you a widow, and your money and estate will go to your brother-in-law?"

Lady Ackley took a breath that nearly caused her well-established bosom to burst through her low-cut gown. "I don't want to force a fight, my love. I just want you to know that I know every little thing."

She lifted her hand, as though offering it for him to kiss. It took a moment for Rose to realize both that she wore an oversized ruby ring on her thumb, and that it was familiar. Stifling a gasp, she shot a look in Bram's direction. His face had gone white, his eyes focused on the ring.

"I say, ain't that the ring you were talking about before, Bram?" James commented, apparently oblivious to the rising tension in the hallway. "King's ring?" The other theatergoers around them had begun gathering, tittering and gawking.

"As a dear friend of yours, Bram," Miranda continued, lowering her hand again, "I thought I might be able to enlighten Lady Rose about a few of your other acquaintances." She giggled again. "Though they aren't just a few, are they?"

Oh, goodness. Lord Cosgrove hadn't wasted any time before upping the ante, as James would say. And now he'd gone after Bram—because Miranda Ackley clearly wasn't interested in her except to gain Bram's attention.

Bram took a breath, shifting his gaze from the glinting ring to Rose's face. After a heartbeat where she couldn't read his expression, he walked up to her. "Please give my apologies to your family," he said quietly, his voice flat and expressionless. "I will call on you tomorrow." Then he walked past her.

For a heartbeat she couldn't believe that he'd just left her standing there in front of that woman. He'd walked away, just as Cosgrove had said he would. "Don't bother," she returned angrily.

His shoulders stiffened, but he kept going, the other patrons moving aside to let him through until he'd vanished into their midst. Lady Ackley, looking pouty and clearly disappointed, sent Rose one last contemptuous look, sniffed, and left as well.

"What the devil was that?" James asked as everyone resumed whatever it was they'd been doing. "Didn't exactly sound like a lovers' quarrel, did it?"

"Bram and that woman are . . . intimate?" she forced out, giving up on finding a way to make it outside and back before the second act began.

Her brother was nodding. "I think everybody in London knows it but Lord Ackley. Bram says she's round in the right places, but he don't like it when a chit chatters on and on. And what was she talking about, saying she'd tell *you* things. You ain't set your cap for Bram, have you? You're engaged."

"I am not," she retorted, fighting against the sudden desire to cry. "Not for nearly a fortnight. Let's go back into the box before they send Fishton out to look for us."

More than anything she wanted the relative quiet of the box and the play so she could think. Just when she'd begun to believe that she could trust in and rely on Bram, he'd walked away. If she couldn't depend on his help after all, she needed to know it. Immediately, while she still had time to rescue herself.

Because if Cosgrove could send one lover or her husband after Bram, he could just as easily send a dozen. If he couldn't stand up to his own demons, he couldn't very well help her stand up to—or escape from—hers.

In the morning Rose slipped into the morning room while the rest of her family sat at breakfast. Moving as quietly as she could, she opened her mother's writing desk and pulled out the countess's address book. Just as swiftly she closed the desk again and retreated back upstairs to her bedchamber.

Once there she sat at her small writing table and copied down the address of every one of her mother's acquaintances who didn't generally come to London for the Season. Of course she couldn't ask a friend of either of her parents for employment for herself, but she could tell them about a friend of hers in need of employment and ask if they could recommend any family that might be seeking a governess or a companion.

Her stomach felt terribly unsettled this morning, and she'd already vomited once. At least it gave her a reason to forgo breakfast, and she sipped at her peppermint tea as she wrote. She was somewhat surprised she hadn't already suffered an apoplexy, with the way her nerves felt stretched to breaking. Hope, despair, fright, anger— she preferred this new resolve of hers, but at the same time she wished there hadn't been a need for it.

Bram's words, his promises, and his touch, had made her feel special and protected. She supposed, though, that he wouldn't have gained his reputation for being a rakehell if he hadn't been able to charm all those other women. A tear ran down her cheek, and she brushed it away.

She wanted Bram to be the man she believed him to be now, not the one he'd been previously. But she couldn't afford to wait and see whether he would call on her again, help her again, and whether he would be her hero or just that blasted scoundrel she'd disliked before she'd met him.

Yes, thank goodness she still had time, even if she might no longer have an ally. Brushing at another tear, Rose kept working.

There was, Bram had discovered several years ago, an art to being useless. And he'd completely mastered it. And after all that effort, he had only now begun to realize that the talent didn't serve him well at all.

"Blast it," he snapped, closing his newspaper and slamming the thing onto his seldom-used breakfast table.

"Ill news, my lord?" Hibble queried, leaning over to refill Bram's coffee cup.

"No news. How the devil am I supposed to discover anything if no one is talking to anyone else? The damned wags are not doing their jobs."

"I don't know, my lord."

"Well, you're no help at all."

"No, my lord."

Bram looked over his shoulder at the butler, but the man seemed perfectly serious. "How long have you been in my employ, Hibble?"

"My lord?"

"You heard me. How many years?"

"Nine years, my lord."

"Yes, nine years." Bram turned his chair a little to face the servant. "And what would you say I'm good at?"

The butler's cheeks paled. "I need to go polish the silver, my lord."

"Come now, don't be a coward. In your years of service, surely you've made some observations. At what activities or skills do you believe me proficient?"

"I'd prefer not to say, my lord."

With a sigh, Bram reached into his pocket and produced a ten-pound note. "You won't be sacked, whatever you say. And if you come up with something, this is yours."

"You ride well," Hibble answered after a moment.

Yes, he did, actually. "What else?"

"I believe your wagering skills are legendary."

"You are correct. And?"

"The ladies, my lord. You're quite popular with the ladies."

Hm. He'd been looking to hear some revelation, some

skill he hadn't realized he possessed. Mathematics or science or something. "Anything else, Hibble?"

"You have a very neat hand. I've heard several compliments to your writing. Oh, and I believe you to be a crack shot, and a fair hand with a team. And your dress has always been impecc—"

"That'll do, Hibble." He handed over the blunt.

The butler pocketed it. "Thank you, my lord. I hope I was of some assistance."

"Absolutely none."

"I—"

"Name a true gentleman," Bram broke in again, "someone of wit and refinement and of true gentlemanly character and bearing. Respectable and respected."

"Your brother, my lord," the butler replied promptly. "Lord Haithe."

"Although I'm deeply hurt that you didn't name me, I am in agreement. Have Titan saddled."

With a grateful sigh, Hibble practically bolted from the breakfast room. Bram sat back and toyed with the breakfast that remained on his plate. He needed some advice. A few weeks ago if one of his lovers had approached him with threats, veiled or direct, as Miranda had delivered last night, he would have seen to it that she had more public attention than she wanted. He would have been ruthless and brutal, and utterly uncaring of the consequences to her and to himself.

Last night he'd fled, keeping watch only long enough to see that, the object of her ranting gone, Miranda had left as well. Cosgrove had clearly found a way to get to him—by threatening social or physical injury not to him, but to those for whom he cared. Anyone could be next. Phin or Sullivan, their wives—especially Alyse Bromley, who had already seen more than her share of difficulty. Phin's brother, William, already confined to a wheeled chair, or his young sister, Beth, naive enough that she'd mooned over *him*. Cosgrove could destroy her.

And there he was, proficient at one thing—scandal. Clearly he needed to . . . to tidy up his life. Become a better man than the one he was. And not just for Rosamund's sake, but for his own. It had just taken becoming acquainted with a very fine, very troubled lady to finally make him realize that. He only hoped it wasn't too late. Only eleven days and eight thousand quid remained between her and disaster, and he found himself willing to do anything to protect her. Even ask for advice from a brother who'd given up offering it.

As soon as Titan was saddled, they trotted over to Marsten House. He hadn't bothered to check the calendar, but luckily the House of Lords didn't meet until the afternoon and his brother was home.

The butler ushered him into the library, where August sat in a large chair, Oscar at his feet and reading aloud from *Robinson Crusoe*. It all looked so domestic that for a moment Bram stood in the doorway to watch, fascinated. Had he ever sat at the duke's knee for any reason? He couldn't recall a single instance, though he did remember being bent over said knee to have his arse tanned on several occasions.

"Uncle Bram!"

"Hello, Oscar," he said with a smile. The boy scrambled to his feet and came forward with a tight hug. Bram ruffled the lad's dark hair. "I'm pleased to see that someone, at least, reads to your father."

"Oh, I'm quite good at it. I shall read to you, if you like."

The fact that Oscar had made the suggestion proved that the boy didn't know very much about his uncle. And that was definitely for the best. "I actually need a word in private with your papa, if you don't mind."

"Not at all. Mrs. Edmonds is making pastries. She always wants me to sample one of them." With a wide grin Oscar scampered through the door.

Bram closed it behind him. "Do you have a moment?"

August looked at him. "What did you do this time, and to whom?"

"Spare me. You know I never tell you ahead of the spread of the gossip. It spoils the surprise."

"Then what is it?"

A warmer reception would have been nice, but August had certainly had his hand bitten enough that he hesitated to offer it. Bram could hardly blame him for being skeptical.

As for himself, he had no idea what he should even be asking, if anything. "I just thought we could chat," he offered, wandering over to the window and gazing out at the street.

"About what?"

Bram frowned, his stretched temper beginning to fray. "I don't know."

"Then get me a whiskey, will you?"

"It's a bit early for that, isn't it?"

He heard August climb to his feet. "Yes, but you're here to talk and you don't know what about. I'll end up with a drink eventually, so I might as well have one to hand."

That made sense. Bram picked up the decanter and poured them each a drink. When he turned around, August was eyeing his trousers. "What?" he snapped. "They're blue. That is not a crime."

"I haven't seen you wear anything but black since you took off your army uniform."

"Perhaps I'm trying to become a new man."

His brother took a breath. "How is the Marquis of Cosgrove?"

"Why the devil are you asking me that? You detest Cos—" He stopped. "Ah. It's because you saw me arguing with him the other night. I'm not playing dance around the mulberry bushes. If you have a question, ask it."

"Your conversation with him didn't look friendly. He's not a man to cross lightly."

Bram snorted. "You don't need to tell me that."

"So you're finished with him?"

"Yes. I'm finished with him. Except for taking measures to keep him away from me and mine. As you saw, we didn't part well."

"Does this have something to do with Lady Rosamund? I am aware of her family's agreement with Cosgrove."

Of course he would know about it; Levonzy knew, and the duke and his older son were thick as thieves. Bram shoved back his annoyance; time enough for that later. "She's been put in an untenable position. I am attempting to help her. Which has put me at odds with King." He shrugged. "But if your next question is whether I'll tire of this game and take up with Cosgrove again later, the answer is no."

"And why is that?"

"God's sake, August," Bram snapped. "If you're going to continue peppering me with the same damned questions, I'll take myself elsewhere."

"I'm attempting to decipher why you've taken yourself here if you have nothing to say."

That was a fair statement. And he didn't precisely have a plentitude of time to wander about and decide how much his pride would allow him to say. Bram closed his eyes for a moment. "I find," he began slowly, feeling as though he was picking his way through a patch of briars, "that I have been in error about some things."

His bear of a brother started to his feet and then sank back again. "Go on."

Bram glanced over his shoulder at August. "That's not enough?"

"You tell me. This is your visit."

"Bloody hell. Fine. I've done some things that were mainly aimed at taunting the duke. Pricking his pride, I suppose. But doing the same thing time and again is dull, so I went on to other things, and then more deeds beyond that." He took a breath, attempting to solve the equation in his mind even as he spoke the components aloud. "The point, I suppose, is that I'm so far off the path that I have no idea what the devil I'm doing or how to return to the road again. If I want to return again."

"Sit, Bram."

He turned around. "Ah, you have all the solutions and want my full attention before you cure me." Walking forward, he dropped into the chair opposite his brother. "Please proceed."

"For years," August began, slowly swirling the whiskey in his glass, "I have thought of you as Hal."

Bram blinked. "Hal. You thought mother and the duke gave me the wrong name. Well, while this is highly . . . insightful, I really must be off."

"Hal as in Henry. Henry the Fifth." When Bram started to interrupt again, August pointed a finger at him. "Hal before he took the throne. When his closest adviser and confidant was Falstaff."

"Cosgrove."

August nodded. "Precisely."

Actually, it wasn't a bad analogy, at least on the surface. Falstaff, according to that Shakespeare fellow, had been the older, corrupting influence to the young prince, drawing him farther and farther away from the honorable, princely behavior he should have been demonstrating. And then Hal had stood against his old mentor, emerging as a wiser, more worldly king than he might otherwise have been *because* of what he'd experienced in Falstaff's company.

"Except that you're the next king or duke or whatever title fits the tale," Bram countered after a moment. "I'm the spare. The second spare, now that you've Oscar to follow you."

"I'm speaking of character, not inheritance."

"Cosgrove's true character has never been much of a secret. I knew what I was stepping into." Deepening his frown, Bram emptied half the whiskey down his throat.

A few years ago it would have burned like the devil; now he barely felt it going down. "I wasn't misguided, either. I went looking for him, as a matter of fact. No. I reject your hypothesis."

August actually chuckled. "It's not a hypothesis. I only said that that was how I viewed you."

"That's still not the least bit helpful."

"How about this?" His brother sat forward, elbows on his knees. "You're one of the most brilliant men I've ever met. Frighteningly brilliant. You have it in you to figure out what you want and how to achieve it. So do that. I certainly can't." He downed his own drink. "But whatever you think of my analogy, it is my dearest hope that you set Hal by the wayside right alongside Falstaff, and become Henry."

Putting the glass aside, Bram stood again. "You're a sentimental fool, August."

"I'm a hopeful fool. And you're the one who came to see me, brother. Not the other way around."

Halfway to the library door, Bram stopped. Whatever he thought of his brother's conclusions, he did know one thing that he wanted. "Would you lend me eight thousand pounds?"

"I can't."

Narrowing his eyes, Bram turned around again. "Can't, or won't?"

"Can't. I've strict orders. If you ever come to me for money, I'm to send you on to Father."

With a curse, Bram turned away from the door again. "I may be young Hal, but at least I'm not the duke's damned lapdog."

The bear rose to his feet. "Before you insult me

again for the way I've chosen to live my life, look at your own. If you want eight thousand pounds, ask Father."

Bram sent his brother a two-fingered salute and stalked out the door. Hal, Falstaff, hope, and the duke's bloody purse strings—it was all a damned cartload of shit. Yes, he wanted to change, but he couldn't pull free from Cosgrove until Rosamund could. He wouldn't— couldn't—abandon her.

He wanted to see her. Immediately, and with a need that troubled him. It was entirely possible that he was losing his mind, because only around Rosamund could he seem to think rationally any longer. Just the sound of her voice filled him with all kinds of noble sentiments that previously would have had him vomiting in the gutter. He'd wandered, meandering through sin after sin, until she'd stopped him in his tracks.

Whatever it was she'd done to him, he enjoyed it. He craved it, and he craved her. So much so that he hadn't looked at another woman since they'd met. Even Miranda's challenge last night had only annoyed him because it had been aimed partially at Rosamund. Yes, his former mistress had clearly been intimate with Cosgrove, but the marquis was welcome to her. In fact, he only wanted one thing from Miranda—his ring. Other than that, he seemed to be irretrievably obsessed with Rosamund Davies.

She was angry with him, he knew; he'd heard her last muttered words to him at the theater. How, then, could he manage another meeting? Without August's assistance he would have to visit the clubs again tonight, but that still left the early evening.

As he swung back up on Titan, he stopped. Clearly he couldn't ask Lester to join him somewhere and expect her to tag along. How lucky, then, that he happened to be acquainted with two respectable married ladies whose husbands owed him several favors.

Chapter 15 _____

"You need a wedding gown," Lady Aber-
nathy said into the silence of the upstairs sitting room.

Rosamund looked up from the table and her correspondence, ostensibly to friends, but in reality a second
dozen letters to households well outside London. A
single acceptance on behalf of "her friend" would do,
but having a choice would be heavenly. "I have several
dresses that will suffice," she commented. "None of us
needs to go to the trouble or expense of decorating a
farce."

"Your wedding should look well," her sister put in, of
course agreeing with their mother.

Ha. She didn't intend to be in London to attend her
wedding. "If we're still pretending this is a surprise
love match, I wouldn't necessarily have time to arrange
for a wedding gown to be made."

"I would like her to be in a flowing white gown."

Gasping, Rose twisted to view the doorway. Lord Cosgrove stood there, James directly behind him. Swiftly she buried her correspondence beneath her appointment book. "What are you doing here?" she asked stiffly, rising in the wake of her mother and sister.

"I'm calling on my friend James and finding myself drawn to his charming sister," the marquis replied.

"Beatrice?"

"Oh, pl-please," Bea stammered, and fled the room.

"Spin whichever lies you choose," Rose continued, returning her attention to Cosgrove, "but I've no intention of spending any time in your company until I must." She only added that last bit for effect; if he had an inkling that she meant to run from London, he would likely have her chained to a chair.

"Rose!" her mother chastised.

Gathering up her things and trying to keep her hands from shaking, Rose looked up again. "I may be expected to spend the remainder of my life under his thumb, but you'll have to forgive me if I choose not to begin that before I must." She walked up to the doorway and stopped, gazing as calmly as she could at the man who blocked her escape and practically daring him to hit her with her family present to witness it.

"Such spirit," he drawled, taking a moment before he stepped aside. "How very invigorating."

Clenching her jaw closed, Rose kept walking until she reached her bedchamber. Dimly she heard James suggest that the two men play billiards to pass the time, and Cosgrove's agreement. She paused before she closed the door. James hadn't suggested a game of cards, friendly or otherwise.

Had her brother finally listened to Bram's repeated and creative warnings? Oh, she hoped so. If her family managed to pull themselves out from under the debt they owed Cosgrove, at least it wouldn't happen again. Of course one instance of intelligence hardly made for a pattern, but it could make for a beginning.

All that, though, made her think about Bram again— as if a moment passed when she didn't. She missed being able to talk with him even after his flight of last evening. Cynical and jaded or not, he'd never failed to be amusing and even comforting. That craving for him, the heat that coursed just beneath her skin when she thought of him—she had to fight against them every moment.

Perhaps it was a good thing he'd turned away when he had, because if she knew one thing, it was that the marriage he'd proposed would never suit *him*. Faced with a choice between one potential disliked husband who would terrorize her and one she felt affection for who would surely stray and break her heart, she had to take the third alternative and run. Far, far away.

A light knock sounded at her door, and she jumped. "Who is it?" she called, wishing she'd jammed her chair beneath the handle again.

"Elbon, my lady. A runner has just delivered you a note, and is waiting for a reply."

Rose pulled open the door just far enough to accommodate the butler's silver salver. "Wait here a moment," she said, lifting off the note and unfolding it. Swiftly she read through the brief missive. "Please tell the runner that the answer is yes."

The butler bowed. "Very good, my lady."

Closing the door again, she leaned back against it. Even with Cosgrove in the house, some light managed to shine through. Alyse Bromley had invited her to a cozy, informal dinner. It wasn't a complete escape, but it would do for one evening.

Rose stepped down from her father's coach and climbed the trio of steps to the Bromley House front door, her maid behind her. From the nearly identical expressions on her parents' faces as she'd left Davies House, they'd realized that the amount of control they wielded over her was slipping. She would have to be more cautious, or before she could manage her final flight she would find herself locked in her bedchamber with a chair jammed against the *outside* handle.

Lord Quence's butler led her to the upstairs drawing room. "Lady Rosamund Davies," he announced, and stepped aside to allow her entry.

"Rose!" Alyse came forward, smiling, to greet her, while all the men present, with the exception of Lord Quence, stood as she walked into the cheery room. "I'm so pleased you could join us."

"Thank you for inviting me." Smiling in return, she continued forward to offer her hand to Viscount Quence, the family's patriarch. She owed Bram a debt for introducing her to these people, however short their acquaintance would be. They seemed so different from her own family. They'd become their own family, friends without the ties of blood; they looked out for one another, and supported one another. She only wished she'd met them under better circumstances.

As she greeted Tibby Waring, standing with her husband Sullivan's arm around her, Rose's gaze shifted beyond the couple to the lone figure standing at the back of the room, watching her. *Bram*.

Abruptly flustered, Rose took a step back. "Was this his idea?" she asked, her voice shaking.

"The timing was," Alyse returned. "Not the invitation."

"Oh." Perhaps she'd expected too much, hoping for a grand gesture from Bram, something that said he regretted leaving her at the theater and he wouldn't do such a thing again.

"You're disappointed that I didn't set an ambush for you?" Bram said abruptly, stepping forward. "I thought you'd had more than your fill of that."

"You left me standing there with that woman!" she snapped back.

"That's what your angry ab—"

"Perhaps you'd like to make use of the billiards room for this conversation," Lord Quence interrupted, emphasizing the word "conversation."

At least someone still had an eye for decorum. "That would be acceptable," she said stiffly.

"We'll be in the billiards room, then," Bram said more loudly, gripping her hand hard.

"Bramwell."

He paused, glancing over his shoulder at the crippled viscount. "I heard you. I'll behave."

"Very well."

"He took you at your word," Rose noted, somewhat surprised, as Bram ushered her across the hallway into the billiards room and closed the door before her maid could follow.

"When I give my word, I keep it." Bram tilted his head, black eyes gazing into hers. "Miranda wanted to provoke me," he said abruptly. "I knew she wouldn't leave unless I did."

"And what if she'd decided to begin pulling my hair or something?"

"I was close by, you know. I didn't leave the theater until she wandered off. I wouldn't have let anything happen to you."

Oh, she wanted to put her arms around him, to kiss him until they were both breathless. Instead she walked over to roll one of the billiards balls across the table. "*You* are what's happened to me, Bram."

The hairs on the back of her neck rose as he stepped up close behind her. "What's that supposed to mean?"

"It means I would rather be in the middle of an argument between you and your latest mistress and know you mean to stand with me than see you run off. I've—"

"I did not run o—"

"I've put my trust in you. If I shouldn't have, then I need to know."

"I made you a promise. Ten thousand pounds or my assistance in getting you out of London. As I said a moment ago, I don't give my word often, but when I do, I keep it."

Rose swallowed. "I'm not certain I believe you, Bram."

His hand touched her arm, very lightly. A heartbeat later it dropped away again. "But you want to believe me," he said after a moment.

"I want to *know* that I can believe you." She turned around, then wished she hadn't. He stood so close, and her gaze focused on his serious, sensuous mouth. Oh, the things she wanted of him. "You were friends with that monster Cosgrove. And that stupid woman is the sort of female you prefer. What in the world are you doing, saying you'll help me?"

Bram took a breath. "Before I met you, I was perfectly content with the unbridled mayhem of my life. I never expected to encounter anyone interesting enough to make me reconsider things. Everything, actually."

Her insides heated. How could she not feel flattered, with someone as compelling as Bram Johns telling her that he found her interesting? But that didn't make him trustworthy. "And tomorrow or the next day you'll find someone or something else to interest you. Don't—"

"I won't," he interrupted. "You and I have more in common than you probably realize. And you've . . . managed your situation with much more dignity and honor than I ever did.. I feel like . . ." He trailed off again, almost absently reaching out to twine his fingers with hers. "I feel like you're my chance. That one moment that comes around and gives you the opportunity to set things right. If you don't want me about later, I will accept that."

"Bram." If he continued, she was going to lose all her bearings and simply throw herself on him, regardless of the consequences.

"All I'm trying to say—badly, obviously—is that I'm attempting to change. For you, and for me. And yes, I'm asking you to trust me. Give me that chance to prove myself, Rosamund. Please."

She had the distinct feeling that "please" was not a word he used often. But she had less than a fortnight to plan an escape. If she put a stop to that again, left it all up to him, she would literally be trusting him with her entire future. With her life. She looked down, then up at his face again, her mind running in a thousand different directions. "You're wearing all black again," she noted.

A brief smile touched his mouth. "I'm in mourning for my old life."

"I want to be certain you won't return to it."

"How can I? I love you, Rosamund."

The words hit her like a blow to her chest, stunning her, stealing her breath. Her heart absolutely stopped beating. Bram Johns, the wildest man and most sought-after lover in London, loved her. Tall, too curved or not curved enough, barely noticeable her.

"It's all I can give you at the moment," he went on, "but if you allow me the chance I will set things right. I swear it."

Slowly, still half dazed, Rose nodded. "I will trust you," she whispered.

Letting out the breath he'd apparently been holding, Bram closed his eyes. Rose lifted up on her toes and kissed him. Immediately he seized her, wrapping his arms around her, returning the kiss with a deep one of his own. Shaking, she wanted to crawl inside him, to give in to the dawning feelings of joy and desire that pulled at her.

But she didn't dare. Not yet. This was the one chance for both of them. They were going against Cosgrove. If he failed, it was entirely possible that neither of them would live to regret her decision.

"Bram, your hair's on fire."

He started, looking over at Phin. "What?"

"You see, Alyse," the former colonel continued, "he is alive."

"We'd begun to think you'd expired and had already been pickled by the alcohol in your veins." Chuckling, Sullivan offered him a toast.

"I was thinking," Bram snapped, annoyed at being caught at it. "And what a surprise that you two wouldn't recognize a thoughtful pose."

"I liked it better when you were staring into your plate." Phin shifted. "Beth, would you mind fetching me th—"

"Oh, no, you don't," his sister interrupted, all hazel eyes and brunette hair. "I'm part of this family, and I'm an adult now. Tibby's only three years older than I am. You're finally going to talk about whatever's brought Sully and Tibby in from the country, and I'm not going anywhere."

"Beth," Quence countered, "your heart is still very young. I would like it to be able to remain that way for a while longer."

"No. By the time you were my age, Phin—and Sully, *and* Bram—you'd already become notorious. I haven't done anything but see Prinny once kissing Lady Jersey on the cheek when he thought no one was looking. And that's not even very scandalous."

Bram forced a grin. "That is somewhat pitiful, my dove, but we've really nothing much to discuss," he drawled.

"But Lady Rose was surprised to see you here, and she was furious with you. Now you're holding hands beneath the table."

He hurriedly untangled his fingers from Rosamund's. Blast the keen observations of children. Even nearly grown ones. "Her fingers are cold, and she forgot her gloves," he improvised.

"Her gloves are on the table right beside her." Beth pointed at them. "Now I've caught you in a lie, and you have to be my partner for charades."

"Devious infant."

"I'm not an infant. The Marquis of Cosgrove has even begged a kiss from me."

All the air seemed to leave the room. Phin shoved to his feet. *"What?"*

For a bare moment Bram thought Quence might make it out of his chair on the power of pure fury. "Elizabeth Anne Bromley," the family's patriarch snapped, "you tell me precisely what transpired. Now."

The eighteen-year-old's cheeks flushed. "It was only on the hand," she stammered. "For heaven's sake. He's a friend of Bram's, so I thought it would be wicked."

Devil take it. That was precisely what he'd worried about. Cosgrove was already moving against those dear to him. Bram opened his mouth to tell Beth the precise value of his friendship with Cosgrove, but Rosamund put a hand over his clenched fist, this time on top of the table where everyone could see.

"Cosgrove is quite handsome, isn't he?" she said quietly, her meadow green eyes on Beth.

"Yes, he is," Beth agreed, shifting away from her practically combusting brothers.

"The thing is, Beth," Rosamund continued, "I have recently discovered the difference between wicked and monstrous. And I'm afraid that Cosgrove knows of Bram's fondness for you and your brothers, and he may be looking to cause trouble."

"But you and Cosgrove are friends," Beth argued, facing Bram.

Damnation. Being good wasn't nearly as fun as either

being bad or simply not caring. "We used to be friends," he said slowly. "We're not any longer. King overstepped a line not even I could cross." He scowled. "And however surprised you may be by that, I am even more so. It's not a challenge to how grown up you are, Beth, because you are a stunning young lady. If I wasn't terrified of you— Well, I am, so there's no getting around that. Be cautious of him, my dove. Keep your distance from him. Will you?"

Beth swallowed. "Yes," she answered, her lilting voice unsteady.

The ladies excused themselves from the table after that, and Bram sent a regretful look after Rosamund. Clearly he was becoming irredeemably softheaded. As a new experience, being in love was powerful, and at the same time petrifying.

With the way he'd spent the last ten or so years of his life, someone else's approval of his behavior or his actions—intended or already perpetrated—should have meant less than nothing. But where she was concerned, that wasn't so. Not even nearly.

Rosamund hadn't scoffed when he'd again offered his assistance. Nor had she thrown herself at his feet and begged for help, ever. She was more levelheaded than he, and more circumspect. *Love*. He didn't think he'd ever said the damned word before except in the sarcastic recitation of poetry or to poke fun at others. It didn't mean what he'd expected.

As he'd said it, he hadn't been thinking of what *he* wanted or what *he* needed. He'd been solely and utterly concerned with the well-being, happiness, and safety of Rosamund Davies. He'd teased Phin and Sullivan about domestication and castration, but he didn't feel weakened. Just the opposite. And all this without her saying that she loved him back.

An awful pain bit into his chest. Her lack of response wasn't any of her fault, though. He was barely human, a wreck of drinking, fornicating, gambling offal. But she hadn't run away. She'd agreed to give him the chance to save her—and thereby to save himself, as well.

"Thank you, Bram," Quence said heavily, once the chits were out of earshot. "I don't think Beth would have listened to anyone but you."

Bram took a swallow of port. "It was my fault." He stared into the glass, the slow anger he'd felt at Beth's confession spreading through him, out to the very tips of his fingers. "You lot should keep clear of me. That's only a warning shot where King is concerned."

"A fairly devastating one," Phin observed, his own expression grim.

"I say we kill the bastard." Sullivan refilled his own glass and downed it.

"Finally a suggestion I can embrace." Bram pushed to his feet. Games were well and good, but not when those dear to him could be hurt. He would do the deed, of course; no sense getting his friends hanged or transported. At least Rosamund would be safe. She couldn't very well be forced to marry a dead man.

"Sit down," the viscount ordered. "I won't have murder plotted at my table."

"Then we'll go outside," Phin retorted. "It could have been worse than a kiss, and you know it."

"No." Bram shook his head, seating himself again. "You lot are keeping clear of this. It's me he's playing with. After he sent Miranda to bait me last night I should have—"

"He what?"

Damn Phin and his need for facts. "I enjoyed Miranda because she didn't put any demands on my intelligence. Unfortunately she doesn't become more brilliant in my absence. Cosgrove's making use of her stupidity by giving her my old signet ring and having her flaunt it in front of me."

"She's another man's wife, Bram."

"And I'm no saint, William." He took a breath. None of this was Quence's fault. "If it makes any difference, I turned her away weeks ago—which probably made it easier for Cosgrove to get beneath her skirts. But it still comes back to me."

"And to Lady Rose."

Bram sent a glare at Sullivan. "She's the only innocent party in all of this. Well, aside from Beth."

"An innocent party to whom you proposed."

"What?" For one of the few times he could recall, Phin looked genuinely stunned. "I think my head's going to explode."

Sullivan leaned forward. "Alyse didn't tell you? After I informed Tibby and then revived her with smelling salts, she and Alyse were all aflutter about it."

"Will you lot stop meandering off the bloody path?" Bram growled. "I proposed; she turned me down. Hardly a surprise, given that she's . . ." He trailed off. He'd nearly begun to rattle off a string of adjectives like "perfect" and "miraculous" and "magnificent," and that would never do. "She's good, and I'm not."

"Bram—"

"I have ten days to either get Cosgrove ten thousand quid or spirit Rosamund away to be a governess somewhere. I'm trying to avoid the latter, because she actually feels responsible for her daft family." And because he couldn't stand the thought of not being able to see her again.

"Where are you going to get ten thousand pounds, then?" Sullivan asked. "Most of my blunt's in livestock right now, but I can give you a thousand."

"We can spare about the same, on short notice," Phin put in, glancing at his older brother. Quence nodded.

So they stepped forward, when his own brother turned him away. "No. I'm not taking money you're using elsewhere, and don't you dare try to tell me you're not." Bram smiled grimly. "I think we can all agree that I'm proficient at a few things, gambling being one of them. I'll manage it."

"Not if you want her."

"Yes, well, that's the blasted rub, isn't it, Sullivan? I damned myself years ago, and as . . . as much as I'd like to ride in on a white horse and win the fair maiden, all I can do at the moment is attempt a rescue the best way I know how. And hope that if I don't cause too much destruction, maybe she'll . . . I'll . . . devil a bit. I don't know. I just need to help her."

"God, Bram." Phin visibly shook himself. "As easy as it would be to make fun of you for finally acquiring a soul, you're a clever bastard. Figure something out."

"Everyone's being so bloody helpful these days."

"If I may," Quence put in after a moment, "I can't claim to have fought the French or performed suicidal acts of bravery, but—"

"William."

"Steady, Phin. I'm making a point. I haven't done those things, but you have. You don't have to own a white horse. Just do the correct thing."

If it were only that easy. Bram frowned. "I am not—"

"Act the hero," Quence cut in.

Sullivan sat back. "Faint heart never won fair lady."

Phineas grinned. "Charge."

"You lot are damned idiots. You do know that."

"Yes, but we're loyal ones." Phin's expression sobered. "Go do what you need to, but for God's sake, remember that we're here. Ask us for anything, and it's yours."

"Now you're going to make me weep." Standing again, Bram finished off his glass. Shoving back at an emotion that felt oddly like hope, he offered them a crisp salute. "See that she gets home safe."

"What *are* you going to do?" Sullivan asked belatedly.

"I'm going to retrieve something that belongs to me, and then I'll see if I can manage to act anything like a hero."

Chapter 16 _____

Despite the fact that the Black Cat had emerged as the most effective way yet to aggravate the duke, Bram had to admit that he'd lost the urge to take things he neither wanted nor needed from other people's homes. Whether this new reluctance to hurt others had anything to do with his meeting Rosamund or whether that was just a large, unlikely, tremendous coincidence, he didn't care to debate.

The fact remained, the Cat was finished. In a week or a month his exploits would be forgotten, and some new offense would take his place in the gossip-riddled minds of his fellows.

Well, he was nearly finished, Bram amended silently. Crouching into the shadows, he tied the black half mask across his face. Whatever supposedly inspiring words with which his friends had gifted him, he needed to see to one thing before he could set aside at least the most obvious trappings of his own villainy. After that—well, Ulysses was considered a hero, and he was exceedingly crafty. Cunning and not above tricking his enemies, even. Perhaps Bram could manage to be that sort of hero. After tonight.

The last of the lights finally went out in Lord and Lady Ackley's rooms above stairs. Knowing Cosgrove, Miranda had probably earned the ruby signet ring rather than being gifted with it. The fact remained, though, that it hadn't been Cosgrove's to give her. Nor was it Miranda's to have now, whatever position she'd lain in to receive it.

And if he could reclaim a bit of his family's good name, perhaps he could begin to reclaim a bit of his own.

He'd stashed Titan two streets away in Lord Greethy's old orchard, and hopefully the big fellow wouldn't give himself a sour stomach from eating green apples. The black was nearly as recognizable as his rider, though, and neither of them could be found near a burgled property.

Jamming his fingers deeper into his black leather gloves, Bram waited another twenty minutes or so before he straightened from his hiding place and made his way closer to the house. His heartbeat quickened as he shoved at the breakfast room window and felt it give.

In addition to the satisfaction he found in annoying the duke, he enjoyed the challenge of getting in and out of somewhere he wasn't supposed to be. Even if he might otherwise have been invited to come calling.

It was only the latest thing he'd found with which he

could amuse himself; one sin, one vice after another had fallen before him. Bram slipped in through the window and closed it again behind him. No sense letting a stray servant know something was amiss.

For once the thing he'd come to steal was his. It felt like the closing of a chapter; he would make himself whole, and then he would stop. And he wouldn't look back. For the first time since he could remember, he had something ahead of him. Someone whose heart he wanted to win, just as she'd already won his.

Luckily in this instance not only did he know the layout of the house, but he also knew where Miranda put the little gifts she wished kept from her husband. And he knew that Lord Ackley was in Surrey—which didn't necessarily mean Lady Ackley would be alone, but it changed the dynamics of the household.

As he considered it, he'd been a supreme fool, going from one unavailable woman to another ostensibly to keep himself amused, but more likely to keep from having to spend a night in his own damned company. As if dallying with married women would ever leave him anything but alone. And how interesting that lately he'd been discovering that his own company wasn't as bad as he remembered.

At the top of the main staircase he turned down the north hallway, his boot steps silent on the long carpet runner. He couldn't recall that Ulysses had ever stolen back a trinket from a former lover, but then Bram hadn't given it to her. He'd lost it through being a fool, and he wanted that part of his life finished and over with. Therefore, he needed the ring back.

Miranda's bedchamber and Ackley's were joined by a long dressing room. Moving cautiously, he pushed open the door to the master bedchamber. It was dark, and thankfully deserted. This was proving to be as simple as some of the break-ins that had annoyed him previously, but this time he was thankful for it.

The dressing room door stood partway open. He leaned around it to peer inside. The door to Miranda's private rooms stood open, as well.

Bram paused, listening. After a moment he made out the distinctive panting sounds of Lady Ackley being serviced. If her visitor was Cosgrove, the task at hand became trickier—and at the same time more satisfying. Taking the chicken out from under the fox's nose, as it were. Or the chicken feed, rather.

With a quiet breath, he lifted a pair of hatboxes from a shelf and set them aside. Behind them sat a third hatbox. Though he couldn't make out the details in the dark, he knew it to be an unattractive shade of olive, dilapidated and peeling. To Miranda this clearly signaled that whatever was inside must be equally unappetizing. As a burglar, it would have been the first thing in the room to pique his interest—a woman as vain as Lady Ackley didn't keep tattered boxes about unless they held something of significance.

The sounds in the bedchamber grew louder and more urgent. A few weeks ago that might have been he. Another wasted evening with someone for whom he felt a general contempt—contempt that he also felt for himself. God, what an idiot he'd been.

Was still, if he couldn't win Rosamund. Bram shook himself. Time for self-assessments later. He was in the middle of a damned burglary, for Lucifer's sake. Swiftly he pulled the lid from the box. Tilting the thing to try to catch some reflected moonlight, he looked inside.

It contained all the baubles Lady Ackley wished to keep from Lord Ackley's notice. A pearl necklace, several bracelets and ivory hair clips, French perfume—an adult's version of a child's treasure box. And inside an enameled bowl, a trio of rings. Including his ruby signet ring.

His hand unexpectedly unsteady, Bram lifted it out of its nest. For thirteen years he'd seen it on Cosgrove's hand, and figured he deserved the perpetual punishment. And now it was his again. He clenched his fist around it.

"You can't be seen walking about my house in only your trousers," Miranda's voice came. "Ackley has a dressing robe across the foot of his bed."

Damnation. Moving swiftly, Bram picked up the entire hatbox, then slipped out of the dressing room. Tucking his ring into a pocket, he hurried through the master bedchamber and out into the hallway. Whether Miranda would know what had happened to her trinkets or not, *he* would greatly enjoy knowing that St. Michael's Church had either sold them off or distributed them to the poor.

If she hadn't given her little performance at the theater he might have forgone the theft, but any charity he'd felt toward her had vanished when she'd insulted Rosamund. She would just have to begin her collection all over again, and without his contribution to the lot.

With a grim smile he returned to the breakfast room, shoved open the window, and swiftly climbed back outside. There. One last visit to St. Michael's and the Black Cat would finally be retired. Hopefully a hero would rise in his place.

* * *

The Marquis of Cosgrove stepped back from the breakfast room door. If he hadn't half expected that Bramwell would attempt to retrieve his ring, he would never have noticed the two out-of-place hatboxes and the third missing one. What he hadn't anticipated was that Lord Bramwell Johns would be wearing a black half mask, especially with rumors of the Black Cat flying everywhere. Now *that* had some distinct possibilities.

Shrugging into the shirt he carried bunched in one hand, Cosgrove padded barefoot through the back of the house and outside to where his horse waited behind the stable. Swinging up, unmindful of the chill in the air, he set off in the direction Bram had been heading.

Three minutes later he spied big Titan, Bramwell on his back, headed southwest. Cosgrove stayed well behind the horse and rider; even with the streets nearly deserted, another rider wouldn't be unusual—unless he happened to be following the one other rider out at this hour. Moving at a slow trot, he trailed them out of Mayfair and into Knightsbridge. Wherever the troublesome lad was going, he knew the way.

Finally Bramwell stopped beside a small church and dismounted. Taking the missing hatbox down from the saddle, he climbed the stone steps and pulled one of the double doors open to slip inside. Moving just as quickly, Cosgrove caught up, leaving his horse on the far side of the building, and slipped up to one of the stained glass windows.

The lad was bold, to willingly enter a church with some of the deeds he'd committed. As the marquis watched, Bramwell's dark, distorted image walked up to the front pew and set down the hatbox. Then he walked to a door behind the altar, knocked three times, waited, rapped twice more, and exited the building again. Slowly Cosgrove returned to his own mount.

That knock had been a signal—one that he'd clearly used before. Bramwell Lowry Johns, second son of the Duke of Levonzy, *was* the Black Cat. In retrospect, it made sense, the clever bastard.

In the morning King would return to this little house of worship and have the priest sign a statement attesting to that very thing. A generous donation, or better yet, threats, would be just the thing to convince the godly fellow.

He believed in manipulating his own luck, but nothing less than providence could explain this. Because he'd expected for some time that this would end with Bramwell dead. What he hadn't realized was that he could have the legal system of England see to it for him. And just to make things a bit more interesting, he would inform his bride-to-be tomorrow that there would be a slight change in their wedding plans.

"Are you certain you wish to walk?" Rosamund asked, taking Isabel Waring's arm as they dismounted from the barouche they'd borrowed from Lord Quence.

"Oh, yes," Tibby returned emphatically. "Driving has become far too bouncy for my comfort, but I can't abide sitting about all day. I even miss horseback riding, and two years ago I was petrified of horses."

That was interesting, considering that she'd married the foremost horse breeder in the country. Rose instructed their driver to go ahead and wait for them at the far end of the park. "I feel as though I've been sitting about far too much with nothing but my own addled brain for company, as well."

"I do thank you for joining me," Tibby said, chuckling. "Beth insisted that Alyse go shopping with her this morning. Beth shopping equals a run all the way from Marathon to Bond Street."

Rose laughed. Her own stomach had found the barouche less than pleasing, but as they began their stroll along the pretty paths of St. James's Park, it settled once more. Until she thought of Bram, which made her feel fluttery all over again.

He loved her. Even if by some awful chance she couldn't escape Cosgrove's trap, Bram Johns loved her.

"What are you smiling at?" Tibby asked, hugging Rose's arm.

"Oh, I don't know. I suppose I actually don't have much to smile about, these days. But it is a pretty morning."

"It is, indeed. And Bram is a very charming man."

Rose blushed. "A few days ago, weren't you attempting to caution me about him?"

"It would have been remiss of me not to. But I have to tell you the truth about something. I've never seen him—ever—act the way he does when he's around you."

Her heart skittered. "Is that a good thing?"

"Yes, I think it is. And I would hate to be the man or woman who crossed him."

"Would you now?"

Ice went down Rose's spine at the low drawl behind them. She wasn't certain what frightened her more—that Cosgrove was there, or that he could find her wherever she seemed to be. "Keep walking, Tibby," she whispered.

"Oh, I wouldn't advise that. I would hate to see Mrs. Waring trip and fall in her delicate state."

Immediately releasing Isabel's arm, Rose turned to face the marquis, putting herself between him and her friend. "What do you want?" she demanded.

Angelic blue eyes leisurely looked her up and down. "I hardly think you'd approve my saying in public what it is I want of you."

"If you're here only for threats and innuendos, I suggest you write them all down and send them to me later, so we may continue on our walk."

"My, my, you're full of courage this morning. I'm glad to see it, because I have some splendid news. Well, splendid for me, at any rate."

Isabel took Rose's arm again. "There are witnesses here, my lord. I suggest you watch your words and your manners."

"I find myself all aflutter."

Cosgrove took a slow step closer, and Rose steeled herself to keep from moving backward. A casual observer would probably wonder whether the increasing frequency of her encounters with Cosgrove meant he was courting her—which was what her father had wanted. Only up close would anyone be able to sense the tension and dread in the air.

"If you won't leave, then state your business and be done with it."

"Careful, my dear, or I'll begin to think you don't like me. And with the announcement of our betrothal sent to the *Times* and scheduled to run on Saturday, we can't have anyone thinking—"

"*Saturday?*" Rose creaked. All the air felt sucked from her body. "That's four days from now. You said—"

"Yes, I said we'd make the announcement at the end of the month, but you haven't been very cooperative, have you? I could have arranged for the announcement to appear tomorrow."

"Why didn't you, then?"

"Because, my dear, half the fun is the anticipation. I wanted you and Bramwell to have a few days to consider new developments."

Oh, God. Could she even arrange to leave Town in under four days? She would have to flee with nothing but the clothes on her back—and nowhere to go once she left. And no Bram to talk with, to kiss, to see ever again.

"There you go," Cosgrove said softly.

Isabel shook her shoulder, and Rose blinked. *Think,* blast it all. "You said development*s*. What else have you done?"

"You're becoming quite clever at all this, aren't you? Very well. I sent one of my men to Canterbury's office. Just yesterday he returned with our special license." Cosgrove showed his teeth in a smile. "We could be married tomorrow. We could be married by sunset today."

In the distance a church bell chimed eleven o'clock, mocking her. Isabel's arm was probably bruised, Rose held it so hard. But she couldn't let go. If she did, she would collapse to the ground. "I will not marry you," she finally ground out.

"Not even to preserve your family's reputation? I could put them out of their home, you know."

He didn't seem at all concerned, and that worried her further. "You've given no guarantee that you'll leave them be if we *did* marry."

The marquis gazed at her for a moment. "So clever," he finally murmured. "There is one other thing to consider, Rose."

She refused to ask what that thing might be. Instead, she clamped her jaw shut and glared, hoping her shaking wasn't bad enough that he would notice it. If she were a man, she was fairly certain she would have pulled out a pistol and shot him.

The marquis seemed to know everything she was thinking. His smile deepened. "I should keep it a secret from you," he finally said, "but I hate when my friends don't have all the facts necessary to make an informed decision."

"Keep it to yourself," she threw back at him. "I don't care what you say. I will not marry you."

"I have proof that Lord Bramwell Johns is the Black Cat burglar."

Rose began to retort that he was mad and desperate, but at the same moment Isabel gasped. Not in surprise, but in horror. *Oh, heavens.* It couldn't be. She'd begun to decipher him, and this was . . . it was too much.

"If you don't agree to announce our marriage in four days and to marry me in five, I'll have him arrested. And then I will use every shred of influence I have to see him hanged." He reached out, taking her chin in his fingers. "Do you understand?"

She pulled away. "You are wrong about Bram."

"Don't make me angry, my dear," he murmured, "or I'll marry you *and* end Bramwell Johns." Cosgrove sketched a shallow bow. "Good day, ladies."

Rose stared after him as he strolled calmly away. In just a few sentences he'd halved her days of freedom, caused her to reconsider her plan to flee, and announced that the man she'd begun to find . . . irreplaceable was a notorious housebreaker. It was beginning to seem that she had no way to escape at all.

Isabel grabbed her hand. "Come on," she said, and began pulling Rose toward the far end of the park. "I need to tell Sullivan what's happened."

Balking, Rose stopped. "Cosgrove was telling the truth, wasn't he?"

"Rose, I—"

"*You* knew, and I didn't."

"You need to ask Bram about all that. But come along! You don't have much time."

No, she didn't. Neither she nor Bram did. And that meant it was time for some . . . some damned answers. From the man who clearly knew far more than he'd been saying.

Chapter 17 _____

"What do you think?" Bram asked, biting back his impatience.

Mr. Pagey-Wright lowered his magnifying glass. "It's authentic," he said in a reverent tone, picking up the vase and turning the item in his hands again. "Hellenistic era."

"As I said. What's it worth to you?"

"How can you bear to part with such an exquisite piece?" The tobacco merchant faced Bram, pausing as he turned to glance at the Egyptian ceremonial scepter mounted on the study wall.

"The more you compliment it, the higher the price I'm likely to ask."

"Oh. Oh, dear. Yes, of course." Pagey-Wright chuckled thinly. "I'm able to offer you fifty pounds for it."

"Make it a hundred, and the scepter's yours, as well."

The merchant stuck out his hand. "Done and done, my lord. Thank you so much for contacting me when you decided to sell."

Bram shook his hand. "I'd heard you had an interest, and I'm a bit tired of the dust they gather."

With his reputation for doing as he pleased, he could get away with selling off a small part of his collection and still avoid rumors that he had run out of blunt. He'd been pushing his luck a bit even so, but his standing was dented enough that no one would notice a few more nicks.

"I'll have the money for you by three o'clock, if that's acceptable."

"That's fine." Bram made a show of pulling out his pocket watch. "And now if you'll forgive me, sir, I have an appointment."

"Of course. Thank you again, my lord." The merchant preceded him into the foyer. "And if I may, I had heard of your collection, but I was a bit . . . reticent to approach you. I'm glad to say that my impression of you was incorrect."

"No, it wasn't," Bram answered, nodding at Hibble. The butler pulled open the front door. "But this is Tuesday. I'm embarking now on a path to future sainthood."

"Oh." Pagey-Wright chuckled uncertainly. "Oh."

Once the merchant was gone, Bram retreated to his office. He'd barely slept in three days, but taking his latest transaction into account, he had nearly six thousand pounds in cash to hand. With more money now he could make larger wagers—risky, but he had only nine days remaining. And knowing Cosgrove, at the last moment there would likely be a charge of interest, and he damned well meant to be prepared to cover that, as well.

Hibble knocked at his half-open door. "My lord, you have a caller. A female."

"Which one?" Bram queried automatically, keeping his attention on his accounts. He could sell Titan back to Sullivan, he supposed, but that would leave his friend short of cash.

"She didn't say, my lord."

"I'm not in, regardless. Send her away."

"Yes, my lord." With a bow, the butler vanished again.

August hadn't been willing to loan him ten thousand pounds, but perhaps he would be more amenable to five thousand. There was one other place he could go to ask for money, of course, but he had no intention of doing so. Ever. It was bad enough that he had to rely on a monthly stipend from the duke, when Levonzy felt like handing it over. If not for that, he would have made certain he never had to set eyes on the old bastard again. Damned families.

His door rattled again. "My lord? She is insistent."

"So am I. I'm finished with chits calling on me, Hibble." And surprisingly enough, he meant it. Somewhere over the past few weeks, he'd become a one-woman man, whether he could ever have that one woman or not. "Get rid of her."

"I attempted that, sir. She threatened to kick me."

Bram glanced up. "Still no name, then?"

"None, my lord."

Damnation. "Well, what does she look like?"

"Rather plain, especially for your taste, my lord," Hibble returned with his usual haughty expression. "Reddish hair and freckles, even."

Bram shoved to his feet so fast his chair went over backward. Wordlessly he strode past the startled butler and down the hallway to the foyer. It was empty. And so was his ill-used morning room as he passed by it. "Where is she?" he barked over his shoulder.

"On the front step, my lord. I wouldn't let her in without your perm—"

Bram yanked the door open.

Rosamund stood just outside, biting her lower lip and looking supremely uncomfortable. "Come in," he said, glancing at the busy street beyond her. She'd taken a very large risk, calling on him. Whatever was afoot couldn't be good.

"Do you always make callers wait on your front steps?" she snapped, hurrying past him. She removed her bonnet, practically throwing it at the startled Hibble. "That's rather rude, don't you think?"

"Extremely so," Bram agreed, trying to assess what might be wrong. Rosamund seemed supremely frazzled, and angry. "I've lately taken to refusing female visitors. I didn't expect you, so I didn't think to inform my butler that there was an exception."

Stripping out of her gloves, she continued down the main hallway. "Where can we speak?" she asked in the same tight tone.

Bram gestured at the door nearest to her. "My office. Do you wish some tea or something? Coffee? Claret?"

"I won't be staying." She vanished into his office.

Torn between worry and bemusement, Bram gestured

for Hibble to approach. "I don't care if God or the devil comes calling at my door. I am not to be disturbed."

The butler inclined his head. "I shall see to it, my lord."

As soon as he entered the office, he closed and locked the door behind him. Clearly Rosamund's reputation didn't concern her today, and he would likewise keep his attention on her visit rather than its larger ramifications. "What can I d—"

"You're wearing your ring."

Damnation. When logic failed to serve, though, he would always opt for bravado. "It's my ring."

Rosamund flung her hand out. Bram caught it just before it connected with his face. Keeping her hand captive in his, he pulled her closer, glaring into her meadow green eyes. "Don't hit me."

"You're the Black Cat! How dare you come to me, swearing you've changed and that you mean to do good evermore, and all the time you're stealing from people!"

"I have never used the word 'evermore' in my life," he retorted, releasing her before her anger could change to panic. She'd been threatened and bullied enough. "And why does the recovery of my ring make me the Black Cat?"

She stalked back up to him again. "Do not dissemble with me, Bramwell Lowry Johns. I've put my life in your hands."

He contemplated her for a moment, seeing fury buried beneath deep worry. And hurt. Hurt he'd caused her. "Very well," he said slowly. "Yes. I'm the Black Cat."

"Why?" she wailed, tears rising in her eyes. "You don't need to take from anyone!"

Bram frowned. Giving up an old life and explaining it were two very different things, he was beginning to realize. "Have a seat."

"I do not want to sit! You tell me what—"

"I will," he interrupted. "It'll take a moment. I've been stupid for a very long time."

With another suspicious glare she plunked herself into the seat closest to the door, probably so she could escape more easily. Bram didn't like that, but he could certainly understand it. He took the chair beside hers and turned it to face her before he sat, as well.

"I have to go back a bit, or it'll make even less sense. So bear with me, will you?"

Rosamund swallowed, then nodded briefly. "Very well."

"Thank you. I'm not accustomed to confession." And he badly wanted a drink, however little that would help. "When I was sixteen," he began, "I did something that displeased the duke. I don't recall precisely what it was—a fight at school, I think. At any rate, my conduct embarrassed him, and he called me down to London to tell me my exact place in the family. I'd been born only because he needed a second son, in case something should happen to the first."

"I'm sorry to tell you, Bram, but that's hardly unusual."

"I know that," he snapped, then tried to pull his own temper back. "I'd known it practically since I was born. But August had just married, and I was never much for rules. 'A handful,' I believe tutor number eight called me. It was the way the duke said it. That once

August produced an heir I would be completely useless, as opposed to the mostly useless state I'd previously achieved. The analogy he gave was that I was the pair of boots he disliked, that he kept beneath the bed on the off chance his good pair of boots should be wrecked beyond repair."

"That was unkind," she said, her tone calmer.

"I thought so. My reaction was to decide to become a pair of boots that was so dark and dastardly and large and full of thorns that it would prick him from beneath the bed, keep him awake nights, no matter how hard the duke tried to ignore it. Two days later I tracked down Kingston Gore and told him precisely that. He agreed to mentor me."

"You took up with him at sixteen?"

"Willingly so. I chewed my way through all the deadly sins and most of the frowned-upon ones." He shrugged. "It did get the duke's attention, which I suppose was the point. Levonzy began threatening to cut me off or disown me or force me into the army. He managed that last one. And considering that I had one friend, and that he joined as well to keep me from blowing my own head off, and that we both met Phin Bromley there, I suppose it did correct my course a little."

"Sullivan Waring?"

"Yes."

"But that was several years ago. The Black Cat's only been striking for a few months."

Bram eyed her. "Persistent, aren't you?"

"I have to be."

"First I need your word that the next bit I tell you will stay between us. Do what you will with my nonsense, but this concerns my friends."

She looked at him for a moment. "Very well. You have my word. About your friends."

God, she was stubborn. "When Sullivan returned from the Peninsula he discovered that his mother's paintings had been stolen from him. With me informing him when and where I found the various pieces, he stole them back. You weren't in London then, but I believe the papers dubbed him the Mayfair Marauder."

"Good heavens."

"You've heard the name, then."

"Yes. Mama refused to let us come to Town that year, because of the thefts."

"Well, he doesn't do it any longer. Last year, though, Phin left the army to aid his brother. For reasons I won't go into now, he rode about Sussex disguised as a highwayman."

"You have . . . interesting friends."

"Yes, I do. At any rate, their actions gave me the brilliant idea to let myself into the homes of some of the duke's friends and relieve them of a few baubles. And then I told the duke precisely what I was doing. Hence me not at the moment having the money to hand to pay off Cosgrove for you."

"That's why he cut you off."

"He would have cut off my head, if he could have found a way to do it without causing an uproar. But if it matters, I've stopped. I went one last time, last night, to recover my ring, and that was the Black Cat's last appearance."

"Why did you decide to stop?"

"Because I encountered someone with a legitimate reason to despise her own family, yet who insisted on remaining loyal to them long past when she should have, simply because it was the right thing to do. Made me realize I was being an idiot, and that I'd turned myself into the waste of breath I'd been accused of being."

Color touched her cheeks. "I would like a glass of something now. What is it that you prefer? Whiskey?"

"It's the nastiest."

"Yes, that will do."

Wordlessly he went to his desk and pulled a bottle and two glasses from the bottom drawer. Filling them, he handed one over and took his seat again. "I recommend one fast, generous swallow. Don't hold it in your mouth."

She did as he suggested, then began coughing furiously. Bram took the glass from her fingers and set it on the desk before he drank down his own. It would be impolite to allow a lady to drink alone, after all.

"Good . . . heavens," she choked out. "You make it look much easier than that."

"Practice." He waited until her coughing subsided. "Do you hate me?"

It was an idiotic question, but that didn't explain his immense relief when she shook her head. "If I'd been a man, and younger, when all this happened, I'm not certain I would have acted any differently."

"Yes, you would have," he countered. "You're a better person than I am." He touched her arm, then dropped his hand again. "What gave me away as the Cat?"

"Cosgrove did. He must have seen you last night," she said, abruptly paling again. "Otherwise he wouldn't have waited until now to make his new threats."

Bram blinked, every sense suddenly alert. "I'm afraid you need to catch me up a bit," he said, as calmly as he could. "What new threats?"

"He found me this morning, walking in St. James's Park with Tibby. He said that he had proof you were the Black Cat, and that if I tried to escape, he would have you arrested. And he's sent the betrothal announcement to the *London Times*. It's to appear on Saturday."

"*Saturday?*" All the blood left Bram's face. Four days. That left him only four damned days.

"With the marriage to take place the day after that. He said he already has a license from Canterbury."

He would, too. Cosgrove didn't forget details. Bram pushed to his feet. "We need to get you out of London. Now." Striding to the door, he pulled it open. "Hibble!"

The butler appeared from down the hallway. "Yes, my lord?"

"Have my coach readied."

"Right away, my lord."

Rose watched, torn between terror and something her mind wouldn't quite let her put words to, as Bram shut the door again and went once more to his desk. "You're taller than Alyse, but Tibby or Beth might have something you can borrow until you get somewhere safe." He pulled a billfold from a drawer and handed it to her.

"What's this?"

"Just under six thousand pounds. I have another few hundred coming in, but it's a bit scattered at the moment. It should see you nicely settled somewhere. If you're careful enough with it, perhaps invest some of it, you won't have to find work."

"What about you?"

"Cosgrove's probably having the house watched. He'll know you've come to see me. I'll provide a distraction while you take the coach to Bromley House, get some necessities and a maid, and go."

"Bram, he'll have you arrested."

He sent her a glance before he went back to rummaging through his desk. "If part of atoning for my misdeeds means getting arrested for them, then so be it. It's certainly not something you're going to pay for." A moment later he produced a pistol. "Do you know how to use this?"

"My goodness. No."

"I won't load it, then. Ask Phin or Sullivan to show you, but don't stay there longer than an hour. I can't guarantee any distraction will keep King away from you for longer than that."

Her heart rose, pressing painfully against her chest and stealing her air. "I'm not leaving," she said, setting the billfold back on the desk.

"Of course you're leaving. With that special license he could drag you to any church and coerce some priest to marry you. He's not touching you again."

"And your plan is then to sit back and be arrested, because that way he'll have you to play with while I flee?"

"He couldn't have me arrested if I hadn't done anything wrong."

"I am not going."

Bram circled the desk to grab her arm. "You *are* going. Don't be so bloody stubborn on my account, Rosamund. You're better rid of both of us."

"You are not him, Bram."

"Don't be so sure of that."

Grabbing his hair with her free hand, she pulled his face down to hers. "I am," she whispered unsteadily, and kissed him. "And the only way I'll leave is if you come with me."

With an unsettled-sounding breath he kissed her back. "I can't run from this, Rosamund." He kissed her again, warm and intimate and very arousing. "If I do, I'll never be able to stand still again."

"Then we'd best think of something else. Because I find myself becoming very fond of you." The thought of him sending her off to safety and remaining behind, however much he might believe he deserved whatever befell him, made her physically ill. "Whether we had ten days or four days, Bram, we made an agreement. If you're staying, I'm staying."

"Stubborn chit," he muttered, but he didn't seem all that upset by her mutiny. Especially not after he kissed her nearly senseless. Finally he lifted his head, gazing down at her as she sat in the chair. "You need to leave."

"Yes, I know I do. My family thinks I've gone to chat with my cousin." She snorted. "As if Maggie or my aunt and uncle would want anything to do with the nearly-betrothed of the Marquis of Cosgrove."

"I'll tell you what," he said, running a forefinger along the neckline of her gown. "If you mention marrying Cosgrove again—every time you mention marrying him—I will do this." Slowly he pushed up her skirts, sliding his hand beneath until he touched her most intimate place.

Rose gasped. "Stop that."

"I'm not finished yet. After that"—and he gently parted her folds with his fingers—"I will do this." Bram lowered his head, nibbling and licking.

"Good God," she bit out, arching her back, digging her fingers into the padded arms of the chair.

He chuckled, the sound and the feeling reverberating into her. With another mewling, panting gasp, she came apart, writhing and pulsing beneath his mouth and his fingers.

How could he do that to her so easily? How could one man's touch push her beyond anything she'd ever known?

Finally Bram lifted his head, looking up at her through the dishevelment of her skirts. He opened his mouth, but before he could say something typically charming or even cynical, Rose sank onto the floor in front of him. Wrapping her arms around his shoulders, she pushed him onto his back, going down with him.

"Brute," he murmured, grinning.

"I know what I want." She kissed him, luxuriating in his strong, hard body beneath her, and the arousal she could feel between his thighs.

"Do you, now?"

"Has anyone ever told you that you talk too much?"

A laugh burst from his chest, his black eyes lighting with surprised amusement. "Only my friends," he replied.

"Then I must be a friend."

"Oh, that you are, Rosamund. Though I've never done this with any of my friends." Reaching between them, he unfastened his trousers and shoved her skirts back up around her waist again.

Slowly she sank down on his member, relishing in the tight, hard slide of him inside her. So no woman he'd ever been with had been his friend. She panted, lifting up and down hard and fast as he groaned beneath her. She rather liked hearing that.

Bram clutched onto her hips, pushing up as he pulled her down on him. She watched his eyes, the pleasure and lust there, as he moved harder and faster and then with a primitive growl found his release deep inside her.

Rose collapsed against his chest, her heart pounding so hard she thought it must explode. He closed his arms around her, holding her close. For a long moment they lay there, breathing together, their hearts beating to the same rhythm their bodies had just shared.

"Now I should go," she finally murmured.

"One day very soon," he returned, relenting when she pushed up against his chest, "you and I are going to spend an entire day—no, an entire week—naked together."

"A week?" she repeated, shifting up to the chair again and smoothing down her skirts, fascinated by his naked lower half. Magnificent, he was. "We shall both be dead at the end of it."

Bram grinned. "And that is the way I very much want to die."

The thought of a week together, naked, rather made her want to think of living. Because an hour, a day, a week in his company was something she very much looked forward to. If they both survived.

"What are you going to do?" she asked as he unlocked the door and pulled it open again.

"We have four days—three to be certain we can have the announcement removed from the newspaper. I have some ideas, but it would take longer to tell you than to set them into motion." He flashed her a grin. "You'll have to trust me, Rosamund."

"I do trust you, Bram," she returned, meaning it.

He kissed her on the tip of the nose as his butler reappeared. "Thank you. Now go home, and stay away from him no matter the circumstance." Bram's expression darkened. "Cosgrove may think he taught me everything I know, but he's about to find out that he's mistaken."

Chapter 18 _____

"He approached you in the middle of St. James's Park?" Sullivan paced to the window of Bromley House's upstairs sitting room and back again. And people called *him* a bastard. "You're not going anywhere else in this damned Town without me."

"He actually approached Rose," Isabel said, sitting on the low couch to one side of the hearth. "I just happened to be there. And please sit down, Sullivan; you're making my head ache."

Immediately he left off pacing and sat beside her. Blowing out his breath, he slid an arm around her shoulders and drew her against his side. "What worries me," he said slowly, kissing her golden hair, "is that he didn't bother to pretend the circumstances were other than what we know them to be."

"You think Cosgrove wants Bram to react."

"That's my guess. I don't know what kind of victory it'll be for the coward if Bram hangs for killing him, though."

"Well, he doesn't intend to be killed, obviously."

Sullivan looked at his wife, resting comfortably against him. Isabel brought him a contentment he'd never thought to find in his life. And at the same time a perpetual, heart-pounding excitement. It would take him a lifetime to decipher the way her quicksilver mind worked, and he looked forward to the challenge.

"What are you thinking?" she asked.

"I'm thinking that you're correct, and that in order to avoid being killed, Cosgrove will have to move first." He leaned over and kissed her softly, at the same time placing his palm over her rounding abdomen. "I'm thinking we need to be ready to help Bram because he won't ask on his own. And I'm thinking I love you to a rather alarming degree."

She chuckled against his mouth, kissing him back. "I'm not alarmed at all."

Bram sat on Titan and stared up at the broad gray and white house on the corner. Today had been a damned foxhunt. Up and down, this way and that, until he felt so twisted around he could barely stand. At breakfast he would have been willing to sell off every possession he owned to keep Rosamund in London. By luncheon he wanted to see her gone without delay, full knowing that he had every intention of getting himself imprisoned or killed to make certain she stayed safe.

And then she'd admitted to being fond of him. *Fond.* Like a fellow was of his horse or his dog. And even that pittance had been enough to turn him around again. If she intended to stay, then he intended to make certain she could do so safely.

Which ended with him pacing on horseback fifty feet from the front steps of Johns House. He'd been there before, of course; hell, he'd grown up there. Over the past few years, though, his visits had been only in response to a formal summons—his monthly or so browbeating, with a side dish of threats and contempt.

With two nights safely remaining, he could probably win the funds necessary to pay off Kingston Gore. Unfortunately there was also the possibility, slim though it might be, that he would have an off night and fail to win. Or worse still, lose some of what he'd accumulated. Large figures meant large wagers and large risks, after all.

And the one thing he couldn't afford in this instance was to fail. Squaring his shoulders, he kneed Titan and sent the big black up the short, half-circular drive. He would keep his temper, he would mind his tongue, and he would get what he needed. That was the only option.

The hulking, broad-shouldered butler pulled open the front door as he reached it. "Lord Bramwell," he said, inclining his head.

"Spake. Is His Grace in this evening?"

"I believe he is dressing for dinner. If you would care to wait here, I shall inquire."

So he was to wait in the foyer. The duke no doubt thought he might pilfer the candlesticks if left alone in the sitting room. Levonzy clearly didn't realize that the object of the game had been to aggravate him while having as little to do with him directly as possible.

"I am not changing my mind," the duke said from the top of the stairs. "You are cut off."

"Yes, I know that," Bram returned, resolutely keeping the lid on his own temper. "That's not why I'm here."

"What is it, then? August and I are to dine with the cabinet ministers this evening."

"I require a private word." Spake might keep the duke's secrets, but Bram wasn't going to entrust Rosamund's to the butler.

A muscle in the duke's cheek twitched. "The music room, then," he said, and turned on his heel.

Bram ascended the stairs, following him. It interested him that Levonzy would choose the music room; it had been the duchess's favorite room in the house, and it was the only place Bram could conjure images of her. Victoria Johns, the one ray of sunlight in Johns House. He didn't have to wonder whether his life would have turned out differently if she'd lived past his tenth birthday; he knew it would have.

They'd never conferred in this particular room before. Was it deliberate, then? Was the duke gambling that Bram would behave himself in there? Bram kept his gaze on his father. He did mean to behave, regardless of the setting, but if the duke felt he needed the memory of his wife to hand, well, perhaps Bram's activities had had more of an effect on the old man than he'd realized. And at this particular moment, that was not a good thing.

The duke moved to the far window as Bram stepped

into the cheery yellow room. Deliberately he turned
and closed the door behind him. "Thank you for seeing
me."

Levonzy pulled out his pocket watch. "You have
three minutes."

"Then I'll get right to it. You know of the agreement between Cosgrove and Abernathy. Why didn't
Abernathy ask you for the ten thousand pounds he
needed?"

"Because he would still have to repay it. An exchange
made far more sense fiscally."

"But you would have lent him the money if he'd asked
for it."

"Why should I have? The daughter would have continued to cost money for her upkeep, and in the event
she married later, he would have had to provide a
dowry. A fairly substantial one, no doubt, given her age
and ordinary appearance."

While Bram's first instinct was to demand an
apology because Rosamund was the least ordinary
woman he'd ever met, something in the duke's argument caught his attention. And it chilled him to the
bone. "Abernathy *did* ask you for a loan," he said, his
voice clenching despite his best efforts. "You talked
him out of it."

The duke shrugged. "As I said, it made more sense
financially to trade the daughter and erase the debt."

"You believe Cosgrove will make her a good husband
then, do you?"

"What I think of Cosgrove I will not say in this
room."

"Then why would you condemn a good-hearted, innocent lady to a life with him?"

"Clearly he wanted her enough to pay well for her. What better purpose would she ever have served?"

This was going to be even stickier than Bram had expected. He walked over to the harp and ran his fingers lightly along the strings. Even the discord of sound they produced was pretty. "What would I have to do to warrant a loan of ten thousand pounds from you?"

Levonzy snorted. "Be someone else."

Bram faced him. "Who would you wish me to be?"

"Ha. It's too late for that. You've shown me nothing but contempt and disrespect for better than ten years. Is she one of your mistresses? Is that why you want to purchase her back? Good God, she's not worth that much! I'm certain your good friend the marquis would share her with you for a much more reasonable price than that."

"Eight thousand pounds, then."

"No."

"Six thousand. And you'll have it back, with interest."

"You've probably stolen more than that amount from my friends. Use *it* to pay for her."

"I haven't kept what I took. I gave it to a damned church."

"Then why—ah." The duke sank onto the deep windowsill. "You went to a great deal of trouble to annoy me, then. Congratulations on your success. Don't expect me to give or loan you anything after what you've done."

"It's not for m—"

The door burst open. "Thank God," August panted, stepping into the room and shutting them in again. "No weapons drawn."

Bram scowled. All he needed was for the golden child to make him look even more tarnished in comparison. "This does not concern you, August. I already went to you, and you sent me here. Get out."

"He's my heir," Levonzy retorted before August could reply, "and he's welcome inside my house. You are not. Your three minutes have expired. Good evening, Bramwell."

"Has he asked you for the money, then?" the Marquis of Haithe asked, leaning back against the door and creating a better barrier than a stack of chairs.

"Yes, he has, if you can believe his gall. As if I would cut him off and then bestow money on him."

"For the last damned time, it's not for me, blast it all!" Bram growled, the lid exploding off his temper.

"No? You don't mean to see that your dear friend can claim ten thousand pounds from an admired member of the *ton*? I'm certain you and he will laugh about it to our faces."

Bram blinked. Was that how the duke saw this mess? As a way for Cosgrove—and for him—to gain a laugh at the literal expense of the good *ton*? "My only thought is to remove Lady Rosamund's obligation to Cosgrove. And you won't be losing any funds. I will repay you. Not the sort of thing I generally laugh about."

"Do you think I've become senile?"

"I believe Bram to be telling the truth, Father," August put in unexpectedly.

A heartbeat of silence echoed in the room. Both Bram and his father stared at Haithe. Bram clenched his jaw before it could fall open. It looked as though Levonzy was having the same trouble.

"Are you taking his side?" the duke finally snapped.

"I'm saying that I think his motives are pure."

"All talk. It's all talk. Give me one shred of proof that this isn't a bloody conspiracy, another attempt to make me look foolish and to make me part with ten thousand pounds I'll never see again."

At least Levonzy wasn't still slamming the door on his face—which was no more than he deserved. Taking a breath and sending up a quick prayer that God would take pity on Rosamund if not on him, Bram pulled the signet ring from his finger and placed it on top of the pianoforte.

"I've broken with Cosgrove," he said quietly. Perhaps a murmur would have a greater effect than shouting. "Permanently. I stole that, in case you're wondering how I've come to have it back. And I'm returning it to you. I know you regret ever giving it to me."

"Yes, I do." Stalking forward, Levonzy snatched up the ring and retreated to the window again. He examined it, as if checking to see whether it had been tainted.

"That was my last burglary, as well."

"Oh, and why is that?"

He hesitated. Saying it aloud, especially when Rosamund hadn't returned the sentiment, seemed foolish. And if she never did . . . "I've assessed my life. Reassessed it, I suppose. I didn't like where it was going."

"And you do now?" Levonzy retorted, sarcasm flowing from him in waves.

"Yes. I love someone. I'm in love with her." *There.* Love was naturally foolish, he supposed.

"Whose wife is she?"

"No one's, yet. In four days she'll be officially betrothed to Kingston Gore."

"God's sake, Bram," his brother murmured. "It's about damned time."

"You may believe this load of turnips he's selling," Levonzy broke in, "but I'm having none of it. And I won't be pulled into some scheme so you can further embarrass me."

That was it, then, Bram realized. He'd been a black-hearted scoundrel for too long to remove the costume. It had melted into his skin. "If you'll excuse me, then, I'm off to the tables. I have another four thousand—no, eight to be safe—quid to win before Friday." That was the limit. Beyond that, and Cosgrove or Abernathy wouldn't have time to withdraw the betrothal announcement from the *Times*.

"Eight thousand?" August echoed. "I'll lend it to you."

Bram froze in mid-step, his heart thudding again with that odd hopefulness he felt in Rosamund's presence. "You said I had to go to Levonzy for any funds."

"Which you've done. I find your reasons to be sound. Come see me in the morning."

Torn between the sudden desire to hug his bear of a brother and wanting to flee before Haithe could change his mind, Bram settled for nodding. "Thank you, August. Truly."

"You're welcome."

And thank God or Lucifer or St. Joan or anyone else who might have had a hand in it. He could save her. His Rosamund. He had a chance to save himself. Speaking of that, though, he needed to make one more confession. "You should know that Cosgrove believes me to be the Black Cat."

"We'll deal with that as it comes."

Levonzy gave a rumbling growl. "I'll disown you, August, if you give him so much as a shilling."

August lifted his head. "Then you'll be out an heir, Father."

"I'll name Oscar. The dukedom will pass you by."

"That's your right, of course. Though I doubt my son would refuse to give his uncle eight thousand pounds."

"Then I'll cast aside the lot of you, you ungrateful, undeserving scoundrels."

The Marquis of Haithe shrugged. "So be it. Enjoy being the last Duke of Levonzy, Father, if you won't open your heart enough to give Bram one last chance."

The duke glared from one to the other of them. Bram doubted that August would actually risk losing his entire inheritance and the ability to support his family over a declaration by his wayward younger brother, but the question was whether Levonzy believed it. Or at least believed the gesture was sincere.

"Bah," the duke finally muttered, waving a dismissive hand at the room in general. "Do what you will, August. I'll not have a part in aiding the blackguard."

August nodded. "Then let's be off to dinner, shall we? I'll see you at ten o'clock tomorrow, Bram."

Bram recognized an exit cue when he heard one. He opened the door as his brother stepped aside. "I'll be there."

"We'll never have time to get you into a proper wedding gown now," Lady Abernathy said with an annoyed sigh. "So I suppose you'll get your way and have to wear something we've all seen you in before."

"Yes, Mama." Rose finished fastening on her necklace and wished that her mother would stop hovering in her bedchamber doorway. The idea that she was somehow getting her own way in this was ridiculous—though if she had any say in the matter, she intended to do just that. In a perfect world, she wouldn't marry Cosgrove, and she wouldn't have to flee to the countryside.

Except that she wasn't entirely certain this world was anywhere near to perfection. And she did have one reason still to marry the marquis, and that was to protect Bram. She'd meant it when she'd said that she wouldn't flee without him—whether the robberies had anything to do with her or not. He'd been hurt, and he'd reacted very, very badly to it. Surely the hope and the help he'd given her outweighed a handful of petty thefts.

"Come along, Rose," Beatrice called from halfway down the stairs. "When Fiona says we should arrive at seven o'clock, you know she means half six."

"Yes, Bea." Fiona, Lady Thwayne, did like to pretend that her dinner parties were far more important than they were. And for the first time Rose hadn't changed anyone's clocks, so her mother had been ready for an hour, Bea was still changing hats in the foyer, and James was dozing in the billiards room. And she didn't feel an ounce of guilt about any of it.

Her mother and Bea continued chattering away as they waited in the foyer for her father to drag James down the stairs. Thankfully the two of them didn't allow a space for anyone else to interject, because Rose was far too distracted with her own thoughts to pay much attention to their conversation.

Only a very thin barrier of hope and faith lay between her and absolute panic. She believed that Bram would do everything possible to set things right. She still had to wonder, though, whether he could accomplish it in three days, and whether he could do so without destroying himself.

His well-being seemed to consume her now. As much as she'd wanted to do the right thing and remain to see her own family protected, she'd ultimately decided to save herself. And now she'd turned around and put herself back into harm's way again in order to give him the chance to prove himself—and to keep *him* safe. Life was a blasted, twisted muddle.

And because she'd begun to feel unaccountably optimistic and happy at moments when she least expected either feeling, something was bound to go horribly wrong.

At that moment she paused halfway into the coach. Out of the corner of her eye she caught sight of a shadowed form at the side of the house. He shifted a little, motioning her toward the stable yard. *Bram.*

"I'll be right back," she said, returning to the house. "I want my other wrap."

"Hurry, Rose, for goodness' sake. I don't wish to be late."

"Yes, Bea."

She rushed through the house. Had something gone wrong? Had he come to tell her they'd run out of time and needed to flee after all? Had he decided to join her? She almost hoped so. A lifetime with Bram, even in hiding and in sin, seemed so much better than the future her parents had planned for her.

Just outside the kitchen door, Bram grabbed her arm

and turned her to face him. Before she could draw a breath, he closed his mouth over hers in a delirious, heart-stopping kiss.

Rose leaned up into him, wrapping one hand into his lapel and tangling the other into his hair. When had it happened, that no matter what lay around her, touching Bram Johns made her heart soar?

"Hello," he murmured after a moment, nipping breath-stealing kisses against her lips.

"Hello." Oh, she didn't want to ask if something had gone badly. "What brings you here?" she settled for.

He kissed her again. "You do. I want you, Rosamund."

She shivered deliciously. "I'm expected at the coach."

"Yes, I saw that." He brushed a strand of hair back behind her ear. "Good thing, since I was about to climb through your window again. Where are you off to?"

"One of Beatrice's friends is holding a dinner. They're terribly pretentious, but she insisted that I come. I think Bea told her I'm to marry Cosgrove, and now Fiona feels threatened because I've netted a marquis, and she only managed a viscount."

"You are not about to marry a marquis."

He said it so . . . possessively. Coming from someone—anyone—else it would have alarmed her, but several times now she'd argued against what he wanted, and he'd given in. She didn't think anyone had ever chosen her wants and needs over their own before. For a long moment she simply looked at him, his intelligent black eyes, lean, handsome features, the excitement and growing amusement in his gaze. Rose furrowed her brow. "What's happened?"

"I have the money."

His words took a heartbeat or two to sink in. "You have . . . you have the money," she whispered, her voice suddenly shaking.

Bram nodded, grinning. The unaccustomed expression lit up his face, lifting him from handsome to—to something that pulled at her heart. "Not all to hand, or I would have called at your front door with it. But August's agreed to lend me eight thousand quid in the morning. With the blunt I already have, it's enough to repay Cosgrove and whatever interest he's likely to demand."

"You have the money," she said again, more strongly. A hundred pounds of sand lifted from her shoulders. She pulled him down to kiss him over and over, the heat, the fire, rising in her.

He'd done it. He'd saved her. Abruptly realizing what her sudden affection must seem like to a hardened rake like him, though, she pulled back.

"I'm not kissing you because you have the money," she stammered, flushing. "I mean, I am, but it's not—well, it is, of course, but—"

"You're relieved," he broke in, still smiling. "And you're happy. There's no fault in that. And frankly, Rosamund, I just enjoy kissing you."

Something else abruptly began to pinch at her insides. *It didn't matter*, she told herself. And she didn't need to know why. Except that apparently she did. "Why do you like kissing me?"

One dark eyebrow arched. "Beg pardon?"

Rose hesitated. "I am so, so grateful to you, and I will do everything I can to see that you're repaid, but—"

"Nonsense," he broke in, his smile fading. "But what?"

"I'm tall, Bram. I'm flat-chested. I have freckles. I'm not a great beauty. You've known a great many women more attractive than I am. And if you feel some obligation to show me affection, you absolutely need not. Or if it's because you see the similarity in our relations with our parents or something, a kinship, you know, that doesn't mean you have to—"

"To what?" he interrupted, scowling now.

"To say you love me. I have no expecta—"

"Oh, that is enough of that." Bram put his hands on her shoulders, meeting and holding her gaze as if by sheer willpower, because she truly wanted to look away. "As you said, I'm no virgin, Rosamund. I've seen the world, and I've cut quite a swath through the middle of it. I've bedded more women than I care to remember. Do you think my heart is swayed by obligation or pity?"

Slowly she shook her head. "No. But—"

"You are the most interesting, beautiful, and true-hearted woman I have ever—*ever*—encountered. I like just chatting with you, and I never chat with females. You've been a . . . a candle in my darkness. And if I should ever be so lucky as to win your affection as you've won mine, I will . . ." He trailed off. "Please don't ever belittle yourself in my presence again."

Goodness. "Thank you, Bram," she whispered, tears gathering in her eyes.

"Yes, well, thank you. And all this sincerity has made me light-headed, so unless you wish to join me in the stable for a bit of naked frolicking, you should return to your family. At once."

Ah, but she did want to frolic naked with him. And she wished he would propose again, because after his speech she felt very much as though she wouldn't mind spending the remainder of her life with him, scoundrel or not. She actually liked the scoundrel bits, as a matter of fact.

Only when she'd taken her seat in the coach with her annoyed and impatient family did it occur to her—he had the funds to help her, but he hadn't said anything about what he meant to do to aid himself.

Chapter 19 _____

Bram went out riding at first light, taking pains to avoid the usual parks and pathways he'd frequented in the past. Since Isabel Waring had been with Rosamund to hear Cosgrove's latest threats, Sullivan and Phin would know of them now, as well. They would be plotting some sort of clever rescue for him, and frankly he didn't want one.

Yes, ideally this would end with Cosgrove falling into a bog or being satisfied to have his money. Bram would propose to Rosamund and she would accept, and the duke would grant him permanent use of Lowry House. Flowers and children would bloom, no one would ever confront him about his notorious past, and he would be a good lad forevermore.

The trouble was, he felt fairly close to being the same scoundrel he'd always been. His friends had broken the law for reasons that he considered righteous. He'd done it because he found it exciting in a life growing ever more dull. The mere fact that he'd fallen in love while trying to commit a single good act hardly made up for all the ill he'd done. And Rosamund had been very correct when she'd called him trouble.

At precisely ten o'clock he arrived at Marsten House, half surprised when he didn't see the duke attempting to block him from the entrance. August actually had the eight thousand pounds in cash, sitting on his desk.

"How did you manage that?" Bram asked. "I thought I would have to take your note and raid half the banks in London."

"I have my ways. Not as mysterious or exciting as yours, but I do have them."

"I'm not about to argue with that, this morning."

They added the blunt to the satchel where Bram already had the six thousand he'd raised. It was a damned fortune, and part of him was still tempted to snatch up Rosamund and make a run for it.

"Now, about this Black Cat mess," August said, settling a haunch onto one corner of his desk, which had the good manners not to creak. "Do you think—"

"I think that you have a family and an inheritance, and that it's nothing you should concern yourself with."

"Bram, you can't mean to—"

"I'm a scoundrel, August, as you've experienced firsthand. Thankfully everyone knows that I'm fairly estranged from the entire family, so any gossip or scandal shouldn't affect you overly much. I'll see that it doesn't." He climbed to his feet, slinging the strap of the satchel over his head and across one shoulder so he wouldn't lose it. Then he stuck out his hand. "Thank you. I'll repay you if it's the last thing I do."

August shook hands with him. "I know you will. And for what it's worth, you and Father may have your differences, but there's no reason you and I can't continue as we have these past few weeks."

No reason except a hanging or a transportation to Australia. Bram nodded. "I would like that."

"Be careful."

"Not for years."

By eleven o'clock he'd reached Davies House. His heartbeat increased—not because he was about to gift a large sum of money to a very proud and likely suspicious man, but because he had a chance to see Rosamund again. His Rosamund, at least for the moment.

There was no way around the fact that he'd gone mad. And what would happen when he asked for her hand for the second and last time—if he wasn't dead before then—he didn't want to contemplate. Perhaps an arrest would be the lesser of two evils. At least then he could imagine that she would have accepted him.

He rapped the brass knocker against the solid oak of the front door. Silence. For a pained moment he worried that the family had trotted off to present Cosgrove with his bride early. As he was beginning to consider kicking open the door, it opened.

"My lord," the butler said, managing to look aloof and displeased at the same time. Quite a skill, that.

"Is Lord Abernathy in this morning?"

"If you'd care to wait in the foyer, I shall inquire."

Ah. Stuck into the foyer again. With a short nod

Bram entered, leaning back against the interior wall and folding his arms across his chest. Leaving him to stand there was fairly presumptuous of a family about to unite themselves with a dog like Cosgrove. But perhaps after this, barring his arrest for theft, of course, he would be invited into a room with a chair.

"What is it you want?" Abernathy asked, emerging from his office, the butler on his heels.

"Just a word with you, my lord."

"I'm quite busy this morning. Perhaps you could leave your calling card and return tomorrow."

Bram rolled his shoulders and stepped forward. "I think you'll want to hear this."

Scowling, the earl moved aside to allow Bram into his office. "Make it quick, will you? I'm on my way to Parliament."

"Certainly. The door, if you please."

Once Abernathy closed it, Bram pulled the satchel off his shoulder. Then he dumped the contents onto the earl's desk. "That's fourteen thousand pounds," he said. "Cosgrove will more than likely demand twelve thousand, but you'll be able to meet whatever he asks for."

The earl stared at the money. "I don't understand."

"What's to understand? Pay off Cosgrove, and distance your family from his influence."

"And be indebted to you instead? I fail to see how this improves anything. Rose's marriage will erase a debt. This"—and he gestured at the mound of money—"only burdens me to a different devil."

Whatever had happened to the old adage of not looking a gift horse in the mouth? Much less throwing shit at him? "It's not a loan. It's a gift."

"A gift."

"Yes."

"To what purpose?"

"Oh, for God's sake." Not waiting for an invitation he wasn't likely to receive anyway, Bram went to the liquor tantalus and poured himself a glass of port. "Consider it to be my way of easing my own conscience. I did help to lead your son astray, so I must be partly responsible for his debts."

"Yes, but what do you want from me in return?"

Your daughter. The same deal that Cosgrove negotiated would be nice. "Nothing."

"No one gives a gift of this magnitude without expecting something in return. Especially not someone like you."

Bram narrowed his eyes, considering. He disliked the notion of putting all his cards on the table, as it were, without first knowing what they were. But if Abernathy decided that selling off Rosamund was easier than a possible entanglement with him, this would all be for nothing. He'd have to put together a midnight run to Gretna Green, after all. "Very well. I have one request in exchange for the gift of the money."

"I knew it. Your father always said you couldn't be trusted to look out for anything but yourself."

"My lord, considering what I'm attempting to do, you might wish to keep a tighter rein on your insults." He took a breath. Fighting with his potential future father-in-law wasn't all that wise, either. "All I ask is your permission to court your daughter."

"Rose?"

"Yes, Rosamund." He would stick a billiards cue through his head before he would voluntarily spend time with the chirpy fish woman.

"So you want to steal her out from under Cosgrove, do you? I still see no difference between what you offer and what he does."

"I'm not demanding Rosamund's hand in marriage. I want the chance to see her. Whatever she ultimately decides, whomever she wishes to marry—or not—the money is yours. The debt is erased. *That* is the difference."

"What if I say no to your . . . courting of Rose?"

"The money is still yours, as long as you give it to Cosgrove and remove your daughter from the bargaining table." He swallowed half his glass. "And if you accept, you won't have to dine with Cosgrove, stand with him at soirees, or holiday with him about. You won't have to suffer the humiliation of seeing him publicly flaunt his mistresses in front of your daughter, and no one will know that you sold her to cover a gambling debt."

"No one knows that now."

"They will, if you don't agree to free your daughter from this mess. I'll see to it. I am doing a good deed, but I never claimed to be a good man."

Finally Abernathy sagged into a chair, as though all the air and pomposity had fled his body. That was it, Bram realized. Care and concern for his daughter wouldn't sway him, but pride and fear of embarrassment would. Hm. Perhaps Rosamund had an even worse father than he did, after all. It was a rather stunning idea.

"Why don't you present him with the money your-self?" the earl finally asked, the last blustering of a defeated man.

"He wouldn't accept it from me. We're not on speak-ing terms. And I don't owe him the blunt. You do."

"Very well. But I won't be grateful to you or thank you, because I know you've arranged this to gain yourself something. The details can't elude me for-ever."

"All I'm attempting to gain is a chance at salva-tion." Bram set the glass aside. "Be certain Cosgrove withdraws the betrothal announcement from the newspapers."

Abernathy bristled a little at the order, but with an-other look at the money on his desk, he subsided. That was that, then.

"Good day, my lord."

Bram left the room, shutting the door quietly behind him. Only then did he close his eyes to send up a quick prayer of thanks to whoever might be listening. He hadn't won the lady, he was now eight thousand quid in debt to his brother, and he'd made an enemy of a very dangerous man. And he still felt like shouting and dancing a jig.

The hair on his arms lifted, and he opened his eyes again to see Rosamund looking down at him from the stair landing. He put a finger to his lips, indicating the office behind him. All he needed was for Abernathy to overhear them and think there was indeed a conspiracy afoot.

With a nod she descended to the second step. A glance at the foyer showed the butler to be elsewhere. Bram reached up, putting a hand at the nape of her neck, and drew her face down to kiss her. Soft as a sigh, it sank into his soul.

"Thank you," she whispered, lifting her head to look down at him, one hand touching his cheek.

"You are exceedingly welcome."

"And now we need to rescue you."

Bram broke away from her. "I'll deal with it."

"But you've helped me. I want to return the gesture."

"*You* were an innocent party in this," he whispered, clenching his hands to keep from pulling her over the railing and into his arms. Self-discipline. He'd never been much good at it, and he'd chosen the devil of a time to attempt to master it. "I am not innocent. I want—I want to declare myself to you, and in front of everyone. But if I need to pay for some of my sins, I'll do it without dragging you down with me."

"There's a chance Cosgrove was bluffing about having proof, don't you think? That he was only trying to force your hand?"

With a half grin, Bram rose up and kissed her again, openmouthed. "You are becoming quite the expert with the wagering terminology. And yes, he could be bluffing. I suppose we'll find that out after your father calls on him." He glanced over to see the butler returning to his post. "I need to leave."

She reached out to grab his sleeve. "Are you attending the Clement soiree tonight?" she asked.

Smiling, he backed toward the front door. "I am now."

"Any sign of him?" Sullivan asked, reining in his big black, Achilles, brother to Bram's Titan.

Phin shook his head. "You know he's dodging us on purpose."

"And unfortunately he knows London better than you and I combined."

In the middle of Haymarket Street they were fairly damned obvious, but clearly the plan of scouting places Bram was otherwise unlikely to be wasn't working. Uttering a curse, Sullivan swung Achilles in a tight circle.

"The least likely place I can imagine him going is to Johns House," Phineas said after a moment, scowling.

"Levonzy? Not even if it snowed in Hades." Sullivan glanced around them again. "Let's give it a try then, shall we?"

"You lead. I don't even know the damned address."

Bram sat on a barrel behind the duke's stable. Munching on a peach, he paged through the Roman history book he'd borrowed from August earlier in the day. It had cost him five pounds, but the grooms and stable boys had sworn not to reveal his location to anyone, least of all Levonzy. And Titan seemed to be enjoying grazing on the grass in the shade.

Hiding from friends probably wasn't very heroic, but it was the surest way he could think of to keep them out of this muddle. It was amazing the way one good deed had so irrevocably knocked his entire way of thinking, his entire life, on its arse. Now he wanted everyone to be safe and happy—and the best way to see to that seemed to be by keeping away from them.

"You owe me a quid," Phin's voice came from the corner of the stable.

"He's actually not inside the house," Sullivan's low drawl returned, "so I'm not certain you've won the wager."

Rolling his eyes, Bram snapped his book closed. "You two louts are more clever than I expected," he grunted, taking another bite of peach. "Huzzah, you've found me. Now go away."

"We've been to see Lord Haithe," Sullivan continued, dragging another barrel over and taking a seat on it. "Have you given the blunt to Abernathy yet?"

"August is a damned wag. Yes. I gave the money to Abernathy."

"And?"

"And what?"

Phin leaned against the tree trunk opposite. "Nice weather we're having. A good day for a duke's son to be arrested as a burglar, don't you think, Sullivan?"

"No, the wind's a bit too easterly," Sullivan took up. "A better day for fleeing to Scotland, say, until this mess gets cleaned up."

"Hm. You may be right. What do you think, Bram?"

"I think I'm attending the Clement soiree tonight and dancing with Lady Rosamund Davies. You can go holiday wherever you like."

"So you're not going to attempt to find a way around this?" Sullivan picked up a stone and hurled it toward the garden. "You know damned well you didn't keep anything you took. It more than likely went for a better cause than it ever would have been used for, otherwise."

"That's not the point."

"Then what is the bloody point?" Phin snapped.

"The bloody point, Phin, is that I want to clean my slate. I'm finished with being a fool for no damned good reason. I don't want to evade this. I want to face it head-on. And the only reason I'm in hiding at the moment, other than to avoid you two, is because I want one more chance to see, to dance with, Rosamund before Bow Street comes to collect me. There. I'm sentimental and maudlin, now. Hardly worth the effort of rescuing."

"And of course if you *are* arrested, you won't have to risk proposing and being turned down a second time. One last dance and a romantic, cowardly farewell."

Bram pushed to his feet. "What would you have me do then, Sullivan?" he snarled. "Deny that I've done anything wrong? Blame it on someone else? I've been a scoundrel. I only see one way to make amends for that."

"That's well and good and noble, I suppose," Sullivan shot right back at him, "but it also leaves Cosgrove free, and no one to look after your Lady Rose."

"*You* two will look after Lady Rose." Bram stalked over to Titan, slid the bit back into the black's mouth, and swung into the saddle. "Do yourselves a favor. Stay home tonight."

Sullivan and Phin exchanged a glance as Bram exited the property. "So we're to protect Lady Rose from now on," Sullivan muttered.

With a grim smile, Phin shook his head. "That's not what he said. He said we're to look after her. Which I would take to mean we're to see that she's happy."

"Ah. Well, we'd best take care of that, then."

Rose held her breath until her father and James returned to the house, the promissory notes her brother had signed over to Cosgrove back in their custody. With a puff of smoke from the morning room fireplace, her obligation to the Marquis of Cosgrove ended. For a long moment she perched on the couch, intense relief pressing at her. Just as quickly, too soon for any real elation, reality crashed back down around her shoulders. She sat there, keeping her expression cool and pleased for the benefit of her family. At this moment no one else could know what had dawned on her this morning—that her monthlies were a bit overdue.

She pushed that thought away. Going from one thing she couldn't control to another, was too much. Later she could decide whether she was mistaken, whether this could be another chance for a changed life or the tombstone to decorate the old one.

"I have to say," her mother commented, as they watched the papers burn, "though it would have been lovely to see you as a marchioness, Rose, Lord Cosgrove's reputation left a great deal to be desired."

"It did, indeed," her father agreed. "There's a bit of madness to that fellow, and I sincerely hope our paths do not cross again." He sent a pointed look at James.

"Yes, Father," the young viscount said, his demeanor uncharacteristically subdued.

That didn't bode well. Her sense of impending trouble deepened. "James, would you assist me with retrieving a book from the top shelf in the library?"

"Of course."

"Rose, you are unattached again," Lady Abernathy pointed out. "Gaining a reputation as a bluestocking will not help your prospects."

"Yes, Mama." Clearly she was never going to be appreciated as anything but exchangeable goods. She wanted to leave them to their own self-concerned lives, and there they were, back to the way everything had been before Cosgrove. Except for her, that was. She had changed. Irrevocably.

As soon as she and James were alone in the library, she grabbed his arm. "Tell me what happened. Everything that happened."

He shrugged her off. "It was just business. You don't need to hear that boring drivel."

"James Elliot Davies, you tell me—"

"Devil a bit, Rose. King was surprised. Startled. Like we'd caught him with his trousers down. I ain't ever seen him caught off balance before. And he wasn't happy. At all."

"But you got back the notes. He accepted payment."

Her brother took a deep breath. "He pushed for information, and Father told him we were gifted with the funds to repay my debt. Cosgrove asked if it was Bram. He said Bram had played a good hand, but he would lose the game. It was so . . . odd. All this time I thought he was at the top of the pole, with the rest of us ranged below him. But now I ain't, I'm not, so certain it's not Bram looking down at the rabble—except that he had nothing to gain by giving us the blunt." He faced her squarely. "Did he?"

"Don't you dare, James. You caused this mess. Simply because Bram and I like one another doesn't mean he had anything but altruism in his heart."

James gave a short laugh. "You just used 'like,' 'Bram Johns,' and 'altruism' in the same sentence."

Rose smiled reluctantly. "I will concede that it's an

unlikely combination. But he has some things at risk, too. More than you realize."

"A few weeks ago you wanted to punch him in the nose."

"A few weeks ago I was only acquainted with the tales you told about him." Her smile fading, she gazed at her younger brother. "Both you and I have been given a second chance, James. Tell me truthfully— are you going to gallop back to Cosgrove's side now and lose shocking amounts of money to him all over again?"

He shook his head. "No. I saw a side of King this morning that . . . well, frankly it repulsed me. And frightened me a bit, too." James grimaced. "If Bram don't—doesn't—mind me hanging about him, I'd like to learn some of his skills, though."

Oh, splendid. "What skills would those be? More gaming?" He'd merely shifted his idolatry from one rake to another. If James had learned anything from this mess, he seemed to be keeping it to himself, except that his grammar was improving.

"No. Well, perhaps a bit. But mainly the way he knows things, and how he walks into a room and everybody notices."

Hopefully that wouldn't include losing money, then. And if James wanted to emulate anyone, she much preferred that it be the Bram she'd come to know over the past few weeks. If he had the chance to do so.

Her chest constricted. If Cosgrove had been as angry this afternoon as James claimed, public accusations could be the least of Bram's worries. Oh, why hadn't she made a greater attempt to talk him into fleeing with her? The thought of not seeing him, of being unable to chat with him and touch him and kiss him—it hurt so much that her mind kept turning away from it. Especially now, when the connection between them had literally become a tangible presence. Or it could, it would, in eight months or so.

"Rose?"

She shook herself. "What is it?"

"Father said that Bram means to call on you. I don't want to be blamed for getting you into another mess, so do you want me to warn him away?"

It would be like trying to separate a moth and candlelight. "No. That's not necessary."

"Very well. Now did you actually want a book lifted down, or may I go?"

"Go." She took his arm again as he walked by her. "There is one thing you could do for me," she continued in a lower voice.

"I'm not going to murder anyone for you."

"What? Oh, good heavens no. Did Papa have any money left after he repaid the marquis?"

"About fifteen hundred pounds. Why?"

Rose hesitated. James wasn't precisely her first choice of confidant. At the moment, though, she didn't seem to have much choice. And technically the money belonged to Bram, anyway. "Bram and I may need to flee London."

"Beg pardon?"

"Oh, dear." She took a deep breath. "Bram is the Black Cat, James. He's stopped his burglaries, but Cosgrove knows. If he does as he threatened and makes his accusations in public, Bram will be arrested."

Her brother stared at her. "Bram's the Black Cat?"

"Yes."

"But he wagered ten quid it was the Duke of Storey. It's on the book at White's." James frowned. "Come to think of it, Storey only has one leg, and he's eighty years old. Bram had to know he wouldn't win the wager."

"This isn't about a wager, James. Please pay attention. Is there any way you can find out where Papa put that money? If we have to leave Town, we'll need some ready cash."

"If *he's* accused, why are *you* leaving?"

"Because . . . because as I said, I've become quite fond of Bram. Exceedingly fond."

"I'm fond of him, too, but that doesn't mean I'd let myself be ruined because of something he did."

"He became involved in this because of me. That makes this partly my burden to bear."

The look her brother sent her was impossible to decipher, but after a moment he nodded. "Father's not likely to trust me enough to tell me where any blunt is, but he's only got three hiding places here. The man has no imagination. Give me a couple of hours to get around him, and I'll let you know."

"Thank you, James." She leaned up and kissed him on the cheek.

"Don't thank me yet," he grumbled. "When Father realizes what's happened, I'm likely going to be running close behind you."

The afternoon remained quiet, and though Rose jumped each time the front door opened, no word arrived about either Bram's thefts or his arrest. She began to hope that Cosgrove *had* been bluffing, and that he didn't have any proof of Bram's activities after all. If that aggravatingly handsome, charming, dark-haired man would bother to simply stop by the house and inform her one way or the other, perhaps she could stop pacing and finish her blasted handkerchief embroidery.

For heaven's sake. If she'd been a man, she would have ridden out to find him. And then she would punch him in the nose, not because she disliked him, but because she was so blasted worried she couldn't even think straight.

Chapter 20 _____

By eight o'clock in the evening there was still no sign of Bram, and no word that he'd been taken anywhere against his will. Rose dressed in a new gown, a rich burnished copper creation with a low, swooping neckline and a shimmer that brought out the red highlights in her hair.

"You look very nice, my dear," her father said, as she descended the staircase.

"Thank you," she returned, giving a shallow curtsy.

"Stay close by tonight if you can," the earl continued, dropping his tone. "We've paid off Cosgrove, but he may approach you anyway. Try to be civil; as far as anyone knows, you are only friendly acquaintances. We want nothing to alter that perception where our fellows are concerned."

For a heartbeat she'd thought him concerned over

her safety and well-being, until she considered that he was only attempting to preserve the facade—that the Davies family had no troubles, past, present, or future. "I've never wanted anything to do with him. I intend to make every effort to avoid him."

"Avoid his friend, too. I have no wish for this family to be caught in the middle of a disagreement between Cosgrove and Bram Johns. It's a damned coil of snakes."

The family *was* the middle of the disagreement. She was, anyway. "You have nothing to worry about where Bram is concerned, Papa," she said aloud. "He and I are friends."

"Tell yourself whatever you like, Rose, but Bram Johns is only a friend to someone who has something he wants. Best guard your virtue, or he'll have you as another of his light-skirts, and I'll have you out from under my roof."

For the space of a heartbeat Rose was tempted to tell him that she'd lost her virtue several times over to Bram, that she was likely carrying his child, and that it had been her idea to begin with. Thankfully her mother and James appeared before she could seriously contemplate that foolishness.

It was more likely, anyway, that having lost this game, Cosgrove would go on to torment someone else. She would once again be the chit no one noticed, doing her best to keep her silly family from looking foolish and wondering whether that would be the sum total of her existence—except for that lingering, growing hope that one man would be looking directly at her. A warm tremor ran down her spine.

"I hope it's not too crowded tonight," her mother was already complaining. "You know how I hate a crush."

"You love a crush, my dear."

Rose sighed. It was true that she had very little respect remaining for either of her parents, but it was also true that they'd done nothing more or less than what custom and the law dictated. She was wise enough never to expect anything more of them. Bram, however, had gone well beyond rule and custom to help her.

And he had more than her loyalty or her friendship or her respect. He had her heart.

He had her heart. She loved him. Rose put out a hand to steady herself against the stair balustrade.

"Rose, are you ill?" James asked, taking her elbow.

"No, no. I just got dizzy for a moment," she stammered.

Oh, goodness. Why had she just realized it? She knew she enjoyed his company, and she certainly enjoyed his attention and his touch. But somewhere in this tangle and in her dawning realization that deep down he was a decent man, a good man, with a dented but very strong moral compass, he'd become . . . indispensable.

"Do you wish to stay in tonight?" her mother asked. "I can't say I would be disappointed to avoid any chance of encountering Cosgrove and his cronies this evening."

"I want to go," she said, too sharply. "We could all stand a bit of celebration tonight, don't you think?"

"Definitely," James seconded, guiding her to the door.

As the coach rolled toward Penn House and the Clement soiree, it was all Rose could do not to sit forward on her seat. She wanted to see him, wanted to know that he was safe. What a change, from being so concerned about her own future to being consumed with him and his well-being. And aside from that, she just wanted to have him gaze at her in that warm, possessive way he had when they kissed.

The street in front of Penn House was solidly blocked with vehicles. They had to stop the coach two full streets away and walk the remainder of the way to the front door. Once inside, there was barely room to move.

"What a crush," her mother exclaimed. "How will they ever make room on the dance floor? I can't even see my hand in front of my face."

"We're opening a second anteroom, my lady," a footman said, offering them selections from a platter of cheeses. "And the second ballroom, if necessary."

"Thank goodness for that," Lady Abernathy returned, fanning at her face. "I suggest you do so at once."

Indeed, several minutes later the crowd seemed to ease a little, and they were able to make their way upstairs into the main ballroom. Rose cast her gaze in every direction, looking for Bram. This wasn't the sort of party he enjoyed, but he had said he would attend. And he had to know she would be worried over him, blast it all.

As she looked about, she couldn't help noticing guests looking back at her. Men, specifically. The moment she had a chance, she glanced at herself in one of the wall mirrors. Nothing hung from her teeth, her gown remained covering all the bits it should have, and no bird or bug had set up residence in her hair. What the devil were they staring at, then?

"Lady Rose."

Her heart stuttered until she realized the voice belonged neither to Bram nor to Cosgrove. She turned around. "Mr. Henning, isn't it?"

The rotund man smiled, sketching an elaborate bow. "Indeed. I was wondering if I might claim a spot on your dance card. There are to be two waltzes, you know."

And she hadn't even procured a dance card. She rarely had enough requests to warrant one. "The first quadrille is available," she decided. She'd seen him dance, and a waltz seemed far too dangerous an enterprise.

"I will be honored." With another bow he straightened, gave an uncertain smile, and wandered off into the crowd.

"I shall have to get a dance card, apparently," she commented.

"I'll fetch you one," James said, and walked off.

She wasn't certain whether he was being belatedly conciliatory for the mess he'd caused, or whether he'd wanted to escape their parents' reach, but he was gone before she could ask him. By the time he returned with a card and a pencil, though, she had three other spots taken. What in the world was going on? At most she danced a cotillion or two with elderly widowers or the chinless sons of the Earl of Banbury.

As she scribbled down her partners' names, the throng to her left stirred. Like the Red Sea parting, space opened up and revealed a black-and-gray-clothed Adonis. Her breath caught as his black gaze swept the room and then found her. From then it didn't waver.

Bram strolled up to her, other guests simply moving aside for him as though they sensed danger, a predator, in their midst.

"Good evening," he said, stopping in front of her. Reaching out, he took both of her hands in his and brought them to his lips.

"Bram," she returned, her voice catching a little. She wanted to throw her arms around him to be certain he was real and he was safe. She wanted to ask whether he'd meant it when he'd said he loved her, and whether he would say it again just so she could hear it.

"Lord Bramwell," her father interjected, making her jump. She'd forgotten anyone else was there.

Bram's eyes narrowed for a moment, and then he released her fingers to shake the earl's proffered hand. "Abernathy. I hope you had a productive day."

"I did indeed. And you have an angry friend."

"He's no friend of mine, but thank you for the warning." Bram inclined his head, then lifted the dance card Rose hadn't even realized he'd taken from her. "Henning?"

"He asked. Everyone's been asking. I have no idea why."

Bram regarded her for a moment. "You don't, do you? You're beautiful, Rosamund. It's just taken this long for the rabble to notice it." He scribbled something down, then handed card and pencil back to her.

Rose looked at the card, her cheeks warming. "You can't take both waltzes."

"Watch me." His mouth curved in a slow, heart-stopping smile. "I don't want you in anyone else's arms," he murmured.

Goodness. As lovely, heavenly, as that sounded, however, it was more than likely meant mainly to distract her from the large measure of trouble that was still dogging them. Him, specifically. "Have you seen . . . him?" she asked, lowering her own voice.

"'Him'?" he repeated. "You're thinking about another man while I'm flirting with you? I'm pierced to the heart."

"Be serious, will you?" She took a step closer, unmindful of the fact that people were probably watching. People always watched Bram. "James said he was practically foaming at the mouth when they took him the money."

"Then we'd best not miss the first waltz." He glanced over his shoulder. "Your quadrille is here."

Drat. "Please, Bram. If you see him—"

"I'll keep him well away from you."

"That is not what I m—"

"I know what you meant." Bram touched her cheek briefly, as though he couldn't not touch her. "I won't be killed or dragged off before I've danced with you." His eyes went cold and serious. "I swear it."

That might have been a bit too vehement, Bram reflected as his Rosamund turned and stepped on the dance floor opposite the clod Francis Henning, but he very rarely swore to things. And when he did, he kept his word. Always.

If Cosgrove knew anything, he would know that the Davies family would be in attendance at the Clement soiree. And he would then easily puzzle out that the man who'd paid off their debt would be there, as well.

He might have stayed away and avoided Cosgrove, but that would have left Rosamund to face the bastard alone. No, this was better. More dangerous for him, but that hardly signified.

Keeping half his attention on Rosamund, he watched the two separate entryways leading into the main ballroom. Thus far Sullivan and Phin were absent, and while he was a bit surprised that they'd listened to him, he was also glad they'd done so. He appreciated their loyalty more than he could ever express aloud, but he didn't know how to make any clearer the fact that they had more important concerns than protecting him from his own short-sighted stupidity.

"Bram?"

"What is it, James?" he asked, keeping his gaze on the flow and ebb of guests into the room.

"I thought you should know," Viscount Lester said, his tone uncharacteristically low and cautious, "Rose has it in her head that if Bow Street should come after you, the two of you will flee London."

Bram frowned. "I wouldn't drag her off to ruin," he muttered back, for the moment ignoring the fact that Lester seemed to know of his nefarious activities. If Rose had chosen to tell him, then she'd had a reason for doing so.

"What bothers me is that she thinks you'd want her with you. If you've been leading my sister down the garden path, or worse, then I want you to know I'll do whatever I can to see you put into gaol."

"I want her with me," Bram grunted, irritated at being dressed down by a pup. "But first I want her safe. I need to see to this mess before I can do anything else."

"And if you're arrested?"

"I'm not fleeing, with or without Rosamund." He frowned. "I don't appreciate explaining this to you, but at least you're finally seeing to your sister's well-being."

"I think I've learned my lesson," the viscount said stiffly.

"Good. I think I've learned mine, as well. And I'm willing to pay for it."

The quadrille ended to general applause, and he walked forward to meet her for their waltz. He *was* willing to pay, after a dance.

"Shall we?" He held out his hand to her.

Rosamund wrapped her gloved fingers around his bare ones. From the look on her face she intended to begin ranting at him again about the chance he was taking by being out in public. If it helped clear any guilt from her conscience he was more than willing to listen to it, but he could think of better ways to spend the few minutes he would have in her company.

The music began, and he slid a hand around her waist as she placed one on his shoulder. Together they swept into the waltz. "You avoided Henning's feet with admirable skill," he drawled.

"Thank you." She took a breath, her body trembling a little beneath his fingers. "I've been thinking."

"About what?"

"About the relatively minor nature of your crimes compared with what they're likely to do to you when they catch you."

"Ah. You're going to serve as my solicitor."

"Don't jest, Bram. Do you truly think your mistake is worth years in gaol or transportation or a hanging?"

"Do you have any idea how much I want to kiss you right now?" he murmured, pulling her a breath closer.

"I will not be distracted."

Of all the conversations they might have had, the question of whether he was worthy of a rescue was not one he would have chosen. "I want you to realize something, Rosamund," he began softly, turning her to the music. "I studied under a monster on and off for more than a decade. And this past year, even when I'd made friends whom I truly value and admire, I went back to him because I was bored. Even that, though, wasn't enough for me, and so I stole from people simply because they called my father friend. As much as I want to be the one who shares your life, I can't do that until I've made some sort of amends for being the . . . the utter scoundrel that I have been."

"You are not like Cosgrove," she returned, her voice shaking.

"I am exactly like Cosgrove. The only difference is that I fell in love with you."

"You are so far apart from him that I can't believe how thick you are not to see it."

"Or you're so good-hearted that you imagine it."

She opened her mouth and then closed it again. "How many other of Cosgrove's pupils have successfully completed their education under his tutelage?" she finally asked.

The question stopped him for a moment. "I don't know."

"Yes, you do. You told us about the one who killed himself. And then there's James, who would have been lost if not for you. Who else is there?"

He thought about it for a moment. "Roger Avelane."

"And where is he?"

"A cemetery somewhere. He bedded the wrong man's

wife. Or he got the blame for it, anyway." As far as he'd been able to tell, the straying cock had belonged to Cosgrove.

"Heavens. That leaves you, Bram. The only one who's seen through Cosgrove and survived him, and has decided to reclaim his own life. That's why he's so angry with you."

"Well, you make me sound quite heroic," he commented, trying to make light of what she'd said, even though it shook him deeply. He'd never viewed his life as being a triumph simply because he'd survived it and parted ways with his mentor. "In a week you'd have me aiding orphans."

"Make fun if you like, but you, my friend, are a good man."

"Now you're pouring the sauce on too thick."

"Bram, don't make me punch you."

He laughed. The idea that this woman could so easily turn his life and his thinking upside down simply stunned him. "I wish I was dramatic enough to ask you to wait for me, my sweet Rose, but neither of us knows how long that will be. All I can do is ask that you find someone who makes you happy."

Tears filled her eyes. "*You* make me happy."

The music crashed to a close. Reluctantly he let her go to join in the applause. Even so, he couldn't stop looking at her.

She thought him a good man. Of course Rosamund meant it as a compliment, but now he felt the absurdly strong urge to prove her right. Stepping out of his life and closing the door behind him to begin anew—men who'd left a trail of destruction behind them as he had didn't get to do that.

And if he'd been content to remain a damned scoundrel, he wouldn't have hesitated to leave his troubles behind and abscond with Rosamund Davies to live a life of lust and sin. *Damnation*. Being bad definitely had some advantages. "I'd best get you back to your parents," he muttered.

As he turned around, he stopped in mid-step. The Marquis of Cosgrove stood just inside the ballroom doorway, his angelic blue eyes focused directly on Bram. Ranged around him, unmistakable in their crimson waistcoats, were a half-dozen Bow Street Runners. He meant to do it tonight, then. In front of everyone.

"Bram," Rosamund whispered, digging her fingers into his forearm.

"I'm sorry," he whispered back, pulling his arm free. "Forgive me." He moved away, leaving her standing.

"You don't need my for—"

"There he is," Cosgrove said in a carrying voice, attracting the attention of the few people at the edges of the room who hadn't noticed the uninvited guests in the doorway.

The largest of the six men stepped forward, a pair of wrist irons in his hands. "Lord Bramwell Lowry Johns," he enunciated, in the too-loud voice of someone who wasn't certain of his welcome and wanted everyone to know he had a legitimate reason to be where he was, "you are under arrest. Please come peaceably and we can be out of here without too much fuss."

Frowning with the effort of keeping himself still when all he wanted to do was begin throwing punches, Bram nodded. At the Runner's gesture he held out his hands. "Go back to your parents, Rosamund," he murmured as the shackles clicked shut. She seemed inclined to stand in the middle of the floor, far too close to him, whatever anyone said.

"What are the charges?" someone from the crowd called. Someone who sounded suspiciously like Phineas Bromley. Damn it all, he'd told them to stay away.

"Lord Bramwell Lowry Johns is accused of being the Black Cat burglar. Now everyone please move aside and let us do our job."

"That's impossible," Sullivan Waring's voice came from another part of the room, unlikely as it was that he would ever attend a Society event. "*I'm* the Black Cat burglar." And then Lord Dunston's illegitimate son stepped forward.

Bram grimaced. For God's sake, Sully had a pregnant wife. "Leave off, Sullivan," he ordered.

"Excuse me, but you're not the Black Cat. I am." Phin moved to the front of the crowd.

"I don't know what you lads are talking about." August emerged onto the cleared dance floor. "*I* am certainly the Black Cat."

Good God.

"Say whatever you like," Cosgrove broke in with his silky voice, "but I have proof. A signed declaration from Father John of St. Michael's Church stating that Bramwell Johns regularly delivered stolen goods there for distribution to the poor."

A deep, cynical laugh sounded from Bram's left. "Bram Johns couldn't step through the doors of a church without being struck by lightning." The Duke of Levonzy came forward. "I'm as likely to be the Black Cat as he is."

Murmured agreement and a scattering of laughter sounded around the room. Bram, though, couldn't take his eyes off the duke. The man hadn't precisely lied for him, but he had definitely dissembled. Levonzy. For him.

"I'm the Black Cat!" James Davies appeared, taking Rosamund's hand, but not attempting to lead her away.

Abernathy walked onto the dance floor, as well. "We're both the Black Cat. We work together."

A heartbeat later, amid a chorus of male voices proclaiming themselves the Black Cat, he heard another round of declarations from the direction of the refreshment table, led by Lord Darshear and his older son, Phillip—Sullivan's in-laws.

Viscount Bromley rolled forward in his wheeled chair. "You seem to have a problem, sir," he stated to the lead Runner, "because *I* am the Black Cat."

"But m'lord, you're crippled."

"Nevertheless, I am the Black Cat. And given these confessions, I suggest you either arrest half the House of Lords or release Lord Bramwell." He turned his attention to Cosgrove. "And you, my lord, had best find a better way to vent your jealousies."

Clearly realizing he was both outnumbered and outranked, the Runner unlocked the shackles and stepped back. "I beg your pardon, my lord. We didn't realize this was a matter of personal animosity."

Bram rubbed his wrists, more to be certain he was actually free than because the shackles had hurt. "You can't be faulted for doing your duty, sir," he replied. "After all, I suppose I'm as likely as anyone else to be the Black Cat. And perhaps knowing how many men claim his identity will discourage him from continuing his thefts. I would say you've done an admirable job tonight."

The man bowed, clearly relieved that he and his men were being allowed to leave without suffering any repercussions. "Thank you, my lord. Good evening." Sending a glare at Cosgrove, he and his men left the ballroom.

King gazed for a moment between Bram and Rosamund, his expression unreadable and his face pale, before he turned on his heel and followed the Runners out the door.

Chapter 21 _____

In the ensuing broil of laughter and self-congratulations from the oh-so-clever members of the *ton* who joined the fun of claiming to be the Black Cat because everyone else was doing it, Rose kept her attention on Bram.

He looked dazed, as though he couldn't quite fathom what had just happened. She wasn't so certain, either, but tonight she meant to send up a quick prayer for everyone who'd stepped in to help. Every one of them, whether they'd done it as a jest or to preserve their own reputations or not.

"Do you need a seat?" Phineas Bromley asked, as the group of Bram's friends made their way outside into the small garden.

"I need a whiskey," Bram growled. "You risked too damned much."

"For a minute I thought you were going to insist on being arrested, regardless of all evidence to the contrary." From somewhere Sullivan Waring produced a glass and handed it over.

"I might be attempting a new path, but I'm not an idiot, either," Bram returned, humor finally touching his voice.

"That should shut up Cosgrove, at least," James chortled, apparently ecstatic to be included in such a formerly notorious group of gentlemen.

Bram sent him a glance, but didn't say anything. The warm flutter in Rose's stomach cooled a little. Did he think Cosgrove remained a threat? As she considered what she knew of the marquis, a public humiliation had likely done nothing but make him more determined to win this game, as he termed it. *Oh, dear.*

"How did you get to Levonzy?" Bram asked, lowering his voice despite the fact that music for the next cotillion had already begun inside. In fact, the three couples and James seemed to be the only ones out of doors. Her cheeks warmed. She was part of a couple, at least for the moment—until Bram thought up some other reason he wouldn't be good for her.

"We didn't," Sullivan answered. "We spoke to August, and I went to Darshear and Phillip."

"I figured out what you were doing, and thought I'd best step in," James put in again.

"Which is what we hoped might happen," Phineas took up. "Didn't expect Levonzy, though. Or Abernathy."

Rose nodded. "I was standing beside Bram. It would have looked poorly for our family if he'd been arrested then."

"Which is why you were supposed to leave," Bram murmured, reaching over for her hand and pulling her closer. "You clearly have no sense of self-preservation." He twined his fingers with hers, looking down at their joined hands as if they fascinated him.

"I believe the mighty have fallen," Sullivan said quietly, amusement in his deep voice.

"You have no idea," Bram returned, shaking himself to glance at his friend. "Thank you. Both of you."

Sullivan shrugged. "You've helped us." He put his arm around Tibby's waist. "Despite what you seem to think, Bramwell, there are people about who like you."

"Hm." Bram gave him a short nod before returning his gaze to Rosamund. "I would like to call on you in the morning, if I could. Would you be amenable to that?"

Actually, she would have preferred a declaration of love and undying devotion in the middle of the Penn House garden, but evidently he had other ideas. "Yes, I would be."

"Good. I have one thing to see to, first, and it might take me a few hours. I will be there by noon. I promise."

What that thing was, she had no idea, but she'd seen the look Bram and Cosgrove had exchanged right before the marquis had left the room. "Don't do something that will set you down the wrong path again," she murmured.

His eyes narrowed. "There are things I'm willing to risk, and there are things I'm not willing to risk. You are one of the latter."

She swallowed. "That's very nice, but I hope you will

keep in mind that *you* are one of the things *I'm* not willing to risk." Rose put a hand on his shoulder and leaned up to kiss him on the cheek. She would have preferred his mouth, but they did have company. For a moment she debated taking him aside to tell him of her suspicions about her own condition, but he didn't need those additional complications tonight, and she didn't want him making the wrong decisions for the wrong reasons. For both their sakes that bit of information could wait until tomorrow. "I will expect you by noon."

"Need any company for this outing, then?" Sullivan asked. "You know how much I enjoy Society gatherings."

Bram shook his head. "You've done enough. More than enough. And this is something I need to see to on my own, anyway." He wrapped Rose's hand around his forearm. "I do think I can manage one more dance first, however."

Worried or not, she had to admit that Bram danced magnificently. "I would be agreeable to that." She would more than likely spend the rest of the night awake and pacing and conjuring all types of disasters, anyway. Anything that could keep Bram from calling on her tomorrow—up to and including his own poor opinion of himself.

Bram stretched, rolling his shoulders. This was far from the first time he'd stayed awake past dawn, but he couldn't ever recall doing so from the roof of someone's home. Particularly not from the rooftop of the house belonging to the family of the woman he loved.

With the sun rising, the servants down below would be stirring, the house no longer asleep and unguarded.

Standing to brush off his trousers, Bram made his way to the edge of the roof and clambered over the side to descend using the drainpipe.

At Rosamund's window, he paused. Tempted as he was to call on her before the time he'd selected, though, he needed to move quickly now. Cosgrove had likely spent the night stewing, nursing the wounds to his pride and plotting his revenge. Since that revenge was likely to include Rosamund, the marquis needed to be stopped. Permanently.

Once on the ground he made his way out to the street and hired a hack to return him to Lowry House. Bram ordered Titan saddled and the morning paper brought to him before he ran upstairs to change.

"Make it quick, Mostin," he ordered his valet as he shrugged out of last night's clothes.

"But you want to look presentable, my lord, do you not?"

"Presentable, yes. Perfection isn't required."

"My lord?" Hibble knocked at his door.

"Enter."

The butler stepped inside, the *London Times* in his hands. "I haven't had a chance yet to iron it for you, my lord. And you have a letter, from Mr. Waring, I believe."

"That's fine." He dumped Sullivan's missive into a pocket. "No one called last night?"

"No. We placed a watch as you requested, but nothing stirred."

"Good. If anyone comes by this morning, I'm not in. If it should be Cosgrove, tell him I'm aware of his . . . ire, and am acting accordingly."

"My lord?"

Bram stomped into his boots, settling for a single knot to his cravat despite his valet's hand wringing. "And if he tries to get past you, shoot him."

"I . . . Yes, my lord."

Taking the newspaper, Bram perused it quickly. There it was, on the top of the Society page. Thank God for wags. Swiftly he pulled out a paper and dipped a pen to write out what was probably the most important bit of literature he'd ever attempted. Then, tearing out the newspaper article, he folded and stuffed it and his note into a pocket as he tromped down the stairs. "See to things, Hibble," he said, leaving the house again to collect Titan.

Galloping along the streets of Mayfair was both frowned upon and difficult to manage, but he didn't much care about the former, and the latter problem at least kept his mind occupied. Finally he turned up Winsley Street to one of the smaller, older mansions at the outskirts of Mayfair. Tying Titan off, he hurried up the front steps and rapped on the door.

After a moment he heard shuffling and grumbling, and the door opened. An ancient-looking butler still in his nightshirt and a robe blinked at him. "May I help you?"

Bram dug into his pocket for a calling card. "I'm here to see Mr. Wyatt. Is he in?"

"Mr. Wyatt is still to bed, my lord," the butler returned, looking down at the card and straightening a little. "It's barely seven o'clock."

"Yes, I know. This is urgent, though. Might I wait for him?"

"I . . . Yes. Please, come inside. There's a fire going in the morning room."

Finally, an invitation into a room with a chair. Things were definitely looking up, and in more ways than one. Of course this morning he was too restless to sit, but at least he might have if he'd wished to.

He'd memorized the square footage of the room before the door opened again to reveal a man a year or two younger than himself, with light brown hair and bespectacled gray eyes. "Lord Bramwell Johns?"

"Yes. You're Thomas Wyatt."

"I am. What's so urgent that you had to call on me at this hour?"

"I don't mean to alarm you, but several things have come to my attention, and I think it's time they were dealt with. Might we sit down?"

The young man gestured at the chairs on either side of the fire. "Of course."

"As you may know, I am a close acquaintance of your cousin."

Wyatt's expression hardened a little. "Yes. I'm aware of that."

Bram tilted his head. "I was given the impression that your relationship is not a close one. That would be correct, I assume?"

"Yes. What's this about, my lord?"

"I don't think there's an easy way to say this, so I'll just come out with it." Bram paused for effect. "I believe your cousin to be mad."

The young man's brows drew together. "Kingston Gore is mad. Are you serious?"

"I am. A few weeks ago he began a 'game,' as he calls it, which would have culminated with the kidnapping of a young woman of good birth for the purposes of torture and ruination."

"I . . . My God, do you have proof of this?"

"I do. He attempted to blackmail her family into handing her over. Luckily we were able to stop him. And then last night—well, have you seen the newspaper this morning?"

"No. My wife and I were still to bed when you—"

"Yes, of course." As he'd expected. Bram dug into his pocket for the article and handed it over. "You need to take a look at this."

Thomas Wyatt read through it, disbelief and—unless Bram was greatly mistaken—an odd satisfaction crossed his thin face. "He accused you of being a burglar."

"In front of half the *ton*, and after bringing a half-dozen Bow Street Runners into his delusion." Bram sat forward. "You know he drinks absinthe."

"I'd heard that."

"He drinks it nightly. Never before sunset, but every night. He claims it will make him immortal."

"Again, you have proof of this?"

Cosgrove had enough enemies that he could think of a dozen men who would agree they'd heard him say that. And so he willingly broke that ninth commandment, the false evidence one. "Yes. And there's one more thing."

"What might that be?"

"The lady he attempted to abduct is about to become my fiancée. I believe once he hears that she and I are to be married, he will react violently."

"My God."

Nodding solemnly, Bram settled back again. "If I'm not mistaken, you have your own worries about your cousin's sanity."

"Yes. Yes, I do. His treatment of me and my family has bordered on sadistic."

"He's mentioned to me that he wagers with your income each month, and only gives it to you if he wins."

"I'm painfully aware of that."

"Given that Lord Hawthorne, one of the patrons of a certain mental facility, was in attendance at the Clement soiree last night, I would imagine you have grounds to see your cousin committed."

Wyatt stared at him. "At Bedlam?"

"Yes, at Bedlam. Bethlem Royal Hospital. For his own safety, your safety, and the safety of myself, my fiancée, her family, and anyone else he imagines to have wronged him."

Slowly the young man stood, walking over to the fireplace. "You think this . . . commitment should be done immediately, do you not?"

"I believe it should be done before he has a chance to injure someone. They do say that absinthe corrodes the brain."

"I'm his heir, you know, since he hasn't married or borne any children."

"I believe the absinthe renders him sterile." It sounded as though it should, anyway. And Bram wouldn't have been surprised by that fact.

"Given your close friendship and your long acquaintance, you would attest to the fact that the Marquis of Cosgrove is unfit to maintain his position. Is this correct?"

Bram pulled another piece of paper from his pocket. "I've already put it in writing."

Reading through it, Wyatt stared into the fire for a long moment. "He's an evil man, you know."

"I'm aware of that. I've witnessed it." As for his own activities, this was about survival. And he'd survived. And he'd chosen to become a better man. Cosgrove would only grow into a worse one, if given the chance.

"I wouldn't wish Bedlam on anyone, but I have two young children to think of. Frankly, having him put somewhere where he can't hurt anyone else would be a relief."

"I agree."

Thomas faced him again. "You wouldn't happen to know Lord Hawthorne's address, would you?"

"I'll accompany you there, if you wish."

"Give me a few minutes to dress and inform my wife."

As Bram had anticipated, Hawthorne was another of the many men who'd grown tired of the machinations of the Marquis of Cosgrove, as were the additional witnesses he'd decided on. By ten o'clock they had a warrant ordering the marquis delivered to Bedlam.

"You'd best not be with us, my lord," Mr. Wyatt said as they approached Gore House. "We don't want a fight if we can avoid one, and you are very likely to set him off."

"As you wish. Best of luck, Mr. Wyatt."

Damnation. He wanted to be there, to see the look on Kingston's face when they came to cart him away. It made sense, though, damn it all, considering that the purpose of all this was to protect Rosamund's future, whatever she decided about him.

Being the cynic that he was, though, he did want to make certain Cosgrove's removal actually happened. He waited, positioning himself down the street close enough to see and hear but hopefully to be unseen, himself. Five minutes after Wyatt and his fellows entered Gore House he heard arguing and yelling and glass breaking. With a frown he urged Titan a little closer. If Cosgrove escaped, he would be out for blood.

The sounds became more muffled and then subsided. A few minutes after that, a half-dozen men emerged from Gore House, Wyatt at their front and Lord Hawthorne behind. In the middle and securely bound, a gag across his mouth, was Cosgrove.

He fought, but they pushed him to the waiting coach. As they hoisted him up, he sent a frantic glance around him—and saw Bram.

Bram met his gaze, resisting the urge to smirk or salute or wave. After all, he'd just condemned a man to a fate worse than death. Given that he knew Cosgrove probably better than any man alive he couldn't regret it, but neither could he rejoice. If not for meeting Rosamund, that might one day have been his own family getting rid of *him*.

Once the coach rolled out of sight, he drew in the reins and sent Titan to Davies House. He checked his pocket watch as he topped the steps. Five minutes of noon. Apparently he'd become prompt as well as benevolent.

"If you'll wait in the foyer, my lord," the butler said.

Oh, damn. Back to that again. "Very well."

While he kicked his heels and waited to see whether Rosamund had come to her senses and changed her mind about him, he reached into his pocket for Sullivan's letter. The former soldier in him found it rather amusing that out of everything he'd done over the past weeks, this moment of this morning was the one that terrified him.

"Don't be foolish simply because you're grateful to him," Rose's father said. "If he even makes an appearance."

"Isn't that why we're all hiding in the library?" Rose returned. "Because you think he *will* make an appearance?"

"Tell her what you told me, Lewis. About his prospects." Lady Abernathy returned to her embroidery.

"Levonzy cut him off four months ago. Unless he makes his living from wagering, he'll be destitute by the end of the year."

"Especially since he gave you eight thousand pounds!" Rose retorted. What hypocrisy. So Cosgrove had been acceptable despite his monstrous behavior simply because he had wealth. And a title, of course.

"The fact remains, he has a terrible reputation, no hope of inheriting a title or a fortune, and his one source of income has been removed."

Elbon knocked at the door and leaned in. "My lord, you wished to be informed when Lord Bramwell Johns arrived. He is here."

Rose's heart skittered. He'd come. And on time. The craving to see him had been growing in her since they'd parted company at the soiree last night. Now, knowing he was just downstairs, all she wanted to do was flee the room and go to him.

"Thank you, Elbon. That will be all."

With a nod, the butler vanished again. Lord Abernathy looked from her to his wife. "I'll get rid of him for you, Rose. You needn't do it yourself."

"I don't want to get rid of him, Papa. Haven't you listened to me at all?"

"I don't listen to nonsense."

Rose clenched her jaw. "I—"

Taking a deep breath, James stood from his seat on the windowsill. "Go down to see him, Rose," he said. "As you said before, you've been given a second chance. Take it."

With a swift smile, grateful to have even an unlikely ally, Rose pulled open the door and hurried down the hallway to the main staircase. Bram stood in the foyer, a piece of paper in his hands and an absorbed look on his face. She paused on the landing just to look at him.

Today he wore gray and tan. The only black thing on his person, other than his eyes and hair, were his polished Hessian boots. He looked so handsome. And he thought her beautiful.

"You know I can see you up there," he drawled after a moment, facing her.

"I didn't wish to interrupt your reading."

"Ah. Thank you, then. Now come down here, if you please." With that, he backed into the morning room.

As soon as she crossed the threshold he was on her, pressing her back against the wall with the force of his kisses. She surrendered to the sensation, opening her mouth to him, moaning as he stroked his hands down to her hips, pulling her against his lean, hard body.

"That's better," he murmured after a very long time, leaning his forehead against hers.

Rose swooped in for another kiss. "I think you should marry me," she whispered, sliding her hands into his hair.

He froze, then lifted his face up a few inches to look down at her. "I was going to do that, you know."

"I wasn't certain. You seem to have a very bad opinion of yourself, which I don't share."

"Mm hm. First I need to confess something."

A slight chill went down her spine. "Confess what?"

"I did one last bad deed this morning."

"You didn't burgle someone else's house, did you?"

With a far more solemn expression than she wanted to see on his face, he shook his head. "No. I went to see Cosgrove's cousin. His heir presumptive."

"Oh. Why?"

"To convince him that the absinthe had made King mad, and that he needed to be carted off to Bedlam. I seem to have broken another commandment."

Oh, heavens. She studied his expression for a moment, half expecting him to wink or to confess that he was just making a jest. Instead he sighed.

"He began this game, and I finished it. And we both know that while he was a monster, he wasn't mad. But he'll have a difficult time convincing anyone of that now. Ever."

"You mean they've already taken him away?"

"Yes. If he could have been reasoned with, I wouldn't have gone to that extreme. But I've known him for better than ten years, and I've seen him leave death and sorrow in his wake. I couldn't risk that. Not now." He ran a finger along her cheek. "I wanted you to know before we proceeded." He cleared his throat. "Now that you know, should we proceed?"

Oh, heavens, he was nervous. And as awful as Cosgrove's fate might be, she couldn't help believing that he deserved every minute of it. For a brief moment she considered how lucky both she and James and the rest of her family had been that Bram had chosen to take their side in this. As caring as he'd been toward her, she never, ever, would have wanted him as an enemy. The marquis should have realized that, as well.

"Rosamund, you're going to give me an apoplexy."

She shook herself. "Yes, that would be acceptable."

He took her hands, guiding her over to a chair. She seated herself, and then, her fingers still clasped in his, he sank to his knees. "The letter I was just reading changed what I was going to say to you," he said quietly, his lips curving. "I was going to say that I would make amends to my father and do my utmost to be a good son so that he would reinstate me and resume giving me my monthly stipend."

"You're not planning on taking that path now, I presume?"

"No. Sullivan has in his considerable wisdom decided to leave London again. He doesn't like Town very much, as you may have gathered."

"Yes, I had that feeling."

"Well, with the way his reputation and his business have been growing, he's offered me the task of arranging his London showings and sales. He's actually offered me a partnership in his business. Since I don't wish to drag him into ruin, I will very likely attempt to do a fine job at it. How does that sound to you?"

Rose chuckled. She couldn't help it. "I think it sounds wonderful."

"Good. Because I'm finding that I rely on you to be my conscience—at least until my own grows past the infant stage."

If he didn't have hold of her hands, she would have hugged him. "Your conscience is a beautiful thing as it is," she said, her voice breaking a little. "And if I haven't said so already, I love you. So much that I wouldn't care if you decided we should be pirates and roam the seven seas."

Bram lifted an eyebrow. "Truly? Because that sounds a great deal more fun than horse breeding."

Before she could respond, he leaned up and kissed her again. "I love you." Another kiss. "You've given me back a future I didn't think I would have." Another kiss. "I will be a good husband to you." Another kiss. "I will never, ever stray. I swear it. I swear it twice."

A tear ran down her cheek. "I know that. As I keep telling you, you are an honorable man."

"But perhaps I could still remain a little bit of scoundrel, yes?"

She laughed. "Yes. A little bit."

"Then marry me, Rosamund. Will you?"

She gazed into those witty, compassionate, clever black eyes. "Since you have a confession, I have one, as well."

His smile faded a little. "What is it?"

"In eight months or so, there's a fairly good chance that you are going to have a larger family than you might have intended."

He blinked. He stared at her. And then Bram Johns let out a whoop, shot to his feet, and pulled her out of her chair. Holding her around the waist, he swung her in a circle. She knew she'd been right not to tell him before, because in the back of his mind he would always have questioned whether he'd become this new, exceptional man out of a misplaced sense of responsibility or because that was what he'd wanted.

"I still want to hear you say it, Rosamund. Say you'll marry me."

Oh, she would marry him twice, if she could. "Yes, I will marry you, Bram. There's no escape for you now."

With a soft chuckle, he kissed her once more. "I have no wish to escape."

"Good. Because that would be very troublesome."

"I love you," he said again, laughing harder as he set her down. "By God, you're an unusual woman."

"I love you, Bram. And you are an unusual man."

"Together I believe we have a very good chance of setting Mayfair on its ear quite regularly."

Oh, she hoped so.

Epilogue _____

Three years later

"How the devil did this happen?" Bram folded his arms over his chest and leaned against the door frame of Sullivan Waring's upstairs sitting room at Amberglen in East Sussex.

"The mess?" Phin asked, looking up from his seat on the floor and the tower of playing cards in front of him.

"Or . . . this?" Sullivan, seated on the couch, gestured at the room in general.

"Both." Pushing upright, Bram made his way around the pile of wooden pull toys and a rocking horse to take the chair in front of the fire. "I went looking for a bottle in your desk, Sullivan," he drawled, "and do you know what I found?"

"I'm afraid to ask."

"I found a bottle. Except that instead of whiskey, it was full of dirt. And worms."

"Ah. That would be Henry's," Sullivan said, grinning. "He knows worms like dark places. Last week I found a sock full of them in one of my boots. Before I stepped into it, luckily."

"And what is young Henry planning on doing with all of the worms in East Sussex?" Bram pursued, lifting an eyebrow.

"They're for fishing," young Henry Waring answered, grimacing as he carefully lifted another pair of cards onto Phin's tower. "I did it, Uncle Phin!"

"You've a steady hand, Henry," Phin congratulated him, reaching over to lift up the crawling infant heading for the tower and aiming the cheeky little chit in the opposite direction.

"Splendid, Phin, send your daughter toward the fireplace." Sullivan leaned down to pick up the baby. "Your papa has hay for brains, Sarah, yes, he does." The infant giggled in response.

"I knew you were there," Phin grumbled. "And yours has vanished by the by, Bram. No idea where to find her." He angled his chin behind the chair where Bram sat.

"I should have known you lot would lose my daughter as soon as I left the room," Bram said, stretching. "Now I've lost my April. Whatever will I do?" Curling his left arm back, he touched silky hair. "Wait a moment, what is this?" Walking his fingers up, he laid his palm over a small head. "I say, I've found a pumpkin!"

A shriek of laughter answered him. "It's me, Papa!"

The lithe, dark-haired sprite swarmed around the side

of the chair and climbed into his lap. Even at just over two years old, April Marie Johns was a beauty. And far too wise for her years. He kissed her on the forehead, still dazed as he considered that he and Rosamund had made this little miracle.

"Would you have thought, Bram," Sullivan said as he played pince-nez with Phin's nine-month-old daughter, "that we would ever end like this?"

Bram took a slow breath. Peace was a new and rare sensation for him, and it was one he coveted. "No, I would not." His gaze lifted as Rosamund strolled into the room, Alyse and Isabel behind her. His light, his heaven, his joy, all the more precious because he'd thought never to deserve such a gift.

"What are you smiling at?" she asked, taking a seat on the arm of his chair and coiling an arm around his shoulder as she leaned against him.

"That you're foolish enough to have yet another infant with me," he murmured, lifting his free hand to twine his fingers with hers.

"Another one?" Sullivan repeated, straightening. "You've lost any chance now to escape him, Rose. You do realize that."

Rosamund gave an exaggerated sigh. "Yes, I know he's a bit of a scoundrel, but he does clean up well, at least."

Amid the general laughter and congratulations, Bram kept his gaze on his wife. Somewhere in all of his past misdeeds he must have done at least one good turn, to find such a woman. And to find such friends. They hadn't done poorly at all, for such a group of notorious gentlemen. Not bad, at all.

At Avon Books, we know your passion for romance—once you finish one of our novels, you find yourself wanting more.

May we tempt you with . . .

- **Excerpts** from our upcoming releases.

- Entertaining **extras**, including authors' personal photo albums and book lists.

- Behind-the-scenes **scoop** on your favorite characters and series.

- **Sweepstakes** for the chance to win free books, romantic getaways, and other fun prizes.

- Writing **tips** from our authors and editors.

- **Blog** with our authors and find out why they love to write romance.

- **Exclusive content** that's not contained within the pages of our novels.

Join us at
www.avonbooks.com

AVON *An Imprint of* HarperCollins*Publishers*
www.avonromance.com